Dedicated, with gratitude,
to the Ladies of the Carpe-Libris Writers Group,
for their unfailing support; to my agent, Lucienne Diver,
for her persistence; and, most of all, to my husband, Matt,
for his eternal patience with the "little writing thing" I do.

THE GOLDEN CITY

CHAPTER 1

THURSDAY, 25 SEPTEMBER 1902

Lady Isabel Amaral plucked another pair of drawers from the chiffonier and tossed them in her companion's direction. Oriana caught the silk garment and folded it neatly while her mistress disappeared into the dressing room.

Oriana laid the drawers in a pile with the others, surveyed the collection spread across the bed, and shook her head. Even after two years living among humans she was still bemused by the number of layers a proper Portuguese lady must wear. Chemises and underskirts, drawers and stockings and corsets: they all lay neatly prepared to pack away, none of them meant to be seen. It was a far cry from the comfortable—and less voluminous—garb Oriana had grown up wearing out on the islands that belonged to her people. She rarely noticed her heavy clothes any longer, but seeing all the lace-bedecked items displayed on the bed before her, Oriana found the quantity of fabric in which Isabel swathed herself daily rather daunting.

What was missing? Even with all that lay in front of her, Oriana was sure Isabel had left *something* out. She puffed out her cheeks, mentally cataloging the garments on the bed.

She wished Isabel hadn't waited so late to inform her of the plan to elope. If she'd known in advance, she would have packed Isabel's best clothes neatly. She could even have sent a couple of trunks ahead via train to the hotel in Paris. Being rushed at the last moment was her own fault, though. She'd made her disapproval of the match known early on, and Isabel probably wanted to avoid an argument. But it was also Isabel's style to wait until the last moment. That made everything more of an adventure.

Unfortunately, adventures didn't always turn out well . . . particularly if one didn't have the proper undergarments.

Aha! Oriana suddenly placed the oversight. "You haven't any corset covers."

Isabel peered around the edge of the dressing room door and waved one hand vaguely. "Pick some for me. I only need a couple. Marianus will buy me new ones after we're married."

Isabel disappeared back into her dressing room, leaving Oriana shaking her head. She had to wonder if Marianus Efisio knew he would be spending the next few weeks shopping. While Isabel's family possessed aristocratic bloodlines tracing all the way back to the Battle of Aljubarrota, they had very little money. Everything supplied by the various milliners and dressmakers who'd rigged Isabel out in style had been bought on credit. Isabel's mother was counting on her beauteous daughter's marriage to a wealthy husband. Luckily, Mr. Efisio did meet that requirement.

Unluckily, he was already promised to another woman: Isabel's cousin Pia.

It was an arrangement made when he was just a boy and Pia an infant. Even so, it wasn't fair to simply ignore the arrangement. At any rate, Oriana didn't think so.

Isabel had waved away Oriana's concerns, claiming that Mr. Efisio wasn't suited to Pia's placid disposition. The elopement would cause a scandal, and Isabel's rarely present father would be livid. Nevertheless, Isabel's popularity in polite society would help her survive the disgrace. In time, Mr. Efisio would be forgiven for breaking his betrothal, particularly if Pia were to marry well. He had money, which always seemed to temper society's disapproval.

Isabel was like a tidal wave, though. She always did as she wished, and the gods would merely laugh at anyone who stood in her way.

Clucking her tongue, Oriana sorted through the contents of the rickety chiffonier's top drawer and selected the two best corset covers. She'd just laid them neatly on the bed when Isabel emerged from the dressing room, her arms overflowing with skirts and shirtwaists. She dropped them atop the garments Oriana had already folded, and a narrow line appeared between her perfectly arched black brows. "Am I missing anything else?"

"A nightdress," Oriana answered. She eyed the wreckage of her neatly folded stacks. Isabel probably hadn't even looked before dumping the clothes she'd carried. *Oh, well.* There was nothing to do but start over. Oriana nodded briskly and lifted the top skirt off the pile.

A knock came at the door, and she jumped. She instinctively hid her bare hands in the fabric of the skirt. She was usually so careful, but she'd taken off the mitts that normally hid her fingers so she could help Isabel pack. Then she realized she was wrinkling the skirt terribly and forced herself to let it go. She took a calming breath, hoping her voice would sound normal. "Who is it?"

"Adela, Miss Paredes," one of the maids responded from the hallway. "I have what my lady asked for."

Oriana cast Isabel a questioning look. What was Isabel plotting?

Isabel hurried to the bedroom door herself. Oriana stayed by the bed and shoved her hands behind her back. Other than Isabel, no one in the Amaral household knew her secret. Oriana wanted to keep it that way.

Her webbed fingers would give her away, and being caught in the city would mean arrest and expulsion, if not worse. They were her great flaw as a spy. She'd finally made the decision to have the webbing cut away, as her superiors insisted, and *had* planned to take her half day off this weekend to have it done. But Isabel's sudden decision to elope had fouled those plans. Oriana hadn't decided if she was vexed . . . or relieved.

Isabel opened the door only wide enough for the maid to pass her something and closed it quickly. She turned back to Oriana, a mischievous grin lighting her face, and held up a pair of maid's aprons and two crumpled white caps. "See what I have?"

Oriana stood there with her mouth open. Why would Isabel ask for *those*?

Isabel rolled her eyes. "A disguise," she explained. "See? If we wear black, we can put these on over our skirts and we'll look like housemaids."

Well, the only thing more scandalous than engaging in an elopement had to be exposure while doing so. The disguise *would* make the two of them less noticeable at the train station; most people in Isabel's circles didn't notice servants. Surely none would comment on a couple of housemaids dragging luggage about for their mistresses, even this late in the evening.

"I understand," Oriana said, trying for an enlightened expression. The black serge skirt she currently wore would pass for a housemaid's, but her white cambric shirt and the blue vest wouldn't. "I'll need to change my shirt, but it should do."

Isabel tossed the aprons atop the chiffonier and grinned. "See? It will all work out."

"I'm certain you've planned for everything," Oriana allowed, inclining her head in Isabel's direction.

A dimple appeared in Isabel's alabaster cheek. "When it comes to marriage, one must."

Oriana laughed softly. Isabel always had a clever retort on her silver tongue, a talent she envied.

She regarded the pile of garments atop the bed and tried to think of the best way to tackle the task ahead of her. An open trunk waited on the old cane-backed settee at the foot of the bed, although she would have to fold and tuck judiciously to get all these garments into it. She would likely have to add a portmanteau as well. Mr. Efisio had gone ahead to Paris, but he had ordered his coach to pick them up no more than a block away. She could carry their luggage to the coach in two trips if needed.

Isabel watched, tapping one slender finger against her cheek. "Now, what have I forgotten?"

"Nightdress?" Oriana reminded her.

"Oh, I mustn't forget that." Isabel dashed back to the dressing room.

Oriana folded the blue skirt from the top of the pile and set it in the trunk, located the shirtwaist Isabel wore with it and tucked that in next, and then headed into the dressing room to hunt down the matching jacket. She found Isabel standing before the full-length mirror in the cluttered dressing room, holding up a nightdress. It was her most daring, a white satin that bared much of her bosom like an evening gown.

Isabel glanced over one shoulder at Oriana, her face glowing with excitement. "Do you think he will approve? It's not too shocking, is it?"

Isabel was blessed with an ivory complexion and thick black hair. She had delicate features, delicate hands, delicate feet. Her hazel eyes had been the subject of many a wretched suitor's poem, and her rosy, bow-shaped lips had earned their own paeans. She was everything that Oriana wasn't—beautiful by any standard. A good thing too, as Isabel's sharp tongue and cutting wit might have earned her enemies were she less lovely. But she'd gathered a court of suitors and held them fast while waiting for a man of both adequate means and malleability to come along. Mr. Efisio had never had a chance once Isabel made up her mind to have him.

Oriana's eyes met Isabel's in the mirror. "I'm certain he'll like it, shocking or not."

"Good." Isabel smiled contentedly at her reflection, but turned back to Oriana, her face going serious. "I know you don't approve. I'm grateful you're coming with me anyway."

Oriana opened her mouth to apologize for her earlier arguments with Isabel over Mr. Efisio's fate, but paused. She still didn't approve. She nodded instead.

"I do love him," Isabel said then, the first time she'd told Oriana so. "Have you never been in love?"

Oriana gazed down at her folded hands, her throat inexplicably tight. She was only a few years older than Isabel, but her situation in life had never been amenable to courtship. How many times had her aunts pointed that out? Unlike women within human society, among her people a female often remained alone; there simply weren't enough males. Those females not meant for a mate were destined to serve their people instead, as Oriana did.

That thread of Destiny that bound her soul to some other's? Oriana didn't think it existed. She had resigned herself to that years ago . . . or she'd thought she had. Seeing Isabel so excited about her upcoming nuptials made Oriana wish she'd been one of the *others*—those for whom Destiny had chosen a mate. "No," she admitted when she found her voice. "I've never been in love, so I suppose I can't understand."

Isabel's brows drew together. "Do your people believe in love? Or are your marriages all arranged, like Pia's?"

Oriana mulled that over. "We believe we are destined for one in particular, or—"

"Then perhaps you just haven't met him yet," Isabel interrupted with a blithe wave of her hand.

Apparently Isabel believed that if *she* were to have a husband, then everyone must. At least Isabel's interruption had saved her from admitting aloud she was destined to be forever alone. Oriana nodded again, as if she agreed. She was realizing she did that quite often.

Isabel surveyed the mess on the bed with narrowed eyes, plotting how to subdue it, no doubt. "Now, why don't you go pack your own bag, Oriana? I'll finish up in here."

Oriana cast a glance back at that chaos and suppressed a shudder. Isabel would simply cram her clothes into that trunk. As she wasn't taking a maid along, Oriana would end up ironing everything later. She hated exposing her delicate hands to all that heat, but she would do so to help Isabel start off in her new life properly. One last thing she could do to repay Isabel for her kindness.

She tugged on her black silk mitts to hide the webbing between her fingers. "I'll be back shortly, then."

She slipped out the bedroom door and walked down the hallway, rubbing her hands up and down her arms to warm herself. The Amaral household was one of contrasts. In the public areas of the house no expense was spared. Fires would no doubt be burning merrily in the parlors to chase away the September evening's chill. The silver was regularly polished, and the china lovingly displayed in a fine oak sideboard in the palatial dining room. The rugs and tapestries were of the finest quality, many dating back to the family's wealthier days.

The social elite of the Golden City seemed to believe that facade of affluence, counting the Amaral family among their most important members. Isabel and her mother were invited to all the important affairs, the balls and picnics and soirees. They attended the theater regularly. Isabel's approval was sought by younger girls, and her hand by all the men.

But while the Amaral family worked hard to present an affluent image downstairs, they didn't bother upstairs. The second floor, where Isabel and her mother had their bedrooms, was left unheated. The draperies and rugs were threadbare, and the hall runner had begun to unravel along one edge. Only half the gaslights were turned up, leaving the hallway murky.

The areas of the house where the servants lived and worked

were worse. When Oriana reached the narrow back stair leading up to the third floor, it was altogether unlit. But since her eyes were better than a human's in the dark, she didn't bother to fetch a lamp to climb its creaking length. The servants' quarters were cramped and cold, the floors covered only with aged floor cloths. Like most houses on the Street of Flowers, the Amaral home had been transplanted to this spot in the Golden City in the previous century, moved stone by stone. The servants lived in rooms that hadn't been improved since that time: no plumbing, no lighting, and with peeling paint on the walls. Small wonder the maids so often fell ill.

Being Lady Isabel's hired companion, Oriana had a room to herself. She was grateful for that. Her little room was a safe haven, a place where she need not hide her hands or her gills or the inhuman coloration of the lower half of her body. While she looked more human than most females on her people's islands, those things simply couldn't be escaped.

Oriana opened her door and slipped inside. Once she'd lit the lamp on her nightstand, she stripped off her silk mitts and stretched out her fingers. The webbing between them glowed iridescent in the flickering lamplight. Although they protected her from exposure, the fingerless silk mitts pushed down the webbing between her index finger and thumb. This pair she'd sewn herself. That ensured they were better made than the ones she could buy at the market *and* long enough to hide all but the tips of her fingers. Even so, they made her hands ache.

Oriana sank down onto her narrow bed, rubbing that sore spot. She kept her nails trimmed close. Otherwise they would curve downward over her fingertips like claws. That was easy to hide. Her webbing was a different matter. At least the other maids didn't question her refusal to bare her hands. Not long after hiring her, Isabel had cleverly let slip to Adela that Oriana had psoriasis—rough, red patches on her skin—marring her hands and throat. That lie provided a ready explanation for continually wearing mitts and her penchant for high-necked gowns, even in summer. It also meant that the maids never associated with her, for fear it was catching. Whenever she wasn't in Isabel's company, she was alone in this cold and unfriendly house.

Over the past year Isabel had become more than just her employer. She'd become a confidante as well. But once Isabel was securely married to her Mr. Efisio, there would be no need for a companion to play chaperone. Oriana would return to the Golden City, alone and without employment. There was little chance she would find work as a companion again, not after having been a party to an elopement.

That didn't concern Isabel, though, and Oriana didn't blame her. Mistresses had no reason to concern themselves with the fate of servants they left behind. Isabel was busy planning her marriage and her future; it would only spoil her enjoyment to hear her companion fretting about her own predicament. But without a letter of reference, Oriana was going to have difficulty finding a new position.

Because she'd not yet had her webbing cut away, her initial assignment in the city had been trivial. The sereia spymaster in the Golden City, Heriberto, had grudgingly taken her on, but he'd done little to help her. Oriana had managed to secure a position in a dress shop on her own, one favored by less-wealthy members of the aristocracy. She'd listened to the gossip of the ladies as they came in for their fittings, reporting back to her master on which of them might be sympathetic to nonhumans and welcome their return to the Golden City. When Isabel—a regular customer at that shop—had offered Oriana a position in her household, it had been a step up, with greater access to the aristocracy. It had been a coup for a spy whose master insisted on treating her like an untested child.

Now it would be back to the cramped dressmaker's shop on Esperança Street, or possibly even home to the islands to wait for another assignment. She would simply have to see what Heriberto ordered. Oriana sniffled and snatched up the handkerchief off her nightstand. This was no time to feel sorry for herself. She would have to press on. She would reschedule her appointment with the doctor. The webbing was sensitive, and its absence would leave her hands with phantom pain for the rest of her life. Nevertheless, if she was going to be useful to her people, she needed to get it cut away.

She had little left of the things that had been important to her as a child. Her mother had died when Oriana was only twelve. Four years later her father had been exiled for sedition. Oriana had never learned exactly what he'd done or said, but he'd been raised by an indulgent mother who'd taught her only child that he was the equal of any woman on the islands. Unlike most males, he'd even been educated. Oriana's mother had been proud of her clever mate, no matter his tendency to defy convention. But his political beliefs had clashed with almost everything the government held true, and after his exile Oriana had been left alone to care for her younger sister, Marina. They had aunts who'd taken them in, but weren't ever close to them. Citing Oriana's natural talent for *calling*, those aunts had pushed her relentlessly to join the Ministry of Intelligence, claiming again and again that it was her Destiny to serve her people. Oriana had refused.

Until three years ago. When Oriana was away visiting their paternal grandmother on the island of Amado, Marina had run away to search for their father. Somewhere along her path to Portugal, she had fallen prey to a merchant ship's crew.

Oriana wiped away a tear with the back of one hand. That had been *her* failure. Marina hadn't been happy living with their aunts on the island of Quitos, but Oriana hadn't believed she would take such a desperate step to escape them. Her parents would have expected Oriana to keep Marina safe, but she hadn't.

After Marina's death, Oriana had given in, joining the ministry. She'd hoped to protect her people from the threat of subjugation under human rule. She'd also hoped to extract a small amount of vengeance, but never learned anything further of her sister's death. The humans she'd met in the past two years had turned out to be no worse than her own people. And she'd seen no firm indication that Prince Fabricio intended to seize control over her people's islands anytime soon. There were rumors, of course—those were as commonplace as seagulls—just no proof.

But Prince Fabricio had acted against her people's interests in the past. The prince had several seers in his entourage, whose words purportedly ruled many of his actions. One of them had prophesied that the prince would be *killed* by one of the sea folk—the sereia, the selkies, or the otterfolk—and fear of that had led the prince to ban all nonhumans from the shores of Northern Portugal decades before, when Oriana was just a child. That decree had cut her people off from their primary trading partner and crippled their economy. Many of their people had lost their property and their livelihoods. And because of that same ban, Oriana now wore mitts that pinched her webbing, and high collars on even the hottest days.

It was simply the price she had to pay. Determined to squarely face whatever chapter lay ahead in her life, Oriana rose and set about the business at hand: packing. As her presence was meant to lend Isabel countenance in this ramshackle flight, she needed to look severe but ignorable. That wouldn't be difficult. She didn't have Isabel's beauty to catch male eyes, and once she was mentally classified as a servant, most people dismissed her from their minds.

That had been helpful over the past year. Her dark eyes were larger than most humans'. Her brown hair, when dry, had a non-Portuguese reddish cast that prompted the maids to whisper that she'd suffered a mishap involving tincture of henna. Those things would have drawn curious eyes if she were a lady, but for a mere companion no one took note. She faded away.

Oriana changed into a black shirtwaist that, under the borrowed apron, would pass for a housemaid's. Then she moved her nightstand away from the wall and used her shoehorn to pry up the short floorboard underneath. In an old netted handbag tucked under the board, she'd hidden every last mil-réis she could save. It wasn't much, but the stash of coins would pay for a place to live while she searched for a new position. She weighed it in her hand, then tucked the small bag into the bottom of the portmanteau and arranged her clothes and hat atop it.

She closed up her case with a touch of room to spare. She might be able to retrieve her other garments when she returned to the city. She unpinned her hair, combed it out, and braided it, making a simple knot at the nape of her neck. She checked the small mirror on her wall—yes, she did look like a housemaid.

But at least she would be a housemaid who had seen Paris, the French City of Lights.

Oriana checked her left sleeve, feeling the reassuring stiffness of the dagger strapped to her wrist. Perhaps Isabel was correct and everything would work out. Even so, it was better to be armed than trusting.

The clock in the hallway struck ten just as she reached Isabel's bedroom. She let herself in and was greeted by the sight of Isabel standing proudly by her trunk, all the catches closed and the strap already buckled. "See? I did it all by myself," Isabel said, a sly look in her eyes. "I know you didn't think I could manage it."

Oriana inclined her head, granting Isabel that point. She didn't comment on the additional portmanteau half-hidden behind Isabel's skirts. "I am impressed."

Isabel chewed her lower lip. "Now, how do we get these downstairs without the butler noticing?"

The other servants were all aware that the family needed this marriage in order to pay the bills, but the butler had old-fashioned opinions about what was appropriate for the daughter of an aristocratic family. He'd created one difficulty after another to keep Mr. Efisio away from Isabel.

"Carlos will help," Oriana decided. The first footman hated the butler with a passion. He might do it just for spite. "Do you have a couple of mil-réis to spare?"

Isabel produced them from her little handbag, and Oriana slipped downstairs to bribe the footman. As she'd expected, Carlos was on the back steps of the house, smoking a cigarette. He proved willing to help and, a few minutes later, carried Isabel's two pieces of luggage out to the corner of the courtyard.

The court behind the row of houses was private. Beyond the courtyard were the mews that served the wealthy homeowners of the Street of Flowers, and the scent of dust and horses carried in the cool night. Under the streetlamps, it was bright enough to see the whole alleyway, but Oriana couldn't make out a coach waiting in either direction. She turned to Isabel, who, with her white cap and apron, almost looked the part of a housemaid, although an impudent one. "Where is Mr. Efisio's coach to meet us?"

Isabel pointed to the farther end of the block with her chin. "On Formosa Street. His driver is to wait for us there."

Oriana groaned. That was several houses away. She should have bribed Carlos to carry the luggage all the way there. Casting about, she spotted the small stair leading from the cobbles down to an old basement entry, the coal room. Reckoning no one would be using that door tonight—no shipment of coal was due for another month at the earliest—she took the two portmanteaus down and tucked them by the steps, where they wouldn't be seen. Then she and Isabel picked up the trunk between them and began the trek down to the far end of the alley.

Isabel had thrown herself into the adventure of the moment. She didn't complain about having to carry her own luggage. She didn't complain about the weight of the trunk, or how far they had to go. She simply picked up her end and led the way. Oriana had to admire her for that, because the trunk was damnably heavy. They'd nearly reached the end of the alley when a coach approached slowly and eased to a stop.

"Thanks be to God!" Isabel said passionately, tugging on her end of the trunk to draw Oriana along faster.

The driver of the coach set the brake and jumped down to help them. They lowered the trunk to the the ground as he opened the coach's door and folded down the steps. Isabel went to climb inside while Oriana spoke to the burly driver. "I need to go fetch two more bags," she told him. "I'll only be a moment."

He grunted his assent, and Oriana turned to dash back to the Amarals' courtyard.

A hand grabbed her hair, fingers tightening about the braided mass at the nape of her neck. Off balance, Oriana stumbled backward toward her attacker. Before she could cry out, he pressed a cloth over her mouth and dragged her against his body.

Oriana bit down hard. But biting only drove the cloth into her teeth, a strange sweet taste on her tongue and in her gills. She struggled wildly as the fire in her stomach died back into cold fear. The big man had her pinned helpless against him. She kicked at his shins, but her heel tangled in the hem of her skirts, like seaweed wrapping about her legs. It was getting harder to move. *All these damned skirts . . .*

The man set her down, shaking the hand she'd bitten. Oriana swayed on her feet. She tried to loosen her shirt cuff to draw her dagger, but her hands wavered in her vision. A surge of nausea rose, leaving her hot, then cold.

What was wrong with her? She should *do* something . . .

As if at a great distance, she heard Isabel cry out. Oriana spun that way, reaching one arm out to her. Then she was tilting, falling toward the night-dark cobbles.

CHAPTER 2

Oriana dreamed she was bound. It was dark. Her head ached fiercely, her stomach felt hollow, and everything was wrong.

Ah, gods, no. It wasn't a nightmare.

She was tied firmly in place. She was upside down, seated in a chair, bound fast to it by ropes about her arms and chest and ankles, and that chair was secured to the ceiling. Her wrists were tied, forcing her hands to lie flat on a metal surface—a table or tray. Her ragged breath echoed in the small space.

She jerked against the ropes, but they didn't give. Instead, the whole world swayed around her. A whimper escaped her lips. *What is happening?*

She couldn't seem to think straight. *I've been drugged, haven't I?* There had been something bitter on the cloth the driver held over her mouth. Was he one of the Special Police, the branch dedicated to hunting down nonhumans like her? Had someone turned her in?

She had to find a way out of this place. She could smell wood and cork, the pungent scents of resins and paint, and, faintly, the river. She held her breath and could hear muted sounds, but nothing that made sense. Her eyes began to adjust to the blackness, better than human eyes for that sort of thing.

And then she realized she wasn't alone. Isabel hung in a chair across from her. The cobwebs that cluttered Oriana's mind blew away in a sudden rush. "Isabel," she cried. "Wake up!"

Isabel's head swayed and her eyelids fluttered, but she didn't respond. She must have been drugged, too.

Oriana's hands curled into fists against the table's surface. She had to get Isabel out of this place. She yanked against the ropes that bound her arms again, but couldn't make out how they were tied. The knots must be behind her back.

She surveyed the shadowy room then, taking stock. She could make out its size now, not much larger than the inside of a coach. The walls looked featureless, dark and plain. There was only her and Isabel and a small round table nestled between them. The ropes pressed her hands down on one side of the table, and Isabel's hands lay opposite them. Oriana could see that the surface was patterned somehow, but the room was too dark for her to make it out.

What is this? Why would anyone put us here?

Her breathing sounded harsh in her own ears, overloud in the tiny room. She forced it down, not wanting to frighten Isabel. She had to come up with a plan. Then she heard a new sound through the walls: the metallic rattle of shifting chains. There had to be someone nearby. "Let her go," she cried, hoping they would hear. "She didn't know I'm not human. She's not a Sympathizer. It's . . ."

Everything moved. Oriana had the terrifying sensation of falling, then her body slammed to a stop against the ropes that bound her. She hissed and followed that with every foul word she'd ever heard her aunts say. The initial flare of pain ebbed after a moment. They were on water now. The room bobbed like a boat.

"It's me you want," Oriana screamed into the darkness. "Not her, damn it!"

There was no response save for the continued clatter of chains.

Oriana's breath suddenly went short. This room couldn't be watertight, not if she'd heard the chains so clearly through the walls. Water was going to fill this space, and quickly. "Isabel, wake up!"

Isabel moaned in response, her eyes fluttering open. "Where am I?"

She heard water bubbling into the structure that trapped them. Something was dragging them deeper. They didn't have much time. "I don't know. We have to try to get loose."

"Oriana? Where are you? I can't see." Isabel began to cry helplessly then, like a lost child.

Oriana tried to keep her voice steady for Isabel's sake. "It's very dark, Isabel. That's why you can't see. Now listen to me. You have to try to get your arms loose."

"I can't," Isabel sobbed.

Oriana couldn't see the water yet. It was above—no, below—her head, seeping upward. She could hear it and smell it, though. Cold fear knotted in her gut. They were going to run out of time.

No, she wasn't going to give up that easily. "I'm going to untie myself," she told Isabel. "Then I'll untie you."

"How?" she whimpered.

Oriana didn't take time to answer. She grasped the edge of the table and shifted in the chair that held her, twisting so her teeth could reach the rope about her right wrist. Her teeth *were* sharper than a human's, something that rarely proved an advantage. The rope splintered and shredded in her mouth.

The water continued to seep upward, inexorable.

"Oriana? Are you still there? Oriana!"

Oriana paused. The fear in Isabel's voice tore at her heart, but she needed to get loose more than Isabel needed an answer, so she kept chewing. But she did stop and glance up when Isabel screamed.

The water had reached the top of Isabel's head. Isabel began thrashing wildly. "No!" she screamed. "No!"

This was *cruel*. Crueler now that Isabel had figured out the fate planned for them.

"Isabel, be quiet." Oriana used her voice to *call* Isabel, the one magic she possessed. She wove the imperative into her words—not a spell like a human witch might use, but simple desire, *yearning*. It would have been more successful with a human male, but she could hold almost any human's attention for a few minutes, and even prompt her to action. The magic drew Isabel's gaze to her and, although she didn't think Isabel could see her, it forced Isabel to focus on her words. Oriana hoped she could buy them some time. "Isabel, bend forward as far as you can," she ordered. "Right before the water gets to your nose, take a deep breath and hold it."

Isabel's ragged breathing was interspersed with sobs, but she obediently bent forward, her dark head almost touching the table.

Oriana prayed that would be enough. She set her teeth back to the rope. It gave suddenly, and she yanked it with her mouth. It had been wrapped around several times, so she had to pull each loop loose. Chilly water touched the back of her head. Cold fingers of water spread along the back of her housemaid's costume, grasped her shoulders, climbed up her garments.

It reached her mouth, and she took it in. Her gills opened involuntarily and her throat closed, stealing her voice. She breathed in the familiar water of the Douro River as she dragged her arm free of the loops of rope.

No! The rope holding her other arm hadn't loosened at all. They were *separate* ropes. She would have to chew through each one individually. She tore at her shirtsleeve, but her wrist was tied too tightly to get her dagger loose, not until she could get that hand free.

There was no time. Oriana didn't want to look, but she couldn't stop herself.

Across from her in the darkness, Isabel's eyes were stricken in the pale oval of her face. The water had nearly reached her waist. Oriana didn't know how long Isabel had been holding her breath, waiting to be rescued.

If she could just reach Isabel, she could breathe *for* her. Oriana jerked against the rope trapping her left arm, but it didn't give an inch. She tried to shove the ropes binding her chest down to her waist, but they tangled in the fabric of her apron.

Isabel's bow-shaped lips opened. A flood of bubbles streamed from her mouth, the last of her breath. Her body jerked convulsively against the ropes that bound her to the chair. Her eyes were wide with terror.

Unable to reach her, Oriana pounded her free hand on the surface of the table, setting off painful vibrations through her webbing. She wanted to scream. She wanted to beg Isabel's forgiveness. But her voice was gone underwater. She reached out her throbbing hand and laid it over Isabel's fingers. What could she do?

She couldn't sing underwater, but she could *hum*. Oriana wove a *call* into the tune to comfort Isabel, using her memories of an old lullaby her father had sung to shape the sound. It was all she had to give.

Isabel's expression eased, the fear in her eyes fading.

Then she was still.

Oriana's song faltered to a stop, and soundless sobs shook her body. The water had stolen her ability to cry. She could taste Isabel's death in the water, the sudden tang of a voided bladder—loss of control along with the loss of life. Oriana tugged the silk mitt off her hand with her teeth and spread her fingers wide, stretching the webbing between them. She could feel the vibration of her own heartbeat.

From Isabel there was nothing.

And then a glow crept across the surface of the table between them, almost like blood flowing from a wound. Letters imprinted on the surface gave off a pallid light, forming words that made no sense to Oriana's eyes. A ring of words circled the table's edge. Inside that was another ring of nonsense symbols, shapes she didn't recognize, and in the center a third ring held a collection of straight lines. The glow crept to the center of the small table and then stopped as if it had hit a wall.

The table had come alive in response to Isabel's death.

Oriana looked back at her friend. She tried to touch Isabel's face. Her fingers fell short, so she grasped Isabel's hand again, as if Isabel could still feel her there. Isabel's head began to sway loosely with the motion of the water, a single strand of hair floating past her open mouth and snagging against her lips.

Oriana squeezed her eyes shut, unable to look any longer.

She didn't know how long she stayed like that, trembling against the ropes that bound her. The water continued to rise about her. It swallowed her legs. The cold seeped into her tight-laced shoes.

Then the last of the air slipped out of the room and the whole thing began sinking quickly, some anchor drawing it down. The pressure of the water made the wood groan. Then it came to a stop, far gentler than that first slam into the surface of the water. Now that the room was flooded, they should sink to the bottom of the river, but for some reason they continued to float.

Oriana opened her eyes. At a deeper depth it was even darker, but the table's surface continued to glow, lighting Isabel's motionless features. Oriana stared at that tabletop for a long time, those meaningless words and lines burning into her mind.

She felt wrung out and dull, like a chemise whose dye had all seeped away into the wash water. She needed to escape this place, but there was no longer any need to hurry. She had all the time in the world now—now that Isabel was gone.

Someone had put them here to die, but it hadn't been the Special Police. They would have known a sereia could breathe as easily underwater as above it. No, this was a trap meant for *humans*. Someone had wanted Isabel to die terrified and helpless.

But that someone had made one mistake.

They hadn't weighed Oriana Paredes into their equations, no

doubt thinking her simply another housemaid. They'd tried to drown a sereia. And she was going to make them pay.

Not for herself. During the year she'd trained to be a spy, she'd been taught that her own life might be forfeit. She'd accepted that possibility. No, she would make someone pay for doing this to Isabel, who had started the day with such great hopes and ended it with terror. She would hunt the murderer down and, one way or another, they would see justice.

It seemed a long time later that Oriana bowed her head and began to chew at the other rope. Once she got that hand free, she was able to draw her dagger and cut the remaining ropes that bound her to the chair. She pushed herself out of it, lightheaded when her body righted itself.

In the darkness, she touched Isabel's face, a final farewell. Isabel's ebony hair had held to its coiffure, save for that one loose lock. It streamed upward now, almost reaching Isabel's lap, a streak of darkness against her white maid's apron. Lit by the table's eerie glow, Isabel was lovely even in death, her face at peace. Tiny bubbles of air worked loose from the shadowy wooden structure about them, glistening in the darkness.

Oriana's throat ached, but she couldn't cry. She clasped the unmoving fingers one more time, and then swam to the top of the little room.

She wedged herself next to the fixed chairs, crowding Isabel's bound feet. She hammered against that floor or ceiling with one hand. Each impact sent uncomfortable vibrations through her webbing, so she wrapped one arm about the base of the table and used her feet to kick at one of the corners instead. After a few good kicks, she felt it give. Nails tore loose from the wood. She slid her hands into that narrow opening and pushed with all her strength.

The boards gave enough for her to squeeze through.

After one last glance at Isabel's lifeless form, Oriana wriggled through that space. Her skirt caught on a nail, and she had to rip it to get loose.

She was free.

She let herself float there for a moment. Her skirts were heavy, but her natural buoyancy kept her from sinking too quickly.

The river's surface above her was dark. Before her Oriana saw shapes floating in the water, more traps like the one she'd just escaped. They were twenty feet or so under the surface, trying to float but prevented from rising any higher by thick chains that tethered them to the river's murky bed below. Why didn't they sink to the bottom? Oriana kicked away from her prison, trying to grasp the bigger picture of what she was seeing. In the nighttime waters she could make out two neat rows, stretching on for some distance. There must be more than twenty of these prisons under the river's surface.

It was *The City Under the Sea.*

Oriana had read of the great work of art being assembled beneath the surface of the Douro. The newspapers often opined about it, ever since the pieces began appearing in the water almost a year ago. Each was a replica of one of the great houses that lined the Street of Flowers, the street of the aristocrats. Shrunk down in scale to no larger than a coach, the replicas were constructed in wood. They were all upside down, enspelled so that they would float, yet chained to the riverbed so they could never escape. They swayed in the grasp of the river's outbound current, all moving in eerie unison.

Oriana looked back at the house in which she'd been imprisoned. It was a replica of the Amaral mansion, Isabel's home. To one side was the copy of the Rocha mansion, and on the other the elegant Pereira de Santos house.

Had Isabel been killed merely for the sake of this . . . artwork? Had others awakened in the darkness only to realize, like Isabel, that their death was seeping in about them?

Oriana gasped, drawing in water, and corruption touched her gills. The water tasted foul, reminding her of a shipwreck, bodies left behind in the water for the fish and other creatures to pick clean. Nausea sent a flush of heat through her body. She slapped a hand over her mouth and nose, as if that could protect her from breathing in the death that was all about her. Oriana kicked hard, fighting the weight of her garments. She had to get to the surface, away from this graveyard.

She swam toward a spot of light that must be the moon's reflection on the water. But when she broke the surface, her head banged against the hull of a small boat, hard enough to disorient her. She instinctively shoved away. The stars spun. In the distance she saw the lights of a city, although she couldn't tell which one. She let herself slip back under the water, the only safe place. She spread her fingers wide so she would feel in her webbing when the boat moved away.

Instead she sensed someone diving into the water. Oriana kicked back down toward the depths, but her pursuer kept after her. She drew her dagger again, but before she could turn about, a large hand clamped down on her hand. She had no leverage to jerk away, and it took only a second before the man attached to that hand managed to pry the blade loose from her fingers. It spun away down through the water, quickly obscured. The tang of blood floated in the water; the dagger had cut her hand when he'd wrestled it away. The man wrapped an arm about her chest and dragged her back up toward the surface.

When she broke the surface again, a second man dug his hands into her sodden dress while the man in the water pushed her up and over the edge of the boat. She tumbled into the bilge.

For a second Oriana huddled there, hands balled into fists, trying to catch her breath. Her head throbbed and her hand did as well. Blood leaked from the palm of her right hand, but she didn't dare look. If she opened her hand to check the wound, her captors would surely see the webbing. Who were these men out on the water in the dark?

The boat rocked as the man who'd pursued her into the river climbed back aboard. She had to face them eventually. Oriana took a deep breath and struggled to right herself between the planks of the rowboat. A moment later she was seated on a bench, wet skirts tangled about her legs, facing an older gentleman. Her pursuer settled behind her. The man before her was sixty or so, still handsome, with gray hair and a stern, square jaw. She recognized his face but couldn't place it. Where had she seen him before?

"Are you well, miss?" The older man had a blanket in his hands. Oriana flinched back as he leaned forward. He persisted, wrapping the blanket about her shoulders.

Oriana began to shiver. Her garments and shoes were soaked through. She lifted one hand to push her hair from her face, remembering to fold her fingers to hide the webbing. Where she'd banged her forehead against the side of the boat, it was already tender.

Had they seen her hands? When they'd pulled her into the boat, had she had her fingers spread? She buried them in the blanket. Perhaps they'd been so busy they hadn't noticed. *Please, gods, let that be the case.*

The man repeated his question. He sounded kindly. He sounded concerned.

He thinks he's rescuing me. Oriana nearly laughed at the thought. She cleared her throat instead. Her breath still came shallow, and too fast. "Yes," she mumbled. "I'm . . . well enough."

"That's good," he said. "We were worried when we saw you in the water."

Her hands balled into fists again under the cover of the blanket. She needed to think faster, smarter. Why was this man out on the river? The Special Police patrolled the waters of the Douro every night, and she thought they had extra patrols over *The City Under the Sea*, but this little rowboat wasn't one of theirs. Had these men slipped past their patrols? The moon hadn't risen yet, and the only light came from a shuttered lantern set on a hook at the fore of the little boat, so it was possible they might not have been seen. The boat began to move, the large man behind her handling the oars, smelling of river water and musk.

The gentleman laid a gloved hand on her sodden knee. "Now, miss. How did you get out here?"

Oriana tried to gather her wits. She shook her head jerkily.

"I had a vision," he said then, "that there would be a girl in the water. I came here straightaway to see you safe, miss."

Vision? With a sinking in her stomach, Oriana suddenly placed his face. The man before her was Paolo Silva, one of Prince Fabricio's favored seers. She had seen the man before, although at a distance, at more than one of the balls she'd gone to with Isabel. She hadn't wanted to attract his attention then, and she didn't want it now. Her lips trembled. The shivering was worse now, and not just from the cold.

This man was close to the prince who so hated her people. If Silva knew what she was, he would surely turn her in. She could try to dive back into the water, but she wasn't sure she could get into the river before the oarsman grabbed her. Her twisted skirts and the blanket would make that easy for him. And attempting escape would confirm that she had something to hide. She swallowed hard. There was still a chance they hadn't realized her true nature.

Oriana tried to keep her voice from shaking. "Thank you, sir," she managed.

"Good," Silva said. "You've found your voice. Now, do you recall how you got out here, miss? I'm amazed you managed to keep your head above water."

Her head *hadn't* been above water. If she told this man she'd been trapped in the houses below, he would know for certain she wasn't human.

"I was dumped off one of the bridges, I think," she lied quickly. "I was drugged, but I remember falling." She sounded pathetic enough to lend it plausibility.

The small lamp swayed with the motion of the boat, casting Silva's features in light, then shadow. "How terrible! Shall I take you to a hospital, then, miss? Or the police station?"

Neither one of those options would end well for her. "No," she said quickly. "I must get home to my mother. She must be terribly worried. She lives right on the quay."

"Of course, miss," Silva said solicitously. "I'll escort you to your door myself, if you wish."

Oriana caught her lower lip between her teeth. Did he actually believe she'd been thrown off a bridge? Perhaps he suspected she'd thrown herself from one of the bridges. In the dim light of the swinging lantern, his face was unreadable. "No," she told him firmly. "No. If you'll take me to the quay, I can get home from there."

"I feel responsible for you now, miss," he said gently.

She didn't want to be around this man any longer than necessary, no matter how kindhearted he seemed. "Please, sir," she said, "you've done enough."

"May I know your name, at least?" he asked.

When people realized that Isabel was missing, her own name would surely be mentioned in the gossip. Silva might remember having seen her in Isabel's company, so lying would only draw suspicion. "Paredes," she said. "Oriana Paredes."

He reached over and patted her blanket-covered shoulder in a grandfatherly way. "I'm glad I followed the promptings of my gift tonight, Miss Paredes. I suspect our meeting must be propitious. I know we shall meet again."

Not if I can help it.

They had neared the tree-lined avenue of Massarelos—almost a mile from where they'd found her—far sooner than Oriana expected. The oarsman used a hook to drag the boat over to one of the stone ramps leading up to the street level. Oriana rose carefully. Hand folded to conceal the webbing, she grabbed for the rail and managed to wrangle her wet skirts about to get her footing on the stone. Once out of reach of either man, she felt far safer. She started to unwrap the blanket from about her shoulders.

"No, you must keep it," the seer insisted. "You must go home immediately and change into warm clothes, miss."

"Thank you, sir," Oriana repeated dully.

She walked up the ramp and glanced back to see the oarsman shoving the small boat away with an oar. Beyond the feeble glow of the streetlamps, the boat's inhabitants were quickly rendered invisible.

Now that she'd escaped her unwanted savior, Oriana desperately wanted to curl up somewhere and cry. She wanted warm clothes. And dry shoes. And a bath to get the foul taste of the water near *The City Under the Sea* out of her gills. She wanted to sleep. Perhaps she would wake to find that it was all a dream.

But first she had to tell Lady Amaral that Isabel was gone. Somewhere in the bottom of her heart she would have to find the strength to do that.

CHAPTER 3

FRIDAY, 26 SEPTEMBER 1902

A vague sense of foreboding kept Duilio Ferreira from sleeping. An idea fluttered about in his mind, refusing to be caught. Something was wrong; he simply had no idea what.

He lay in his warm, draped bed, staring up into the darkness. He toyed with the idea of rising, turning up the lights, and attempting to read, but hadn't quite given up on sleeping. His limited seer's gift had something it wanted him to know. He simply wasn't sure whether he wanted to spend his night trying to figure it out. He would rather be sleeping. The clock on his mantel, barely visible across the murky dark of his bedroom, ticked past three.

He groaned and tried turning onto his side. It was something about *water*. Something had happened or was going to happen in the river.

He was helping the police investigate the work of art being slowly assembled near the river's mouth, *The City Under the Sea*. Surely his edginess was related to that. The artist, Gabriel Espinoza, had taken into his mind to re-create the grand houses that lined the Street of Flowers. He'd anchored the first replica in the water a year ago, yet only recently had the Security Police—the regulars—begun to investigate those houses, suspecting that something more sinister than art might be driving the creation. They had immediately been ordered to close their investigation, although it was unclear from how high in the government that order had come. That had only served to pique Duilio's interest. As a private citizen, he could still ask all the questions he wanted.

The latch of his bedroom door turned with a faint click.

Reflex more than anything else got him onto his feet before the door opened halfway. He didn't feel the twinge of warning that usually alerted him to danger, but he snatched up the revolver that lay on his nightstand and held it ready as he turned to face the intruder. A shape stood unmoving in the doorway, startled by his sudden action. Someone else waited in the hallway with a lamp, casting the intruder into silhouette.

His visitor was female, even though she clearly wore trousers. That didn't mean she was harmless; a woman could be as dangerous as any man. But Duilio felt sure there was no reason to fear this visitor. He let out a breath he hadn't realized he'd been holding. "What do you want?"

"You're him, aren't you?" a feminine voice asked, confirming her gender. "Erdano's brother."

Well, any woman who knew *that* wasn't likely to be a threat. Duilio lowered the revolver and set it back on the nightstand. His visitor had to be one of Erdano's women—part of his brother's harem.

Duilio buttoned the top button of his nightshirt and started hunting for his felt slippers. "Give me a moment, please."

Very few humans had any inkling the Ferreira family possessed selkie blood, and those who did were polite enough not to let themselves into his bedroom in the middle of the night. It was, of course, an open secret among their employees that Duilio's mother was a selkie. While most selkies spent their lives in seal form, every moment in the sea or on a beach, she'd been raised among humans. But for a time she *had* lived as a seal among the nearest harem, to the north of the mouth of the Douro River at Braga Bay. Erdano was her child by that harem's master. He often visited the Ferreira household, but tonight he'd sent one of his women instead.

Duilio cursed under his breath. His valet had hidden his comfortable-but-worn slippers again, an unsubtle reminder that the man wanted Duilio to replace them. He gave up on finding them, crossed to the mantel, and lit the gaslight there. It wasn't likely that bare feet would offend this woman anyway. He turned up the light enough to cast a feeble circle of illumination about the armchair and table waiting before the hearth, then looked back at the unknown woman. "Do you have a message from Erdano?"

"Yes." She stepped into the light, revealing pointed features set in a heart-shaped face. Light brown hair fell sleekly over her shoulders. She was a lovely girl, but as soon as Duilio caught the scent of her, any thought of getting to know her better fled. Evidently before she walked barefoot into the city to find him, she'd simply borrowed some of Erdano's garments. The clothes—a man's trousers and shirt cinched tight by a wide belt at her waist—reeked of musk. Duilio resisted the urge to pinch his nose closed. Even though he was only half selkie himself, he had never much liked the scent of other males.

"Sir?" a voice asked from the hallway, dragging Duilio's attention away from the girl. João, the young boatman who stayed down on the quay with the family's boats, stood there, his sheepish expression evident in the light of the lamp he carried. "She came onto the yacht looking for you, sir. I thought it best to bring her here to the house. I . . . I thought she would knock, but . . ."

"It's fine, João." Duilio knew better than to expect polite behavior from this girl. Selkies didn't have the same manners as humans. She stood gazing up at the gaslight distrustfully. "Give me a few minutes," Duilio said, "and then you can escort her back."

"Yes, sir." The young man nodded quickly and withdrew into the hallway, pulling the bedroom door shut as he went.

Duilio wished João hadn't closed the door. The girl wouldn't be concerned for her reputation, but Duilio would prefer that the servants not get the wrong idea. He plucked his velvet dressing gown off the end of his bed, drew it on over his nightshirt, and belted it. Then he returned to the girl's side, leaning closer to get her attention. "What did you need to see me about?"

"Oh. There was a woman in the water," she said, watching the flickering gaslight as if concerned the flames might suddenly jump out of the fixture.

A woman in the water? That had to be what his gift had been yammering on about. "Where?"

The girl glanced at him for the first time. Her eyes slid toward his velvet dressing gown, her brows drawing together. "What is that?"

She'd probably spent most of her life in the sea and would have little familiarity with human luxuries. Duilio held out his arm so the girl could touch his sleeve. "It's called velvet."

She laid a tentative hand on his arm. The corners of her lips lifted as she ran her hand over the fabric's nap. Her warm brown eyes were, in the gaslight's glow, quite lovely. "Pretty. Can I have it?"

In addition to their ability to change form, most selkies purportedly had magical abilities in the area of seduction—selkie charm, it was often called. Duilio doubted this selkie was more than eighteen; young in human terms, but likely experienced in many things human girls of that age would not be. He patted her hand in his best fatherly manner. "What is your name?"

"Aga." Her eyes flicked toward the bed and then up to meet his. "Tigana said I could stay with you. You could give me the velvet."

God help me. Duilio pressed his lips together, weighing his response. Tigana, the queen of Erdano's harem, had control of the harem's many females. It wasn't the first time she'd sent him a girl, apparently believing he must be in dire need of a woman. Duilio had never been sure of the rules of harem politics and, not wanting to cause friction between Erdano and his queen, he'd always refused the gift. Well, save for the first time. Since then he'd tried to handle it diplomatically.

"Can you tell me what you saw, Aga?" he asked, reminding the girl of the reason she'd come. "Where was the woman?"

The girl's mouth drew down in a moue. "Over the rotting houses."

The rotting houses were what the selkies called *The City Under the Sea.* The houses themselves were all new, even the oldest not showing much wear from being underwater yet. All the same, the selkies had noticed a scent of rot in the water about them—a detail that Duilio feared was linked to several reports of missing servants. They had only made a connection between those missing servants and the work of art a few weeks ago, when Lady Pereira de Santos had reported two of her maids missing only a day after the replica of her house had been mentioned in the newspapers. They'd wondered if their bodies might be hidden within those houses. Aga's sighting firmly linked Duilio's sense of foreboding to *The City Under the Sea*, but he was still missing some vital clue. "Was she swimming?"

Aga shrugged fluidly. "Yes, but then she was in the boat."

Duilio felt his brows drawing together. When had a boat entered the conversation? "How late was this, Aga? Had the sun set?"

She sighed as if vexed by all his questions. "Only a little while ago. I swam to the mouth and then to the big boat . . ."

The "big boat" would be the Ferreira family's yacht, moored out past the Bicalho Quay. "I see."

". . . and then I walked here with the man."

Duilio chewed his lower lip as he calculated. Aga had swum out to the mouth of the Douro, almost three miles against the current, back to the yacht, and then she'd walked nearly a mile up the steep streets of the Golden City. How long had that taken her? Perhaps two hours? Three? "So, was it before the moon rose?"

"Yes." Her tone suggested he might be dense.

Women did not swim in the river in the middle of the night. Most human women never learned to swim at all. "Did you see the woman, Aga? What did she look like?"

The girl stepped closer and laid graceful hands on his velvet-covered chest. She didn't quite reach his chin. "She wore black. And white."

His gift told him that this conversation was *important*, that he needed to know something this girl was telling him . . . or not telling him. He wasn't sure what questions he needed to ask. "Were you close?" he pressed. "Did you see her face?"

Aga rubbed her cheek against his chest. "No. Wrong way."

He wished Tigana hadn't been in a mood to be generous. He didn't need this sort of distraction now. Duilio set his hands on the girl's shoulders, stepped back, and tried again. "This is important, Aga. Can you tell me anything else? Did she fall out of the boat?"

"No, it was waiting when she came up," Aga said, her shoulders slumping.

Came up? From the houses? Why would someone come *up* from the houses? If they wanted a better look at them, they could ride out to the site on one of the submersible boats that sold tickets to curious folk who wished to see the work of art. He'd even gone to look at them himself. And at night it was too dark to see them anyway.

"You don't want me?" Aga's hands began to roam his chest, drawing Duilio's wandering mind very firmly back to the present.

Oh, what a vexing question. His body had clearly noted the girl's lithe form. Heaven knew she was attractive enough, and once he got her out of Erdano's garments, the disturbing scent of male selkie would be greatly diminished. But she was part of Erdano's harem . . . and there was a servant outside in the hall, waiting. Both factors dampened any ardor she aroused in him. "He's my brother," he told her. "I want to keep on his good side."

"Why?" She sighed again, sounding petulant. "Tigana said . . ."

He held her at a distance. "All the same."

"They said you were nice," she added plaintively.

Oh, good Lord. The only time he'd gotten involved with any of the women from Erdano's harem had been when he was fifteen. That was half a lifetime ago, and evidently they still talked about him being "nice." Well, it could be worse. "I'm sorry, Aga, but I need to sleep."

That only made him sound like an old man.

Her lower lip thrust out in a pout. "What do I do?"

"There's a room down the hall where Erdano sleeps when he's here. You can stay there for the rest of the night or go back to the boat if you wish."

Her face took on a calculating look. "Is the handsome man from the boat still here?"

Duilio resisted the urge to laugh at her eager tone. *Poor João.* "I believe so."

The corners of her pretty lips lifted. "Is he nice?"

Duilio wasn't going to speculate about whether João was nice. "You would have to ask him, I suppose."

"I'll do that," she said brightly, then her brows drew together. "Do I leave now?"

"Can you think of anything else to tell me about the woman in the water?"

Aga took a deep breath and appeared to be thinking hard, her lips pinched together. She finally pronounced, "She had webbed hands."

Like a thunderclap inside his brain, Duilio *knew.*

That was the fact he'd been fishing for. His gift confirmed it.

A woman with webbed hands. Duilio set his own hand under the girl's elbow and drew her back toward his bedroom door. When he opened it he found a very flustered-looking João right outside. The young man must have been listening at the keyhole.

"Sir," João said quickly, "you asked me to wait."

Seeing the young man's flushed features, Duilio held in a laugh.

"Yes, João, I did. Can you escort Miss Aga to Mr. Erdano's room at the far end on the left? Or back to the yacht, if she wishes."

João's eyes slid toward the girl. "Yes, sir."

Recalling the girl's request, Duilio slipped off his dressing gown, bundled it up, and handed it to her. "In trade for the information, Aga."

She petted the bundle of velvet like a pup. "Pretty."

She didn't even look back, but happily followed the boatman away, the light of his lamp fading as they went down the hallway. Duilio shut his door, content to leave his little problem in João's capable hands. He returned to the hearth, settled into the leather armchair, and stretched out his legs.

A woman had been out in the water, near the submerged houses. That woman had webbed hands: a *sereia*, not a human. Unlike selkies, who were called selkies all over Europe, the sereia bore different names in other countries. The French called them *sirènes*, the English mermaids, and the Germans knew them as *Lorelei.* No matter how they were named, they weren't allowed in the Golden City.

Selkies weren't either, but the ban hadn't ever kept his mother or Erdano—or him, for that matter—out. For all Duilio knew, there could be dozens of selkies living in the Golden City. Unlike the sereia, once they'd shed their pelts they were almost indistinguishable from humans. Without a selkie's pelt, one couldn't prove that they weren't human. The sereia's webbed hands, their gills, and the scale patterning of their skin were all elements of their nature that they *couldn't* put aside.

Duilio laced his fingers together and propped his chin atop them. He could recall seeing sereia walking the streets of the city when he was young, in the days before the prince's ban. Although they kept their distance from human society, a few had owned houses in the city or in Vila Nova de Gaia across the river. They had traded with the locals, but not any longer.

When Prince Fabricio came into power following his father's demise, he had issued a proclamation banning all sea folk from the Golden City on pain of death. He'd been told by his seers he would one day be killed by one of the sea folk. Duilio had his doubts. He found it hard to believe a seer could reliably predict anything far into the future, and it had been almost two decades since then. Too many factors had changed in the interim.

Whatever the impetus behind the prince's order, for the first few years following its issuance the Special Police—whose explicit mandate was to carry out the orders of the prince, whether or not those orders served the best interests of the people—had obediently rounded up every sereia or selkie they could find, along with many of those who protected them. Sympathizers had been jailed and their property seized. The sea folk themselves had been executed. Otterfolk rarely came into the city, and most selkies slipped in and out, interested in little beyond a night's pleasure, so the majority of those executed had been sereia. And although Duilio hadn't heard of an execution in the past few years, most citizens believed the Special Police still carried them out, just not publicly. There *was* actually an ambassador from the Ilhas das Sereias—the islands of the sereia—at the prince's court, but the man lived under house arrest at the palace. And while Duilio had long *suspected* there might be sereia hiding in the city, he hadn't been sure until he met Miss Paredes.

He closed his eyes, remembering that day. It had been a brief encounter, back in the spring. Everyone else had watched the stunning Lady Isabel Amaral. Duilio's attention had been captured instead by the lady's companion, a woman somewhere near his age, modestly dressed and attractive, although he wouldn't have called her beautiful. Pretty, perhaps, but nothing special. Well, she had exceptionally nice lips, lips made to kiss. He recalled admiring her tiny waist and rounded hips, although that might simply be her corset. Her flat-brimmed straw hat had cast a shadow across her face, but as she shifted the parasol she carried to better shade her mistress' alabaster skin, he'd noticed her dark eyes.

His breath had gone still. He had *known*, in that way his gift worked, that she was more than just a hired companion. She was special. That had been enough to make Duilio look again.

And for the six months since that brief meeting, his gift had kept telling him the woman was *important*. He didn't know how, exactly, but he didn't take the feeling lightly. He'd watched her from a distance. He bribed a servant in the Amaral household to discover her given name, Oriana. He'd investigated her background. Before becoming a lady's companion, she'd worked in a dressmaker's shop. He discovered little else. It was as if she hadn't existed before then.

He'd often attended the same social events as Lady Isabel and her companion, even if he didn't travel in the Amarals' elevated stratum of society. They were *old* aristocracy, while the Ferreiras were newly moneyed and not worthy of their conversation. Duilio had watched Miss Paredes carefully, though. She often kept her hands in her lap. She wore silk mitts rather than gloves, an old lady's affectation. She always chose high-necked shirts, even at formal occasions, carrying her modesty to an unfashionable extreme, although he'd heard a rumor from one of the servants that she had spots . . . or something *catching* on her hands.

Taken individually, none of those things had given her away. But the longer he thought about it, the surer he became that all of those foibles combined were signs of a sereia hiding her true nature. Duilio opened his eyes and stared at his cold hearth. He had no proof that Miss Paredes was a sereia, but his gift assured him it was true.

Just as there might be dozens of selkies hiding in the city, he was willing to accept that sereia might be living here as well. But it was more dangerous for them. Their nature was harder to hide. The most reasonable explanation that he could come up with was that she was a spy, although what she could learn in the Amaral household mystified him. While the Amaral family had impressive social ties, their political ties were limited.

And if she were a spy, what had she been doing out by *The City Under the Sea*? Did her people find the taste of death in the water as objectionable as did the local selkies? Or could she have had some other reason for being there? A vague frisson of worry snaked out of the back corner of his mind, his gift trying to give him another clue to unlock the bundle of questions.

Black and white. Aga had said the mysterious woman with webbed hands wore black and white. That had been important. Duilio closed his eyes and concentrated, hoping to force a direct answer out of his gift. He took several slow breaths. *Was it Oriana Paredes out on the river near* The City Under the Sea*?*

His gift supplied nothing in response.

Duilio rubbed one hand across his face and groaned. *Stupid.* That was the wrong question. That event was in the past already, and his gift only looked forward. He reformulated his mental question and asked himself, *Will I learn that Oriana Paredes was out on the river tonight near the rotting houses?*

And then he *knew*. Sooner or later he was going to discover that Aga's mysterious woman with webbed hands was, indeed, Oriana Paredes, companion to Lady Isabel Amaral.

Duilio suspected it was for this very night that his gift had called her to his attention that day as she stood in Isabel Amaral's shadow. Tonight she had been seen in the river near *The City Under the Sea.* Surely she had some reason for that, some information that might be helpful to his investigation.

Black and white. Why was that important? His gift never answered the why of things, which was always the part he needed most. He sat back in his chair and sighed. In the morning he would visit the Amaral house and ask to speak with Miss Paredes.

No, I won't. His gift told him she wouldn't be there. She had left the Amaral household for good, which was damnably inconvenient for him.

Duilio got up and turned down the gaslight. If he wanted answers to his questions, he first had to find her.

CHAPTER 4

Oriana jolted awake when the milkman's cart rattled through the alleyway. A momentary panic seized her, but she too quickly recalled why she had fallen asleep out of doors.

Lady Amaral had cast her out. When she told the woman that Isabel had been taken, Isabel's mother claimed it was merely part of her daughter's scheme to elope. Oriana hadn't been able to tell her the truth; she'd barely gotten a chance to speak at all. Lady Amaral had just returned from a ball or party and was in a foul mood, so in the early hours of the morning she had the butler escort Oriana out of the house.

It had been too early and too dark to go anywhere, and Oriana had been too exhausted to search for a place to stay, in any case. After a dazed moment standing in the court behind the house, she recalled the stairwell that led to the house's coal room. The two bags she'd left the previous evening were still there, so she'd curled up on the cold stone next to them and cried until sleep overtook her.

Oriana forced herself to sit up. The morning air was cold but bearable. Her black skirt was ripped. Her clothes were almost dry, although her shoes were still damp. Her forehead was tender, and her fingers found a small lump there. She checked her right palm, wrapped with strips torn from her apron. The narrow slash her rescuer had made when wrestling her dagger out of her hand had scabbed over, although one end began to bleed afresh when she removed her makeshift bandage.

She heard someone speaking then with the milkman up at the back door of the house—meaningless chatter, but it reminded her she wasn't alone here. She grabbed the portmanteau she'd left there the evening before, dragged it to her side, and searched through the contents until she found another pair of mitts. Hiding her hands came first. She tugged the right one on over her scabbed palm, making sure that all of her webbing was covered.

She was donning the other when Carlos, the first footman, leaned over the rail that led down to the coal room stairs. "Miss Paredes? Are you still hiding down there?"

Oriana clutched both hands to her chest, her heart slamming against her ribs. She took a deep breath and rose unsteadily, grasping the rail with her left hand. "Yes, I'm here."

He came a few steps down, not crowding her. "The dragon won't be awake for hours, so Arenas won't notice if I'm missing for a few minutes." He held out a napkin-wrapped offering in one hand. "Were you serious about Isabel being grabbed?"

Oriana took the napkin. It held a croissant, a rare show of kindness from Carlos. She wasn't starving yet, so she tucked it into the mouth of her portmanteau. "Thank you. Yes. I fear something terrible has happened."

Carlos nodded. "Efisio's driver came by here just a few minutes ago. He said he was supposed to pick up the two of you last night. They drove around and around but they never saw you."

Of course the driver would have missed Isabel! "Has anyone told Lady Amaral that?"

"Wake the dragon?" Carlos laughed shortly. "Not after the way she treated you last night."

It had been a terrible display of temper on Lady Amaral's part. Oriana didn't want to relive it again. "There was a coach at the end of the alley," she told Carlos. "We thought it was Mr. Efisio's. *They* took us. They drugged us and threw me into the river, but Isabel . . ." She shrugged, not wanting to lie outright.

Carlos nodded, his lips pursed. "I'll be changing my bets, then."

What did he mean by that? "Bets?"

"On whether they'll get married or not," Carlos clarified, brushing a croissant crumb off his black sleeve with white-gloved fingers.

Oriana felt a flare of anger. Carlos didn't care about Isabel—or her. He just wanted to make certain he didn't lose money on a bet.

"You can't stay here," Carlos added, glancing pointedly down at the two bags near her feet. "Arenas will find you for sure. Do you have somewhere to go?"

There were places she *could* go, but Oriana didn't know if she'd be welcome in any of them. She could go to her master, Heriberto, but if she went to see him, he might order her back to the islands and she wouldn't be able to pursue Isabel's murderer. She could try one of the sereia who lived here in the Golden City, the exiles, but as they'd been banished by the very government she represented, they had no reason to help her. She doubted any of them would, not even her father. In any case, contact with the exiles was strictly forbidden by the ministry.

She raised her chin. "I'll think of something," she told Carlos.

He fished a slip of paper out of a pocket and passed it to her. "My grandmother's sister rents rooms. Tell her you know me, and she'll give you a good rate."

The paper had an address on it, one down near the river. It wasn't a good neighborhood, but she couldn't afford a good neighborhood, not with what little she had stashed in her portmanteau. Oriana looked back up at Carlos. He was watching her, but had one eye on the house's back door, she could tell. "Thank you, Carlos."

His eyes focused on her, one corner of his lips twisting up into a smirk. "And if you can't pay, I'm sure we can work something out."

I should have known Carlos wasn't acting out of kindness. A paid companion was considered *above* the household servants, but given her current circumstances, the footman might well think a dalliance with her within his reach now. She'd had some of Isabel's suitors try their hand at seducing her before. It had been an easy matter to frown at them and shake her head, but she'd been under Isabel's protection then. Now she had no one to guard her against unwanted advances. Still, while she might not like Carlos, she needed a place to stay, a place where they wouldn't ask too many questions about a woman showing up in her bedraggled condition. She forced herself to smile at him. "We'll see."

Carlos spotted the butler come out looking for him then. He winked at her and jogged up the steps toward the back of the house, nose in the air as he went.

Oriana leaned back against the stairwell wall and covered her face with her hands. *Why do things keep getting worse?*

Duilio's mother sat alone at the breakfast table. He stopped at the threshold and gazed at her, worried. She looked completely human and had human manners. She had excellent taste in clothing, always comported herself in a manner befitting a Portuguese lady, and had elegantly decorated the Ferreira home, managing to work in the occasional garish item brought back by her seafaring husband. None of the social set who knew her would have any reason to guess that she was a selkie.

At the moment, she stared toward the dining room's west-facing window, her hands cupped in her lap. She absently rubbed the tips of her fingers with her other hand as if they ached. With her somber garb and desolate countenance, most would assume she mourned her husband's death still. Duilio knew better.

She was pining for the sea.

He hated to see her this way. When he'd left the Golden City to travel abroad, she'd been vivacious and mischievous—a loving, attentive mother. She'd helped oversee the family's business investments and kept firm control of the household. Now most days all she did was sit in the front parlor and gaze in the direction of the river. It seemed her spirit had slipped away from her body.

And, to some extent, that was his fault. If he'd stayed home, perhaps none of this would have come to pass. Perhaps he could have stopped . . .

His mother's head turned as if she'd caught scent of him standing there. "Duilinho?"

He smiled. She persisted in calling him by his childhood pet name. He settled next to her at the table and covered her hand with his own. "I'm here."

Her seal-brown eyes fixed on him, a rare moment of concentration. "Are you well?"

He must look tired after his sleepless night. Even as distracted as she was, she always worried for him. "I'm fine, Mother."

Her eyes slipped back toward the window, and she turned that direction as if she heard the sea itself calling her.

Duilio pressed his lips together. It troubled him that she spent most of her days cooped up in the house. His father had been dead more than a year now. Duilio expected that his mother would prefer to remarry eventually. She was a lovely woman, even approaching fifty as she was. But her social reemergence must be put off until she was better.

One of the footmen brought him his regular breakfast, a large plate of eggs and *chouriço* along with a pot of coffee. Duilio waited until the man left before starting in on his food. Between bites, he told his mother of the bizarre information he'd gotten very early that morning. He wasn't certain she was attending. Her coffee was almost untouched, and she'd eaten only half her croissant. Her preferred newspaper—the trade daily rather than the *Gazette*—lay unopened next to her elbow. He talked to her anyway, in the hope that she caught something of his words. He would hate for her to feel neglected.

"So I'm going to go see Joaquim," he finished, "and ask if he can help me find her."

His mother continued to stare at the window.

"Shall I bear your greetings, Mother?"

That caught her attention. She blinked and turned halfway toward him. "To Filho?"

Apparently she *had* been paying attention. Just as she addressed Duilio by his childhood name, she called Joaquim so also. Joaquim Tavares and his father shared a name, so Joaquim was simply Filho—"son"—to her. He set down his napkin. "Yes, Mother."

Joaquim and his younger brother had lost their mother at an early age and had come to live with their cousins, the Ferreira family. They had stayed for the next eight years, until their father retired from his sea travels to take up boatbuilding. The younger son, Cristiano, had joined that business, but Joaquim had chosen to make his career in the police.

Duilio might have selected that profession himself, had his own father not been set on his sons being *gentlemen*. He'd dutifully studied law at the university in Coimbra—an acceptable profession for a younger son—but then had proceeded to travel abroad for the next five years to work with various police agencies on the continent and in Great Britain. His father had not been pleased. But when his elder brother Alessio died, Duilio had been forced to return home to shoulder the responsibility of managing the family's considerable investments . . . and to take care of his mother.

She brushed her hands along her skirts and picked up her newspaper, a rare show of energy. "Please tell Filho to come visit me."

"I'll ask him, Mother," he promised.

"I wonder . . ." She laid down her paper and touched the smooth brown hair dressed in a simple knot at the nape of her neck.

Duilio hadn't inherited that hair. He had his father's, darker and with a tendency to curl. The only feature he'd inherited from his mother was her eyes. He wished he resembled her more, as Alessio had.

He waited for her to finish her sentence, but instead she stared down at her newspaper as if she had no idea what it was doing there. Sighing inwardly, Duilio rose and took his leave of her, kissing her cheek in farewell. Her maid, Felis, bustled past him, no doubt eager to get her mistress up and about her silent day. Duilio paused and watched the elderly woman fussing over his mother's unmoving form.

His mother's pelt was missing, stolen from the house three years before. In a feat of magic that Duilio's intellect never could grasp, a selkie could remove his or her pelt and be left in human form. Half-human, Duilio couldn't do that himself, but he'd *seen* it done many times. It still baffled him. And even in human form, that pelt remained part of the selkie, an eternal tie to the sea and her life there. Without her pelt, his mother couldn't go back to the ocean she loved.

Duilio hadn't been around at the time of the theft. If he had, he might have stopped it, but he'd been in London instead, studying the police force there. Alessio had written and mentioned a theft, but hadn't told Duilio *what* was stolen, a gross oversight. He would have come back to hunt the thief himself if only he'd known. But Alessio and Father had thought they could find the thing without help. Unfortunately, that hadn't been the case.

Then Alessio had died.

His death nearly a year and a half ago had been suspicious. He'd gotten involved in an argument over a lover and ended up dueling another gentleman in a clearing outside the city. Both parties had seen it was foolish and in the end both men deloped, firing their guns into the air. Yet somehow Alessio was shot through the heart. Duilio had talked to witnesses, and none had any idea from where that fatal shot had come. With no evidence to the contrary, the police had called it an accident.

Duilio wondered if that stray bullet was linked to Alessio's hunt for their mother's pelt. In his journals, Alessio had indicated he was close to a breakthrough right before his death. But he hadn't recorded that breakthrough, whatever it was, leaving Duilio in the dark.

It turned out they actually knew who'd taken the pelt from the house: a footman hired only a month before. The man had pinched both the pelt and a strongbox from the desk in the library. When Alessio had located the footman's apartment, the strongbox and the pelt were already gone. And they couldn't question that false footman about it. He'd been strangled to death. That made it likely he'd merely been *hired* to find the pelt and steal it. Whoever hired him had probably killed him to keep him quiet.

Duilio's father had continued the search for the pelt, but one damp night while out hunting, Alexandre Ferreira contracted a chill that all too quickly became pneumonia. He died before Duilio could make it home from Paris. In the intervening year, Duilio had reconstructed every last step his father and brother had taken in their searches, with no more success. His gift had proven singularly unhelpful in this particular quest.

The thief hadn't destroyed the pelt; Duilio knew that much. His mother would have died if that were the case. No, it was secreted away somewhere, an item of indescribable magic. Without it she would never be whole again. If she were to answer the call of the sea, she would be as vulnerable to the waters as any human. She fought that desire constantly.

After one rueful look at his mother, Duilio headed to the door to collect his things from the long mahogany table in the front entryway. He hadn't found her missing pelt yet, but perhaps he could find one missing servant.

The butler, an elderly man who had served the Ferreira family his entire life, bustled up the hall in time to hand Duilio his gloves. "I've heard your sleep was disturbed last night, sir. I am so sorry . . ."

Duilio tugged on the kid-leather gloves and shook his head. "No need to worry, Cardenas," he said reassuringly. "It was an important message, and I was awake anyway."

"I'm concerned about security is all, sir." The butler handed over Duilio's top hat. "I don't like strangers in my house."

"I do understand, Cardenas. I'll ask Erdano again not to send others from his harem here." He hoped that would placate his ruffled butler. He didn't want the man worrying himself into an early grave. "Is the young lady still in the house?"

Cardenas blushed. "Yes, sir. In Mr. Erdano's room."

Duilio managed not to grin at the man's vexed tone. His long-suffering butler tended to consider Erdano and his women a nuisance. Their presence invariably disordered Cardenas' well-run household. "I'm certain she'll leave soon enough."

The butler's spine was ramrod straight. "She's not alone, sir."

Ah, that explains the blush. Well, it meant João hadn't spent the night out at the quay, but that was permissible as long as he had all the boats in sailing shape when they were needed. "Be patient, Cardenas. I believe this morning is João's half day anyway," Duilio lied, giving the butler an excuse not to throw out the boatman. "Now, I'm off to meet with Joaquim. I'll likely be gone past luncheon, so don't hold the meal for me."

"Yes, sir," Cardenas said with a brisk nod.

Duilio headed out the door. Once on the flagstone steps, he heard the door lock behind him. As his gift had lately been warning him of impending danger, Duilio patted the flap pocket of his frock coat to verify that his revolver was there, then tucked his newspaper under his arm.

The Ferreira house was set back from the cobbled street by a small garden, the flowers all faded so late in the year. A tall fence of wrought iron about it warded away trespassers. An unpretentious manor of dark brown stone, the house had originally been built to adorn a *quinta*—a vineyard. The owner moved it to the Street of Flowers nearly a century before, stone by stone, but died with no child to inherit it. It had passed to the Ferreira family then, to Duilio's newly wealthy grandfather. Although the house had been in his family for more than sixty years, they were still considered newcomers.

The traffic on the Street of Flowers was brisk that time of morning. While the broad avenue was forbidden to wagons and commercial carters, its width invited all other manner of traffic. Pedestrians bustled past the wrought-iron fences separating the street from the houses, either heading down toward the river or up toward the palace or the government ministries centered in what had once been the Bishop's Palace. Finely dressed gentry and government officials shared the busy street with fishermen and boatmen.

A tram ran up the center of the road, the gold-painted car rattling by all day long. The line had been electrified at the turn of the century, eliminating vast quantities of mule manure that had required collecting almost hourly. Fortunately for the sanitation workers, the horses drawing private carriages and hired cabs up and down the street ensured that they still had jobs.

Duilio walked down to his gate and let himself out, standing back as a lovely lady in a stylish peach-colored walking suit passed him. Her poodle tugged on its leash, trying to get a better sniff of him, no doubt thinking him an oddly shaped seal. Dogs always found him perplexing. The woman cast him an appraising glance, smiled coyly, and slowed her pace, her hips swaying attractively. *One of the demimonde*, Duilio decided, *hunting for her next protector*. He admired her lush figure for a moment. She was tempting, but he nodded to the woman politely and resolutely walked the other direction, up from the river.

It was a steep climb. The Golden City rose from the north bank of the Douro River near where it fed into the sea, spreading across several hills. The Street of Flowers traversed the distance from the quay up to the palace itself. While it had once been a narrow lane occupied by goldsmiths and fabric sellers, less than half a mile long, businesses and churches and homes alike had all been demolished to make room for aristocratic newcomers. The country had been embroiled in a civil war, the throne claimed by two young twin brothers—or, rather, their advisers. The Liberals in the south pushed for political reform and a break from the Church, while the Absolutists in the north preferred the status quo.

But when an earthquake destroyed much of Lisboa in 1755, the war had fizzled out. The southern prince, Manuel III, threw all his efforts and his army into helping his city recover. In the north, Prince Raimundo refused to take advantage of his twin's distraction. Instead his councilors set up a rival capital, cutting Portugal into two princedoms rather than a single united kingdom. Prior to that time, the Golden City had been modestly known as the Port, a city of commoners, although many would argue it had belonged to the Church instead. That was easy to believe, given the number of spires that dotted the hills, the tower that marked the city's heights, and the grand cathedral that rose above the river.

Nevertheless, the aristocrats *had* come, along with their prince, and had changed whatever suited them, for good or for ill. They had moved their houses from the farthest edges of the city, from the resort of Espinho to the south, or from the countryside. Some homes, like that of the Queirós family two doors up from Duilio's, were newer, built in the neoclassical style, with pillars and pediments, the marble imported from far away. Others had the whitewashed walls and red tiles common to the area about the river. It made a jumble of a street, the houses unmatched save for their arrogant consumption of space.

Duilio had always felt a touch guilty about living there. He didn't believe that having inherited his home and wealth made him any better of a person than João, the young man who watched his boats. That was one reason he'd chosen to continue his work with the police, hoping to, in effect, earn what he'd been given.

He passed several more houses before reaching the crossing of

Clérigos Street and the Street of Flowers. Clérigos had less traffic, so he turned west on it and began the steep walk up to the higher levels of the city. Built on one of the highest points, the baroque bell tower of the Clérigos church had long served as a landmark for sailors, a slender beacon of ornate gray granite. The thing also made the navigation of the old city's narrow streets easier for those on foot. Once Duilio reached the heights, he walked along, keeping one eye on the tower as he unfolded his newspaper and hunted for the social page. He brushed past other pedestrians as he did so, but not sensing any danger on the streets that morning, he didn't worry.

The social page listed the normal comings and goings of the aristocracy—who was seen where and with whom. For those readers unfamiliar with the persons listed, the significance of the entries was limited. The news that Lady X had visited Lady Y at her home meant nothing if one didn't know of the long-standing feud between the families. But as Duilio acted as an interpreter of these affairs for the police, it was his business to keep apprised of all the foolishness of the upper crust. He read through the first column of entries, making mental notes as to what needed further investigation. Nothing in particular jumped out at him until he reached the second column.

He stopped in the midst of the foot traffic, causing a portly gentleman in a brown tweed suit to bump into him. Duilio apologized to the equally apologetic gentleman and stepped back against the wall of the building to his right to get out of others' way. Then he read the notice in question again.

Lady Isabel Amaral and her companion left the Golden City for Paris Thursday night via train, following the evening departure of Mr. Marianus Guimarães Efisio. Friends of Mr. Efisio expect they will be married in Paris within the week.

Duilio frowned down at the page. He should be shocked that Efisio had eloped with a woman other than his meek betrothed, Pia Sequeira. But that wasn't what troubled him.

Miss Paredes had been in the river at midnight last night, but if he recalled correctly, that train left for Paris via Lisbon at ten in the evening. She couldn't have been on that train.

He felt a chill, not simply because of the cold stone wall behind his back. Had his gift been wrong? For a moment Duilio stared up at the tower, realizing only then that he was in the square before the church itself, the baroque facade of the building looming almost as if in accusation.

Fortunately, the Church in Northern Portugal didn't hold his natural talent against him. Here the prince himself employed seers, and it was common knowledge that the Jesuits had many witches within their ranks. Not so in Spain, where seers and healers and any other stripe of witch were made to disown their gifts or be imprisoned.

Duilio had more than once considered trying to disavow his gift, trying to ignore it, not using it at all. But his gift was a part of him, just as his mother's pelt was a part of her. Now was not the time to start doubting it. He closed his eyes for a moment, arguing with that inner voice. It insisted again that Aga's mysterious web-fingered woman *was* his Miss Paredes.

Opening his eyes, he glanced down at the paper clutched in one gloved hand. He read the entry again as a group of young girls walked past him, whispering among themselves. He pondered the disparity for a moment and a horrible possibility occurred to him. What if Isabel hadn't been on that train either? He closed his eyes again and asked himself a different question: *Will Isabel Amaral marry her Mr. Efisio?*

His gift told him that Lady Isabel Amaral was not to marry Mr. Efisio. That she was never to marry Mr. Efisio. That she was never to marry at all. *She was already dead.*

Duilio opened his eyes, the sense of urgency in him rising. From the beginning there had been something wrong with those damned houses in the river—they stayed afloat long after they filled with water. There were buoyancy charms carved on each house, but after

Duilio and Joaquim had begun investigating the houses, Cristiano had told them that such charms were next to useless. That revelation had led them to the disturbing conclusion that the missing servants were being *sacrificed* to keep the houses floating, that the taste of rot the selkies found so objectionable came from slowly decaying bodies hidden inside those houses. What if they'd been wrong?

What if a new house had been added to the artwork while he'd slept fitfully? That house might have held Lady Isabel and her companion. What if one of the two had been *alive* at the time? Or both had?

He had wondered why Miss Paredes was seen out by the houses at midnight. His mind had spun out several different scenarios, most involving her people's government investigating the artwork. Now he felt certain that wasn't the case at all. He quickly searched the newspaper's front page, hunting for any mention of a new house being added to *The City Under the Sea*, but didn't find any. It usually took a couple of days for the news to trickle out. And if Aga had witnessed that happening last night, she hadn't mentioned it. Perhaps she'd simply arrived too late.

Will I learn that Oriana Paredes escaped from inside one of those houses? he asked himself. The answer his mind gave him sickened him. *Yes.*

Jaw clenched, Duilio folded up the newspaper and tucked it under his arm. He headed on out of the square, settled in his intention to hunt down the mysterious Miss Paredes, who was *not* on her way to France, no matter what the paper had to say.

CHAPTER 5

A short while later, Duilio stood before the threshold of the small apartment Joaquim Tavares rented on Restauração Street. The tall, narrow house was well maintained by grace of the elderly widow who owned the building and kept a hawklike eye on all her tenants.

Duilio knocked on the door and heard a request called back to wait a moment. Only a second or two passed before the door swung open, revealing a half-dressed Joaquim, still buttoning his shirt cuffs. He wore a matching waistcoat and trousers in a beige check—a casual suit. He seemed surprised to find Duilio waiting in the narrow hall. "What are you doing here?"

Although a cousin, Joaquim was closer to Duilio than either Alessio or Erdano in both temperament and appearance. They had the same height and build, and their faces bore the stamps of the Ferreira family: square jaws and wide brows. But what made for pleasant features on Duilio's face translated to handsome in Joaquim's case, possibly because he had inherited his Spanish mother's darker coloration. Duilio smiled ruefully at Joaquim's apparent annoyance. "Who were you expecting?"

"Mrs. Domingues, bringing a pastry for my breakfast."

Duilio rolled his eyes at the idea of such a skimpy morning meal. "Are you going to invite me in or not?"

Joaquim grabbed Duilio's shoulder to draw him inside. "Yes, but I'm about to leave for the station."

"I'll walk with you." Duilio closed the door while Joaquim went to fetch his suit coat. The apartment was furnished in items cast off from other houses, either the Tavares or the Ferreira home. Two worn armchairs, one upholstered and one covered in leather, waited near the single window in the front room. The leather one had been in Joaquim's room in the Ferreira house as a child.

Duilio felt as much at home here as he did in his own library. He turned to peruse the mismatched bookshelves that lined the wall next to the door. Joaquim had always had an interest in history and philosophy, which showed in the selection of books neatly lining those shelves. After laying his folded newspaper on one shelf, Duilio ran a finger along the rows, hunting for the requisite volume of Camões that must lurk there.

"A woman was seen out near the houses last night," Duilio called in the direction of the bedroom. "I need to find her." Joaquim had a talent for finding lost people, one of the many skills for which the police valued him.

"Which houses?" Joaquim returned.

"*The City Under the Sea*." Duilio located the book he was looking for, the epic poem studied by every Portuguese schoolboy wherein the author detailed the voyages of Vasco da Gama.

Joaquim came back into the room, tugging on his loose suit coat. "Doing what?"

An inspector's pay didn't afford him the same quality of garb he'd had as a child in the Ferreira household, but Duilio knew better than to comment on the coat's poor fit. He could afford a fancy valet like Marcellin to turn him out in fine frock coats and silk waistcoats. In fact, he could easily afford to pay for a valet for Joaquim, but his cousin was prickly about money matters, so Duilio didn't interfere. He pulled out the book he'd located instead. "She was in the water. . . ." he answered.

Reaching for the tweed hat on the shelf nearest the door, Joaquim paused. "Swimming?"

"Yes. That's not what's important. I think she was in one of the houses."

Joaquim cast a perplexed look in his direction.

"She was meant to be a victim, Joaquim. I think she *escaped* from it."

Joaquim went still as he worked out the ramifications of that. They'd assumed the victims were sacrificed to keep the houses floating, but such a use of necromancy would have to be enacted before the houses were placed in the river. The possibility that the victims had been put into those houses *while still alive* had never occurred to them. "If that's true, we need to find her. How did *you* find out?"

"Aga saw her and told me."

Joaquim rubbed a hand over his face, a sign of frustration. "Aga?"

Starting at the beginning would take too long. "One of Erdano's girls. The thing is . . . I think I know the woman she described to me. It's Miss Paredes, who's companion to Lady Isabel Amaral." Duilio slid the folded newspaper off the bookshelf and pointed to the questionable item on the social page. "Rumor says Lady Isabel eloped last night, in that same companion's company, with Marianus Efisio."

Joaquim perused the notice, a doubtful expression crossing his features. He set the paper back on the shelf. "If she eloped, how would the gossips already know?"

Duilio shook his head. That wasn't the point. "Lady Amaral must have spread the rumor last night herself. To stave off her creditors, I'd expect."

Joaquim rolled his dark eyes. "Oh yes. I recall the woman now."

Duilio resisted repeating anything he'd heard of the impecunious noblewoman.

"So, what makes you think this companion was in one of the houses," Joaquim asked, "if she's supposedly off eloping with two other people?"

Duilio dropped into the upholstered chair, the one he usually took when visiting, and continued flipping through the book. "She wasn't eloping with them. He went ahead. The companion was probably going along as a chaperone until the wedding."

Joaquim settled in the other chair. "Get to the point, Duilio."

"If I'm correct," Duilio said, "the Amaral house was added to the artwork sometime last night, and we'll find out that Miss Paredes wasn't the only one who didn't get on that train."

"You're suggesting that Isabel Amaral was in that house as well." Joaquim's fingers tapped loudly on the leather arm of his chair. "We knew we were about due for a new house to show up."

New houses had been appearing in the artwork at roughly two-week intervals. Duilio found the passage he was looking for, stuck a finger in the book to mark the place, and closed it so he could focus on Joaquim. "My gift tells me that Isabel Amaral is dead, no matter what the newspapers claim."

Joaquim closed his eyes and made the sign of the cross. Duilio's gift had been passed to all males of the Ferreira line. A cousin on the *distaff* side of the Ferreira family, Joaquim didn't have the gift, but having grown up around Duilio and Alessio, he knew very well how it worked.

Duilio went on. "The only thing that makes sense of her companion's appearance in the water at midnight is that neither of them reached the train station. To find out exactly what happened, I have to find Miss Paredes."

"Won't she return to the Amaral household?"

As soon as Joaquim asked, Duilio shook his head. "No. I don't think Lady Amaral would take Miss Paredes back once she told her what happened. That woman needs people to believe her daughter alive to keep her creditors at bay. She would be more likely to hide the truth."

Joaquim nodded slowly. Apparently, he too believed the woman would put concern about her creditors over concern for her daughter's fate, a sad commentary on the woman's priorities. "Then the police," Joaquim said. "Surely your Miss Paredes would have taken her story to the police if her employer was killed."

No, that was one place she wouldn't go. They would ask how she could have survived if Isabel hadn't, and Miss Paredes couldn't reveal that. "She will not go to the police," Duilio said firmly. "We're going to have to hunt her down."

Joaquim frowned. "Is that your gift speaking, too?"

How could he answer that without lying to Joaquim? He wasn't ready to hand over all the truth yet, not until he was *sure* she was a sereia. "I have reason to believe she won't go to the police."

Joaquim's expression showed he recognized that evasion for what it was. "I'm not supposed to be investigating this any longer."

That had never stopped Joaquim before.

"I'll go talk to the submersible captains," Duilio told him, "and ask if they've seen a new house in the water." A handful of entrepreneurial captains had invested in submersible crafts that could be attached to their ships, pumping air down into vessels that would allow their passengers to go underwater and view the artwork. Despite the cost of maintaining what were essentially oversized diving bells, the investment had reportedly paid off. Their tours of the artwork were filled by the idle wealthy and the curious. Duilio had even gone down in one of the vessels a couple of times himself. He tapped his fingers on the chair's arm, weighing what he most needed from Joaquim. "Could you put together a list of places an upper servant might go if left on her own? Between positions, perhaps. Not a lot of money. A hotel or apartment?"

"More likely a rented room." Joaquim fell silent, probably mulling over what needed to be done. "I'll stay late tonight," he said after a moment. "I'll put together a list and drop it off by the house."

Duilio hid a smile. While Joaquim might not be allowed to expend further police time and resources on the investigation, Duilio hadn't had any doubt that he would help on his own time. Joaquim had a revolutionary streak in his soul. He counted every one of those missing servants the equal of Lady Isabel Amaral, and kept their names in neat files in his cabinet at the station.

Once they'd made a connection between the missing servants and the work of art, it hadn't taken too long to confirm that each of the servants, all of whom worked in great houses along the Street of Flowers, had disappeared within a few days of the appearance of their masters' homes in the artwork. Most of those servants had claimed they'd been offered positions elsewhere. Others said they were going home to visit family in the country. It had taken time to determine that those events hadn't ever happened. It had taken a good deal more effort to determine that *every* household represented in the artwork had lost two servants. Most hadn't bothered to report their servants' absence, assuming their employees had indeed moved on to other positions.

Even so, they couldn't *concretely* tie the missing servants to the houses. When the police had made inquiries about opening one of the houses, an order had come back almost immediately to shut down the investigation.

Joaquim's hands had been tied after that, but he had still helped Duilio in his efforts to track down the artist, Gabriel Espinoza. Unfortunately the man had disappeared from the city completely, but he couldn't be doing the work alone. There had to be a number of coconspirators to create an artwork of this size, not only builders and watermen to get the artwork into the river, but someone had to be funding all of that as well. They had researched how the houses were built and how they were chained to huge weights on the river's bed. They had tried tracking down some of the building materials, from shipments of wood to the proper grade of chain. Unfortunately, so far all their leads had gone nowhere. Duilio hoped that finding Miss Paredes would breathe some new life into the investigation.

"I can't help you look today," Joaquim finally allowed, "but I can ask the officers at the front desk to tell me if they hear anything from the Amaral woman."

"Thank you," Duilio said. "I'll see what I can find out at the Amaral household as well."

"Don't talk to the servants, though. I'll do that on my way by the house tonight." Joaquim would be better to handle that as he didn't have a presence in society. The servants would perceive a policeman as closer to their class.

"I'll see if I can wheedle Lady Amaral into admitting something, then." Duilio doubted he'd be successful. He lifted the copy of Camões and glanced down at the section where the poet described Vasco da Gama's discovery of the Ilhas das Sereias in 1499—a violent introduction that had sown distrust between the sereia and the Portuguese for the past four hundred years. To this day, the islands of the sereia didn't appear on any map, although it was said the Church knew where they were to be found. The sereia preferred to stay hidden. "Can I borrow this book for a bit?"

"You have a copy," Joaquim said, sounding bewildered now.

It was a safe guess that the book could be found in most libraries in Northern Portugal, but if Joaquim said there should be one in the Ferreira library, there was. "I don't have it *with* me," Duilio pointed out.

Joaquim rolled his eyes and rose. "Fine."

"So, will you come for dinner tonight, then?" Duilio asked, rising and slipping the book under his arm. He retrieved his newspaper as well. "Mother would like to see you."

Suddenly somber, Joaquim rubbed a hand over his face. "How is she?"

"The same as yesterday." Duilio pressed his lips together, but then added, "I know how painful this is for you, but for her sake, please. It helps her to see us."

"I know." Joaquim sounded guilty. "I'll come."

That was a relief. "Thank you. Now shall we go?"

Joaquim collected his hat and paused with one hand on the door latch. "How do you know your Miss Paredes hasn't fled the city?"

Another good question. Duilio just couldn't believe he'd seen the last of her.

CHAPTER 6

SUNDAY, 28 SEPTEMBER 1902

Oriana had spent several hours Saturday in the back rooms of the *Porto Gazette*, trying to locate every last article they'd printed covering *The City Under the Sea.* They had stacks of old papers carefully shelved, but no one could tell her in which days' newspapers to look, so she'd hunted through them issue by issue, taking down every scrap of information she could find on the artwork and its creator. No one seemed to be aware that the water around the artwork tasted of death, that Isabel could not have been the first to die there. Who those other victims might be Oriana didn't yet know. And the only hint of magic mentioned was the presence of buoyancy charms inscribed atop each house meant to keep them afloat, the sort boatbuilders used. What she needed was an ally who knew far more about human magic than she did. Fortunately, she knew where to find one.

Nela wasn't precisely a scholar, but the old woman had studied human lore with Oriana's grandmother prior to being exiled from the islands for sedition. When Oriana first recognized the old woman walking along the street almost two years before, Nela had nodded at her once. Nothing more passed between them. But that bare instant of recognition had given Oriana the courage to contact the woman, no matter that it was a clear violation of the ministry's directive not to interact with the exiles. Nela had consented to meet with her, although it hadn't come for free, and Oriana's supply of coins was dwindling quickly. Nevertheless, she was relieved she'd found someone willing to aid her, so she'd gladly said she would wait until Sunday afternoon to visit.

Nela's druggist's shop on the first floor was closed that afternoon, but Oriana and its owner were in the tiny apartment above. The woman handed Oriana a cup of tea and settled across from her in a chair upholstered in a faded blue floral. A white cloth with fringe about the edging covered a small square table, and atop that lay the sketch Oriana had drawn that first morning after settling into her rented room.

Oriana turned it so that Nela could read the letters. "Does this mean anything?"

Her drawing showed the half circle of the tabletop that had lit following Isabel's death. Oriana had remembered the four words that circled the perimeter of the table. There had been another ring of figures inside that, but those hadn't been familiar to her at all and had faded from her memory before she'd had access to paper to record them. The center of the table—the half she had been able to make out—was occupied by a large T with a dash under one arm and a line above it. That meant nothing to her either.

Nela's scarred fingers traced the words in the outer ring. Oriana watched the old woman's hands, wondering who had done the surgery to remove her webbing. It had been poorly done, leaving her with ugly scars on the sides of each finger. Perhaps Nela had done it herself. But she *was* able to wear gloves, which meant the woman was far safer than Oriana in this city.

"*Ego autem et domus*," Nela read musingly. "That's Latin, I believe, but I'm not very familiar with the language. I don't know what it means."

Oriana didn't either. "I see."

"Where did this come from?" Nela asked.

"I don't think I should say."

The old woman regarded her doubtfully. "Child, don't waste my time."

Oriana swallowed. She would have to trust someone if she was going to find out who had created this monstrosity. With her gray-shot hair, this woman reminded Oriana of her own grandmother, her father's mother back on the island of Amado. Her grandmother had been a woman one could trust. "It's from *The City Under the Sea*."

Nela sat back, her dark eyes narrowing. "You didn't go down there, did you, child? The Special Police patrol that part of the river well."

"I know," Oriana said. The newspapers had noted the frequency of police patrols in that area, particularly at night.

"Someone saw this there and told you about it?" Nela shook her head. "That doesn't make any sense."

Oriana took a deep breath. "It's not important where it was. Is this a spell? A charm?"

Nela tapped her nose with one finger. "Spells, I think, since they're combined. A charm has to be kept simple. We have two languages represented: Latin and whatever the next ring is written in. Choice of language is purely stylistic in human witchcraft, so the two disparate languages imply two *different* spells. The symbol in the center means nothing to me, especially given that I'm only looking at half of it. Why do you have only half?"

How could she answer that without telling Nela everything? The addition of the Amaral house to the work of art hadn't been mentioned in the city's newspapers until Saturday morning, and Oriana hadn't seen anything yet about Isabel's absence. Lady Amaral apparently hadn't told anyone, which meant the police probably weren't even looking for Isabel. Nothing had been heard from Mr. Efisio either. Perhaps the man was still waiting in Paris for Isabel's arrival.

"It was dark. A girl was seated at the table, with her hands tied to it. She died, and"—Oriana's stomach twisted, but she forced herself to go on—"and when she did, her half of the table lit. This was inscribed on the surface of the table."

Nela picked up her tea and took a slow sip, eyeing Oriana over the rim. After a moment, she set the cup aside. "Lit how?"

"The symbols themselves glowed. I think they were metal set into the wood."

Nela's dark eyes were wary now. "That sounds like necromancy, needing death to feed it. What have you gotten yourself involved in, child?"

"It was not by choice," Oriana said with a quick shake of her head. "I need to find the person who *made* this spell. I need to stop him before he does it again."

Nela gazed at her appraisingly and gave one sharp nod. "You need to talk to the Lady."

"Which lady?" Oriana asked, baffled.

The old woman leaned over and set a hand on Oriana's arm. "*The* Lady. She doesn't have a name. She's an expert on human magics. She would be able to tell you what this is."

That sounded promising. "Where can I find her?"

"You can't," Nela said. "No one finds her."

Now it *didn't* sound promising. "But . . ."

"I'll tell a few well-placed people that you're looking for the Lady. If she wants to, she'll find you. Can you give me your direction?"

Oriana hesitated. She didn't want to give Nela the address of the boarding house on Escura Street. Not just because she was afraid of being tracked there, but she already knew she would have to find somewhere else to stay. She was running out of funds and had no intention of paying for her room in the fashion Carlos had in mind. "I'm not sure where I'll be."

"Then come by here in a few days, and I'll tell you what I've learned." The old woman rose, rubbing her hands together as if they ached.

Oriana realized that meant their interview was over. She set down her cup, folded up the sketch, and tucked it into her notebook as she got up. She opened her handbag to dig out her payment. "We agreed . . ."

Nela laid a wrinkled hand atop Oriana's mitt-covered ones. "Don't bother. Consider it a favor, for your grandmother's sake. You look like you need it more than I do."

"Thank you," Oriana mumbled. She took in the shabby apartment one more time. "If there's anything I can do for you . . ."

The old woman pushed her gently out the door. "Go on, child. If there's a necromancer out there, he needs finding and killing."

Oriana nodded helplessly as she went down the stairs to the building's front door. She paused at the landing, her stomach churning. Was *that* what she was doing? Hunting a necromancer?

If so, she had wandered into a shiver of sharks.

On the southern shore of the Douro River, Duilio waited on a low wall in the shade of an old olive tree next to one of the wineries that crowded Vila Nova de Gaia. The vintner had sold him a case of brandy, giving him ample reason to sit in the shade and sample a leisurely glass. He gazed across the river at the Golden City, tapping one foot against the wall.

He wished his contact would hurry. If this appointment hadn't been set the previous week, he would have put it off. He had a woman to find. Despite having a couple of friends in common with Marianus Efisio, it had taken Duilio the better part of the day Friday to find someone who knew what hotel the man was fixed at in

Paris. He'd sent a telegram to Mr. Efisio, explaining briefly that Lady Isabel was missing. He hadn't revealed what he suspected, not wanting to cause the man grief until he had proof. He hoped he would find Mr. Efisio's response waiting when he got back to the house. He'd spent much of Saturday hunting down every boarding house on Joaquim's list, scouring the old town for the elusive Miss Paredes, to no avail.

On the opposite side of the river, the painted walls of the Ribeira rose above the quay, a jumble of reds and yellows, creams and grays in the afternoon sun. Houses had been crammed into every inch of space, sometimes at odd angles, on the ancient riverbank. The red-tiled rooftops rose layer after layer up the hills. From his vantage point, Duilio could see the Clérigos tower crowning one hill and the fanciful palace topping another. The tower had been the higher—as had been the power of the Church—until the current prince's grandfather, Sebastião II, built the ornate palace. To ensure his structure would be the taller, the second Sebastião had the hillside built up, an effort to put the Church in its place, no doubt.

Duilio had always loved the city. It had changed since he was a child, but not as much as it should have. Part of that was the stultifying influence of the Absolutists so powerful in the north, but even normal progress had ground to a stop here.

Prince Fabricio had halted all his father's and grandfather's plans for modernization. Many projects started in the 1880s had simply been abandoned or had idled for the two decades since he ascended the throne. The new port north of the city at Leixões was left half-built, accessible to the navy but not practical for shipping. The funicular at the base of the Dom Sebastião III Bridge had never been finished. The trams that climbed the city's steep streets had been electrified only through *private* funding.

Prince Fabricio's refusal to change had left Northern Portugal and the Golden City behind its contemporaries, with Liberal-led Southern Portugal becoming more powerful every day. The current prince of Southern Portugal—Dinis II—had made many improvements there, and Lisboa had become a destination for vacationers. Just in June, the city had announced that all Lisboa now had electricity. In the north, the Golden City's infrastructure had begun to fall into disrepair. Duilio had never taken much interest in the politics of the country, but he found he sided more with the Liberals and their desire for progress than he did with the Absolutists, who wanted everything to stay as it was.

He turned his eyes toward the Dom Sebastião III Bridge, an elegant creation of iron that stretched between the Golden City and Vila Nova de Gaia. Two levels of traffic moved over the river there, one atop the grand iron arch coming from the heights of the city to the mount on the far shore. The other traveled across at the level of the quay. And from that direction, a tall and gangly Englishman approached Duilio's perch on the low wall, striding up the lane under the shade of the olive trees.

Duilio held out the bottle when he got closer. "Would you like a taste?"

The Englishman, one Augustus Smithson, took it and downed a healthy drink before he folded himself onto the wall. "I've made inquiries, Mr. Ferreira," he said in English, "but I can't find any information on your footman, Martim Romero."

Smithson was the fourth investigator Duilio had hired in the past year, hoping an Englishman might be able to bring fresh connections to the search for his mother's pelt. Duilio answered the man in his own tongue. "Any idea who hired him?"

"None," Smithson rumbled, shifting as if the stone wall was digging into his bony backside. "There *are* people who collect magical artifacts. Most of them are secretive about it. They don't want the others to know what they have."

Duilio didn't actually believe that his mother's pelt was in the hands of a *collector*, but it was a possibility he had to consider. "Do you have any names or not? I'll pay what you want."

Smithson's shoulders hunched as he leaned closer. "What I have is a neatly worded note, Mr. Ferreira, left on my desk in my own sitting room, informing me I was to drop the matter. Whoever left it easily entered my home without leaving any trace behind." He glanced about nervously. "A witch. It had to be. That means I might wake up dead one morning."

Duilio had *never* seen evidence that a witch existed who could transport himself into a locked room—it was the stuff of fantasy. However, he'd met plenty of thieves who could get in and out without leaving a sign. Either way, though, Smithson wasn't going to be any more help to him. Duilio sighed and pushed himself off the wall. "Please send your bill to my man of business, Mr. Smithson."

Smithson rose and shook his hand, his expression sheepish, likely embarrassed by having been frightened off. Duilio headed back to where his driver waited with the carriage in the vintner's front court. He climbed into the carriage and settled back against the leather seat. The ride across the bridge and up the steep streets to his own home gave him time to think.

It was interesting that the man was so determined to keep the pelt that he chose to interfere with the investigators Duilio hired . . . and to do it in such a dramatic way. He could have bought off the investigators rather than writing cryptic notes. That spoke of an obsession with secrecy . . . or a childish streak of melodrama.

Duilio hadn't been able to *prove* who'd hired Martim Romero, the fake footman, but he had a good idea. There was one man who'd disliked Duilio's father enough to strike at him by hurting his wife: Paolo Silva. It wasn't for anything Duilio's father had done, but because Duilio's father had been the legitimate son, whereas Paolo Silva was merely his bastard brother, gotten on a housemaid. Silva had spent his first ten years in the house that Duilio now owned, kept out of sight of the Ferreira family. Then his mother had died of a fever and young Paolo had been shunted off to a distant relative out in the countryside. Alexandre Ferreira, only seven at the time, hadn't even known that the boy who lived in the servants' areas was his half brother.

But Silva had never forgotten his expulsion. He had disappeared for years, only to return to the Golden City just as Prince Fabricio ascended the throne. Silva quickly wormed his way into the young prince's favor. He'd become the prince's favorite seer, displacing Alexandre Ferreira as an adviser. While always polite in public, Silva had privately told Duilio's father that it was his intent to ruin the whole Ferreira family for their treatment of him.

If only his grandfather had been a little kinder—or faithful to his wife—Duilio suspected he wouldn't be hunting for his mother's pelt in his spare moments.

CHAPTER 7

In the slanting light of late afternoon, Oriana walked along Escura Street, clutching her notebook to her chest as she headed back to the boarding house. Her feet ached. Her shoes had been too small before, but the soaking they'd gotten in the river meant they were tighter now.

She had hoped that the sketch would tell her something definite, but Nela's words had only left her with more questions. Her time searching the newspapers suggested that the creator of *The City Under the Sea* had fled the Golden City. How was she supposed to hunt him down if he was miles and miles away?

None of the newspaper articles had mentioned that Gabriel Espinoza was a necromancer, but that didn't surprise her. The Portuguese Church forbade this type of magic, so if he studied necromancy he certainly wouldn't tell anyone. But it was far more likely he wasn't working alone. There had to be workers to build the houses, others to lower them into the river at night, and someone to dive down to affix the chains to the weights on the river's floor. Surely she could find one person among those willing to talk. Surely *one* of them found this monstrous.

But she was nearing the end of her rope.

She couldn't go to the police. She'd considered posting an anonymous letter to them, but no matter how she imagined that playing out, every possibility led back to them asking her why she had lived when Isabel had died. The truth would land her first in the Special Police's holding cells and then on the gallows.

There were other possibilities. Her father lived in the Golden City . . . but she wouldn't go to him. Not unless she became *truly* desperate. Not having made such a mull of her life. Not after Mariana's death. She didn't know if she could ever face him, having failed to keep her sister safe. And he had a new life here, a fresh start, where he was allowed to pursue his own goals and dreams without the government's disapproval of a male getting out of his place. Her father was a businessman now. Oriana was proud of him for his enterprise . . . and was equally furious that he had replaced her dead mother with a human lover, one of his employers, Lady Pereira de Santos. Oriana had heard it whispered in the Amaral house—one over from the home of the lady in question—and it stung.

It was a childish reaction, she knew, but when she occasionally saw him, she felt such a welter of conflicting emotions that she always kept her distance. She only hoped that no one else realized he was her father. Heriberto might use that information to force her hand if he learned of it—he could turn her father in to the Special Police—and she didn't want to give her master that sort of advantage over her.

No, she must simply find some manner of work, a position that would allow her to stay in the city and pursue the person who had ended all of Isabel's dreams. She could go to an agency, perhaps, or start checking with dressmakers to see if any needed a seamstress. She glanced down at her worn black skirt. She wouldn't make a favorable impression wearing this.

A voice broke into her musings. "I've been looking for you."

Oriana glanced back at the store she'd just passed. Tucked into the first level of the building beneath an overhanging balcony, the tiny shop sold lace and fabrics and ribbon. The man waiting for her there could not look less like one of their patrons. An older man with graying hair in untidy curls, he dressed like a fisherman in worn brown trousers and a stained white tunic. A red kerchief hid his throat from view.

Ah gods. He was the last person she wanted to see now. Oriana mentally steeled herself, squaring her shoulders and lifting her chin. "Heriberto. How did you find me?"

The sereia spymaster stepped out of the shadows into the lesser shadows. In this part of town, the cobbled streets were jumbled and narrow. With the buildings tightly packed on either side, reaching up four stories high, it was a wonder anyone here ever saw sunlight. Heriberto gave Oriana a false smile. "Your employer eloped, I hear." He leaned closer, his voice lowering conspiratorially. "And you missed your scheduled report. Why?"

He hadn't answered her question, Oriana noted. This wasn't an ideal location to have a private discussion anyway. Escura Street was busy this time of day, with pedestrians wanting to get past them and on to their dinners. Laundry flapped in the murky breeze overhead, run between and along the balconies, snapping and spraying them with fine droplets of water. "I have something I need to take care of."

He raised one scarred hand to touch a finger under his eye, the gesture for disbelief. "You have no business other than what I tell you to have. You had an appointment with Dr. Esteves Saturday afternoon. Remember? I set it up for you, yet you're still dragging your feet about getting your hands cut. Gods, you're useless."

Oriana was as tall as he was, so she could look down her nose convincingly. "You forget, Heriberto, I'm the only one you've got with access to the aristocracy. Who warned you that the navy was moving out on exercises last April?" she whispered. "Who told you that the Marquis of Maraval has friends among the Absolutists?"

They had been important bits of information, whether Heriberto wanted to admit it or not. The first had come from a naval officer who'd wanted to impress Isabel at a ball, puffing on about how the exercises—which would have taken the navy far too close to the islands—couldn't proceed without his navigational skills. The other tidbit had come from Isabel herself, simple chatter while Oriana had been repairing a rent in one of Isabel's dresses. Of course, Isabel didn't see the Absolutists as a threat—after all, her own father was one of them. But the Absolutists believed in the divine right of the royal family, and therefore that the prince's ban on the sea folk was perfectly legitimate. The Marquis of Maraval, the powerful Minister of Culture, was supposed to be neutral. If he shifted his views in favor of the Absolutists, it might adversely affect her people. Northern Portugal had always leaned in that direction anyway.

Heriberto ignored her reminders. "Your access to the aristocracy just fled to Paris. The papers claim you went with her, but I hear her mother threw you out on your ear."

Her blood pounded in her ears, and Oriana pushed down the sick feeling that welled up at his claim. *How did he know?* She glanced down the street at the door of the boarding house. Her expulsion would have been fodder for servants' gossip up and down the Street of Flowers for the past few days. It wouldn't have cost him more than a beer or two to hear *that* tale, but only Carlos had known she was coming to stay with his elderly kinswoman. He must have told Heriberto where to find her. Oriana lifted her chin, trying to appear confident, and lied through her teeth. "When she gets back, Isabel will give me a reference. I'll find another position then. I just need a couple of weeks to get my feet under me."

"Weeks?" Heriberto snorted and made an obscene gesture with his hands that, fortunately, no human would recognize. "To get your feet under you? I heard you're going to be spending that time on your back to pay your rent. Are you stupid enough to trust a human with the color of your stripe?"

Most sereia had skin too thick to blush. Oriana was grateful for that at the moment. The warmth flooding her face wouldn't show.

People were passing them on the street, none looking very interested in a petty squabble. Fortunately, the reference to the color of her dorsal stripe—a euphemism for promiscuity back on the islands—wouldn't mean anything to the passersby who overheard it.

Oriana had no doubt Carlos had claimed she'd agreed to become his lover, but Carlos had never had a chance of seeing her dorsal stripe. "Don't believe everything you hear," she told Heriberto.

"Oh, I never do." He stepped closer, grasping her sleeve to keep her from escaping. He kept his voice low. "No one's *ever* seen your stripe, from what I hear. You know, I could make your life here a great deal more comfortable, girl, if you're interested. And I'm well liked back home. I could get you a better position in the ministry."

She'd heard that other girls who'd come to the city had done just that, taking Heriberto as a lover in exchange for easier assignments and faster advancement. It bothered her that he had that much influence. Not because he was male. She had no problem with males in positions of authority. But no one should have that much influence over his workers, especially when he was inclined to abuse it. He made a mockery of his posting. She would take Carlos as a lover before Heriberto. No, she would rather turn herself in to the Special Police first.

He laughed shortly, as if he'd read her mind. "I'll give you two weeks. If you don't have a sound position by then, I'm sending you home. I'll even make another appointment with the doctor for you, next Friday. I expect you to show up this time. My superiors aren't as tolerant as I am, and I'm tired of making excuses for you."

"I understand." Oriana jerked her arm free and turned away before Heriberto could say more, almost colliding with a burly carter carrying a cask on his shoulder. She managed to sidestep out of the man's path, an awkward dance set to the sound of Heriberto's laughter. Clasping her notebook closer to her chest, she strode away.

"Be there Friday at three," he called after her.

She glanced back and nodded sharply in acknowledgment. She'd won one concession.

"And someone is hunting for you on the streets," he yelled. "Asking for you by name. Don't bring trouble back to my door."

There was little chance of that. His "door" was a little fishing boat moored on a quay farther from the old town center. She had no intention of going there. Oriana strode out of the narrow, confined street onto wider São Sebastião. When she glanced back over her shoulder, Heriberto was nowhere in sight.

Her ire faded. Heriberto set her teeth on their sharp edge—he always had. But now that she was out of his sight, the sick and hollow sensation in her stomach returned with a vengeance. Now she had *more* to worry about. She stopped on the corner and pressed one mitt-covered hand to her belly. *Who's looking for me?*

Surely it was too early for Nela's mysterious Lady to be doing so, and Carlos already knew where to find her. Could it be Silva, the prince's seer who had pulled her out of the river three nights before? Or could Lady Amaral have gone to the police after all and blamed her in some way for Isabel's absence? The last thing she needed was the police hunting her.

A gentleman in a dark suit brushed against her as he passed, startling her. He tipped his hat apologetically before he went on his way. Oriana shook herself. She couldn't afford to be standing here on the street corner like a lamppost. She walked on, feeling shaken.

She waited for an opening between the carriages traveling São Sebastião, and headed toward the quay. Once there, she stood on the quay in the noontime sun, gazing up toward the old tile roofs of the houses that lined the river. The smell of the water was comforting

It had seemed clear at first. The police had no inkling of Isabel's fate, so it was up to her to seek retribution, wasn't it? She'd been angry. She hadn't questioned what it would cost her to find the artist and expose him. She hadn't allowed herself to doubt. But now she knew she was hunting a necromancer. Not only was she hiding from the police, as always, but now she had to duck Heriberto and Carlos as well. She had little money and few friends and no idea where to look next. But none of that would stop her.

She'd never been able to avenge Marina. She wasn't going to fail Isabel in the same way.

The library of the Ferreira home was Duilio's favorite room. It housed a collection of items his father had brought back from his travels. An array of giant clam shells, bleached almost white, sat atop the middle of a large circular table covered with marquetry, supposedly liberated from a pirate's lair in the South Seas. A chandelier hung above that display, delicate branches of white coral holding two dozen candles—a fixture too fragile to refit for gas lighting. That came from the street bazaars of the desert city of Marrakech. Many of the books that lined the room claimed equally unlikely origin. His father's desk in the corner—his desk now—supposedly came from Brazil, but Duilio had no idea if that was true either.

Cardenas had left a telegram atop that desk, and Duilio picked it up. Sent from Paris, it told him exactly what he'd expected. Marianus Efisio was there, but neither Lady Isabel nor her companion had ever arrived. Efisio intended to remain there until he received word from Isabel. Duilio tucked the telegram into a pocket, uncertain whether he felt sorry for Efisio or not.

Felis, his mother's maid, appeared on the threshold of the library and fixed him with her hawklike eyes. "What is this about you wanting to see *me*, Duilinho?"

Her voice had an angry edge to it, as always. But the woman's bark was, as it was said, far worse than her bite—most of the time. Duilio smiled at her and withdrew a small bundle from his other coat pocket. The bribe should definitely come first. He'd seen a woman selling barnacles on the quay—Felis' favorite treat. "Please, Miss Felis. I've been looking for a few days now, and I can't find someone. I thought perhaps you could help."

She exhaled loudly but walked over to the chair he held out for her, her eyes on the bounty of barnacles. He closed the door, and when he returned she was happily chewing away on one of the briny treats. She drew a tattered box of cards from her apron pocket, removed the deck, and slid them toward him. "What do you need to know, Duilinho?"

Felis wasn't a witch, he felt sure. Her talent lay in getting someone to organize their thoughts *around* the cards she presented, making it seem as if the cards knew what was in their subconscious. At least, that was what Duilio suspected she did. While his gift usually only told him yes or no, her card work seemed to bring out more complete answers for him. He didn't often ask this of her, though, as he didn't want her to think he took her for granted.

He picked up the deck, shuffled it, and put it back in her wrinkled hands. "There's a woman. I need to find her."

Felis withdrew one card and lay it facedown on the polished surface of the table. "This is your card, Duilinho." She started to deal the cards out into three piles. "Is she a criminal?"

"No," he said quickly. Many would argue that point since she was in the city illegally, but he didn't see Miss Paredes that way. "A witness. A victim."

Felis picked up one of the stacks and turned over the first card, the two of spades. "Yes, she's under a cloud. Is she in hiding?"

He wasn't familiar enough with Miss Paredes to predict her actions, but hiding was a good guess. "I suppose."

Felis discarded one card and laid out another. "In her place, what would you do?"

He sat back. If he'd been captured and nearly killed, he would have been trying to find the person responsible, investigating. But a woman would be more likely to seek assistance, the police or . . .

He shook his head, annoyed with himself. Why was he assuming she would ask for help? If she was a spy, that implied an intrepid nature, a self-reliance he'd not been factoring into his expectations. If such a thing had happened to *him*, he wouldn't have known whom to trust. He would have tried to solve the problem himself.

"Seven of diamonds," Felis said, drawing his thoughts back to the cards. "Traveling near water, perhaps?"

Miss Paredes might return to her people's islands, he reckoned. "A sea voyage?"

"No, not the sea." Felis continued to deal out the cards, ending up with several facing upward. She spread them wider and scowled down at them. "The river. Hmm. Why would she do that?"

Duilio reached to flip over the first card she'd laid down, only to withdraw his hand hastily when she slapped it. "You said it was *my* card," he protested.

"They're all my cards, boy, so leave it alone."

That seemed unfair. One of these days he was going to find a book that listed the supposed meanings of each card. For all he knew, Felis was making it up as she went along.

She slid the jack of clubs out from where it had been hidden behind another card. She scowled and said, "There's a man involved. A man with ill intent."

Well, he had to agree that the man who'd put Miss Paredes in the river had ill intent. Perhaps the card represented the artist, Espinoza. "I knew that," Duilio said. "Any ideas where I can look for her?"

"Back to the water, boy. She's going back to the water." She looked up then, clearly at the end of her reading. "That's where you'll find her."

Duilio sat back, puzzling over that claim. It was so vague as to be useless. Felis began to retrieve her cards, apparently ready to leave. When she picked up the last card—the hidden one she'd said belonged to him—she chuckled to herself. Duilio leaned around and saw the king of hearts in her fingers. "What does that mean?"

Felis tucked it in among the others, slid the box back in her pocket, and gathered up her handkerchief full of barnacles. "Remember, boy, you don't believe in the cards."

He felt a flush creep up his cheeks. Her tone wasn't remonstrative; more teasing than anything else. But he didn't believe in fortune-telling. Not exactly. He wished he'd thought to dissemble instead of admitting that as a child. He helped her to her feet and opened the library door for her. "I believe in you, Miss Felis, which is more important."

The old woman snorted and walked out without a backward glance.

Duilio paced around the library once, trying to settle his anxious mind. In the far corner, the normal collection of social invitations waited on his desk for his attention, but he didn't sit. The prayer niche between two bookshelves offered no answer at the moment. He contemplated the liquor cabinet and decided that wasn't the answer either; that had been Alessio's favored response to problems, and it had never served him well.

Somewhere on the library shelves, Duilio recalled, there should be a volume in French that told of the strange and barbaric society of the sereia out on their islands, supposedly penned by a sailor who'd been there. His father had brought the book from Lyons or Marseilles, and Duilio had read it a dozen times as a boy. He halfheartedly scanned the shelves, aware that the answer wouldn't be between its covers either. He couldn't find the book, though. It was probably sitting next to the copy of the Camões epic that Joaquim claimed should be in this library; he still hadn't found that.

Duilio finally flung himself onto the sofa and stayed there, fretting.

If he *were* to seriously consider the fortune Felis had laid out before him, then he had to believe Oriana Paredes would go back to the water. Not her home, not the islands, but to the river. Could she be swimming in the chill waters even at this moment, living in the rough, as selkies did? That didn't seem right. Every time he'd set eyes on her she'd seemed to fit in perfectly, not chafing at the restrictions of human society. He could no more imagine Miss Paredes hiding among the moored boats along the quay than he could his own mother. No, Oriana Paredes was living in the city. She was going to the water. *Returning*, Felis had said.

Duilio sat up abruptly. He knew exactly where he would find Miss Paredes; his gift told him he was right. She was going to return to the scene of the crime.

CHAPTER 8

MONDAY, 29 SEPTEMBER 1902

The sides of the submersible groaned, an eerie sound to hear while trapped inside its metal body. Oriana pressed closer to the viewing window. She clutched her hands tighter about her handbag to still their shaking. She didn't trust this creaking metal fish.

She could have simply swum here but couldn't afford to risk being seen. And she hadn't wanted to breathe in that death-laden water, so she'd sold her best pair of embroidered silk mitts to old Mrs. Nunhes at the boarding house to purchase a ticket aboard this rickety contraption. Now she'd begun to question that decision.

Set every few feet along the walls of the submersible's viewing room, the white-painted casings of small round windows dripped water onto the decking, whether from leakage or condensation, Oriana didn't know. Either possibility suggested poor workmanship. Even so, she was only one of nearly a dozen paying customers crammed into the small vessel. Finely dressed citizens of the Golden City pressed against those dripping windows, straining to catch a glimpse of *The City Under the Sea*.

She'd come to this place, hoping that another viewing of the floating houses might reveal some clue she'd missed before. She wanted more to tell Nela's Lady if she agreed to meet with her. They were getting close, so Oriana steeled herself to look at the sunken houses.

The man sharing her window, a gentleman she'd seen somewhere before, craned his neck to look toward the surface above them. She already knew what she'd see. She clenched her jaw, drew out her small notebook, and gazed out the window. Lanterns inside the submersible lit the scale replicas of the Street of Flowers. With the sun shining down on it, the river's surface above them truly did look like a silvery street with its houses lined up neatly in file.

It was art that only those who swam could appreciate. Or those who observed from vehicles such as this, chugging and whirring through the calm waters of the river's edge. It was a shameful waste of money, made all the more sickening by the macabre details that the other observers with her didn't know. No one in this contraption understood what they were viewing, but she had tasted death in that water, many deaths.

The replica of the Amaral house was remarkably accurate, a fact she hadn't noticed that night. There was even a wrought-iron railing on the second-floor balcony. On either side she saw the Pereira de Santos home and the Rocha mansion, just as she remembered. Oriana stared at the houses, unable to tear her eyes away. Who would do this? And if necromancy was involved, what were they trying to achieve?

From one corner of the house's top—its floor—she could make out a sliver of pale light. That had to be the table glowing, visible where she'd pushed the boards loose enough to wriggle out. Had the wood swollen back to close the gap? Odd that no one seemed to have noticed the damage.

"Have you ever seen anything so magnificent?" her companion asked, awe in his voice. The light musky scent of ambergris cologne floated with him when he leaned nearer.

Oriana shuddered, thinking of that dark room where Isabel waited still. And then she couldn't bear to look any longer.

She drew back from the window and, without answering him, returned to the gilt chairs bolted to the submersible's observation deck. She shouldn't have wasted her dwindling funds on this. She hadn't taken a single note. She hadn't learned anything new and, now that she'd seen it, she only wanted to escape this place. She wanted to cover her eyes to hide away from the memory of that night. Instead, she forced her hands to settle neatly on her lap, kept her back straight and her chin up.

They were coming about to return to the quay, the captain announced through his speaker. When he requested that all his guests return to their seats, the other viewers left their windows with obvious reluctance. Oriana drew up the hem of her skirts enough to keep them from the water that flowed across the observation deck as the submersible canted at an angle, glad she'd already taken a seat.

She felt the sting of tears at the back of her throat. She didn't want to embarrass herself, not here, not among these people who had no understanding of what they'd seen.

The ambergris-scented gentleman settled next to her. He hadn't sat next to her on the ride out to this spot, so it was a matter of choice. Oriana clutched her handbag and favored him with a weak smile.

"They say the artist will do the entire city eventually." His deep voice was low enough that others wouldn't overhear the discussion—surely intentional—but his tone carried admiration, hinting that Oriana shouldn't say anything to disparage the artist in question.

She didn't want to talk to him. He was a gentleman, surely one of the decorative types who did nothing all day long. He would discover quickly that she was merely a glorified servant and be embarrassed to have spoken to her at all. "There would be no room for the fish," she returned without much enthusiasm.

He smiled slightly, his lips pressed together, as if he found that amusing but was too well-bred to laugh. "Ah yes, the fish. I suppose we must consider the sereia as well, and not encroach too much upon their waters."

Oriana resisted the urge to look at him, a flutter of panic swelling in her belly. Had he guessed her secret? Or was his mention of the sereia a coincidence? At least his comment didn't seem to require an answer. She lifted one hand and tugged at the high neck of her cambric shirtwaist, making sure her gill slits were covered. She wished she'd brought a shawl.

The gentleman was named Duilio, she recalled, a nephew or son of one of the merchant-adventurers who'd served the prince's father in days past. She couldn't recall where she'd met him, though. He inhabited the edges of society, if she remembered correctly, a lower sphere than the Amaral family. Isabel wouldn't have favored him with her conversation. Sitting next to him in the confines of the metal ship, Oriana didn't have any choice. The other viewers had all taken seats again, so trying to escape him would only make him curious.

He was an attractive man although not particularly striking. Nothing marked him as out of the ordinary. Taller than average, but only an inch or two taller than she was. His dark hair was short cropped, and he wore a frock coat and trousers in somber hues. He had limpid brown eyes, though, and an amiable manner that made Oriana hope he might be harmless. Where had they met before?

"Don't you agree?" he asked then.

Evidently he *did* expect an answer. She kept her breathing calm and, hoping to evade further conversation, repeated a claim she'd read in the newspapers. "An entire city suspended from the bottom of the river would pose a navigation hazard."

Duilio laughed, his head thrown back, displaying even teeth. "I had no idea you were a wit."

A wit? Oriana shifted uncomfortably on the delicate chair. She couldn't quite tell whether he meant that as a compliment or sarcasm. "I am generally considered quite dull, sir."

He glanced down, fingering the fine scarf that hung about his neck, old gold against the dark gray of his frock coat. "I do wonder if people are mistaken about you."

No, it didn't sound like sarcasm. She appraised him while his hands were occupied. His coat looked custom made—nothing bought ready-made, like hers. His wool trousers appeared freshly pressed and his patent shoes shone, a sure sign that his valet earned his keep. Oriana felt more aware then of her worn black skirt and pinching shoes.

He glanced at her. "May I ask, are you not Miss Paredes, companion to Lady Isabel Amaral?"

She suppressed a groan. She would have preferred that Duilio Who Smelled of Ambergris didn't remember her. She peered at him cautiously. "I was."

He nodded, his eyes going serious. "I hear she's gone abroad. Do you know when she'll return?"

She fixed her eyes on the metal wall straight ahead of her. If she looked at him when she answered, she might give herself away. "I'm no longer employed in the Amaral household," she said. It was an honest answer, one no one would refute. "I'm afraid I'm not privy to their plans."

Despite her determination to appear composed, Oriana's mind brought forth an image of Isabel's face, hair streaming about her in the water, her expression frozen between terror and resignation . . . and the pain of that night swept over her again.

Miss Paredes had been behaving with such calm that Duilio had wondered if he was wrong about her. She had gazed up through the water at the replica of the Amaral house without a flicker of recognition reaching her features. She had fended off his intentionally insensitive comments with drivel that had been printed in the newspapers. She had made him *doubt*.

Until that moment, when he had asked her when Lady Isabel would return.

Something in her eyes gave away her pain. She had been in that house after all. He considered it impressive that she'd chosen to face the scene of what might have been her death. Some victims of crimes never could go back. That argued strength on her part, or stubbornness, or both. And if her grief was a pretense, she should be on the stage at the São João Theater.

He'd been trying to come up with a way to earn her trust, if that was possible. Now he was tempted to console her—perhaps lay one of his hands over hers—which would have been presumptuous of him. He glanced about to see if anyone had noticed her distress and intended to intervene, but the other patrons of the vehicle were happily chattering away.

"My mother is in half mourning," he said. She didn't respond, but he continued anyway. "Eventually she'll go back into society and it would benefit her to have a companion. I wonder, as you're no longer employed by the Amaral family, if you're between positions?"

Her large eyes remained fixed on some terrible vision within.

He kept going. "If so, I think you should apply to my mother to be her companion."

Miss Paredes shook her head briefly, as if rising from sleep.

"She has been searching for one for some time," Duilio lied.

She blinked and glanced up, her eyes meeting his almost by accident.

No, surely not human. The wide dark eyes seemed too large for her fine-boned face, the irises almost black. Eyes made for seeing in the darkness of deep water. Duilio felt he could almost see into her soul. *She's afraid*, he thought. *Alone.*

"I beg your pardon?" she said, sounding perplexed.

Duilio drew a calling card from the inside pocket of his frock coat. "Come by tomorrow afternoon for tea. My mother will be expecting you."

"And what should I tell her?" Miss Paredes asked hesitantly, allowing him to lay the card on her palm. The black silk mitts she wore bared only the tips of her long fingers.

He dangled the bait in front of her. "That you would like to be her new companion, of course. She's sure to like you."

Miss Paredes carefully tucked the card into her purse. "Thank you, sir."

Ah, now he had gone from annoying gentleman to potential employer. As he didn't want her to flee, he set about making inane conversation, one of the skills he'd found terribly useful in his work. A large number of the Golden City's social elite believed him only half a step away from idiocy. They would say almost anything in front of him, never realizing he was listening. *Rather like a lady's companion.* "So, Miss Paredes, have you read yet of Prince Fabricio's new coat? It was in the *Gazette* this very morning. A gift from the ambassador in Goa, they say. India, you know. Very exotic."

She didn't protest the new topic of conversation. She patiently let him tell her all about the new coat as if she were accustomed to gentlemen blathering on about trivial things. He'd read the bizarre news item that morning and recalled most of the details. Those he didn't, he simply fabricated. She continued to nod at polite intervals, the tension in her shoulders slowly easing.

He was relieved, though, when the submersible came up next to the quay, and not only because he wanted to breathe fresh, nonpressurized air again. It had been difficult to maintain his facade of absurdity when there were so many questions he wanted desperately to ask this woman. This wasn't the right time or place, though, and Miss Paredes clearly wasn't the confiding sort. If he pressed her, she would likely run in the opposite direction. No, he needed some leverage to get her to talk to him, and he had an idea what might work.

For the moment he settled for helping her up the wide plank leading from the door of the submersible to the quay. "Remember, Miss Paredes, my mother *will* be expecting you."

She nodded, whatever she felt about that offer hiding behind those dark, now-opaque eyes. Then she was gone.

CHAPTER 9

Isabel Amaral's eyes were wide in the pale oval of her face. One lock of hair had come loose and streamed across her cheek, up to her lap. The air was slipping away, leaving them with the water that would kill Isabel. Her eyes pleaded for help . . . and then her lips opened and a flood of bubbles streamed from her mouth, the last of her breath.

Her body jerked convulsively against the ropes that bound her there. Oriana tried to reach her, tried to do something, anything, but she failed.

Isabel went still. Her head began to sway loosely with the motion of the water, that single strand of hair floating past her open mouth and snagging against her lips. And an eldritch glow began to fill their watery prison, the table with its spells and death.

Oriana turned her eyes toward it, but it blurred, none of the letters or words containing any meaning. And if she didn't figure it out, she would have to watch Isabel die over and over again.

TUESDAY, 30 SEPTEMBER 1902

Oriana sat up abruptly in her narrow bed, her gills agonizingly dry. She pressed her hands hard against the sides of her neck, putting pressure on her gills to force the pain to subside. Tears slid down her cheeks, a reaction to the terror that had pursued her beyond her dream.

After a moment, she wiped her tears away and covered her face with her hands. Instead of figuring out some new method of hunting Espinoza, she'd spent the whole evening curled on the bed in her rented room, crying. Not just for Isabel, but for everything she'd lost, all the pain and regrets of her life catching up to her at once.

She needed to pull herself together. She took several deep breaths, praying for strength.

And she did feel better then, as if her night's misery had floated away on her breath. The sun had already risen. Her windows faced west, so it was still dim in the room, but she forced herself to get up and lay out the cleanest of her remaining garments, a black suit that flattered her pale complexion. She'd sewn blue ribbons around the hems of the skirt and the jacket's bodice to smarten it up. The seat of the skirt was shiny with wear, but no one would note that unless they were seeking to find fault. She hoped it would be good enough; she had an interview this afternoon.

The decision had been an easy one. If she wanted to stay in the city long enough to find justice for Isabel, she had to get money somewhere. Should she secure this position, it would give her both an income and a place to live without the threat of Carlos and Heriberto finding her. She didn't have time to deal with either of them as they deserved.

All the same, she couldn't be certain Mr. Ferreira wasn't after the same thing as Carlos. Women usually made the decisions in the home; if a gentleman offered a position, that hinted at seduction. The fact that he was a gentleman didn't make any difference. She'd had more than one improper proposal from among Isabel's circle of suitors, all of them gentlemen. She didn't think Mr. Ferreira intended the same, though. He'd involved his mother in his offer, something that went beyond the realm of acceptable behavior if he planned a seduction. A gentleman did not include his family in his transgressions.

And she was qualified for the job. She had, after all, been Lady Isabel's companion for more than a year. Although she had no letter of recommendation from Isabel's family, she must be considered experienced. She also had her abilities as a seamstress to offer, which had helped convince Lady Amaral to hire an unknown woman as a companion in the first place.

Oriana looked at her pale face in the spotted mirror and nodded sharply. She had to take the chance. Having made her decision, she drew her hair down about her shoulders and neck to hide her gill slits, picked up her pitcher, and headed downstairs to the kitchen to fill it.

It wasn't the same as a bath, but it would ease the ache in her gills. After days without being able to bathe properly, her skin was beginning to feel dull and dry. And she should sponge off her skirt as well. If she was going to ask after a position in a fine lady's household, she had better be presentable.

The Ferreira family lived near the end of the Street of Flowers, not far up from the Church of São Francisco—an indicator of the family's social status. When the aristocrats had built along that street, the most influential located nearer the palace, closer to their prince. The lesser nobles and the gentry had been relegated to the far end near the river. When she'd lived in the Amaral mansion, Oriana would have had to travel some distance downhill to reach the Ferreira household.

Of course, to get from the boarding house to the Ferreira home, she had to go *up* the steep hills. Climbing had never been easy for her. She'd been told once that the air bladders on the outside of a sereia's lungs were vestigial. That didn't matter; they took up space. Her smaller lungs made the steep streets hard going. She might have taken the tram, only she didn't want to spend what few coins she had—not when she didn't yet have a position.

So Oriana headed up the Street of Flowers, carrying her

portmanteau, her heels clicking along the cobbled edge of the road. When the cool wind tried to pluck away her plain straw hat, she held it with one mitt-covered hand as she walked. Glancing up at the sky, she saw that clouds were rolling in, rain in them. She hoped she would have a place to spend the night.

She felt a sudden pang of homesickness for the house on Amado where she'd grown up among her father's family. She missed her grandmother's tile-roofed home with its terrace where she and her sister would sleep under the stars. She missed the beaches and the red-sailed fishing boats that cluttered them. She missed the heady smell of flowers on a summer breeze. Amado was, of all her people's islands, the most similar in culture and architecture to Portugal, but it wasn't crowded and formal and stuffy like the Golden City. For better or worse, she'd left it behind long ago. Now she had to make the best of the situation she'd landed in.

When she reached the Ferreiras' address, she paused, caught her breath, and pulled the bell chain. After a moment, a gray-haired butler appeared at the door.

"I am Miss Paredes." Fortunately, she didn't sound winded. "Mr. Ferreira asked that I speak with Lady Ferreira regarding a position here."

"Yes, Mr. Duilio said you would be coming, Miss Paredes." He took in her tired costume with perceptive eyes and gestured toward the bag clutched in her hand. "Why don't you set that on the table over there, miss, and I'll take you through to meet our lady."

Our lady. It was a possessive title, suggestive of an elderly woman or an invalid. Oriana did as the butler suggested, leaving her single bag on an exquisitely carved table of dark wood. A fine mirror hung above it, so she took a quick moment to check her hair and make certain her clothes were neat, and then obediently followed the elderly butler through to the front sitting room.

It was elegant, all ivory and gold, and the fine furnishings made Oriana curious to see the remainder of this house. Nothing about the couch or the low tables or chairs was ostentatious, but having worked with fabric in the past, she could tell that each was constructed of quality materials. The brown figured rug under her feet appeared to be wool and silk. The whole room suggested wealth but not extravagance. She wondered if that were only true of the public areas, as in the Amaral home.

Enthroned in one of the chairs across from the sofa, Lady Ferreira sat alone, a wistful expression on her face as she gazed out the window in the direction of the river. A great beauty, the woman had her son's dark, clear eyes. The lady wore a dark brown suit, suggestive of a working woman's efficient garb—no frills or lace—yet shantung silk that fine would never be seen in the city's offices. The skirt was trimmed in black velvet that matched the smart velvet cuffs and lapels on the jacket. Jet earrings dangled next to the lady's slender throat. A newspaper lay abandoned on the small table next to her right hand, along with a cup of coffee.

"Lady, this is Miss Paredes," the butler intoned. "Mr. Duilio said she would come by."

The lady stared out the window as though she hadn't heard him.

"Lady Ferreira?" Oriana tried. "I'm Miss Paredes."

The lady moved then, as if a new voice had been enough to rouse her. She turned halfway to gaze over her shoulder. "Ah, my son told me you would come." She gestured for Oriana to approach and opened one hand to indicate the sofa. Oriana obediently sat, catching the scent of the lady's perfume, floral with a hint of musk, as she did so. The lady murmured for the butler to bring a tea tray, and then said, "I've not had a companion for a long time. It will be nice to have someone to talk to."

Oriana nodded. "Your son suggested you might consider me for the post."

"Oh, of course," the lady said vaguely. Her eyes drifted back toward the window.

"I've been companion to Lady Isabel Amaral for the past thirteen months."

Lady Ferreira simply nodded, her eyes fixed on the windows.

"I do not, however, have a letter of recommendation from the Amaral family, as Lady Isabel left her home unexpectedly." Oriana waited for a disbelieving response, but the lady simply nodded again. "I am also trained as a seamstress," Oriana added, "and worked previously at a dressmaker's shop on Esperança Street, from which I can provide references pertaining to both my skill and my character."

"That's not necessary," the lady said.

Oriana didn't know quite what to make of that. She'd been let go without a reference after more than a year in the Amaral household. Most employers would see that as the mark of a troublesome employee. "Did your son vouch for my character, my lady?"

Lady Ferreira had returned to staring out the window. She rubbed the fingertips of one hand with the other, a gesture that reminded Oriana of Nela's arthritic hands. "He says you need to be here."

Need to be here? Oriana wondered again whether the man planned this as a prelude to seduction, but couldn't bring herself to believe he would involve his mother in such a scheme, particularly not when his mother seemed to be . . . less than completely aware of her surroundings. It didn't sound like Lady Ferreira actually wanted a companion so much as she'd been told to accept one. No matter how it affected her situation, Oriana refused to be party to forcing the woman into company against her will. "Are you certain, my lady? Do you truly want me to stay?"

The woman sat unmoving for a moment, her expression distracted. Then she looked at Oriana directly, the first time she'd done so. "It will be nice to have someone to talk to. Felis is so busy, and has no interest in business. I . . ."

The lady's gaze had drifted over to the abandoned newspaper.

One gloved hand reached for it but paused midmotion. She seemed frozen.

"Felis, my lady?" Oriana prompted after a moment.

"My maid," Lady Ferreira said, shaking herself. "I do not have visitors. We are still in half mourning. But I enjoy reading the newspapers."

The half mourning explained the lady's soberness, but *newspapers*? Isabel would never have chosen such a thing, preferring to read sensational novels, such as the works of Collins or Sheridan Le Fanu. Or, rather, Isabel liked to have them read to her. Oriana suspected that Isabel had fancied herself one of those gothic heroines. In retrospect, newspapers seemed a safer choice.

Oriana gestured toward the paper lying by the lady's elbow—the trade daily. "Would you like me to read it to you?"

Lady Ferreira's eyes had drifted to the window again. She rose in a cascade of brown silk and went to stare out at something beyond the glass. Oriana followed, but saw nothing out there save rooftops and the distant waters of the river.

The gray-haired butler had returned on cat feet, leaving a tea tray on the table. He touched Oriana's elbow, bowed, and softly said, "Miss, I've been instructed to show you your rooms."

She was being herded away. Oriana murmured her excuses to the lady and followed the butler out to the hallway. Lady Ferreira never seemed to note their departure.

"Will Lady Ferreira need me later?" Oriana asked.

The butler inclined his head. "I believe you're to start in your position tomorrow, Miss Paredes. You're to have the rest of the afternoon to settle in."

It wouldn't take her that long to unpack her few garments and press them. "May I walk about the house, Mr. . . . ?"

"Cardenas, miss," the butler supplied. He waited for Oriana to retrieve her bag and hat from the table next to the doorway, and then led her along the main hallway toward an elegant stairwell that led up to the second floor. "The lower floor is all public save for the library," he said. "Teresa will show you around this evening after supper. I assume you'd prefer a tray in your room tonight. . . ."

The butler went on, assuming various things about what she wanted. Since it was a butler's job to be cognizant of the needs of the house's inhabitants, she decided to follow his lead. She didn't want to cause trouble and end up without a position again.

The main second-floor hallway stretched on for some distance, with doors leading off to either side. Bedrooms, she guessed. The stairwell up to the servants' floor would likely be in the back. Mr. Cardenas surprised her by stopping at the first door on the left. He opened it and gestured for her to enter ahead of him. "Miss Paredes."

Gripping the handles of her bag, Oriana stepped into the room.

It was far too grand a room for a servant, even an upper servant such as herself. The colors of the room suggested a man's taste, all dark browns with occasional hints of burgundy. A stately bed occupied the far end, fine ivory drapes hanging from the posts. A small seating area lay to the right of the door, a leather settee and a low table hinting that the owner would have time to recline and read there. Two doors led off to the right, a dressing room, she supposed. "Um," she began, "surely there's some mistake, Mr. Cardenas."

"No, miss. Mr. Duilio said to put you in here."

"Thank you, then, Cardenas," Oriana said, attempting to settle properly into her role in the household. If she became too familiar, it would be difficult to retreat later, and she might end up facing another footman who thought he could take advantage of her. Better to start off on the right foot. "Also, if it's not too much trouble, could one of the maids bring up a tray? I didn't have a chance for luncheon."

The butler inclined his head. "Of course, Miss Paredes. Do you prefer tea or coffee?"

"Coffee," she told him. "With cream."

He bowed and left Oriana there, staring at the opulence around her. She licked her lips nervously. She didn't understand the reasoning behind this elegant room and the courteous treatment she was receiving. Ensconcing her in this bedroom increased the likelihood that Mr. Ferreira intended a seduction. She couldn't imagine any other reason he might place her in what must be a family room. But she wasn't attractive enough to inspire some grand passion in a man she barely knew.

Worry made her empty stomach roil. *Surely this can't be his bedroom.* No, the butler would not have treated her with anything approaching respect if his master's designs had been so blatant. Even so, the room smelled masculine, with a hint of bay rum in the air. It wasn't a room normally used by a lady.

Shaking herself, Oriana gathered her wits. She would need to find the toilet stand shortly, so she'd better start exploring. She set her bag and hat on the settee and went to investigate the entry nearer to the dressing area. It opened onto a small room that smelled still and unused.

The dressing room held a large armoire and a chest of drawers in a dark wood that matched the bed. When she opened the armoire, she found a quantity of clothing, clearly a man's. For a fleeting second her worry that this was Mr. Ferreira's bedroom returned, but the clothing hadn't been touched recently. This was someone else's room—abandoned.

Oriana backed out of the dressing room and cast a quick glance at that second door. It didn't lead to the dressing area after all, so it must adjoin some other room, possibly Lady Ferreira's. At least she hoped so. Bracing herself, she went and tried the handle. The door opened outward, revealing a stunning vista of white porcelain and polished brass.

She laid one hand over her gaping mouth. It was a bathing room. A *private* bathing room.

A skylight overhead illuminated the largest tub Oriana had ever seen, easily large enough for her to lie down in—almost six feet long. It had to have been custom made for this house. The brass fittings, for hot and cold running water, gleamed as if they'd been polished that afternoon. A soft rug in pale beige covered the tile floor, and thick ivory towels waited in a set of shelves against the far wall, next to another door that must conceal a water closet.

Amazed, Oriana leaned down and ran her fingertips along the cool lip of the tub. A collection of brass boxes and delicate bottles clustered on one side of the vanity caught her eye. She suspected the fragrances would be masculine, property of the room's previous occupant. Looking about her at this rare creation, she felt an ache that was almost physical. Her skin sorely needed a long bath after a week without in the boarding house, and she couldn't imagine a better place for it. This room was beyond magnificent. It was perfect.

A sharp rapping at the bedroom door penetrated her reverie. Oriana forced herself to leave the bathing area and found a pretty young maid entering the room, a coffee tray in her hands. Oriana went to take the tray from her, an automatic response.

"Oh no, miss. I'll just put it on the stand here." The maid set the tray next to the leather settee, ran brisk fingers over her tidy apron, and curtsied. "I'm Teresa, Miss Paredes. I'll be taking care of your rooms, and anything else you need."

"There must be a mistake," Oriana said. "These rooms are too grand for a companion."

The girl smiled and shook her head. "No, miss. Mr. Ferreira said it would be easiest to keep you in this end of the house rather than opening up something at the end of the hall. And you're next to the lady here. Makes it easier for us, you know."

That sounded more like an excuse than a reason. "Who usually has this room?"

"It was Mr. Alessio's room," Teresa said, casting a glance at Oriana's bag, where it still rested on the settee. "Before he passed, I mean."

Ah, the mourning. "When was that?"

"Year and a half ago, miss, about. I didn't work here then. I started after the father died."

Oriana puzzled at those statements and decided the girl was definitely talking about two different people. Alessio wasn't the father, then. Perhaps a brother. "The father?"

The girl chewed her lower lip. "Mr. Ferreira, I meant. He died not long after his son. About a year ago, I think."

Lady Ferreira had lost a husband *and* a son within the last year and a half. *How awful.* Oriana decided to try a different tack with her questions. "Do you like working here, Teresa?"

"Oh yes, miss. Mr. Ferreira is a good master. Everyone likes him, even Miss Felis, who's known him since he was born."

Oriana didn't think this girl was faking her enthusiasm; Teresa didn't seem the sort who could lie well. She felt her worries about the man's intentions fading. "That's good to know."

"Do you need anything else, miss? I could press something if you like."

Oriana had always had to press her own garments at the Amaral household. It seemed strange to have a servant do such a chore for her. But since ironing was terribly uncomfortable for her hands, she opened her bag and located her black serge skirt, the blue vest, and her remaining shirtwaist. She surrendered them to the maid. "I thought I would take a bath, so there's no need to hurry."

The girl grinned. "Very well, miss. I'll just leave these on the hooks in the dressing room. Mr. Cardenas said I should show you around the house later this evening, after the supper service. Mrs. Cardoza usually does that, but she's got her hands full with dinner tonight since two of the girls are visiting family out in Madalena. Mr. Cardenas hoped you wouldn't mind."

It would probably be easier to get information out of this open-faced girl than out of a housekeeper anyway, so Oriana didn't argue what some others might consider a slight to her consequence. Instead she sent the girl on her way.

She stripped off her silk mitts and jacket and left them lying over the curled arm of the settee. Determined not to be wasteful, she forced herself to sit down and eat a couple of the tasty sandwiches the cook had provided for her, enough to take away the edge of her hunger. And then deciding that everything left on the tray would be acceptable cold, she returned to the bathing room to consider that lovely oversized tub.

CHAPTER 10

Humming with the sound of moving water, the pipes on the second floor told Duilio his mother's new companion had drawn a bath, which served his purposes well. He had questions that needed answering, and catching her in her bath would give him the leverage he needed. She wouldn't be able to deny who she was.

It might be improper, but it was expedient. He could apologize later.

But he had to smooth his butler's injured consequence first. "This has nothing to do with you, Cardenas. I merely suspect she would prefer to hold both copies."

Cardenas wasn't happy about surrendering one of his precious keys. "And if I should need to get in there to inspect the maids' work, sir?"

"It's only for a short time, Cardenas," Duilio said soothingly. "I'll give it two weeks. If she's comfortable with the arrangement by then, I'll ask her to return the key to you."

"As you wish, Mr. Ferreira." Cardenas frowned as he worked the brass key off his ring.

Duilio couldn't blame him. It wasn't the loss of a key that bothered the man, but the implied loss of control. Cardenas didn't want to give up the ability to check on the other servants in the household, particularly not after the incident with the footman who'd robbed them. Fortunately, the butler wasn't the sort to abuse his power. Duilio slipped the key inside his coat pocket, where it clinked against the master copy he already held. "Thank you, Cardenas."

The perturbed butler took his leave and headed down the stairs to the first floor.

Duilio chewed on his lower lip. *Am I actually going to do this?* He took a deep breath and knocked on the bedroom door. When he got no response, he listened carefully and then let himself in.

It was Alessio's old room—too masculine for a lady's companion, perhaps, but there hadn't been time to make changes. It had a private bath, as did none of the other empty rooms; if he was right about her, she would appreciate that.

Duilio strode across the rug and pressed one ear against the door to the bathing room, but didn't hear any movement within. He unlocked the bathroom door, and, once inside, gazed down into the oversized porcelain tub.

Miss Paredes lay under the surface of the water, her eyes closed. The jangling of the keys must have been muffled by the water, because she apparently hadn't heard him enter.

Duilio stared down at her, mesmerized. A flush of heat surged through his body. She was . . . stunning.

He'd admired her figure before, but unclothed she was as spectacular as he'd imagined. Her breasts with their mauve-tipped nipples were rounded but not overlarge. Her waist didn't owe its trimness to corsetry, and her hips flared down to nicely curved thighs. His hands practically itched to touch her. He'd never been attracted to small, delicate females. Oriana Paredes was the sort of woman he preferred to bed—tall and strong and able to keep up with him in . . .

Oh, good Lord! What was he thinking? She was *employed in his household.* He turned partially away from her, mentally clamping down on his desire.

He was grateful she seemed unaware of his presence, that she hadn't opened her eyes to catch him gaping at her like a schoolboy in a whorehouse. He must be flushed all the way to his hairline. He peeked at her again out of the corner of one eye, firmly reminding himself he was purportedly a gentleman.

Her hair spread about her head, the reddish tinge transmuted to a burgundy glow. Her skin looked different in the water as well, the paleness of her face becoming an opal-like iridescence. Below her breasts, her skin changed to a shimmering silver, a perfect imitation of scales running all the way down to her toes—the reason sailors claimed sereia had fish tails.

Her hands moved slowly through the water, no longer obscured by an old woman's mitts. Translucent webbing showed between her fingers, pearly skin stretching between them up to the last knuckle, so thin he might be able to see through it in the light.

The expression on her face reminded him of paintings of the saints enraptured in the presence of God. She was singing to herself, the notes muted by the water. On each side of her neck, pink-edged gills vibrated with the sound.

But that song could entrap him if she raised her head above the surface. It was said men would throw themselves into the sea on hearing it. And while he wouldn't mind staring at that silver-gilded body for the rest of the afternoon, the last thing he needed was to be enslaved to her, so he discreetly tapped on the side of the tub with one booted foot.

Still underwater, her dark eyes opened wide.

Miss Paredes sat up in a rush, setting the water sloshing about. She scooted back against the side of the tub and pressed her hands over her neck to hide her gills. That forced her breasts together, unfortunately obscuring his view of them at the same time. "I locked the door," she said, her shaky voice betraying alarm. "How did you get in here?"

Duilio spotted a towel on the table near the vanity stand and retrieved it. He was *not* going to blush. "I have the keys, of course."

Selkies rarely showed any discomfiture over nudity. That

French book he'd once read, if he recalled correctly, suggested the sereia shared that view. Her choice of covering her gills—rather than anything else—reinforced the notion. Even so, it would be ungentlemanly to stare at her bared body, no matter how lovely. He held out the towel, resolutely reminding himself to keep his eyes on her face.

"What are you doing in here?" She rose from the water, giving him a glimpse of golden stippling along the outside of her thighs. He couldn't see her dorsal stripe, supposedly one of a sereia's best features, from that angle. She snatched the towel from his hand and wrapped it about her body, keeping her back turned away from him the whole time. Then she fixed him with a hard gaze, raising her brows to prompt an answer to her question.

Duilio leaned back against the vanity stand and crossed one ankle over the other, trying to present a nonchalant facade. "I suspected you were a sereia," he said in a mild tone. "I needed to be sure."

"You could have asked," she said with asperity.

Her teeth barely showed when she spoke. Even though they looked like a human's teeth, he'd heard they were razor sharp. He had the feeling she was considering biting him, so he kept his distance. "You would have lied."

She twisted her dripping hair into a knot with one webbed hand. The movement gave him a better view of a yellowish discoloration encircling her forearms and wrists, faded bruises that might have come from being bound. "It is unacceptable to take advantage of someone in your employ, sir," she said primly.

He felt his cheeks burn again, but tried to ignore it. "I haven't taken advantage of you," he said, "nor do I have any intention of doing so. But we need to talk, and we can speak privately here without being interrupted."

"And I expected that I could bathe privately here, sir," she snapped. "Without being interrupted."

Duilio found himself admiring her nerve. It made him like her better. He doubted he would have maintained such composure if their positions were reversed. "If you're caught here," he began, "the prince will have you imprisoned or killed."

"I am aware of that," she said, sounding as if she thought him dense.

He inclined his head. It had been a waste of his breath to say it. "But in this household, you are quite safe."

One brow rose. "Even from you?"

"As I said, I needed to be sure. This is not a habit."

She tucked the towel more firmly about herself. "How did you know?"

"I've watched you for some time." He smiled, feeling oddly pleased that he was finally getting to tell *someone* how he'd figured out her secret. "Your eyes are large, dark, as one would need to see in deep water. You always seem to hide your hands. I've never seen you wear gloves, always mitts."

"I see." Miss Paredes regarded him warily. "So, what do you want of me?"

"You were pulled out of the river on the night of the twenty-fifth. What happened?"

Oriana stared at Mr. Ferreira, taken aback. *How does he know about that night?*

"Miss Paredes?" he prompted.

And how could she answer his question? She couldn't tell him the truth. . . .

Then again, she had nothing to lose, did she? He already knew she was a sereia. Could she trust this man? He wore a different face now, not the one she'd seen the day before. He'd unnerved her at first, but ultimately she'd taken him for a fop, silly and desperate for approval, prattling on about a stupid coat. The man standing in front of her had direct, intelligent eyes—sharp eyes that she suspected many in the upper levels of society wouldn't appreciate if they realized his frivolous manner hid them.

He'd been hunting her all along, she realized. Mr. Ferreira had to be the one who'd been inquiring about her by name on the streets, the one Heriberto had mentioned. She sat down on the edge of the full tub and tucked her overlarge feet behind its clawed foot, debating internally. Then she lifted her eyes to meet his. "Isabel Amaral died there."

He didn't flinch.

"She and I left her home disguised as housemaids, but we were apprehended in the street. I was drugged. When I awoke, I was tied to a chair, upside down, inside a tiny dark room. Isabel was across from me, bound the same."

He looked neither surprised nor horrified. "And then it was dropped into the river."

"Yes." She gazed down at the bruises that discolored her arms. If she kept to the facts, she could keep the pain at bay. "I heard chains rattling. Then we hit the water and started sinking. The water kept coming in. I chewed at the ropes, but Isabel was dead before I could get free."

His expression remained solemn.

She took a steadying breath. "You knew."

He pressed his lips together, stalling perhaps. "I *suspected.* Can you tell me what happened then?"

Oriana told him everything—about trying to save Isabel, about the glowing letters on the table, and the taste of death in the water once she'd escaped. Her description of the two men in the rowboat drew a scowl from him. She quickly listed what she'd learned since, including Carlos' revelation that Mr. Efisio's coachman had searched for them, her research taken from the newspapers, and the sketch she'd made of the table. She left out only her meeting with Nela, as she was unwilling to endanger another sereia. Mr. Ferreira listened solemnly, asking pointed questions in places, but he never questioned her veracity. "So, this might be necromancy of some sort," she said, "although I don't know what purpose it serves."

"Magic is not my forte. I know whom I would ask if we were in Paris, but here . . . here the Church holds more sway, so no one practices openly." He shrugged ruefully. "In any case, you're the first victim to escape, so what you know far outweighs what the police know."

She sat up straighter. "Are the police investigating this? How long have they known?"

"It took them some time to see the pattern," he said. "A couple of servants would disappear from a household on the Street of Flowers and, a day or two later, that corresponding replica would be found in the river. The police only figured it out a few weeks ago. Most of the missing servants were never reported to the police, and those who were reported were treated as missing. No one believed they might be dead until Lady Pereira de Santos started pressing the police to find her two missing housemaids. Since the houses aren't being placed in the river in an obvious order, the relationship between the two factors was difficult to discern."

Oriana covered her face with her hands. Servants came and went, generally unimportant to their masters, but she recalled Lady Pereira de Santos herself coming to the Amaral house to speak to the butler. Even if Oriana hadn't known the girls, it made her stomach turn to think that they and so many others had died the way Isabel had. She drew another calming breath and laid her hands in her lap again. "Espinoza has taken someone from each household?"

Mr. Ferreira nodded ruefully. "All of the houses have confirmed the abrupt 'departure' of a pair of servants."

And she and Isabel had been disguised as *housemaids*. Oriana laid one hand over her mouth, suddenly wondering if Isabel's silly whim had gotten her killed. She was *not* going to cry. She turned her eyes to the floor so he wouldn't see. "How many have died?"

"We can't be sure, but there are now twenty-five houses in the river."

Oriana shuddered. That meant fifty dead servants out there. No, *forty-nine.* It was a huge number to have slipped past unremarked, showing a damning disregard for the lower classes of society. "That means we only have about a week left to stop him before he kills again. I should have gone directly to the police. I didn't realize . . ."

"No," he said softly. "Turning yourself in wouldn't have benefited anyone. When we went to the commissioners for permission to pull up one of the houses and open it, we were ordered to drop the investigation altogether."

She licked her lips, wondering at his use of *we.* "You work for the police?"

He smiled sheepishly. "Surely you aren't suggesting a gentleman would work for money?"

She preferred a direct answer. "Do you?"

"I *consult* for them," he said, dipping his head.

Semantics. "In what capacity?"

He shrugged. "I have access to levels of society where the police are not welcome."

Ah. The police were using him to access society, just as she'd used Isabel. "But if the investigation was stopped . . ."

"As a private citizen," he said, "I can ask the questions now forbidden to the police. We're hoping that, given enough evidence, we'll be allowed to reopen the investigation. Right now we have no *proof.* We can't even get the newspapers to investigate. They fear being accused of spreading conspiracies by the Ministry of Culture, and supposedly the prince likes the artwork. They don't want to offend him and get shut down. However, the fact that someone other than a mere servant was killed might prove the tipping point."

Far too late to do Isabel any good. "So you sought me out. Why ask me to come here, if you could simply ask me your questions and send me on my way? You could have had them arrest me."

"You are a victim in this," he said, actually sounding regretful, "not a criminal. And you're the only witness we have, the best lead we have in finding the man who's doing this."

"And when we have stopped Espinoza, will you then turn me in to the Special Police?"

He smiled wryly and shook his head. "No. You're safe here. I have never found it reasonable to fear any of the sea folk. And I do not intend to reinforce the prince's fears by exposing an actual spy. Heaven forfend."

He made it sound light, but he could easily send her to her death. "Thank you."

"You are a spy, aren't you?" he asked, as if needing verification.

"Yes," she said. "I am a spy."

He nodded once. "I assume you have a master to whom you report. Do you need to do so?"

No, she wouldn't tell Heriberto. He would not like this development at all. Oriana shook her head. "I'm avoiding him for now. I will find Isabel's killer first and face him later."

One of Mr. Ferreira's dark brows quirked upward. "That's brave."

"I have my reasons," she said. "So, what do I do now?"

"Well, to start, try to entertain my mother a little, which will be harder than you expect."

Given her earlier interview with the woman, she *did* expect that to be difficult. "Should I not speak to the police? The actual police, I mean."

He shook his head. "I don't think it would be wise for me to drag you to one of the police stations. If you don't mind, I'd like to sit down tomorrow, perhaps after breakfast, and go over everything you can remember. I need every detail you can dredge up. Then I'll talk to my police contacts, find out what we need, and we'll go on from there."

"Is that all?" She suspected her frustration came through in her tone.

He pushed away from the vanity where he'd been leaning and added, "I intend no slight, Miss Paredes. I believe you will be key to stopping Espinoza and his cohorts. But we need time to assess your information. Give me one day, please."

He took her free hand—the one not clutching the towel—and pressed two brass keys into her palm. The sight of the webbing between her fingers didn't seem to give him pause. "The butler's copy as well, so you can have some privacy here. And one of these tins," he added, gesturing toward the jumble of gilded boxes on the vanity table, "probably has sea salt in it."

He let himself out of the bath, the scent of his ambergris cologne tickling her nose as he brushed past. Oriana locked the door behind him and rested her back against it.

He had apparently known she was a sereia for some time. That was a humbling revelation. She'd always been so careful, hiding her gills and hands. Isabel would never even have known if she hadn't stormed back into the back rooms at the dressmaker's and caught Oriana with her hands bared. For two years, no one *had* noticed her. Even so, *he'd* known.

At the same time, Mr. Ferreira had utterly fooled her. On the submersible, she'd believed his endless chatter. She'd thought him empty-headed and harmless. He was far more deceptive than she'd ever guessed, and clearly more successful at it than she was. She'd never heard a whisper of his involvement with the police. Society would be livid—and unforgiving—if that ever became public.

She let out a sigh and contemplated the cool water in the tub. After a week without a proper bath, her gills could certainly use more time in the water. And she needed desperately to unravel everything she'd just learned and plot a new course of action.

As she did her best thinking when wet, she went to find that promised box of sea salt.

CHAPTER 11

Duilio waited alone down in the kitchen. Mrs. Cardoza and her helpers had finished with the after-dinner cleaning. Gustavo Mendes, one of the footmen, was playing his twelve-string guitar down in the workroom and singing a mournful song whose notes drifted to the empty kitchen. The music brought back memories of Duilio's university days, of drinking more *Vinho Verde* than was wise and listening to fado in the taverns of Coimbra far too late into the night.

While Gustavo was a talented singer, Duilio had quickly discovered after his return that the young man's true desire was to become a police inspector, like Joaquim. Gustavo had proven to be a help when Duilio had needed to observe someone, break into a house, or be in two places at once. He could have asked Gustavo to wait here, but . . .

Duilio checked his watch again—it was just past ten—and almost missed Miss Paredes slipping down the servants' stair. He rose when he saw her walking along the narrow hallway toward the back door of the house. She wore black again, a skirt and shirtwaist shabby enough to cause him to speculate as to whether it might be what she'd had on that night. "Miss Paredes?"

Her head snapped about. "Mr. Ferreira. What are you doing down here, sir?"

Judging by her tone, his presence wasn't wanted. "I thought if you needed to go out, I might accompany you."

She came down the two steps into the kitchen, her jaw clenched. She looked *trapped*. "I was not to take up my duties until tomorrow, I thought."

He caught her implication immediately. "You are an employee of this household, Miss Paredes, not a prisoner. I'm not here to stop you, but as you are our most important lead in this case, I don't feel comfortable leaving you on your own out there."

She'd listened with her lips pressed tightly together. "Mr. Ferreira, I have been in this city for two years and have never run into trouble."

Duilio felt his brows creeping upward.

Miss Paredes shook her head. "That was a stupid thing to say. But truly, sir, I am only going over to Bainharia Street to see a friend. I won't be gone more than an hour."

Bainharia Street wasn't far, but its short length was dark and shadowy, as was that entire area. It would be an excellent location for an ambush. And he was curious to see where Miss Paredes was going at this hour, so he continued to press her. "Are you armed?"

She caught her lower lip between her teeth, a motion he found strangely appealing, as she adjusted the pin holding on her straw hat. "Do you think that's necessary?" she asked in a tart voice. "There are plenty of streetlamps."

"And someone almost succeeded in killing you before, Miss Paredes." He felt bad for pointing that out. It wasn't as if he'd never walked into a trap himself. "All I'm asking is that you let me follow you. I'll keep my distance, I promise."

She sighed, her shoulders slumping in defeat. "Oh, very well. You might as well accompany me, since it pertains to your investigation."

"Thank you. I am honored you're willing to trust me that far," he said. She cast him a doubtful glance, but didn't protest his statement, so he gestured for her to precede him. When she walked up the steps, he could see that her skirt had been torn in a couple of places, then neatly repaired. Hadn't she said something about her skirt tearing when she escaped the replica in the river? Did it bother her to wear those same garments again?

She stopped at the back door and waited while he picked up his hat and an umbrella. Once outside, he locked the door and set off at her side. "You'd best give me your arm."

She hesitated, but then wrapped her hand about the crook of his arm as they walked in silence down the alleyway behind the houses. He led her along the alley and onto the Street of Flowers, heading up toward the palace. "Can I assume you have some expertise with weapons?"

"Yes. I lost my dagger in the river, though," she said softly enough that he had to lean closer to hear. "The man who dove in after me wrestled it out of my hand." She glanced down at her right palm, covered by her mitt. "I need to replace it."

The traffic on the Street of Flowers flowed all night, although there were far fewer carriages at this hour. Pedestrians kept their distance, moving along the line of fences in clumps. Duilio watched them, unwilling to risk her safety. "I've got a couple of spares. A gun?"

"I know how to use a gun, but the trigger guard can be tricky, so a blade is more reliable."

He almost stopped walking, puzzled by that claim, and then realized that her webbing would make getting her finger through the trigger guard difficult. That prompted a dozen other questions in his mind, most pertaining to her people's military—surely they had a navy—but this wasn't the right time to be asking. Instead he went back to an earlier question. "This man who dove in after you. How did he catch you? Did he outswim you?"

"I'd hit my head on the side of their boat," she said, sounding embarrassed by that fact, "and I was exhausted by then. I just wasn't fast enough."

Her face turned toward him, but he was watching a group of apparently drunken young men stumbling in their direction. He maneuvered Miss Paredes over until they walked next to the fence and made sure he kept between her and the young men. Fortunately, the revelers were too busy insulting each other to bother Miss Paredes. Their chatter faded as they continued down toward the river. "And the other man," Duilio said. "Silva? Did he say anything?"

She turned onto Souto, the narrow street that would cross Bainharia. It wasn't much more than a cobbled alleyway, not wide enough for a carriage. A feeble glow came from a streetlamp affixed to the side of one of the buildings that closed in on either side. "He seemed to think he was rescuing me," she said. "He claimed he'd had a vision about me being in the water and came to save me."

Duilio pursed his lips. He didn't like Silva, but he didn't want to bias her perception of the events of that night. He didn't want to put ideas in her head.

It had been an unpleasant shock when she'd told him his bastard uncle had been the one to draw her out of the river. At first Duilio had assumed the boat was rowed by a collaborator of hers. When he'd realized Miss Paredes was a victim, Aga's mention of the two men in the boat had gone from understandable to *baffling*. How had the small boat gotten out there, past the patrols? Hearing that it was Silva in the boat made it less improbable. The man had access everywhere, and could probably talk his way past any police patrol. But Duilio found his entry into her story disconcerting. "Did you see any other boats on the water nearby?"

"If you're thinking of the boat that dropped the house into the water, it would have been long gone," she said, shaking her head. "Silva and his man must have rowed out from the city."

The City Under the Sea was positioned out of the lanes of traffic, nearer the southern bank of the Douro River. It inhabited an area dredged out in the past decade, ostensibly to create harbor space for naval vessels, but the navy had chosen to dock their vessels at the unfinished Port of Leixões, north of the Golden City, instead. That dredging had created a perfect situation for the artwork. It was just past a curve in the river, so the river's outward current didn't pull too hard on the houses, and protected from the incoming tidal currents by the southern breakwater that kept the sea at bay. It was about a mile from the quays of the Golden City over to that spot, giving it privacy. One had to be going there to end up there, so Silva's appearance could not have been an accident. "Did you believe Silva? About his vision, I mean?"

She walked on for a moment without answering, her heels clicking against the cobbles. "To be truthful," she finally said, "I am not a believer in seers, Mr. Ferreira. I've always suspected they simply pretend to know what will transpire and only point out the times they happened to be correct. Anyone would be right half the time, don't you think?"

Well, I've been put in my place. Duilio smiled ruefully. "Logic tells us that *is* the case, Miss Paredes. So what do you think led him there, then?"

"I don't know," she said. "But he said we'd meet again. That does concern me."

It worried him too. Silva was the showy sort who would create a great fanfare when he revealed that he'd saved a young woman from drowning. Miss Paredes did not need her likeness in the newspaper. He only hoped that it took Silva some time to locate her.

They'd reached Bainharia Street and she gestured toward the dark windows of a druggist's shop in one of the first buildings. "This one. We'll have to go upstairs."

Beyond the wrought-iron guarding a narrow balcony, a light still burned in the second-floor window. Someone was waiting for Miss Paredes. She opened the door and slipped inside. A plain lantern hung from the ceiling, casting the yellow walls in a sickly light. Duilio followed, climbing the narrow stair behind her. She knocked on the door of the apartment above the store.

An elderly woman opened the door and peered out. "Ah, good. You've come. I've had word." She caught sight of Duilio waiting a couple of steps down the stair. "Who is this?"

"My new employer—" Miss Paredes began.

The woman opened the door a bit wider and held up a wrinkled hand. "Don't tell me, child. Heriberto came by this afternoon, trying to find out where you went, so I'd better not know any more. Give me a moment." She closed the door, leaving them in the hallway.

Miss Paredes glanced at him, an apologetic expression drawing her brows together. Duilio shook his head. "I don't need to know."

The worry fled her features then. "Thank you."

He *didn't* need her to tell him. Heriberto was, without doubt, the name of Miss Paredes' superior. That the man had visited the elderly inhabitant of this building hinted that the woman must also be a sereia, despite the evidence that Duilio hadn't seen webbing between her fingers. That raised questions he would love to explore, but they could wait until Miss Parades trusted him more.

The door opened again, and the elderly woman passed out a square envelope. "She left this for you."

Miss Paredes took it. "Thank you. I truly appreciate your help."

The elderly woman waggled one finger at her, a finger that had an ugly scar running up each side. "Be careful out there, child."

"I will," Miss Paredes promised her.

The woman nodded and closed her door, an end to the interview.

Duilio heard the key turning in the lock. "Is that it, then?"

Miss Paredes chewed her lower lip for a second, cast a glance at his face, and then opened the envelope and withdrew a fine, deckle-edged card. She read the words, her dark eyes flicking across the page. "I'm supposed to meet her at the Carvalho ball Thursday night." Her eyes lifted to his face. "Do you know a way I could sneak in?"

Duilio didn't ask whom Miss Paredes was expected to meet.

Not yet. But if she'd asked his help, then this meeting was important to her. "Sneak in? No, Miss Paredes. You and I will walk in the front door. I'm invited."

"I can't accompany you," Miss Paredes protested, her spine straightening. "I'm not . . ."

When she trailed off, he realized that she'd misunderstood his intention. He *could* escort a young lady to that ball uninvited—he knew the Carvalho family well enough to get away with it—but that would attract more attention than he wanted at the moment. And it might prove awkward, since Mr. Carvalho had approached Duilio earlier in the year, hoping to arrange a marriage with his eldest daughter. But Duilio had a different plan in mind. "My mother is invited as well," he clarified. "As her companion, your attendance would be unexceptional."

"Ah. I see," she said, her face lowering as if she might be blushing, although Duilio didn't see any flush staining her cheeks. "Is she well enough to go?"

"Despite her distraction, my mother is made of steel, Miss Paredes," he said. "She can do anything once she makes up her mind. Shall we discuss it with her in the morning?"

Miss Paredes slipped the card back into its envelope. "Yes. Thank you, sir."

Duilio offered her his arm. "Then let's go home."

CHAPTER 12

Wednesday, 1 October 1902

By the time Duilio made it downstairs in the morning, he'd already thought of a dozen things he needed to get done and about a hundred more questions he wanted to ask Miss Paredes. He found his mother and Miss Paredes in the dining room, already eating breakfast. His mother looked more alert than she had in some time, able to concentrate enough to greet him this morning. He went and kissed her cheek before sitting down. Having a companion might suit her after all.

For her part, Miss Paredes looked far more rested than she had the day before. She wore a white shirtwaist with a vest in royal blue that flattered her pale complexion. Her black skirt wasn't the one she'd worn to make her late-night visit, but a finer woolen that looked well made, if not in the most current fashion. Recalling her statement that she'd hit her head against the boat that night, he noted the faint bruising on her temple. She looked serene despite the difficulties of the past several days. That might be a facade. He didn't know her well enough yet to be sure.

Miss Paredes held one of the newspapers in her mitt-obscured hands, stubbornly keeping her eyes on the printed words. Duilio wondered if she was the sort of woman who read the gossip pages, but decided that if she did so, it was only as a part of her job. She seemed too serious. The paper she currently held was his mother's trade daily. He would love to know whether Miss Paredes enjoyed reading that. Personally, he found it a dead bore.

While waiting for the footman to bring his customary breakfast, Duilio sipped at his coffee. "Are you settling in well, Miss Paredes?" he asked.

His mother actually appeared interested in her answer, a good sign.

Miss Paredes folded the paper and laid it down. "Yes, sir. Thank you."

Duilio turned to his mother then. *No time like the present.* "Mother, do you recall that the Carvalhos are having a ball tomorrow night?"

She appeared to consider his query for long enough that he feared he'd lost her attention, but finally said, "Isn't their youngest daughter turning seventeen?"

"Yes." None of the three Carvalho girls had managed to find a husband yet, despite their father's best efforts. Duilio only hoped his mother's attendance at the ball—her first outing in years—wouldn't be misinterpreted as interest in Carvalho's eldest daughter on Duilio's part. "Miss Paredes and I need to speak to someone there. A police matter. Would you be willing to go, Mother, as a favor to me?"

His mother sighed. "Am I out of mourning now?"

His mother hadn't attended a social function of any sort for three years, but mourning wasn't the reason behind it. "You're in half mourning, Mother. It shouldn't cause too much comment as long as you don't dance," he said, "or run off into the gardens with some young swain."

His mother didn't respond to his joke, but the preposterous comment drew a dry glance from Miss Paredes. He rather enjoyed seeing that expression on her solemn face.

"If it will help," his mother said, "I'll manage, Duilinho."

Despite being made to feel about eight years old in front of Miss Paredes, Duilio couldn't help smiling at his mother's long-suffering tone. She had never enjoyed the fripperies and gossip of the social set. "So, Miss Paredes," he asked, "you and my mother have two days to prepare for a ball. Is that feasible?"

Miss Paredes cast a glance at his mother, but nodded shortly. The paper apparently captured her attention after that, for she said nothing else to him. She began reading one of the articles to his mother instead, something about steam trawlers, a type of fishing boat banned from the area. A portion of the family's money—his mother's money—was invested in the boatbuilding industry. Apparently Miss Paredes already knew of his mother's interests there.

Duilio would give anything to have his father and brother back. Among other things, then he wouldn't have to oversee the family's investments. While his grandfather had amassed a decent fortune buying up fabric mills in the north of the country and building a shipping fleet to get those goods to markets, Duilio didn't know a great deal about either; he'd always believed Alessio would inherit. His father had shifted his funds to investment in those industries rather than active participation, removing some of the stench of trade from their hands. Fortunately his man of business kept him apprised of the pertinent news, saving Duilio from reading the trade papers every morning.

After breakfast, Duilio asked Felis to join them in the front sitting room to read to his mother. He hoped that eschewing privacy would stem any gossip about himself and Miss Paredes in the household, so he directed Felis and his mother to two ivory-brocade armchairs set by the window. A few minutes later he was ensconced on the pale leather sofa before the hearth. On the low table before him he laid out the timeline, a sheet of foolscap on which Joaquim had drawn a long dateline across the top, with each pertinent event written perpendicular to that in his tidy hand.

Miss Paredes nodded toward it. "What is this?"

Duilio pulled the sheet of foolscap closer. "We've done our best to put together a chronological chart of every event pertaining to *The City Under the Sea*."

She nodded her head slowly, eyes still downcast. "I found much of this information in the newspapers. I just didn't think to lay it out this way. It's clever."

Duilio shifted closer to her on the couch. "This starts just over a year ago, when the first house, the Duarte mansion, was discovered in the water. And this," he said, pointing, "in early September, was when we put together the reports of missing servants with the timing of the appearance of the houses in the water. Then we were ordered to close the investigation."

"And then it was the Amaral house," Miss Paredes said softly.

Duilio sat back. "Espinoza is the only person we definitely have connected to this," he said, "so several of these entries pertain to our efforts to find him."

She touched a date shortly after the fifth house was placed. "Espinoza stopped giving interviews about this time. The papers said he tired of being hounded by the writers."

"Yes," he said. "That sounds right."

"He lived in Matosinhos before he became famous," she said, naming a town only a few miles north of the Golden City. It was on the Leça River, the site of the unfinished port of Leixões. "He must have come to the Golden City about two or three years ago, I think, but I didn't find anything about where he lives or works now."

"He was renting a flat in Massarelos parish," Duilio said, "but moved out about a year before the first house was placed. We've not been able to trace where he went from there. Not so far. He had to have had space to build the houses and a way to get supplies. But he's essentially building small boats, and there are dozens of boatbuilders in this city and the neighboring ones. He could be hiding among those."

"They're not boats," she pointed out. "The house continued to float after it filled with water. The newspapers say there's a charm on the top of each that keeps them floating. Could you hunt for the person who made those?"

Duilio frowned. "The charms are of questionable effectiveness. They do nothing more than make sailors feel safer. And anyone can put together a charm, I'm afraid, Miss Paredes."

"Oh." She looked back down to the timeline. "How many people do you think it takes to build these . . . *things* and submerge them? The newspaper articles said there must be dozens."

"I don't think so. Keeping a secret with that many people is nearly impossible, and Espinoza has managed. I think we're talking about one dozen at most. Unless there's some cause they're espousing," Duilio added. "If they have a cause, they're more likely to keep their mouths shut."

"What *cause* could this possibly serve?" Miss Paredes' lips thinned, her eyes taking on the same hurt look he'd seen in the submersible. She'd shifted away from him, her black-clad hands clenched tightly in her lap. "What is the point of killing so many, and in such a manner?"

She, more than anyone else alive, had the right to ask that question. Duilio just wished he had an answer. "Perhaps your meeting tomorrow night will give us that information. Did you not tell me that you had a sketch of the table?"

"It's not much," she said. "I couldn't remember any of the symbols in the inner ring, so what I have may not be useful."

"It's more than we had yesterday morning," Duilio assured her. He wanted to set her at ease, talk about something trivial, but he suspected this was better done swiftly. So he asked her questions about the coachman who'd accosted her and drugged her, about the man who'd drawn her into the boat with Silva, about the voices she'd heard from inside the replica, and even the rattling of the chains she'd heard. He tried to recall everything she'd said the day before in the bathroom, so as not to make her repeat herself.

"How did you get out of the replica?" he asked. "Was there a door?"

"No," she said. "I kicked at the upper corner of the roof—well, the floor, since it was upside down—and it gave eventually. I managed to squeeze out. The damage wasn't visible from the submersible, just a line of light from inside. From the table."

He hadn't seen that damage, but he hadn't known where to look either. "And you were wearing the housemaid's costume." That would be the "black and white" that Aga had reported.

She nodded jerkily. "I'd lost the cap but I still had the apron on. I tore up the apron to bandage my hand once I was on the quay."

Bandage her hand? "Then what did you do?"

"I don't know how long I stood there." She was being careful not to look at him, he noted, perhaps trying to keep her words impersonal. "Eventually I made my way to the Amaral house. I went in through the back. The butler found me there and sent for Lady Amaral. I told her that Isabel had been grabbed by someone, but I couldn't tell her what had actually happened."

"She doesn't know you're a sereia?"

She shook her head. "I told Lady Amaral I'd been drugged and dumped off a bridge. I said I didn't know what had become of Isabel."

He could understand the lie. She'd had a lot to lose that night. "Did she believe you?"

"I don't know. She said I was a lying . . ." Miss Paredes paused. "She fired me and ordered me out of the house."

Without a care for her welfare, he surmised, even after more than a year of service. Lady Amaral couldn't afford to act as if her daughter wasn't safely married, so Miss Paredes had to be silenced. He suddenly liked Lady Amaral even less. "So, where did you go from there?"

"I'd hidden my bag next to the coal room steps." Her hands began to shake. "I stayed there, hiding down by the steps until after dawn, trying to plan what to do. I had a bit of money in my bag and some extra clothes. The first footman has a relative with a boarding house, so I went there."

Duilio couldn't imagine what he'd do in the same circumstances, having watched a friend die, left on the quay after midnight with no family to turn to, unable to go to the police, and soaked to the skin. He hoped he would have acted with the same presence of mind.

He reached over and patted her folded hands, hoping to reassure her. "That's all I need at the moment," he said. "I suspect I'll come up with a dozen more questions by this afternoon. I usually stop into the library in the evening before I go up to my room. If you think of something you want to discuss with me, you could leave a note on my desk."

She nodded briskly, her posture still rigid. "Is that all?"

She seemed eager to escape him, so he moved to the end of the sofa. "Yes, I think so."

"Should I go get that sketch for you?"

"I would appreciate that," he said.

Miss Paredes rose, forcing him to rise also. She fell only an inch or two short of his height, tall for a woman but not shockingly so. He stepped to one side to allow her to pass. Her black skirt brushed his thigh as she did so. The contact, even unintentional, startled him.

He found himself looking into her eyes. They glistened. In general, he didn't react to women's tears—they were too often a sham. But everything within him believed Miss Paredes in that moment. He wanted to talk to her, to comfort her somehow. He felt the urge to draw her into his arms, no matter how inappropriate that might be between master and servant. He shook his head to dispel that idea.

"I'll . . . I'll be back directly," Miss Paredes stammered.

Duilio watched her go, wondering if sereia had any powers of attraction other than their *call*, the song that drew men to them. That sudden urge to comfort her, so very out of place for him, surprised him.

Felis read on, her voice sibilant. The maid hadn't looked in their direction, Duilio observed, and so probably hadn't noticed anything amiss. His mother hadn't either, no doubt.

He knew very little about Miss Paredes, but he could remedy that. He would love to spend a few hours talking with her—about something other than death. It was an enticing thought. But it would take longer than hours, he suspected, to learn all he wanted to know. It might take years.

And he didn't think they had that much time. She was a spy. She had her own agenda and was here in his house only until they found Espinoza. Sooner or later, she would be gone. So by the time she returned from her bedroom at the top of the stairs, he'd managed to quell his curiosity. Her eyes were red, making him suspect she'd allowed herself to cry once out of his sight, but she seemed composed now.

He took the folded piece of paper she handed him with a grave nod. When he opened it, he saw the rings she'd described, with three words in Latin. "*Me, however,* and . . . *house.*"

Something teased at the corner of his mind. He *should* know those words. There was something familiar about them.

"Is that what they mean?" Miss Paredes asked. "Is it Latin?"

"Yes," he said. "That's how the words translate, although I have no idea what they mean. I have to wonder what the other half said."

"I'm sorry," she said softly. "I couldn't see anything on that side."

He was impressed she'd recalled all the small details she had. Not all witnesses were as useful. "We'll figure it out, Miss Paredes. Now, I'll be gone most of the day, but I'll keep you apprised. I'm sure my mother will have preparations to make for the ball tomorrow night, so I'll leave you ladies to your work."

Miss Paredes, silk-covered hands neatly folded in front of her, didn't look at him this time. "Yes, of course, sir," she said without emotion. "We'll take care of everything."

A very professional answer, as if she, too, had reminded herself of proper demeanor while upstairs. The mask was necessary if she was to survive in the Golden City. How difficult it must be never to let anyone see who she truly was. She was a sereia first and a spy second, yet neither of those labels told him who she was.

CHAPTER 13

After Mr. Ferreira left, Oriana sat down on the sofa, letting Felis continue to read. She should be doing that herself, but her nerves were rattled.

She hadn't reckoned it would be so hard to discuss Isabel's death again. It had been easier the first time. She'd been able to tell Mr. Ferreira the *facts* of what had happened then, without letting herself feel anything, perhaps because she'd been on the defensive after he'd uncovered her identity. This time, though, he had looked at her as if he felt compassion for her. That had almost been her undoing. She had managed to hold back the tears until she reached the safety of her bedroom, saving herself that embarrassment.

Oriana wiped at her eyes surreptitiously with the tip of one finger, took a deep breath, and went to take over the reading. Felis looked old enough to be Lady Ferreira's mother, but clearly had all her wits about her. Her hawklike eyes raked over Oriana, her attire, her too-narrow shoes, and then turned solicitously back to her mistress. "Lady, are you truly planning on going out Thursday night? I am pleased. It's about time."

The lady nodded. "Yes. Will you pick something for me to wear? Something that would be appropriate. I'll come see what you've picked out later."

Oriana hid her surprise. Isabel would never have let her maid pick out her garb, which hinted that either Lady Ferreira trusted Felis implicitly or that she didn't care what she wore. The maid left swiftly, and Oriana spent an hour reading about the business of building boats. It calmed her nerves and, if nothing else, she would learn about boats while she was here.

Despite the fact that she'd spent the past year dealing with Isabel's fits and starts, entertaining Lady Ferreira did turn out to be more difficult than Oriana expected, just as Mr. Ferreira had promised. She spent the remainder of the morning trying to engage the lady in conversation. At first she read the newspaper aloud, but as soon as she'd completed a few sentences, the lady's attention would wander back to the windows. Fortunately, Oriana was well schooled in patience. Isabel had been prone to dramatic fits of melancholy. Oriana had gotten plenty of practice cajoling her out of those. After a time, she hit on the idea of asking if Lady Ferreira wished to go out onto the second-floor balcony that looked out toward the river.

That suggestion roused the lady from her daydreams. She settled an old-fashioned lace mantilla over her neatly twisted brown hair and accompanied Oriana up to the gallery that led out onto the balcony. She pushed open the door and stepped out into the light. She laid elegant hands on the wrought-iron railing, her eyes seeking the narrow band of water visible from that particular spot on the Street of Flowers.

Oriana took a deep breath of the air, still humid from the previous evening's rain. The sounds of traffic on the Street of Flowers and birds squabbling along the river's edge touched her ears, but neither was as seductive as the distant rush of the water, barely detectable this far into the city. Perhaps it was only her desire that made her hear it. The water called her, always at the back of her mind and heart, the reason few of her people ever strayed far from the ocean.

The lady's eyes rested on the view of the river, gray under overcast skies. "My sons worry if I come out here alone," she said after a time.

Oriana cast a glance at Lady Ferreira's lovely face. The woman had only *one* son now. Surely that was what the maid Teresa had told her. Alessio Ferreira had died well over a year ago. Some scandal had attached to the gentleman's death, but Teresa hadn't supplied any details. She'd shown Oriana a photograph of the man, though, kept on the mantel in the front sitting room in a well-worn silver frame. Alessio had strongly resembled his mother—strikingly attractive, more *beautiful* than handsome. Oriana decided he must remain alive in his mother's mind, prompting her to speak of her sons. "Are they concerned you'll take ill?"

"No." Lady Ferreira hugged her arms about herself. "I miss the sea."

Well, she certainly understood that. It made her think Lady Ferreira a kindred spirit. She touched the lady's elbow. "Can you not go down to the water?"

"Here in this house, Duilinho can keep me safe," the lady said in a firm voice, almost a mantra. She ran her hands along the railing as if it were her cage.

"From whom?"

Lady Ferreira shuddered delicately. "That bastard Paolo. He would see my son dead."

Dead? Mr. Ferreira hadn't mentioned that anyone wanted him dead. And who was Paolo? Oriana leaned forward, trying to read Lady Ferreira's expression. "And what of your other son? Does this Paolo seek to kill him also?"

Lady Ferreira looked up sharply and laid a slender hand on Oriana's arm, her seal-brown eyes fearful. "Paolo mustn't know about Erdano. That's why I can't go back to Braga Bay. He might follow me to Erdano, and then Erdano would die, too."

Erdano? Who was that? Oriana was certain Teresa hadn't mentioned any Erdano. "I won't tell anyone. I promise."

Lady Ferreira wiped one eye with the edge of her mantilla. "I only have my sons left now. I will do what I must to protect them, even if it means never going near the water again."

That didn't clarify much. Clearly Erdano wasn't another name for the dead Alessio, though. He must be yet another son, sired by a different man, perhaps a former husband. Even so, Oriana couldn't imagine why the lady would go to Braga Bay to see him. There was no settlement at that secluded bay north of the city. It was tiny, more a cove than a bay . . . and only the seal people lived on that narrow strip of sandy beach beneath the cliffs.

Oriana gazed down at Lady Ferreira's worried face; her delicate, pointed features; and large dark eyes and something strange occurred to her. Unlike Oriana's own people, the seals took human form—a completely human form—when they shed their pelts. *Could it be?*

Mr. Ferreira had promised her that she would be safe in this household. Perhaps he'd felt safe offering that promise because his mother was as much at risk as she was. That would definitely need discussion when she could catch him next.

Duilio found Joaquim at the café nearest the police station in Massarelos parish. It was Joaquim's usual stop for lunch when he had time—the Café Brilhante. The tables had elegant white cloths and shining cutlery but didn't cater to an upper-class clientele. Duilio liked the place. He wended his way through the crowded café to the table near the back, where Joaquim sat. It was, rather predictably, in a corner with a good view of the entryway, but Duilio managed to sit down before a distracted Joaquim could rise to greet him. "What are you working on?"

Joaquim straightened a handful of papers and slid them back into a folder. "Another case. Nothing for you to worry about."

Duilio translated that as meaning a case Joaquim didn't want his aid on—not yet. Joaquim often investigated cases other inspectors had given up on, usually on his own time. He was too stubborn to quit. "I see. Have you ordered?"

After learning that Joaquim had, Duilio waved over one of the waiters. It was noisy in the place, but everyone seemed inclined to mind their own business. At least he needn't yell at Joaquim, as he must in some cafés. "Miss Paredes took the position as Mother's companion."

The waiter arrived, and Duilio ordered coffee and a large lunch while Joaquim sat shaking his head. Once the waiter had gone, Joaquim frowned. "You *hired* her? Why didn't you just bring her to meet me down at the station?"

"I don't want Miss Paredes near your station, Joaquim." There were no other diners seated near enough to overhear them, so Duilio told the truth. "She's a sereia."

That gave Joaquim pause. "Truly? How do you know?"

He was not going to tell Joaquim how much of an eyeful he'd gotten the afternoon before. It had probably been an unwise action, given the effect the mere sight of her nude had on him. He should probably start looking about for a mistress—although he wouldn't mention that to his cousin. Joaquim had a prudish streak, likely a reaction to having been raised around Alessio and having Erdano as a regular guest at the house. Joaquim had even considered entering the priesthood, choosing the seminary over the university at Coimbra. He'd been relieved when Joaquim finally chose the police instead.

Duilio puffed out his cheeks, deciding how best not to offend him. "I've seen her webbed hands and her gills," he admitted. "I'm absolutely certain she's a sereia. I've honestly suspected it for some time."

Joaquim gave him a flat stare. "And you didn't think to mention that to me?"

Duilio tried for a casual shrug. "I didn't want to bother you with excess information if it turned out to be . . . unimportant."

"Wrong, you mean." Joaquim eyed him with exasperation. "This is why you're right all the time: because you omit all the times you're wrong."

That sounded damningly like what Miss Paredes had said about seers the night before. Duilio waved airily, a gesture he usually saved for his society persona. "Dear Joaquim, I'm simply infallible."

Joaquim laughed, a rarity. "So, what else haven't you told me yet, assuming I don't need to be bothered?"

"Too many things to count." Duilio didn't intend to tell Joaquim any more about Miss Paredes. He wasn't going to mention her striking coloration, her narrow waist, or her lovely breasts. "Unfortunately, I was right about Lady Isabel. She's dead. Miss Paredes can breathe underwater, so she had time to untie herself and escape, but she watched Lady Isabel die."

Joaquim rubbed a hand over his face and sighed, his expression changing to sympathy. "Poor girl. Why did she not go to the police? Wait . . . never mind. She's a sereia; no police. Did she see who put them in the house?"

"No, she was drugged and only woke once inside," Duilio told him. "Lady Isabel was intending to elope with Mr. Efisio, as the paper says, but she and her companion were grabbed by a different coach than the one they expected. They were disguised as housemaids."

"Fatal mistake," Joaquim said softly.

Duilio held up one finger in warning as the waiter approached with his coffee. One never knew where a stranger stood on the matter of nonhumans. Once the man had gone again, Duilio shook out his napkin, laid it in his lap and took a sip of his coffee. It was strong, as he preferred. "I discussed the case with Miss Paredes in detail this morning."

Joaquim perked up at that. "Did she give you any new leads?"

Leaning closer, Duilio tried to tell Joaquim most of what Miss Paredes told him. The mention of the table's inscription coming to life after Lady Isabel's death caused Joaquim to glance about, as if the necromancer might come to the café to find them. Duilio withdrew the sketch from his pocket and slid it across the table.

When Joaquim read the writing in the outer circle, his brows drew together. "I don't understand."

"It's in Latin," Duilio offered sarcastically. Joaquim's Latin was, without doubt, better than his own.

Joaquim gave Duilio a dry look, folded up the paper, and passed it back. "I mean that I don't understand the choice of scripture. Why use that one?"

Aha! That was why he'd felt those words were familiar. "Sorry. Which one?"

Joaquim rolled his eyes. "*Ego autem et domus mea serviemus Domino.* The Book of Joshua, Chapter Twenty-four. 'However I and my house will follow the Lord.' "

It appeared that Joaquim hadn't forgotten any of his seminary training while on the police force. "Could this be the Jesuits, then?"

During the ugly days of the Inquisition, witches had hidden *inside* the Church to escape persecution and most had eventually gravitated toward the nascent Jesuit order. Joaquim had studied with the Benedictines, though, so he didn't have many connections among the Jesuits. He shook his head. "I can't imagine they would condone any part of this, Duilio. And the verse doesn't fit, anyway. It has nothing to do with these crimes."

"There are houses involved," Duilio reminded him, which earned another dry look.

The waiter arrived then with two plates: Duilio's hearty meal of liver and sausage with fried potatoes, stuffed mushrooms, and *broa*, along with Joaquim's fish soup. Duilio couldn't understand how Joaquim didn't starve; Joaquim was the heavier of the two of them. Duilio simply seemed to require more food. Thinking of that, he picked up a fork.

"Miss Paredes is supposed to meet someone regarding the table's inscription tomorrow night," he said. "So perhaps it will make more sense afterward."

Joaquim nodded but didn't ask about Miss Paredes' unknown contact.

Duilio was grateful that Joaquim, such a stickler in some areas, was willing to bend in the important matters. As a police inspector, he was walking a fine line. He hadn't asked why Miss Paredes was in the city, disguised as a human, but surely he'd guessed there was a chance she was a spy. Even so, the less he knew of her, the less he would have to hide.

Duilio had another concern to lay before him. "I should warn you, the man who pulled her out of the water wasn't a fisherman, as I'd originally assumed. It was Paolo Silva."

That made Joaquim set down his fork. "Silva? Your uncle Silva?"

Duilio was tempted to ask which *other* Paolo Silva it might be, but there were probably a hundred other men in the city with a name that common. "Yes, him. He told her he'd foreseen that a woman would be in the river in need of rescue, which Miss Paredes obviously was."

Joaquim shook his head. "No good can come of that."

"True. I'm worried he'll try to make a public show of the fact that he 'rescued' her," Duilio admitted. "She can't afford that sort of attention."

"Neither can we," Joaquim pointed out. "Can you keep her hidden from him? If she stays to the house . . ."

Duilio pushed away his plate. "I suspect that if we ask her to sit by and do nothing, Miss Paredes will disappear and go hunting Espinoza on her own."

"I see," Joaquim said. "A militant sort, is she?"

Duilio held in a laugh. He didn't know enough of Miss Paredes to speculate on her relative militancy. Not yet. "She doesn't strike me as being willing to wait around merely because she's female, and she knows another house will end up in the river in a week or so."

Joaquim crossed himself. "Yes. We'll simply have to work faster."

Duilio only wished they had more to work with. "Will you tell Captain Santiago that I'm working on a new lead? I'd avoid telling him about Miss Paredes, though. He'd probably want to drag her into the station, and I'm not going to allow that."

Joaquim cast him a shrewd glance before turning back to his soup. "I'll be discreet."

Oriana sat in her bedroom, a blue silk dress in a mass on her lap. After consulting with Teresa about the state of Oriana's garments, Felis had picked it from among Lady Ferreira's out-of-date clothing and ordered Oriana to wear it. Since what remained of her wardrobe wasn't suitable for a ball, Oriana acquiesced. The waist needed to be taken in and the skirt was too short, but she could add a flounce made from part of the underskirt, alterations that she could easily do herself, since Lady Ferreira was napping. The dress would be presentable but somber, suitable for a companion in a house recently out of mourning.

The window seat on which Oriana perched looked out over the Street of Flowers, giving her an excellent view of the traffic passing the house. It also offered the best light in the room. Working on dark fabric with dark thread was hard on the eyes, but she hated doing *nothing*.

She leaned forward against the window to get a better view of two men striding along the street. The streets weren't crowded at this hour, so she got a good look at them as they walked in the direction of the quay. One was a fisherman with gray hair and worn shoes—Heriberto. As he walked down the Street of Flowers, he talked quietly with the Amarals' footman Carlos.

Oriana shoved the dress off her lap and stepped over the crumpled mass on the floor. Her mitts lay on the table next to the leather settee, so she grabbed those up and slid them on before leaving her room and dashing down the stairs. Cardenas gave her a startled glance when she passed him in the hall. "I'm going out for a few minutes," she told him. "I'll be right back."

"May I get you a hat, Miss Paredes?" he asked disapprovingly.

Bother. I am bareheaded. She glanced into the sitting room and spotted Lady Ferreira's mantilla lying on one of the tables. She grabbed that and settled the comb into her hair, hoping that the lady wouldn't mind. She tugged the veil forward to cover her face and headed out the door, ignoring Cardenas' worried eyes.

She hurried down the steps and began walking as quickly as would be seemly. In a couple of minutes, she caught sight of the two men just as they turned down one of the side streets toward the Golden Church of São Francisco. Oriana hopped over a pile of mule dung as she crossed the street a few feet ahead of an approaching tram. She didn't want to lose them.

Was Heriberto looking for her again? She hated the idea of being caught unawares, as she had when he'd found her before. She needed to know what he was after.

The two men stopped at the corner, forcing her to walk more slowly. There were a few more words said, and then Heriberto dropped a handful of coins into Carlos' hand. That verified her suspicion that Carlos had spilled her hiding place at his kinswoman's boarding house. Carlos slipped the coins into his pocket and strolled away toward the quay.

The money changing hands disabused her of any notion that his chat with Heriberto was a coincidence. Perhaps she should go to Heriberto and simply ask him what he was after now.

But once Carlos was out of sight, Heriberto walked around the corner onto Infante Henrique Street and up two levels of steps to reach the terrace in front of the church. Under the rose window, he glanced about and walked over to the stone railing that ran along the side. He leaned on the railing, apparently to wait. *For whom?*

On the street below, Oriana paused. Surely he would note a veiled woman walking back and forth. While the mantilla was commonly worn during Mass, it was too late in the day for that. She could go inside the church and pretend to pray, but then she wouldn't learn what he was doing here. If only she'd thought to grab a sketchpad, she could pretend to be drawing the church's stone facade or rose window.

She hesitated there at the base of the stairs, too long perhaps, because he leaned forward, as if he'd suddenly spotted her. She held her breath, prepared to run, but then realized he was gazing past her. Oriana glanced over her shoulder and felt her throat tighten.

Thank the gods she had the veil to hide her face.

The man striding toward her along São Francisco Street was dressed elegantly, a tall hat on his head and a polished cane in his hand. His frock coat and pinstriped trousers could pass for a gentleman's garb, although he was actually a businessman. A handsome man in his late forties, he had only a touch of gray at his temples. He passed her with a tip of his hat and walked up the steps to meet Heriberto.

Oriana pressed her hand against her stomach and closed her eyes. Her father hadn't recognized her, not with a veil hiding her face.

She made up her mind quickly, walking around the edge of the church grounds onto São Francisco Street. She leaned against the wall of the first house before casting a glance back.

It could be a coincidence. That was possible.

She laughed to herself and shook her head. She would have to be an idiot to believe this a coincidence. No, the only reason she could accept for her father to come so far from his home was to meet with the man.

So Heriberto *was* aware her father lived in the city. She had fervently hoped that he didn't know, but Nela *had* commented last night about not divulging information to Heriberto, so apparently the prohibition against communicating with the exiles didn't apply to him. It had been foolish to hope that her father, with his successful business and human lover, would have escaped Heriberto's notice.

Then again, it meant that her father dealt with Heriberto on his own. Perhaps all her worries for his sake had been misplaced. She had feared that if Heriberto knew, he might turn her father in to the Special Police. It was the sort of underhanded thing Heriberto would threaten to get his way. But he hadn't. Why not?

Realizing she'd been in one spot long enough to garner the attention of patrons of the small café, Oriana pushed herself away from the wall. She made up her mind quickly, going up the first flight of steps but not up to the next level to the church. She walked to an inward corner of the wall and paused there, almost directly under where Heriberto stood. She wrung her hands together, hoping she looked like a woman left waiting for a lover who never showed. She held her breath.

". . . and I wouldn't tell you if I did," her father was saying. Snapping, actually. He was angry.

"You *will* tell me if you hear from her," Heriberto said flatly, as if he had the upper hand.

"Or what? What more do you want? More money?"

Money? Her father was *paying* Heriberto? For what?

"I know your secret, Adriano," Heriberto answered. "Did you think I wouldn't find out about her?"

Oriana took a quick breath and didn't catch what her father said in response.

"You want to keep your girl safe," Heriberto said then, derision in his voice, "you'll do what I say. I know where she lives." Again, Oriana couldn't make out her father's response. Heriberto's voice reached her ears clearly, though. "If Oriana comes to you, you tell me. You find out where she is, I want to know directly."

Why *was* Heriberto suddenly looking for her? On Sunday he'd willingly given her two weeks to report in, yet now he needed to find her? Why so soon? Her father was speaking above her head, but

Oriana couldn't make out anything. She pressed her hands together, pacing again. When she turned in the direction of the café, she noted a woman watching her from one of the tables. The woman didn't bother to look away when caught staring.

Oriana turned back, her pulse pounding in her ears. She couldn't panic. If she were to run, it would be a sure sign she wasn't supposed to be there. She doubted she could outrun Heriberto anyway, not in these pinching shoes. So she let her pacing take her back toward the stairwell, losing any chance of overhearing the conversation. The woman was still watching her, but Oriana kept her head down, trying to look . . . troubled. Not difficult at the moment.

She turned as if she'd finally come to some decision and briskly headed back the way she'd come. Even as she walked away, she felt the unknown woman's eyes on her back.

Her temples throbbed. She'd attracted someone's attention, something she couldn't afford to do. The woman must have been watching Heriberto first, and spotted Oriana eavesdropping on his conversation. *Who is she?*

Oriana glanced over her shoulder, but didn't see anyone in pursuit. The woman was bold enough that she hadn't even tried to hide her appearance. She had thick brows and very hard eyes in a pale oval face. Dark hair pinned up neatly. Well dressed, but in stern black with a high collar. Her square jaw hinted that she could be a sereia, although something indefinable had been . . . off about her. Oriana would definitely recognize the woman should she see her again.

If the woman was watching Heriberto, the most likely explanation was that she was *his* superior, perhaps checking up on him. But Oriana had met most of those who currently spied here and in Sintra, to the south, and she was certain she'd never seen that woman before.

CHAPTER 14

Duilio had dropped by the house prior to dinner to return the sketch he'd borrowed from Miss Paredes, only to learn that she'd gone out. Cardenas didn't approve, of course, but Duilio managed to convince the man that Miss Paredes had gone out to run an errand for him.

Unfortunately, a note from the young boatman, João, prevented him from staying for dinner. Erdano had left a message requesting Duilio's company, but neglected to tell João the reason. Since Erdano seldom demanded his presence, Duilio thought it best to find out what his selkie half brother had on his mind.

Erdano currently sprawled on the bench at the tavern, watching one of the waitresses. In human form he made a very large man, taller than Duilio by a hand and half again as broad. They didn't resemble each other much, save about the eyes. He didn't look back to Duilio when he said, "Tigana says Aga saw a woman on the water, a woman with webbed hands, so she sent her to you."

"Yes," Duilio said, not bothering to mentally untangle that sentence. "Tell Aga I appreciate her acuity, please."

Erdano cast a perplexed look at him then, heavy brows drawing together in an exaggerated fashion.

Poor choice of words. Erdano didn't read or write. Erdano's father hadn't seen any use for such things, and had won out over their mother's urgings. Sometimes Duilio forgot that. "I appreciate that Aga was paying such close attention," he clarified. "The woman with the webbed hands will be very helpful to my investigation."

"Oh." Erdano took another swig of his beer and licked his lips. "She's a sereia, right? Is she pretty?"

Conversations with Erdano *always* followed this course. His brother had numerous females in his harem, but was perpetually eager to add more. "Yes," Duilio admitted reluctantly. "She's attractive."

In the corner a woman sang about the old days when the Portuguese had conquered the world, accompanied by a man strumming a guitar. Erdano could find this sort of establishment as if he sensed them with his whiskers: crowded and a little run-down, excellent fish soup, salted cod served on platters of questionable cleanliness, plenty of beer, and appealing girls. Vastly different from the café Duilio had visited with Joaquim that morning.

Duilio glanced at the waitress his half brother watched so avidly, a petite but buxom girl with dark hair and eyes that tilted upward. She wended her way gracefully through the crowded room with a tray perched on one hand. Erdano didn't seem to prefer a specific type of woman; they all interested him. And even dressed in a set of rarely washed clothes and with his long hair uncombed, Erdano attracted them in turn. Women seemed to find him irresistible. *Selkie charm*, Duilio thought wryly.

"What are her markings like?" Erdano asked.

It took a second for Duilio to mentally chase down what Erdano meant. Sereia markings were said to mimic one predatory fish or another—tuna in this part of the world—which hinted that Miss Paredes would have a black or blue dorsal stripe. Duilio sorely wished he'd gotten a look at her backside, but she'd managed to remain facing him. Now his mind burned with curiosity that he suspected wasn't ever going to be satisfied.

He tried to sound dismissive. "I didn't see her dorsal markings."

Erdano regarded him with a surprised expression. "You haven't bedded her yet?"

Duilio clenched his jaw, holding in his growing irritation. Given her sudden introduction into the household, some of the servants had assumed that motivation on his part as well. According to his valet, Marcellin, picking Alessio's bedroom for her only fueled that speculation. Fortunately, while they might talk among themselves, the servants would never spread such rumors beyond the house. "She's in my employ now, Erdano."

Erdano craned his neck to get a better view of his waitress. "No, then?"

His reluctance about discussing Miss Paredes with Joaquim had involved his guilt over walking in on her nude in the bath. He didn't want to discuss her with Erdano for fear of exciting his half brother's interest in her. "It's inappropriate," he said. "Besides, I don't know how long she'll be here."

"You should go ahead and bed her now, then," Erdano said. "No sense waiting."

Duilio let out a laugh, amused out of his annoyance. There were times when Erdano's simplistic view of life had its advantages. "That's why you're going to end up with a kitchen knife in your back someday, Erdano."

His half brother laughed. "No woman would ever hurt me."

To be truthful, Erdano did have a talent for finding women who didn't seem to mind sharing him. "Her husband, then," Duilio said. "I'll keep my distance from Miss Paredes."

"Your loss." Erdano grinned at the waitress, who returned a saucy wink. "She hasn't come back. Are you bedding *her*?"

Duilio stared across the table at him, trying to follow that logic. "Who?"

Erdano blinked at him, head tilting to one side. "Aga. Tigana gave her to you, and she hasn't come back. That's why I wanted to see you."

Duilio had qualms about Erdano's casual way of referring to members of his harem like they were possessions, but as he didn't live in Erdano's world, he chose not to comment. "Aga didn't stay with me. Do you want me to look for her?"

Erdano shrugged. "She has to leave the harem eventually, but . . ."

"Wait . . . why does she have to leave?"

"She's one of my father's get," Erdano said, as if that were patently obvious.

Duilio wished his mother were more aware of things about her, so he could ply her with questions about the rules inside a selkie harem. Evidently there were more than he knew. He'd never considered before what happened to all of Erdano's half sisters once their father died. "I'll see if I can find out what happened to her."

Erdano nodded briskly. "Thanks."

Erdano rarely came to him with a problem, so Duilio didn't mind pursuing the inquiry. Besides, he had a good idea where to start. Aga was likely at João's small apartment on the quay near the Ferreira boats. If Erdano had thought to ask João directly, Duilio probably could have just stayed home and talked with Miss Paredes all evening. Duilio dropped a handful of coins on the table to cover the tab, slid off the bench, and clapped his half brother's shoulder. "Come on back to the house."

With a dramatic sigh, Erdano joined him and headed toward the door. "I'll have to come back for Eva later, I guess."

Eva must be the petite waitress. "Mother *would* like to see you," Duilio reminded him.

He waited on the threshold as Erdano mouthed something at the pretty girl, to which she nodded. And then a twinge hit him, a brief instant of premonition.

His blood roaring in his ears, Duilio sprang forward. He shoved Erdano over as a gunshot rang through the crowded room. Fragments of wood sprayed in all directions when a bullet hit the doorpost where he'd stood.

Amid the screams of the patrons, Duilio landed atop Erdano on the tavern floor. Everything seemed to move more slowly about him as he pushed away from his brother. He heard a second click, but nothing happened. Had the gun jammed? He couldn't pinpoint the direction the sound had come from. His own breath sounded harsh in his ears now.

He was an easy target there on the floor. That realization sent cold rushing through his body. He rolled to one side to get back to his feet.

He'd barely risen to his knees when another body slammed into his from behind, sending him back to the ground. Searing pain burned through the back of his left shoulder—a knife. Duilio hissed in a tight breath. Gritting his teeth, he rolled away, drawing his revolver as he moved.

The sight of *that* was enough to forestall his assailant, a burly, dark-haired man in a checked suit. After a split second of indecision, the man bolted out the tavern door and into the night. Duilio groaned and lay back on the floor, wondering how long it would take his heart to stop racing. *Damnation, that was close.*

There were people bustling past, stepping over him, belatedly trying to escape from danger that had already fled. Fortunately, no one stepped on him.

"You're bleeding," Erdano said helpfully from above. He offered Duilio a hand up.

Duilio took Erdano's hand, grunting when Erdano practically jerked him off the floor. Erdano sometimes forgot how strong he was. Once Duilio was on his feet, Erdano started looking about for his waitress, unconcerned by the aforementioned blood.

Duilio holstered his gun and raised his other hand to his stinging shoulder. It did come away bloody, but he doubted the wound was severe. Had the attack been linked to his recent discussion with Augustus Smithson, tied to his search for the missing pelt? Perhaps he'd gotten too close, as Alessio had at the end.

Then he saw the dagger lying on the floor at his feet. He retrieved it, noting both his blood on the edge of the blade and the sigil stamped on the hilt—the open hand of the Special Police. *Not good.* He slid it into a pocket.

What had changed that had caused the Special Police to come after him? He doubted it was his selkie blood. They had no way to prove he wasn't completely human. No, this had to be something else.

They patrolled the area around *The City Under the Sea*. Could his attacker be involved in that somehow? And if this attack was about that, why now? How did they know he'd made enough progress in the case to become a threat? And if that was it, would they come after Miss Paredes too? He wasn't sure what to make of the timing. He turned to Erdano. "I suspect you shouldn't go back to the house with me after all. I'll send word when it's safe."

Which apparently suited Erdano's plans for the night anyway. He shrugged and wandered off to find his Eva.

After a nearly silent dinner, Felis had helped get Lady Ferreira settled in bed. Oriana spent the remainder of the evening in her bedroom, stewing over the day's happenings as she affixed the new ruffle to the blue silk dress. She was baffled by Heriberto's actions toward her father. What did it mean that her father had paid Heriberto money? And the woman who'd watched Heriberto and then Oriana herself? That was another mystery that she was going to be picking at for some time. At least tomorrow night she might get answers about Isabel's death from Nela's mysterious Lady. That would be a leap forward.

And now that the household was mostly quiet, she could take a stab at unraveling the mystery of her employer's family. In the silence, Oriana walked downstairs and entered a room that had been left off her tour, off-limits to the servants, according to Cardenas. The library had the same elegance as the rest of the house and smelled of ambergris cologne, a hint of lingering muskiness. Well-dusted bookshelves lined the walls. A liquor cabinet held an assortment of bottles, and between the sets of shelves was a niche with a kneeler for prayer.

That niche held her quarry, the Ferreira family's Bible. Oriana flipped through the first few pages and found the information she sought. Among the births and deaths, there were only two sons listed under Lady Giana Ferreira's name: Duilio, who would be twenty-nine, and Alessio, who had died before his thirtieth birthday. No Erdano at all. No previous husband. So although this Erdano must exist, he wasn't recognized by the Church.

Oriana rubbed the back of her neck. Where could she look next?

Then she heard footsteps in the hall. With a startled gasp, she quickly ducked into the shadows on one side of the liquor cabinet, hoping not to be noticed.

Mr. Ferreira strode into the library. He closed the door, trapping her there with him, but she was certain he hadn't noticed her. He leaned on the table for a moment, one hand on its polished surface. Then he sighed, withdrew a holstered revolver from the waist of his trousers, and laid it on the table. He shrugged off his frock coat, revealing a bloodied shirtsleeve. Oriana clapped one hand over her mouth. He tossed the coat over one of the chairs, then removed a small gun from an ankle holster. Apparently thinking he was alone, he pulled down his braces and unbuttoned his shirt, tugged it off, and laid it atop the coat.

He was a well-made man, athletic and lean. Oriana found herself staring at his back, weighing whether the lack of a dorsal stripe detracted from its attractiveness. *No, it doesn't.* There was something fascinating about that span of monochromatic skin.

Her eyes were drawn then to a narrow cut crossing the side and back of his left shoulder. It was still oozing, no doubt the source of the bloodied sleeve. Mr. Ferreira tried to inspect the wound, pulling his arm forward and craning his neck around to do so. Then he turned toward the liquor cabinet and spotted her there. He started and cursed under his breath.

Oriana quickly hid her smile behind her hand. While it hadn't embarrassed her to be caught nude, as it would have a human woman, it had embarrassed her to be caught *at all.* Now she had the upper hand. "A knife wound?"

His cool manner restored, he attempted to survey the slash again. "Yes, but not deep."

As she couldn't go to a hospital herself, she'd been trained to handle minor injuries. She opened the liquor cabinet, selected the brandy decanter, and carried it over to the table. She picked up his bloodied shirt and, once she'd poured some brandy on it, lifted it to his shoulder. "Who did this?"

He hissed when the fabric touched his skin, but otherwise he didn't flinch from her familiarity. "I'm not sure."

"You didn't see your assailant?"

He gazed at her, his expression calculating. "I did, but I didn't recognize him."

She pulled the shirt away. The blade must have scraped along the skin, leaving a shallow cut rather than a puncture, so the wound wouldn't need stitching. "Do you have something to bind this?"

"I was going to use the shirt," he said with a short laugh. "And I was planning on drinking the brandy."

Oriana handed him the sodden garment. "You must have gauze somewhere. Iodine?"

"Open the bottom drawer of the cabinet."

Oriana returned to the liquor cabinet and, from the bottom drawer, extracted a bottle of iodine in a paperboard box that also held a few rolls of gauze and a pair of sharp-looking scissors. The handles were small, but she could probably use the very tips of her fingers to control them. She took a pair of glasses from an upper shelf and returned to the table.

"Who is Erdano?" she asked as she set everything down.

He picked up the brandy decanter, poured two glasses, and slid one over toward her hand. "What did my mother tell you?"

Oriana ignored the glass for the moment and peered at his wound again. There was a bit of skin that would need to be cut away, but it looked clean otherwise. She removed her mitts and laid them aside. "I gather he's your half brother. She said he lives at Braga Bay, but only selkies live there."

He was facing away from her at the moment, so she couldn't see his expression. "And your deduction is?"

"That Erdano is a selkie," she said as she negotiated the small handles of the scissors onto her fingertips. "And that your mother must be, as well."

"Yes," he said, his head bowing. "If my mother were handed over to the Special Police, it would mean her life."

"Don't move, please." She dabbed at the wound with some of the gauze, and then began to cut away the extra skin. So Mr. Ferreira was half selkie himself. That shed new light on his willingness to harbor a sereia in his household. He could ensure Oriana's safety here . . . because she could turn the threat of exposure back on him and his mother. "I'm done cutting." Oriana wiped the scissors on a scrap of gauze. "Your mother's human in this form," she pointed out. "They can't prove she isn't."

He glanced at her over his shoulder. "*Someone* can. Someone has her pelt, which would be ample evidence should that person choose to expose her." Oriana touched iodine-soaked gauze to his wound, and he flinched. "Are you enjoying that?"

"Of course I am," she said, not entirely sarcastically. She sponged the wound and then the skin around it. "Was her pelt taken from her?"

He sighed when she laid down the iodine-dampened gauze. "It was stolen three years ago, and since then she's been trapped in human form. Until we can get it back, she won't get better."

"Is her"—Oriana laid clean gauze over the wound while she tried to find an acceptable term—"*distraction* due to its absence?"

Mr. Ferreira took a sip of his brandy and nodded.

How very sad. No wonder the woman stared out at the water; she couldn't go back. In human form, Lady Ferreira was as vulnerable to the water as Isabel had been. Oriana had Mr. Ferreira lift his arm so that she could wrap a length of bandage about the shoulder, and then he held that tight while she looked through the box on the table. A moment later the bandage was secured with a safety pin, although if he was a restless sleeper it probably wouldn't hold.

Mr. Ferreira drew out one of the chairs, sat, and drank down his remaining brandy in one gulp. Facing her, he looked little different from a sereia male. That thought sent warmth throughout her body that had nothing to do with the brandy. She was glad then that she couldn't blush. She settled across from him and finally took a sip of her own glass. Brandy burned her throat and gills, but Isabel had taught her to stomach it. "Was it this Paolo she's so afraid of?"

He sat with lips pursed for a moment.

"She said he wants to kill you," Oriana added. "That he'd taken away your brother and your father. *Did* he kill them?"

He rubbed a hand across his face in a weary gesture. "About a year and a half ago, Alessio fought a duel over a lover. Despite the fact that the other man fired into the air, Alessio was shot through the heart." He regarded his now-empty glass, then poured another. "I was abroad. I'd been traveling across the continent and I hadn't come home for . . . well, a long time. When my father finally learned I was in Paris and sent a telegram about Alessio, I started home. I had already missed Alessio's funeral, so I didn't rush. A few days before I arrived, my father died of pneumonia."

Two deaths so close together had to have been hard on him. He'd come home from his travels to find no brother, no father, and a mother sliding toward . . . not madness exactly, but Lady Ferreira wasn't whole either.

He rubbed his eyes with one hand as if they stung. Perhaps he was fighting tears. Then he dropped his hand, shook himself, and took another sip of his brandy. "I didn't know how bad things were. They had all been sparing me the worry, you know. But Alessio and Father fought constantly, about everything. It was just easier for me to be elsewhere. I would give anything to go back and change that."

"You didn't know," she said. "You never know when your family will be taken away from you." Her own life had taught her that.

He gave her a wry look. "*I* should have known, Miss Paredes. I should have come home. Instead I was far away, playing police officer when I should have been here, helping search for my mother's pelt."

She wished she had some clever words, soothing words, to placate him, but he would likely always blame himself, just as she did over her sister's death. "So is this Paolo to blame?"

"My cousin Joaquim—who's an actual police inspector, unlike me—he and I investigated my mother's claims thoroughly. We've never found any evidence to corroborate the claim."

"Then why does she think he's responsible?"

Mr. Ferreira sighed heavily. "When the pelt was stolen, the thief also took a strongbox from my father's desk, a box that contained only my grandfather's correspondences. You see, Paolo's my father's bastard brother. Older than my father, but never acknowledged. My father believed his brother stole the letters to find some evidence of his birth he could use to blackmail us, to obtain a portion of the inheritance he didn't get. The pelt was taken in case the letters proved useless. But we've never found any verification of that. No proof."

So they had ample motive, but nothing more. "And your mother's just repeating your father's claims."

He pinched the bridge of his nose. "We have looked everywhere, Joaquim and I. We know the pelt hasn't been destroyed—that would kill her. But each lead we had fizzled away. I personally searched every one of my uncle's properties. My time with the police forces taught me a great deal about breaking into others' houses discreetly."

"*You broke in?*" The idea of urbane Duilio Ferreira breaking into a house seemed fantastic. He laughed, the gloom about the room fading with the sound. At least her incredulity had gotten a smile out of him. "Forgive me, sir. I didn't mean to make it sound . . ."

"Implausible?" he supplied. "That's what makes me valuable to the police. People think I'm useless, but I was instructed by some excellent housebreakers. I'll have you know I'm very good with a skeleton key." He nodded once at the end of that statement. "I'll even stoop to breaking a window if necessary, although I have not attempted the palace."

Oriana wondered if he might be a touch drunk. Or perhaps he was simply fooling her again. "The palace?"

"To see if he'd hidden the pelt there," Mr. Ferreira said.

Something clicked in her mind, a recollection of his wary reaction when she'd first mentioned Paolo Silva the day before. "Do you mean Paolo Silva, *the prince's seer*? The one who pulled me out of the river?"

"Yes." He sighed, his dark lashes hiding his eyes. "He's my father's bastard brother."

Why hadn't he mentioned that when she'd told him of the seer's "rescue" of her? Of course, many families didn't speak of their bastards. But Silva's entry into her story must have made him suspicious. "And what happened to you tonight, Mr. Ferreira?"

"Erdano and I met at a tavern," he said. "We were set upon as we left." He reached back, dug something out of the pocket of his frock coat, and laid it on the table. It was a knife bearing the mark of the Special Police. "It could be a coincidence or stolen, but this doesn't look like a cheap copy. It's regular issue." His eyes rose to meet hers. "I think they're not happy that I'm asking about *The City Under the Sea*. What I'm not sure about is how they know I'm still asking."

Oriana glanced down at the blade. A line of his blood stained the edge. "Do they know about you . . . and your mother?"

"Why would we be alive if they did? No, I suspect this is about the investigation." He regarded her wearily. "I came by earlier to return your sketch, but you were out."

Oriana licked her lips. Was he accusing her of telling someone about his investigation? Did he think she'd provoked this attack on him? "I . . . I saw my master on the street, and . . ."

He held up one hand. "You don't have to explain. I just wanted to apologize for not getting you a knife earlier, as I promised I would. I'll bring one to breakfast."

The coil that had been twisting in her stomach loosened. She didn't want him thinking badly of her. "Thank you."

Mr. Ferreira stood and offered her a hand up. Her mitts lay on the table, but she placed her bare hand in his and let him draw her to her feet. That close, he smelled of ambergris cologne, of blood and brandy, a fascinating combination.

"I should go to bed," he said, "before the brandy goes to my head."

He must be exhausted. She felt guilty now for interrogating him. "Of course."

"Then good night, Miss Paredes." He gathered up his coat and assortment of weapons, including the knife with the sigil of the Special Police. He moved toward the door, but stopped and glanced back over his shoulder. "And if you sleep in the bathtub, you might contrive to rumple the bed anyway. I was already asked by my valet, who had it from the butler, who was told by a maid that you didn't sleep in your own bed last night. Their assumption being, of course . . ."

"That I was in your bed," she finished for him, warmth stealing through her body again. She crossed her arms over her chest. "I'll keep that in mind."

He nodded, and then was gone.

Oriana sat down and stared dazedly after him.

She didn't know why she was reacting this way to him. She had never given a moment's thought to any of the men who'd made up Isabel's court of suitors. Some had been overly familiar, touching her inappropriately or making suggestions, but that had only made her like them less. They simply hadn't interested her.

She wasn't certain why this man *did*. He wasn't strikingly handsome. He was human—or half-human, she corrected herself. He was also half-selkie. Her people tended to regard selkies as savages, choosing to live in the sea like animals. She'd never met one before, though. Lady Ferreira was certainly not a savage, nor was her son.

But selkies also had a reputation for seductiveness. Oriana licked her lips, wondering if that was the source of her reaction. She had gotten close enough to smell his skin. That scent she'd taken for ambergris cologne must have been a selkie's musk. Could that be it?

She shook her head to stop her brain's meandering. She needed to keep herself under control around Mr. Ferreira. She didn't need any more complications.

CHAPTER 15

THURSDAY, 2 OCTOBER 1902

Duilio had expected to toss and turn for hours, but he'd actually fallen asleep facedown on his bed without even undressing. Marcellin had been livid at Duilio's disregard for his attire, more so than he'd been over learning that someone had tried to kill his master. Duilio took it with good humor, though, offering the man the chance to pick out his evening wear for the ball that night as a sop.

By the time he reached the breakfast table, he found Miss Paredes and his mother already halfway through their meal. When reminded of the ball they planned to attend later, his mother promised she would take a nap that afternoon. She appeared unruffled by their plans, which made him feel better about dragging her out into society.

He turned to Miss Paredes, sliding a napkin-wrapped bundle across to her. "I hope this one works for you, Miss Paredes."

She peeked at the knife and its wrist sheath, then quickly shifted the contents to her lap. "Thank you," she said meekly. Her eyes flicked toward the door where Gustavo was entering, carrying a tray with Duilio's regular breakfast and coffee. "It will be fine, sir."

Apparently she didn't want to talk in front of the footman. Or perhaps she was sheepish after her boldness last night. But she seemed withdrawn this morning. Duilio preferred the woman who'd surprised him in the library the night before, who'd spoken to him like an equal. He wondered if that was the real Oriana Paredes.

He wasn't going to find out this morning, he decided half an hour later. Miss Paredes spent the meal reading to his mother about an effort to lift salvage from a Spanish ship sunk decades before near Lisboa. When he left, pleading a need to go speak with Joaquim, Miss Paredes seemed relieved. It was vexing.

A quick side trip down to the marina past the Alameda de Massarelos, where the family's boats were moored, gave him the answer to Erdano's query about where Aga had gone. As soon as Duilio said her name, a furiously blushing João stammered that Erdano's sister had decided to "visit" at his flat for the time. Since he'd probably gotten the young man into that situation, Duilio asked João to come up to the house in a few days to discuss it further. João's apartment was rent free, but the young man would need additional funds if he were to host Aga for any length of time. Duilio didn't mind—after all, Aga was almost family.

Joaquim wore a pleased smile when Duilio finally reached his office. The office in the Massarelos Police Station was small, with a modern metal cabinet for files standing in the corner and a decrepit desk in the center of the windowless room. As offices went, it wasn't particularly welcoming. The plain wooden chairs before the desk were sturdy, though, and surprisingly comfortable—a good thing, since Duilio spent a great deal of time sitting in them.

"I have good news," Joaquim said before Duilio even settled into his usual chair.

Duilio puffed out his cheeks. "Erdano and I were set upon last night."

"Yes, I heard," Joaquim said briskly, waving that away as he sat behind the desk. "Now, Captain Santiago has given me a new assignment—"

"We're both fine, by the way," Duilio said, feeling unappreciated. "Only a knife to the shoulder for me."

Joaquim folded his arms over his chest, an impatient frown twisting his lips. "Don't be childish. Cardenas told me about it when I stopped by the house earlier this morning. He said you came in through the servant's door late last night, looking like hell but on your own feet."

Duilio slumped back in the chair and tugged off his gloves. "You stopped by the house to talk to Cardenas and not to me?"

Joaquim shrugged off Duilio's protest. "You were at breakfast. Mrs. Amaral has decided to be petulant and is claiming that Miss Paredes stole personal items of the daughter's. Some jewelry and—"

Duilio sat up straight, appalled. "That's ridiculous. Miss Paredes—"

Joaquim held up his hands. "It's a baseless charge. However, the charge gives me license to question the Amaral servants. I can get back to work on this case, even if in a roundabout fashion. Fortunately, Mrs. Amaral doesn't know where Miss Paredes has gone or she'd probably demand I immediately arrest her."

"Damnation," Duilio said with a grimace. "She'll know tonight. Remember, we're supposed to go to the Carvalho ball tonight." When Joaquim looked ready to argue, Duilio added, "Besides, servants up and down the street do gossip. It wouldn't occur to them that her *presence* should be kept secret."

"Which is why I spoke with Mr. Cardenas this morning," Joaquim said. "I wanted to ask him to have the servants keep quiet about Miss Paredes."

Duilio stretched out his legs and crossed his ankles under the desk. It irritated him that Joaquim felt unwelcome in his home. There'd been a lot of friction between Joaquim and Alessio when they were young. When his mother's pelt was stolen, Alessio had chosen not to tell Joaquim, even though Joaquim surely would have been helpful in the search. Duilio didn't know what had passed between the two of them, but he suspected *that* was at the base of Joaquim's behavior. And Alessio was dead. "You should have come up and eaten with us."

"I'd already eaten, and I wanted talk to Mr. Cardenas, not you."

That puts me in my place. Duilio sighed. "That will give us until tonight, at a minimum. Has Efisio contacted the police in any way about Lady Isabel?"

"No," Joaquim said with a roll of his eyes. "It's a conspiracy of silence, with him and the girl's mother shielding the criminal while they're trying to protect their so-precious reputations."

Duilio *did* understand Joaquim's disdain for that aspect of privilege. Reputation shouldn't come ahead of the truth. He nodded mutely.

"Now, I have something to show you." Joaquim opened a desk drawer, withdrew a slip of paper, and handed it to Duilio—an invoice from the Castro Ironworks. "I talked with the bookkeeper there a couple of weeks ago, before the investigation was shut down. He didn't recall anything unusual, but left this for me late yesterday. He didn't know where the chain ultimately went, but the bill went to that address."

Duilio frowned down at the paper, an order for three hundred feet of galvanized marine chain. A coffee stain marred one corner of the invoice, as if a cup had been left atop it. The grade of chain, a little heavier than a normal anchor chain, approximately matched what Duilio had seen when peering out through a submersible's windows. The billing address near the bottom was in a less-well-to-do parish of the city on Bonfim Street. "Espinoza?"

"I stopped before work this morning and talked to the landlord," Joaquim said, "one Mr. Gouveia. The renter answers Espinoza's description handily. Middling age, lean, with white hair in a queue. He hasn't been seen there for some time. Gouveia isn't certain exactly how long, but he's still receiving the rent via the mail."

Fortunately, Espinoza's old-fashioned hairstyle made him memorable. "Well, this has promise."

"Here's the best part," Joaquim said. "The tenant rented both the first and second floors and, according to Mr. Gouveia, the first floor has been made over into a craftsman's shop."

"Woodwork, perhaps?"

"The landlord wasn't sure, but it was enough to make me curious."

"Me too." Duilio folded up the invoice. He held it between his palms and asked himself whether it was important. *Yes*, came the answer. Duilio grinned at his cousin. "I'll try to get back with you later today, let you know if I find anything." He quickly rose to take his leave. "By the way, did you get a chance to tell Captain Santiago I had another lead I was working on?"

Joaquim rose as well. He retrieved his suit coat from the back of his chair. "I did, although I didn't tell him what lead or mention the specific case. He would know, since you're only on the one right now. But I didn't feel comfortable talking about your source. Captain Rios was in with him," Joaquim finished, shrugging on his coat.

Duilio paused, one hand in the doorknob. Captain Rios was the liaison between the Special Police and the regular police, and he thoroughly disliked Duilio. Rios considered him an interfering busybody and dilettante. "The person who attacked Erdano and me in the tavern last night? He left his knife behind. It was Special Police issue."

Oriana had been working in the front sitting room where the light was good, but she'd finished the edge she was hemming some time ago. She'd been sitting there just staring at it. The blue silk dress with its layers of skirt and newly attached ruffle was almost ready. At the moment it lay across her lap on the beige sofa, a cloud of darkness that reflected her mood.

She shook herself back to awareness. The day before she'd checked behind her a dozen times on her walk home—using a far more circuitous route than she would have normally taken—and had finally been satisfied that she wasn't being followed. Her brief foray in pursuit of Heriberto had given her a great deal to think about. She'd always suspected that Heriberto wasn't above blackmail. Now she knew that to be true.

He had definitely been threatening her father. It had been a vague threat, but Oriana had heard Heriberto mention his girl. She didn't know whom Heriberto meant by that. It wasn't Oriana herself, because Heriberto had said he knew where she lived. It apparently wasn't her father's employer and purported lover, Lady Pereira de Santos, which hinted that her father was involved with more than one woman. Oriana hadn't yet forgiven him for replacing her mother with Lady Pereira de Santos, no matter that her mother had been dead for fourteen years now. It implied that the tie of Destiny between her father and mother had been false, didn't it? She hadn't been able to reconcile that in her mind yet.

And she was jealous of her father's new life here, where he had a gentlemanly occupation and likely didn't wear shoes that pinched his feet. Here the males had all the opportunities, which would suit her father perfectly. She shouldn't be angry with him. But *she'd* been the one left behind to raise Marina when he'd been exiled. She'd had to hear the news that her sister was dead. She'd been alone then, with no one to comfort her.

Lady Pereira de Santos lived one house over, and Oriana's father came there on occasion. She would peer out the Amarals' windows, trying to catch a glimpse of him as he walked up the front steps of the Pereira de Santos mansion. But she'd *never* contacted him—not even a note. She had played by the rules, done everything as she should, and now she felt a fool.

He'd known she was here in the city. Her father hadn't contacted her, but he hadn't displayed any surprise when Heriberto asked about her either. He'd seemed ready to defy Heriberto for her sake. He said he wouldn't tell Heriberto where to find her even if he knew. Part of that was simply his temper. She'd gotten her hot temper from him, not her mother. But she believed his words.

She'd spent the past two years in fear that Heriberto would blackmail her by threatening her father. Evidently she'd gotten it all backward. And what of the woman who'd watched her from across the street? Oriana sighed, clenching her teeth on the pins in her mouth. She wished she knew what the truth was.

Stop wasting time. She could mull this over and over for hours and still get nowhere. She turned the dress about to take in the waistband.

The door to the sitting room began to swing open. Oriana reflexively buried her bare hands in the mass of fabric in her lap. But it was Mr. Ferreira who stepped inside, leaving the door open. His brows drew together quizzically as he regarded her. "Miss Paredes?"

She abruptly recalled the pins in her mouth and carefully removed them, keeping the webbing between her fingers hidden the entire time. "Mr. Ferreira."

"Please don't rise," he told her. "Whatever are you doing?"

"Alterations, sir." She calmly set the two pins into a small pillow that rested on the table and reset the needle in the fabric. "For the ball tonight. Is your shoulder better?"

"Is that one of my mother's old gowns?" he asked, disregarding her query.

Did he think she'd misappropriated it? "Miss Felis assured me your mother wouldn't mind my wearing one of her old gowns. In fact, Miss Felis insisted. She didn't want me being a discredit to Lady Ferreira due to lack of proper garb."

Mr. Ferreira sat down in the chair next to the sofa, saving her from craning her neck to look up at him. He steepled his fingers and pressed them to his lips. "I doubt my mother would even notice, Miss Paredes," he finally said. "But I recall your wearing several attractive gowns over the past few months. Why do you not . . . ?" When Oriana didn't clarify, he said, "Ah. Lady Amaral didn't allow you to take anything with you when you left. Did she?"

Oriana shook her head. "No, sir. Only the clothes I was wearing that night."

"People continually surprise me with their pettiness," he said. "Although in her case I shouldn't be surprised. She is, unfortunately, the reason I stopped back by here."

That sounded ominous. "Sir?"

"Lady Amaral has gone to the police with the claim that you stole some of Lady Isabel's property when she threw you out. Jewelry was mentioned."

Oriana couldn't help her initial reaction—one of disbelief and rage—but she quickly schooled her features to neutrality. "That is not true, Mr. Ferreira."

One of his dark brows rose. "It never occurred to me it might be, Miss Paredes."

She could breathe more easily then. "Thank you, sir."

"I wanted you to be aware of the charge," he said. "That's all. The police don't credit the idea either. After all, Lady Isabel could have taken the missing pieces with her to Paris. However, if Lady Amaral learns you're living here, she may demand that the police arrest you on *suspicion* of theft. She's influential enough that they might comply without evidence."

Oriana had learned enough about influence in society here that she knew he was right. She'd stood next to the coal room steps that chilly morning and decided *not* to take the second bag, the one that held whatever Isabel couldn't cram into her traveling chest. No matter how pragmatic it would have been, she'd refused to become a thief. Yet Lady Amaral had cast that slur on her character anyway. "She had the butler escort me out, Mr. Ferreira. He would have seen anything I touched. Although I doubt he'd vouch for me to the police," she added with unfortunate honesty. "He has his position to think of."

"I expected as much." Mr. Ferreira smiled ruefully. "Don't worry, Miss Paredes. The police do know what sort of person they're dealing with. She has a history of bringing charges against servants that generally prove to be no more than an excuse to let them go without pay."

Oriana felt her brows draw together in annoyance. Lady Amaral *hadn't* paid her when she'd cast her forth. "I see, sir."

"Yes," he said in a dry tone. "I'm sure you do. I've already talked to Cardenas and told him that if he hears anything about a theft, he's to ignore it."

A maid came in then carrying a tray with a small pot of coffee and a pair of cups. Miss Paredes tucked her hands back into her mending, her vexed expression fading into polite placidity. Duilio rather liked the vexed Miss Paredes, but he wasn't foolish enough to say so. "Thank you, Ana," Duilio told the maid instead. "You may go, but leave the door half-ajar, please."

The girl curtsied and swept her way out of the room, pulling the door almost all the way closed. He should go and open it wider to protect Miss Paredes' reputation, but didn't bother. He appreciated the privacy for now. He poured himself a cup of coffee. "Would you like a cup?"

"Yes, please," Miss Paredes said after a brief hesitation.

He added cream to hers, having seen her do so that morning, and set the cup on the small table near her elbow.

"You're not supposed to serve me," Miss Paredes protested.

Duilio didn't laugh at her wry tone. He broke societal rules regularly enough that this tiny slip in etiquette didn't merit any twinge of insulted propriety on his part. "I don't mind serving, Miss Paredes, particularly as your hands are occupied. Do you enjoy sewing?"

She regarded him warily, as if she feared a trap. "Yes. It's calming."

Well, now he'd learned something. Miss Paredes liked to sew; it wasn't merely a part of her disguise. He smiled down into his coffee. "I believe there's a sewing machine down in the workroom. Did you know that?"

"Yes, but once you've accidentally sewn through your webbing, you tend to stay away from machines. I prefer to work by hand."

Duilio cringed. "I see. The next time you need a gown, it might be simpler to have one made up. I didn't mean for you to spend your hours here mending."

She pushed the rumpled blue mound on her lap into order and then picked up her own cup. "Mending is honest work, sir."

He crossed his legs and peered at her lowered features. Their relationship wasn't a normal one, caused by circumstances to vacillate between that of master and servant . . . and something else. But his remarks about the mending had caused her to revert to servant again, which irritated him. He wanted to *talk* to her, not just exchange pleasantries.

Duilio decided she had the same sort of pridefulness about money that afflicted Joaquim. She didn't want anything given to her, perhaps because that often came with a price.

He'd hit on the simplest way to handle Lady Amaral before he'd even left Joaquim's office: simply have Joaquim take a statement about the value of the missing articles, and Duilio would have his man of business pay the woman that sum. It wouldn't pinch his pocket, and the funds might entice Lady Amaral to leave Miss Paredes alone. Duilio wasn't going to mention the transaction to Miss Paredes; he didn't want her scowling at him more than necessary. He fished about for another topic.

"I have often wondered about your people's culture," he said then, hoping to draw out the woman behind the mask of servility. "It's a shame tourism isn't allowed on your islands."

"Given our history with your people, are you surprised?" she asked tartly.

His people's relationship with hers had not gotten off on the right foot, a story recorded in Camões' epic poem. The islands had been discovered on one of Vasco da Gama's voyages. The sailors, spotting the lovely "sea nymphs" bathing there, decided they were a gift from Venus . . . and took advantage. The poet chose to cast the incident in a heroic light. He wrote of the sereia running away into the woods, depicting their flight as an attempt to further entice the men—as if sailors long at sea required enticement at all. Duilio had always suspected that interpretation of those events; if a sereia wished to attract a man, she could *call* him, could she not? "That incident was some four hundred years ago, Miss Paredes. I would hope my people are a little more civilized by now."

"And yet your Camões is still heralded as a great poet. Did any of those sailors bring their so-called sereia brides back to Portugal? Did they attempt to right the wrong perpetrated against those women?" Her dark eyes turned toward the dress in her lap. She fiddled with the fabric, giving him an occasional glimpse of the webbing between her long fingers. "We have our own history of that incident—*The Rape of Amado*, it's called."

"I am not surprised," he admitted. "What happened afterward is shrouded in mystery. What do your people say?"

"Amado became a prison of sorts," she told him. "It had once been a game reserve, just for hunting, but along with the dozen or so human men who'd stayed behind, all the sereia who were caught up in that incident were sequestered there by their own people. They weren't allowed to return to their home islands, as if they were contaminated. For long afterward, any humans who ended up on the islands, whether by shipwreck or capture—or those missionaries your Church kept sending—were transported to Amado and not allowed to leave."

Duilio sat back in his chair. "That seems very harsh. Is it still sequestered?"

She shook her head. "No. After about two hundred years our rulers lifted the ban on travel. Amado is often called the Portuguese island, though. Its people have the most human blood, their culture is the most like that of Portugal, and a percentage of them are even Christian, which never did spread to the other islands. And thus Amadeans are looked down on by the inhabitants of the other islands who claim pure sereia blood, no matter how untrue that is."

Her tone had grown sharper as she spoke. She must be Amadean herself, given her irritation. "Miss Paredes, I'll promise never to speak fondly of Camões again, if you'll accept my apology for what happened to your ancestors."

She seemed surprised. "Your prince is the one who should apologize."

"Unfortunately, *that* will never happen, Miss Paredes. And I thought we were making such progress. I was hoping to see those islands before I die."

That statement caused her brows to furrow. She picked one of the pins from her pincushion, possibly planning to stab him with it. "Why?"

"I like different places," he said quite truthfully. "I'm curious. I like to travel, see how different people live."

She regarded him warily. "Why our people? There are plenty of others."

He argued with himself over whether to tell her the truth or not, and then shrugged. "When I was a boy, my father brought home a book about your islands. It was in French, I recall, and made many unlikely claims, among them the report that your people wear no clothing, or very little. *That* prompted my initial curiosity."

Oriana stared at Mr. Ferreira, wondering what type of impression he intended to make with that bald statement. "That alone piqued your interest?"

He flushed, a hint of red creeping cross his cheeks. "I had no intention of offending you, Miss Paredes. I was twelve, I believe. Boys that age, I'm afraid, find nothing more fascinating than the possibility of glimpsing a woman in her natural state. I hope that doesn't negate my earlier apology. I am somewhat more mature now than I was at twelve."

Her tone must have been sharper than she'd intended. "I'll not take it amiss, then, sir. I should tell you, though, that we do wear clothing, although admittedly less than your own people. Our women especially don't have to put up with this excessive number of layers." She gestured at her own skirts, hidden under the blue dress.

He inclined his head, as if in acknowledgment of a gift. "I'll have to look for that book. You might find it amusing."

She could only imagine how inaccurate a human-written book about the islands would be. His dark brows drew together, and for a moment he didn't speak. "Mr. Ferreira?" she prompted, uncertain where his thoughts had strayed.

"May I ask a personal question?"

She folded her hands atop the fabric. What could possibly give him pause after admitting having been an imaginative twelve-year-old male at one point? "Of course, sir."

He gestured toward her hands. "The webbing between your fingers seems very delicate. I wondered if you often injure it. You said you've done so when sewing."

She felt the urge to smile at his hesitation. "It's tougher than it looks and heals very quickly. I do prick it on occasion, which jars me to my teeth, but it doesn't hurt that much."

"Jars you?"

She licked her lips, working out the words to explain. "Our webbing is what allows us to sense movement in the water—waves or fish or boats. When I injure it, it's like . . . a loud thunderclap, but not in my ears. In my head."

"Like a seal's whiskers," he said with a slow nod. "How sensitive is it?"

She hadn't realized the purpose a seal's whiskers served, but if anyone would know, he would. She held up her hand and spread her fingers wide, which allowed her to sense him. "At this distance I can feel your breathing, your heartbeat. It's indistinct, but in water it would be far clearer."

That apparently gave him something to think about, as he sat with his lips pressed together, unmoving.

Oriana suspected she knew what he wanted. Isabel was the only other human who'd ever known her well enough to dare ask. She moved to the front of the couch, hands still in her lap. "Would you like to look at them?"

He regarded her cautiously. "Would you find that offensive?"

She didn't recall exactly when, but he'd switched to informal address, speaking to her like a friend, *tu*, rather than just an acquaintance. She did the same. "Will you show me yours in return?"

"It would be a terrible sacrifice," he said with a sly smile, "but I suppose I could."

Then he recognized it for a foolish request. She'd seen plenty of human hands in the past two years. But it was a trade she was willing to make. This wasn't vulgar curiosity or sensationalism on his part. He simply liked to understand.

She leaned forward and held out her left hand—the one without a cut across the palm. The webbing ran up to the last joint on each finger. Their conjoined nature didn't allow her the dexterousness of a human hand, but she found most tasks doable.

"May I touch your hand?" he asked.

Given his walking into her bath unannounced only a few days before, it was an ironic question. He'd already touched her bare hand, once when he passed her the bathroom keys and then the previous night in the library. This was different, though. She just wasn't certain how. "Of course," she managed.

His left hand, ungloved, touched hers. His fingers were warm, sliding under her hand to support it. His thumb rubbed across her palm, distracting her. She spread her fingers wider and let him turn her hand slightly to catch the light on the webbing. The silhouette of his fingers showed through the translucent skin. His heartbeat reverberated through her senses.

He was holding her hand because . . . he wanted to do so.

She swallowed. The sensation of Mr. Ferreira's skin against hers was surprisingly affecting, making her body warm and her heart beat faster. She wasn't accustomed to such familiarity; that had to be the source of her reaction.

His eyes met hers. "You have lovely hands."

She jerked her fingers free of his light grasp, then wished she hadn't. He'd done nothing wrong. "Thank you," she mumbled. "I'm surprised that a . . ."

One of his eyebrows crept upward.

She should stop including Duilio Ferreira in her generalizations about humans . . . and about men. "I have large hands," she said. "I'm given to understand that human men prefer delicate ones."

"I am not entirely human," he reminded her. He held out his own hand, leaning close to let her view it. She could smell him clearly now, that light musky scent she'd originally mistaken for ambergris cologne.

"Can you become a seal?" she asked.

"No," he said with a shrug. "*Too* human for that, it seems."

Oriana gazed down at the hand displayed before her. Larger than hers, with blunt-tipped fingers and neatly trimmed nails. His knuckles looked calloused. She turned his hand over. "What does a palmist make of your hands?"

"I've never been to one," he said. "Have you?"

A man of science, then? "No. You don't trust seers either?"

"Well, I do listen to Felis. She reads the cards," he added in a conspiratorial tone. "I'm not sure if she's a true witch or not, but other than her, I don't listen to fortune-tellers."

She wasn't certain whether he was joking about Felis. "You don't believe their predictions, then? Not even Silva's?"

His warm eyes seemed to focus inward for a moment. "I think

we make our own paths in life. As for my uncle, I've no knowledge how profound his powers truly are."

That comment struck a chord in her memory, but she couldn't place it. "I suspect he's no more than a good guesser."

She caught her lower lip between her teeth. Duilio Ferreira was easy to talk to, a dangerous temptation. She felt as if he understood her far better than . . . well, *anyone*. She could mention the strange meeting between Heriberto and her father to him. It would be nice to have someone else's opinion of the entire matter. But it was a sereia problem and had nothing at all to do with Isabel's death, so she kept her query to herself.

When she said nothing further, he rose, leaving his coffee cup on the tray. "Well, as I need to go break into a building, I should leave. Thank you for the company and for the interesting conversation."

He'd switched back to more formal address with that last comment, so she must have hit upon a raw nerve. "You're most welcome, sir."

He made his way out of the sitting room, but paused at the threshold and glanced back. "And my shoulder feels much better, Miss Paredes," he said, answering her original question. "Thank you for asking."

He pulled the door shut behind him before she could think of a fitting response.

She couldn't recall when she'd had that long of an exchange with any male since coming to the city, her master Heriberto included. She would not mind doing so again.

CHAPTER 16

Duilio watched the building on Bonfim Street for a time. His gift insisted that the place was important, but now also seemed to think it was dangerous. Duilio wasn't sure which warning carried the greater significance. On top of that, he had the feeling he was being watched, an odd itch between his shoulder blades. He could just put this off, but they needed results soon.

The apartment was in a narrow building above a small store that had once sold fabric, its red-painted walls faded to a dry rose in the sun. Buildings pressed close on either side, one facade tiled in white and blue and the other built of plain gold-brown stone. It did appear that the fabric store had been converted into a woodworker's shop. A mechanical saw mounted on a large table dominated one side of a room. Another side held a treadle-driven lathe. Wood was neatly stacked against one wall, along with shelves that held wooden kegs of various sizes. Nothing moved within.

Duilio rubbed his aching shoulder as he walked past the store. On reaching the building's narrow entry he walked briskly up the steps. A quick turn of his skeleton key opened the door, and he stepped inside. The white-painted hallway held nothing more than a closed door that led to the fabric-cum-woodworker's shop and a narrow stairwell. Duilio headed up that to the apartment above.

After a brief moment of fiddling with the lock, Duilio slipped inside and closed the door behind him.

The apartment smelled musty, as if it hadn't been aired in months. It wasn't huge but larger than Joaquim's and probably far more expensive. Two windows on the front wall looked out over Bonfim Street. They had sheer lace curtains, but the dark drapes over those were half-closed, letting in only a pale bar of light. Duilio didn't draw back the drapes; that would surely be seen from the street. He glanced at the single kerosene lamp on a table near the door and discarded that idea as well. He didn't want to alert anyone to his presence.

Those with an artistic mentality were often held to be. . . . messy, and this tenant certainly lived up to that stereotype. Stacks of papers covered every horizontal surface in the front room. A low couch couldn't be sat upon because of the piles of sketches obscuring it. More sketches on foolscap lined the edges of the walls, many of them torn and tattered about the edges, made into nests for mice. That explained the musty smell that was making his nose twitch. Duilio perused the paper-littered tables and then gingerly lifted a few drawings from the couch. He held one up to the light streaming in through the lace curtains. The charcoal sketch was a rudimentary likeness of the Duarte mansion, the first to be re-created by Espinoza and set upside down in the water.

Duilio laughed softly. Joaquim had finally run the artist to ground.

He didn't want to stay in the place too long, but he needed to know what it had to tell him. Like most in the old town, the apartment was long and narrow, so Duilio headed for the door that led to the next room. He listened at the door and when he heard nothing, pushed the door open.

The shadowy room was uninhabited. It was a bedroom, but only identifiable as such because a long, narrow bed had been set against the wall in the darkest corner. A pair of drafting tables with tilted tops dominated the room instead, the sort an architect might use. Both were completely immaculate, a stark contrast to the mess in the front room. The blankets on the bed had once been pulled tight, judging by the neat corners that were left.

Duilio stepped back out into the front room, eyes narrowing. The clutter hadn't been wrought by the missing inhabitant, but by mice. If not for their predations, the stacks would have been neat and organized. He looked at the couch with new eyes; it was a filing system. Apparently the inhabitant simply hadn't ever planned on having guests.

He turned back to the immaculate bedroom. The must-and-mouse smell carried through from the front room, and he could see evidence that the woolen blanket on the bed had been chewed as well. A small nightstand stood next to the bed. Duilio opened the single drawer, but saw only a dog-eared Bible within. He picked it up and checked for any inscription but found none. When he shook it out, nothing fell from between the pages. Sighing, he slid the book back into the drawer and closed it.

He'd hoped to find some clue where the artist had gone, but his gift didn't seem eager to attach significance to anything. "I could use some help," he complained to himself.

Nothing popped into his mind, so he threw his hands up and turned to search the drafting tables. A thorough going-over of the first revealed only the artist's inks, pens, and pencils. The second had a neat stack of paper atop it, all of which appeared to be blank. Inside the drawer, he found a couple of blades for sharpening pencils, along with cleaning cloths and some wadded-up papers. It was unusual, given the neatness of everything else.

His interest piqued, Duilio began removing the contents of the drawer. As he pulled out the last cloth, his fingers brushed something solid crammed into the very back of the drawer. He tugged on it and it came loose, a leather-bound volume.

Duilio felt gooseflesh prickling along his arms, his gift alerting him. "Aha!"

He flipped the book open and scanned the handwritten pages.

He turned to the front of the volume and saw neatly dated entries, the first more than two years old. They appeared to be calculations of the distances from the riverbed to the ideal depths for the miniature houses. Grinning, Duilio tucked the journal into one of his coat pockets.

With renewed energy, he inspected the two doors on the far wall. One opened onto a very dark dressing room that had definitely fallen prey to mice, judging by the odor. Garments lay strewn about. Pinching his nose closed to mitigate the smell, Duilio shoved open the door as wide as it would go and dug through the scattered garments with one boot. They were plain-looking garb in the dim light, more like a workman's than the flamboyancy he expected of an artist. He'd judged the man too readily by his occupation. A basin and pitcher had been knocked from their commode, the pitcher's handle broken off on the hardwood floor. *A struggle?*

He cleared most of the clothing to one side and picked up the broken pitcher, then turned it over to view the unglazed base. Something dark discolored the porcelain, as if it had seeped into the porous material. Duilio crouched down. Near where the pitcher had lain, the cracks in the wood were darker as well. He felt sure it was blood, but couldn't quite tell. Frustrated, he went back to fetch the lamp from the front room.

A twinge of warning alerted his senses before he reached the bedroom door, setting his heart to racing. Duilio sniffed . . . and caught the distinctive odor of kerosene. He heard the sudden *whoosh* of a fire igniting.

Duilio ran back to the front room and stopped in the doorway, aghast at the sight.

Flames leapt several feet high, blocking the doorway, and for a second he couldn't breathe, panic freezing him there in that spot. He clutched at the doorjamb. One of the few selkie traits he *had* inherited was an irrational fear of fire.

Duilio squeezed his eyes shut. *Don't panic. Deal with this.*

He opened his eyes again and tried to take stock. Flames already coursed around the edge of the room, feeding off the scattered papers. His eyes flicked around the room, hunting for some escape.

Damnation! How had the fire grown so fast? He couldn't get near the door. Someone had splashed kerosene all over that wall.

But there were still the front windows. The fire had already reached the couch in front of them, but hadn't yet touched the curtains. He could get out that way. He had to, or else the fire would trap him in the narrow bedroom.

Duilio ran back to the bed and stripped off the blanket, then returned to beat at the flames on the couch. Bits of charred paper flew up with the vigor of his actions, glowing on the edges. He took a deep breath, tasted ash, and started coughing. The flames roared, loud enough to drown out the sound of his harsh breathing. He cursed under his breath.

Calm down.

Covering his mouth with one sleeve, Duilio doggedly beat out the flames on the couch. He grabbed the top edge of the couch and flipped the whole thing over, sending more sparks into the air. But the backside of the couch wasn't afire yet. He got behind it and shoved it over, away from the window. He grabbed the curtains and drapes and yanked them down, all in one heave, and tossed them over onto the upturned couch.

He wiped ash and sweat from his face, then pressed close to the dust-clouded window to peer out. There were a dozen or more people in the street below, pointing and crying out. They weren't looking at him.

A huge groan came from the floor below his feet, and he *knew.*

The woodworker's shop on the first floor was ablaze as well—a place likely filled with stains and resins and other chemicals that would burn hot. For a second his breath stilled. A cold sweat broke out all over his body.

Someone intended to bake him alive.

CHAPTER 17

Duilio looked out the window. It couldn't be more than fifteen feet to the cobbles.

He grappled with the latch and finally got it open, the windowpane swinging out and banging against the stop. That caused another round of cries as glass sprinkled down to the cobbles below. Smoke began to billow over his shoulder, and Duilio glanced back to see that the flames had almost reached his feet. He had no time left.

He climbed over the sill and a second later dangled by his hands from the window's frame. Voices urged him to drop, so he did so. He landed on his feet, but felt that jolt through his very teeth. People were still crying out, and there seemed to be chaos about him in the street.

Then water splashed all over him from behind, startling him out of his numbness. "What in Hades' name are you doing?"

The man holding the bucket clapped Duilio's shoulder. "Back of your coat was on fire."

Duilio instinctively craned his neck, trying to look at the back of his coat. "Thank you," he mumbled as the man strode away.

Something exploded in the shop then, scattering the pedestrians. Duilio backed away with the rest of the crowd. Another barrel or keg blew, this time shattering the front windows, and black smoke began to roil out of them, joining the stream that came from the upper floor. The Corps of Public Safety fought most of the fires in the city, but Duilio didn't think they would get there in time to save any part of the building.

I should not be here when they arrive, he thought with sudden clarity. His sodden and apparently burned jacket would place him as having been in the apartment. He didn't want to try to explain his presence there to them. Pulling up the collar of his coat, he eased away through the crowd, heading in the direction of the church at the end of the street. He felt again the sense of being watched, but was too tired to care at the moment.

Duilio settled on the stone steps before the church. His coat was ruined, so he tugged it off, rolled it up, and tucked it under his arm. His shirt and waistcoat were ruined as well, but weren't as bad. He didn't care, save that Marcellin was going to have a fit of apoplexy over this. A weak laugh worked its way out of his chest, then turned into a cough.

"You need someone to watch your back," a man said in a voice that suggested they'd been chatting for a couple of hours. "That time he almost got you."

Duilio looked to his right. Leaning against the stone wall that surrounded the church's grounds was the man who'd thrown water on him when he'd hit the ground. The man's dark skin and short-cropped black hair hinted he might be from one of the old African colonies. His eyes were an odd shade of smoky green, hard to mistake should he turn up again. His suit looked to be well made, although of a foreign cut. Oddly, Duilio's gift had given him no warning about this man's approach, as if he wasn't there at all.

Duilio rose, keeping the coat under his arm. He didn't want to lose it—or the journal in one of the pockets. "*Who* almost got me?"

"Donato Mata," the man said. "Do you know him?"

"No," Duilio admitted. The name didn't mean anything to him. "And you are?"

"Inspector Gaspar, Special Police," the man said.

A frisson of worry slid down Duilio's spine . . . but it wasn't his gift warning him. It was simply the normal reaction to speaking with a member of that body. The man spoke in accented Portuguese—from Cabo Verde, if Duilio placed it correctly. The inspector extended a card in one gloved hand. "What exactly were you doing up there? Why is he after you?"

Duilio took the card. It bore the man's name, Miguel Gaspar, along with his seal and a stated rank of special investigator. It looked impressive, but it wouldn't be difficult to find a printer to falsify cards. Despite his doubts, Duilio tucked the thing into the damp folds of his coat. The rank put this man above Joaquim. Even above Captain Rios, Duilio suspected. "What did you mean when you said he almost got me *this* time?"

The man fixed his gaze on Duilio's face. "He took a shot at you last night in a tavern. I assume your gift warned you in time, although it didn't do you much good today."

Duilio felt his breath go short again. Did the Special Police know he was a seer? That couldn't be good.

"Then again," the man added, "setting a fire isn't acting directly against *you*, which would allow your gift to miss it. Probably why he chose that method rather than a direct confrontation this time."

"My gift?" Duilio asked.

Gaspar's smoky green eyes narrowed. "You're a seer, although not a particularly strong one. I suspect your selkie blood limits your gift somehow."

His instinctive desire to take a swing at the man and run seemed a good idea now. Why was his gift not helping him? If Gaspar knew that Duilio was part selkie, then he had every right to drag Duilio down to the station and throw him in jail. But he hadn't done so. And *how* did he know? The number of people who were aware of both those things was limited. "I imagine your superiors wouldn't approve of your conversing with me if that were true."

Gaspar smiled mildly. "There are Special Police, and then there are Special Police. And then, Mr. Ferreira," he added, "there are *special* Special Police."

While that answer didn't precisely make sense, Duilio understood. Within any police body there were divisions. He'd not heard any rumor of such, but merely because the regular police hadn't heard of this didn't mean the Special Police weren't at one another's throats. "And what makes you think those things are true about me?"

It was a dangerous question to ask, but at this point why not chance it?

"I see it, Mr. Ferreira," Gaspar said. "I look at people . . . and I know."

Duilio gazed at the man leaning against the stone wall. Did he correctly understand what Gaspar had just intimated?

He'd met different kinds of witches throughout the past several years—not just seers, but healers who could still a man's blood in his veins, witches who could lay a curse that lasted for decades. There were Truthsayers who could weigh a man's words, and Finders who could locate things gone missing. There were a myriad of little talents, and skills benign enough that they didn't have names. But this was something different, a rarity that supposedly appeared only once a generation. "You're a *Meter*?"

The inspector didn't flinch. "Yes, Mr. Ferreira."

Meters were the stuff of legends. A Meter was a witch who could *see* what others were. Duilio wasn't sure how far that talent extended, what Gaspar saw in him, but if Gaspar truly was a Meter, the Spanish Church would love to have him in their clutches. They still hunted witches in Spain, and Gaspar could simply point out each one on the street. "So, what are you doing here?" Duilio asked him. "Were you following me?"

"What were you doing in that building?"

Admittedly, Gaspar had revealed something of himself—clearly hoping to gain Duilio's trust—but he *was* a member of the Special Police. Duilio couldn't be sure where the man stood on anything, least of all investigation of *The City Under the Sea*. For all he knew, Gaspar had set that fire himself or was in league with the man who'd attacked him at the tavern. After all, his attacker had probably been a member of the Special Police. Duilio didn't answer.

Gaspar pushed away from the wall. "It would be helpful to me if I knew why Mata is hunting you, Mr. Ferreira. I understand your hesitation. I'm sure you understand mine."

Yes, he did. It was always a game of trying to figure out whom to trust.

"You should go home, Mr. Ferreira," Gaspar added, giving him a friendly pat on his shoulder. "You look a wreck."

Duilio shook his head ruefully. *Yes, I certainly do.*

Oriana needed to return the fabric scissors she'd borrowed from Felis, so she headed down to the servants' workroom. Halfway down the back stairs, she almost collided with Mr. Ferreira coming up.

She should have been warned by the smell. He carried the acrid scent of burned paper about him like a cloud. His coat was tucked under his arm, and she could see dried blood staining his shirtsleeve where he'd been injured the previous evening. His charcoal-gray waistcoat was liberally streaked with soot and ash. Even his shoes looked ruined. "Do you come home every evening like this, sir?" she asked, horrified.

He laughed, apparently not as perturbed as he should have been.

Is this normal? "What happened?" she demanded. "Are you hurt?"

Mr. Ferreira leaned against the newel post. "Someone walked into a room behind me and set it ablaze," he said, sobering. "And the floor below that. I suspect it was the same gentleman from last night."

Who seemed likely to have been a member of the Special Police. "They certainly don't want you proceeding with this investigation, do they?"

He shrugged and then winced. "I'm beginning to have questions about that, Miss Paredes. I suspect my understanding of the Special Police might be insufficient to grasp what's going on now."

What does that mean? "Are you hurt?" she asked again.

"Oh, I'm fine," he said dismissively, as if an attempt to burn him to death didn't warrant concern. He began to search the pockets of his coat. "I went to investigate the place because we thought Espinoza might live there."

"Did he?"

Mr. Ferreira tugged a leather-bound book out of one of the pockets. "Evidence suggests that he did but hasn't been there for some time."

When he held out the book, Oriana took it. It was damp, the edges of the pages already beginning to curl. "And this is?"

"A journal, likely his."

He certainly disliked stating absolutes. He qualified everything he said. She peered down at the leather-bound book more closely. It didn't seem to have been damaged by the fire, but she was going to have to let it dry. "May I look through this?"

"Yes," he said. "I'm afraid it got wet. Someone dumped a bucket of water on me. I thought you might be able to determine if there's anything useful inside. Perhaps some hint where the man is holed up. It would be helpful if he names any of his compatriots, particularly in the Special Police. Or who's paying for his work. That would be nice to know."

He could have given this to his cousin in the police instead, but he'd handed it over to her. It was a gesture of trust. "Thank you," she said softly. "Were you injured again? Or is that the other wound reopened?"

"The old one," he said, glancing back at his blood-smudged shirt. "Nothing that requires an application of brandy, Miss Paredes, I assure you. I'll get my man to bandage it after I get cleaned off.

If you see Marcellin downstairs, could you mention to him that I'm here? I need to get cleaned up before dinner."

A vast understatement. "I'll do so, sir. Will we still go to the ball?"

"Absolutely, Miss Paredes. If there's one thing we could use more of, it's information. Especially if it helps make sense out of all the other information we have."

Oriana did her best to salvage the journal. Some pages were wetter than others, so she took a towel and carefully dabbed at them, trying hard not to smear any ink. The book had been tightly wedged into Mr. Ferreira's pocket, so the water hadn't crept too far into the pages. He'd been lucky.

She skimmed a couple of pages, most describing building one house or another, along with a few others that contained arcane mathematical calculations. Deciding that she could read it the next day, she laid the journal atop the chest of drawers in the dressing room. She weighed down each side of the cover with what appeared to be unused snuffboxes, trinkets that must have belonged to Alessio, and the pages fanned open. She hoped they would dry by the morning.

They were to leave the house at ten, so Oriana stewed in her room for a couple of hours. If Nela's Lady did show up in the Carvalho's library, what should she ask? Unfortunately she understood what Mr. Ferreira had meant when he'd given her the journal. They had a great deal of information already. They simply didn't know how it tied together. Too many aspects of this didn't make sense. If only she could ask the right question tonight and get the right answer, perhaps everything would become clear.

Teresa had left the blue dress, now freshly sponged and pressed, on the bed. When ten approached, Oriana donned it and tried to make her hair presentable. She usually wore it in the English style with tendrils down about her neck, but Felis had brought her a pair of jet earrings, a reminder that the household was still in half mourning. The dress had a high batiste collar that would hide her gill slits, so Oriana drew all her hair up into a knot at the nape of her neck, better to let the earrings show. It wasn't elegant, but it was the best she could manage on her own. When a knock came at the door, she expected Teresa to enter with some item she'd forgotten, but it was Ana, the second housemaid, instead. "Miss Paredes?"

Oriana quickly drew on her mitts. "Yes, Ana?"

"Teresa said I could come up and see if you needed help with your hair." The young woman sounded uncertain, but she went on. "I'm not a proper ladies' maid, but she's been letting me help her, and we girls all fix each other's hair below stairs."

"I'd be grateful for your help pinning it up," Oriana told her.

The housemaid came in and, once Oriana handed over the pins, brushed out Oriana's hair, braided it again, and pinned it into a neat coil at the back of her head. Ana also produced a jar of dusting powder that covered the fading bruise on Oriana's temple. The girl chattered the whole while, repeating how excited the staff was that Lady Ferreira was going out again. When she'd finished, Oriana had to admire the job the young woman had done. Her hair looked more elegant than any coiffure she'd ever achieved on her own. She thanked Ana, gathered her handbag with the sketch secreted inside it, and went to wait at the side of the house for the carriage.

If she hadn't known that Mr. Ferreira had been attacked twice in the last two days, she wouldn't have been able to spot it. He looked dashing in his black evening jacket and gray waistcoat. Yes, *dashing* was the right word. He carried a satin top hat and a silver-handled cane, which Oriana suspected was more for decoration than for supporting himself. When the carriage rolled up to the side of the house, he helped his mother up first, and then Oriana. It wasn't even a mile up the Street of Flowers to the Carvalho house, but Oriana didn't fancy walking that distance, so she settled next to the lady and clutched her small handbag close.

In the flickering light of the little lanterns inside the carriage, Lady Ferreira looked stunning in a dress of dark brown that bared much of her shoulders and throat. Although brown, the black trim should allow it to pass as half mourning. It shouldn't shock the aristocratic matrons overmuch. A jet parure completed the lady's costume, and Felis had done an excellent job with the lady's hair, pinning it up in a fashion that made her look youthful yet not daring. Some might interpret her dress and her appearance in society as a sign she'd decided to leave mourning behind, but Lady Ferreira's persistently grief-stricken demeanor would surely convince everyone otherwise.

Mr. Ferreira joined them in the carriage. Once he'd settled in his seat, he drew a silver case out of an inside pocket—a cigarette case. It had to be an affectation on his part. She'd never once caught a whiff of smoke on him—except for today. He took out a cigarette and then offered the case to Oriana, one brow raised. She shook her head. Isabel might have taught her to drink coffee and brandy, but she drew the line at smoking. Her gills would never forgive her. "You're not actually going to smoke that, are you?" she asked.

"I don't allow it," his mother said softly.

Duilio returned the silver case to his pocket. "Marcellin already complains enough about the scent of others' smoke in my garments. I don't want to displease *him* more than necessary, much less my mother." He turned to Lady Ferreira. "Are you still feeling up to this, Mother?"

The lady sighed. "Yes. Only I don't wish to stay too long, Duilinho. I've forgotten how to endure late nights."

"Of course, Mother. A couple of the footmen will meet us at the Carvalho house. They'll be able to escort you home should you grow tired." He tapped on the wall of the carriage with his cane, and the vehicle lurched into motion. "Miss Paredes," he said in a cheerful tone, "your hair is lovely in that style. You must wear it like that more often. Off your neck, I mean."

He continued to natter on, talking about the various merits of his mother's dress, and after a moment Oriana's bewilderment subsided. He'd become the inanely chattering Duilio Ferreira she'd met on the submersible, a strange transformation to behold. His voice even sounded different, higher in tone. The cigarette case had to be a prop meant to help him remember his role, much as her garments fixed her securely in her own disguise of a Portuguese gentlewoman.

He'd stopped talking and was regarding her with a questioning expression. Oriana realized she'd stopped listening at some point. *Does everyone do that to him?* "I'm sorry, Mr. Ferreira. I lost track."

His eyebrows crept upward. "I was asking whether you have a watch in your purse. I don't recall if the Carvalho family has a clock in their ballroom. I will come fetch you in time to take you along to their library. Is that acceptable?"

She nodded mutely.

"Now," he continued, "I think it would be easiest to claim that Lady Isabel introduced you to my mother a couple of weeks ago. Planning ahead, so to speak. It's vague enough that no one can refute you. Of course, there will be those who think the arrangement was made with me rather than my mother, but just act shocked that anyone would suggest my mother would allow such a decision to be made for her. . . ."

He went on as the carriage rattled up the street, making suggestions how to handle the many rumors that would be swirling about her. By the time they reached the section of the street where the Carvalho family lived, Oriana felt prepared to take on an army of gossips.

CHAPTER 18

When they stepped into the foyer of the Carvalho home—a stately neoclassical creation in the Pombaline style so popular in Southern Portugal—Duilio passed his hat and cane to the footman waiting there at the entryway. Then he escorted his mother up the grand staircase and through a marble arch to the main ballroom, where they would have to endure the greeting line. Miss Paredes trailed mute behind them, his mother's shawl draped over her hands.

Duilio made his bow to Lady Carvalho and was introduced again to her youngest daughter, Constancia, a round-faced young lady who appeared overwhelmed by the number of people to whom she was being introduced. His mother drifted through the introductions with a fair approximation of attention. She kissed Lady Carvalho's plump cheeks and walked on. Head lowered, Miss Paredes followed his mother around the side of the ballroom.

Duilio paused near the entry arch to scan the room. It wasn't overcrowded. At least, not yet. The sounds of a small group of musicians could be heard over the din of conversation, and in the center of the ballroom a gavotte was in process. Duilio cringed inwardly. He'd never enjoyed dancing and didn't want to end up swinging the three Carvalho daughters about. His knees ached from his hard landing on the cobbles that afternoon. Of course, it would be a different matter should Miss Paredes consent to dance with him—preferably a waltz, where he might get away with holding her closer than propriety dictated. Unfortunately, singling out his mother's companion would only foster gossip, and Miss Paredes didn't need that sort of attention.

Duilio sighed. He checked his watch and saw that he had a good half hour before he needed to escort Miss Paredes from the ballroom. He spotted a cluster of gentlemen to one side of the room near the arches that led out to the balcony. A couple he knew from Coimbra, but most of this set were older than him, and possibly displaying their own daughters tonight. As he approached the group, he could tell they were speaking of a recent scandal, all their eyes on Luís Taveira, who must have the freshest gossip.

"He waited for her in Paris," Taveira was saying, "but she never arrived."

Duilio hadn't been to any social function for a week now, so he hadn't heard whispers yet of the absence of Marianus Efisio and Isabel Amaral.

A few of the young men cast glances about the room, perhaps concerned Lady Isabel might be standing behind one of the potted orange trees. "Where did she go?" a spot-faced youngster asked, nearly splashing his champagne onto his neighbor's patent shoes in his enthusiasm. "Was there another gentleman involved?"

"Efisio doesn't know," Taveira said. "All he would tell me is that his heart is broken and he can never forgive her."

"She made a fool of him," another gentleman said with a sage nod.

"She's gone to the country, no doubt," a third added. "Surely her parents have taken her out of the city."

"No, they're still here packing," another inserted.

Duilio stepped back from that group, not wanting to be there when the suppositions about Lady Isabel turned ugly, as they undoubtedly would. He was relieved when the Marquis of Maraval, the Minister of Culture, stepped in, remonstrating with the younger ones for their gossiping tongues. Maraval was a genial older man who'd always treated Duilio kindly. Careful grooming and application of dye to his hair made him seem younger, but Duilio guessed that the man was close in age to his own father . . . or Silva, even. Relieved that Lady Isabel had a defender, Duilio slipped away.

He found a spot against one of the walls where he could see most of the room. Leaning back against the wall half-obscured by a heavy velvet curtain, he watched the spot across from the musicians where the matrons had settled to observe and pass judgment regarding behavior on the dance floor. His mother was seated among them, looking as if she were half listening to the conversation. Miss Paredes sat slightly behind her in a spot suitable for a companion, out of the way and inconspicuous.

While he watched, Lady Pereira de Santos—a longtime widow in stark black—approached his mother and greeted her. The lady turned toward Miss Paredes next and began to speak, but Miss Paredes looked away. The lady's attention seemed to make her uncomfortable. Since the Pereira de Santos mansion stood next to the Amaral home, Miss Paredes had probably met the lady before. No doubt Lady Amaral had spewed her slander against her former employee to her neighbor. Duilio found himself contemplating a way to remove Miss Paredes from that situation.

It *would* seem odd if he singled out his mother's companion. Then again . . .

It wasn't as if he'd attempted to fix the interest of any of the daughters who'd been thrown at him in the last year. He'd avoided female companionship, not wanting to worry about a woman he might not be able to trust with the truth about his family. But Miss Paredes was different from both the society girls he might be expected to wed and the Spanish girls he would be expected to bed. He liked her better than the women he'd met of either category.

He started to make his way over to where the matrons sat chattering. Unfortunately a blond-haired young woman approached

Miss Paredes first, smoothing a hand down the front of her pale lavender satin dress. It was Pia Sequeira, the betrothed of Marianus Efisio—or she had been until he'd attempted to elope with Lady Isabel, her cousin.

Miss Paredes nodded and rose, and together the two walked to a door to one side of the ballroom, under the curious eyes of half the revelers. Duilio had no doubt the other half would hear about it within minutes.

Oriana couldn't think of a graceful way to get out of an audience with Isabel's cousin. Outside the ballroom, they emerged into an open foyer where a young footman waited, giving the appearance that he was no more than a statue.

Miss Sequeira clutched at Oriana's arm. "Miss Paredes, I've heard you've gone to work for Lady Ferreira. Is that true?"

Pia was delicate and petite and, although nothing alike in coloration, she otherwise reminded Oriana very much of her own younger sister, Marina. "Yes."

"Aunt claimed you trumped up some tale about Isabel being spirited away by bandits to cover her elopement. That she'd been taken by someone other than Mr. Efisio."

"Not a tale, miss, but Lady Amaral didn't believe me," Oriana volunteered, since otherwise it would take Pia hours to get to her point.

"Mr. Efisio wrote to me, making it plain Isabel isn't with him." Pia touched the back of one gloved hand to her lips and sniffled. "If Isabel hasn't run off, then she must be . . . dead . . . or kidnapped. Aunt *must* go to the police."

When Oriana didn't argue the point, Pia looked up at her again. "Have you . . . ?"

"Yes, I've spoken with a representative of the police," Oriana said truthfully. "But as Isabel's parents have said nothing, they have no reason to pursue the inquiry."

"Oh." Pia chewed her lower lip. "Will the police suspect Mr. Efisio of harming her, do you think?"

So the girl was still concerned about him, even though he'd jilted her. "I don't think so."

"Good," Pia said softly, her blue eyes shining. "I would hate for him to be accused."

Oriana didn't know how deep the girl's feelings for her erstwhile betrothed went, but Pia was a kindhearted girl. She would probably forgive him anything.

"He's very angry with Isabel," Pia added. "He said some unkind things about her in his letter, that she was toying with him and only wanted his money. Did she intend to go through with the wedding at all?"

"Yes," Oriana admitted. "She told me she loved him," she added reluctantly.

"His feelings are wounded, then," Pia said, nodding as if that made sense of what she'd read in his letter. "He begged my forgiveness. He said his infatuation with Isabel was a fleeting thing, and asked if he might take up our betrothal again."

Technically, their betrothal never had been terminated. As Oriana understood it, Pia was still betrothed to Marianus Efisio. "Do you intend to take him back?"

Pia lifted her hand to her nose again to cover another sniffle. Then her expression firmed. "No. I won't. I've written to him to end our betrothal. I'd prefer a husband who won't be drawn away by every pretty, clever woman who comes along."

"Good," Oriana said, even though she had no right to comment on Pia's actions.

Pia sniffed wetly, opened her handbag, and began hunting through it. "I heard you, you know, a few months ago when you thought I was still in the water closet." She produced a lacy handkerchief and dabbed at her eye. "I was in the hallway, and I heard you tell Isabel it was dishonorable to try to steal her own cousin's betrothed. I didn't believe you then, but that's how I know how long it was going on. At least four months, so it wasn't just a passing fancy on his part."

"No, I didn't think it was," Oriana agreed. "They should have told you the truth. If he didn't wish to marry you, he should have spoken to you."

"A man doesn't break off his betrothal," Pia said with a helpless shrug, her eyes lowered. "I suppose he thought if he ignored me long enough I would do it for him."

The coward's way out. Oriana wished she had some comfort to offer the young woman. "I'm sorry I couldn't sway her."

"No one could sway Isabel once she'd set her mind to something." Pia took Oriana's right hand in hers again and met Oriana's eyes. "Thank you, Miss Paredes. I hope your current situation is easier than your last."

"It's a good household," Oriana said honestly. "Isabel introduced me to Lady Ferreira a couple of weeks ago. I was fortunate that she needed a companion."

"Especially since Aunt turned you out without a reference. Isabel's maid told me that Aunt accused you of stealing, and kept all your clothing, even. If you need, I can ask *my* mother to give you a letter."

"Thank you," Oriana said, genuinely touched. "I'll keep that in mind."

"I should go now," Pia said, dropping Oriana's hand. "I'm going to tell Mother I want to go home. I don't feel like smiling at anyone any longer."

Oriana understood that sentiment. "Good night, then, miss."

Pia walked past Oriana and into the ballroom, her shoulders drooping like a flower gone too long without water.

Duilio caught sight of Miss Paredes emerging from that doorway a few minutes later, directly after the pallid Miss Sequeira came forth. Miss Paredes scanned the room and then began to edge her way around the dance floor.

She crossed, her head lowered, to where the matrons sat, and settled in her seat again. Miss Sequeira spoke with her own mother, and they made a stately exit from the ballroom under the eyes of every gossip in town. Word of Pia Sequeira's mournful retreat following that talk with Miss Paredes would be aired all over the city by morning. Duilio could spot eyes here and there watching Miss Paredes afterward, but no one approached her to speak with her.

Duilio caught movement in the corner of one eye and spotted Rodrigo Pimental drifting over to the balcony doorway where he stood. He sighed inwardly. Pimental was a few years older and not actually a friend. Well, not a friend by any measure. Always well dressed and careful of his grooming, Pimental presented an image of wealth and success. He held some sort of decorative ministry position, Duilio knew, likely bestowed by the prince for some favor his father-in-law had done. That kept Pimental's well-born wife in silk stockings and furs, but the man was always short on funds. He had an annoying tendency to sponge off others. What Pimental did have was a keen ear and a sharp tongue that could cause no end of trouble if one didn't watch one's words around him.

"Well, Ferreira," Pimental said, "is it true, the whispers I've heard about town?" He held a glass of watered sherry in his hand.

Duilio plastered his most vacant smile on his face. "That would depend entirely upon the whispers, Pimental."

Pimental smiled tightly, his eyes on a pair of dancers on the floor. "That you hired away Lady Isabel Amaral's companion—Miss Paraíso, or something. She has a fine figure, I admit, but there are younger and prettier girls out there. I can recommend a couple if you're hunting a mistress."

Duilio chose his words carefully, suppressing the urge to hit the man. "What a silly notion, Pimental. Miss Paredes is my mother's companion."

"I think not. I saw you watching her." Rodrigo leaned closer, his eyes still on the dancers. "Your mother didn't even have a companion before, I'm told. Or are you killing two birds with one stone, so to speak?"

Duilio pressed his lips together. Most gentlemen would let it go after a simple denial. No, Pimental intended to blackmail him, assuming he would be desperate enough to pay to keep society's approval, yet not outraged enough to challenge him to a duel.

"Of course," Pimental continued, "no one wants to speak ill of another gentleman."

"Of course not." Duilio allowed sarcasm to creep into his voice. "What is it they say about not being lucky at cards? One has fortune in love? Alessio never had trouble in that field." He took out his cigarette case and offered a cigarette to the man. "Then again, you knew that personally, didn't you? Alessio mentioned you fondly in his journals."

Pimental paused, match in midair. "You wouldn't dare," he whispered.

Duilio had skimmed through Alessio's journals, seeking only information regarding the search for his mother's pelt and the duel that took Alessio's life, but he was sure he'd seen Pimental's name somewhere. The man's reaction confirmed it. The journals' contents had often put Duilio to the blush; he didn't share his elder brother's wild proclivities. Duilio might be a sinner when compared to Joaquim, but next to Alessio he was positively a saint.

He returned to watching Miss Paredes with her downcast eyes and prim posture, so much at odds with the woman he'd come to know in the past few days. Pimental might be hypocritical about his reluctance to have his amorous exploits exposed, but he and Miss Paredes weren't any more honest, both hiding what they were. Duilio turned back to him. "You're right; I wouldn't. We all have things we'd rather our friends—and wives—not know about us."

"It was an aberration," Pimental said quietly, his cheeks crimson. "I don't . . . I'm not . . ."

Poor fellow, drawn in by Alessio's selkie charm. Alessio had been able to seduce almost anyone he fancied into his bed, and had suffered from a selkie male's need to maintain a harem. His desires had clashed horribly with the mores of Portuguese society, leading him into one impossible, doomed relationship after another. He'd taken to drink to console his wounded feelings, which in turn only made him less discerning about his partners.

"Alessio had that effect on people," Duilio said, feeling a bit sorry for Pimental. "He could get them to do things they would never normally dream. If I'm to believe what he wrote, there were very many gentlemen and ladies who shared your situation."

Pimental's hand shook as he took a deep drag on his cigarette. "He was so . . . beautiful."

Duilio shook his head. "Forget I mentioned Alessio. But remember this, Pimental: Miss Paredes is my mother's companion and *only* her companion. I would never demean Miss Paredes by taking her as my mistress. Make sure you don't make the mistake of calling her that."

Pimental cast a startled glance in his direction, likely surprised that Duilio had bested him, and then strolled away, looking rather like a cat whose tail had been trodden upon.

The next few days would surely generate some nervous personal inquiries, as he'd confessed that Alessio had left behind *written* evidence of his amorous exploits. Having been raised with a father who struggled to hide his own indiscretions—often unsuccessfully—from his wife and sons, Duilio had tried to live in a manner he wouldn't have to conceal from a future wife or children. It baffled him that others failed to take such precautions. He shook his head, resolved not to worry about it for the time being, but a sharp warning prickled down his spine, his gift jolting awake again.

Duilio stepped deeper into the curtained alcove and scanned the room, wondering what had set off that warning. Then he spotted Paolo Silva framed in the entry archway. His uncle rubbed his chin with one hand as he surveyed the ballroom and its inhabitants with a jaded eye. Why had he not checked with Carvalho to see whether Silva was on the guest list? His mother would *not* take it well should she notice Silva's presence. Duilio shot a quick glance at Miss Paredes to see if she'd noted the man's arrival, but she appeared lost in thought, her eyes on the dancers.

The musicians were in the middle of a set, so Duilio edged his way around the ballroom toward his mother's side. He needed to get her out of here before the man came and bothered her. He wasn't afraid for his mother, but that would not end well for Silva.

Oriana sat to one side of Lady Ferreira as the young folk danced to the reedy music of the quartet. The swirl of color of the young women's gowns, the aromas of cigarette smoke and heady perfumes, the hushed patter of the gossip flowing around them all faded into the background. The waiting was proving irksome. She wanted to be *doing* something.

She'd caught sight of Mr. Ferreira as he stood near one of the curtained doors that led onto the balcony. He'd been talking to an urbane gentleman whose expression appeared to alternate between embarrassment and avarice—Mr. Pimental, who had married the youngest daughter of the Marquis of Davila. After a time that man slipped away, leaving Mr. Ferreira momentarily alone. But now he moved, edging around the dancers and toward the matrons. When he reached their side of the dance floor, he nodded to the matrons and pressed a kiss to his mother's gloved hand. Lady Ferreira smiled vaguely up at her son.

"Mother, would you like to take a walk on the veranda?" he asked, catching Oriana's eye as he did so.

"Of course, Duilinho," his mother said, rising gracefully.

Oriana rose with her, but Mr. Ferreira caught her hand. He leaned closer, the musky scent of his skin touching her nose. "Silva's here," he whispered. "I'll send my mother home with the carriage and be back in a few minutes. Just tell everyone you're waiting for her to come back. Will you be able to handle him if he accosts you?"

His eyes met hers, worried, but she shook her head. "I'll be fine," she told him.

"I'll come back for you as soon as I can." He escorted his mother away.

Oriana settled into her chair again. She didn't know if Silva was guilty of what Lady Ferreira believed, but her own past interaction with him made her amply wary. She was not going to let him get the better of her.

CHAPTER 19

The dancing went on, one set ending and another beginning, while Oriana sat among the gossiping matrons and pretended to wait for Lady Ferreira's return. She watched the swirl of color and wondered how many of Isabel's friends had seen her but chosen not to speak to her. How many mistakenly believed Isabel was still alive?

Where *was* Silva? Oriana glanced about markedly as if anxious for her mistress to return, and finally caught sight of him. He stood at the far side of the ballroom, bowing over a young woman's hand. The pretty girl seemed flustered by his attentions. Silva tucked the young woman's gloved hand into the crook of his arm and led her at a slow walk about the edge of the ballroom floor. It would take them around to this side of the room. Oriana mentally readied herself for the moment the man noticed her. He had said they would meet again, hadn't he?

She could see a resemblance to Duilio Ferreira now that she knew to look. Not as tall as his nephew, Silva had run to stockiness with age. He dressed wisely, though, in well-tailored garments that concealed his thickening waist.

No sooner had he come within hearing distance of the gaggle of matrons about her than old Lady Beja swatted at his legs with her cane. "Let go of that young girl, you old miscreant," she snapped.

"Come sit with someone more your age, who can appreciate you properly. I'll have Torres escort Miss Offley back to her mother."

Silva complied with every appearance of graciousness. The old lady's companion, a black-clad woman nearly as ancient as the lady herself, jumped up spryly, grabbed the girl's arm, and hauled her toward the far side of the ballroom. The girl cast a confused glance back at Silva but apparently never thought to protest. Oriana was glad to know someone else found Silva's pursuit of very young women inappropriate. Isabel certainly had.

"Now," the lady continued, "you've been absent from our company too often recently. What have you been doing?"

"Whatever my prince bids me, madam," Silva said in an obsequious tone. "If my duties take me from your presence, I can only mourn my loss."

Relieved she was sitting behind them and not in their line of sight, Oriana rolled her eyes.

"So, what do you make of this year's crop of girls, Silva?" the lady asked.

"Sadly, they all suffer again this year in comparison to Lady Isabel," he returned smoothly. "Is she here tonight?"

"Surely you've heard? She's eloped," the lady said in a whisper that carried clearly to the ear of all but the deafest matron. "Ran off with her cousin's betrothed. Lady Amaral has taken to her bed, I'm told."

Thank the gods, Oriana thought. That meant Lady Amaral wasn't likely to show here. Her presence on top of Silva's would have been unbearable.

Silva gasped at Lady Beja's gossip. "I've been so busy I hadn't heard a word."

The lady snapped her fan across his white-gloved knuckles, and then pointed at Oriana with it. "Miss Paredes there knows all, I suspect."

Oriana sighed inwardly. Apparently Isabel's disgrace meant

that her own name was now known to every gossip in the city. Oriana turned in their direction, giving in to the inevitable.

The lady crooked an imperious finger. "Come here, Miss Paredes."

She rose and obediently crossed to the lady's other side, feeling Silva's eyes on her. "Yes, Lady Beja. May I fetch something for you?"

The lady fastened a clawlike hand on Oriana's arm and hauled her down into the seat her companion had left empty. "Sit here. Now, where has Lady Isabel gone?"

"I no longer work for the Amaral family, Lady Beja."

"You did until then." The old woman slapped her fan across Oriana's right hand, sending uncomfortable reverberations through her webbing. "No point in keeping secrets for a family who threw you out, miss."

Oriana clenched her jaw, ignoring the fading discomfort. "Isabel introduced me to Lady Ferreira before she left, lady. And if I had secrets about Lady Isabel, I would hold them for her sake alone."

The old lady laughed. "A loyal companion? How unusual. Torres would sell my bed curtains in the market the very day I died."

"I cannot believe that, my lady," Oriana protested.

"Wait and see, girl." She waggled her fan in the direction of her returning companion. "That one's mercenary through and through."

"Tell me, Miss . . . Paredes, it is?" Silva inserted, leaning forward in his chair to favor her with his notice. "Do you know when Lady Isabel and her new husband will return from abroad, then? I would like to pay my respects."

He appeared completely earnest, filled with concern for an old and dear friend. But he was also acting as if he'd never met her before, which set her teeth on edge. She couldn't be mistaken. He'd been in that boat that night. She was appalled at how easily the man lied. That increased the likelihood that Lady Ferreira was right about him.

"The Amaral girl won't be any more receptive to you now that she's a married woman than she was five years ago," Lady Beja snapped.

Silva draped a hurt look across his mobile features. "Lady Isabel misunderstood my intentions completely."

"I doubt that," Lady Beja said under her breath.

Ah, now Oriana knew why Isabel had disliked the man so. He must have tried to seduce Isabel, thinking her as foolish as any other girl of eighteen or nineteen.

He smiled fatuously at Oriana now. "Will you take a turn with me about the floor, Miss Paredes? Perhaps you can tell me something of this fantastical news . . . without betraying Lady Isabel's confidence, of course."

A gentleman didn't parade around a ballroom with a mere companion without having some ulterior motive. "I had better not, sir," she said quickly.

Silva rose smoothly and extended an elbow for her to take. "I insist, Miss Paredes."

Oriana tried to produce a plausible protest, but nothing came to mind. So she laid her hand on his arm and let him lead her along the edge of the ballroom.

"Now, what actually happened to Lady Isabel?" he asked.

Apparently he'd decided to stop oozing courtesy. Oriana licked her lips. "I told Lady Amaral. She was grabbed by the men who later threw me off one of the bridges."

He gazed at her doubtfully. "And you floated all that way down the river?"

It *was* quite a way from the Dom Sebastião Bridge to where *The City Under the Sea* was located. "I barely remember, sir," she protested. "That whole night is a blur for me now."

They were behind another pair of guests who'd abruptly decided to stop and join in some gossip, forcing Oriana to stand there in place and wait. Silva eyed her narrowly. He didn't believe her story. *What does he know?* She tucked her fingers in closer, trying to hide webbing that was already hidden by her mitts.

"Tell me, then, Miss Paredes—" he began, his voice taking on a menacing edge.

"Silva," a dark-haired man interrupted. "I haven't been introduced to your young friend."

Oriana surreptitiously let out a pent breath, grateful that someone had come to her aid. She recognized the man as the Marquis of Maraval, although she hadn't ever been introduced to him. The Minister of Culture, he was known for his civility. Apparently he had seen that she was uncomfortable in Silva's company and had come to her rescue.

Silva smirked. "And you're upset that I got to her first? How amusing. May I introduce to you Miss Paredes, who was once companion to Lady Isabel Amaral."

When Silva told her the marquis' name, Maraval bowed smoothly over her hand. "Miss Paredes," he said, seemingly unruffled by Silva's glare, "may I escort you back to your seat?"

"I would appreciate that, sir. I was concerned that Lady Ferreira might return while I was absent." She should have used that objection to avoid Silva's clutches in the first place.

Maraval settled her hand on his sleeve and turned her back the way she'd come, striding away from Silva. Oriana could almost feel Silva's angry gaze following her. "I'm afraid my contemporary has a reputation for inappropriate behavior toward pretty young women," Maraval said mildly.

If it were only that, Oriana wouldn't have been so flustered by Silva's attempt to drag her off. She had practice ridding herself of overly insistent males. "So I've heard," she mumbled.

"Yes. He tried to entangle Lady Isabel some years ago," Maraval continued as they drew closer to the seats where the matrons sat. "As I'm a close friend of her father's, I took steps to make certain

Isabel didn't fall into his clutches. Although I doubt she would have if left to her own devices. Isabel has always been a clever girl."

Oriana nodded. Maraval hadn't visited the Amaral household while she'd been in residence, but Isabel's father rarely came into the city. Amaral preferred his quiet house in the country to his wife's company.

"Unfortunately, I've never gotten along with Lady Amaral," Maraval added, "but I went to speak with her Sunday after Mass."

Oh, dear. They had reached her chair, and Oriana nodded to him and sank down into her previous spot. She wasn't surprised when Maraval sat next to her. "I didn't know that, sir."

Maraval settled his gloved hands on his knees. "Amaral has been ill, and can't travel here at the moment, but he believes his wife is hiding the truth from him." He sighed heavily, his features lined with worry. "I'm afraid that rumors are beginning to circulate concerning Isabel's absence. That Mr. Efisio jilted his betrothed is shocking enough in itself, but that Isabel may have, in turn, jilted him for someone else is far more sensational. I have managed to suppress any further mention of her name in the papers so far, but if she doesn't reappear soon, the talk might be irreversibly damaging to her reputation."

Ah, Maraval believed she knew where Isabel was. She did, but she wasn't going to tell this man that. Oriana closed her eyes briefly. "I haven't seen Lady Isabel since Thursday night, sir. If she was involved with another man, I know nothing of it."

"If you can think of anything that will help me find her, I would appreciate your help." Maraval dug a card out of his jacket pocket and handed it to her. It gave the address of the Ministry of Culture in the old Bishop's Palace. "Please come to my office if you remember anything. Her father is very worried."

Oriana slid the card into her handbag. At least Isabel's father was showing concern over his daughter's absence. "I will, sir."

"Miss Paredes?" Duilio Ferreira spoke at her shoulder, startling her.

Oriana craned her neck to glance up at him. "Yes, sir?"

"I must apologize for stealing you away from your conversation," Mr. Ferreira said, "but I'm afraid my mother has decided she'd like to go home. She's waiting in the carriage."

Oriana picked up Lady Ferreira's shawl and thanked Maraval, who rose along with her. Mr. Ferreira nodded to him, and then led Oriana from the ballroom.

When they were on the stairwell that led down to the ground floor, Oriana quietly asked, "Is your mother on her way home?"

"Yes," he said. "Gustavo and Tomas will get her there safely. What did Maraval want?"

"He rescued me from Silva," she admitted, "but he did want to know if I could tell him where Isabel is. He's a friend of her father's. Are we late?"

"We have a couple of minutes to spare," he said, showing her his watch as they reached the bottom of the stairwell. "Shall we?"

Oriana laid her fingers on his sleeve. She hadn't thought to ask before how he knew where to find the library in this house. Perhaps he'd broken in to it at some point. The very thought made her smile.

They walked down the hallway, and he opened the door onto a library far larger than his own. The walls held bookshelves with glass doors—some locked—but otherwise there was no resemblance to the Ferreira library. This room was tastelessly decorated with garishly overdone floral wallpaper in pinks and reds. Burgundy couches and chairs surrounded a huge Persian rug in the same shades as the loud wallpaper. Oriana stepped over the threshold into the room, relieved to see it was unoccupied. Fortunately, the gaslights were turned up.

"This will look improper if we're caught here," Mr. Ferreira said, closing the door behind them. He stalked across the room to check behind the couches, perhaps expecting small children there.

"Especially after I had to quash some gossip that you're my mistress. So we'd best not get caught."

Oriana felt heat rising through her body. "Who said that?"

"Pimental," Mr. Ferreira said without hesitation. "I have something on him, though, which will keep him from spreading lies about you."

Good news, although she would rather people not talk about her at all. Especially in a way that might harm the Ferreira family. "What do you have on him?"

"Are you encouraging me to gossip, Miss Paredes?" He looked offended when he said those words, but his eyes laughed.

"It would be best to save the gossip for later."

Oriana spun about at that voice. She pressed a hand against her chest to quell the pounding of her heart.

A woman stood in the far corner of the room.

She wasn't hidden. Mr. Ferreira could not have missed her standing there. For that matter, Oriana had looked too. *Right in that spot.* How was that possible?

The woman walked toward them, her fine dress rustling with the movement. She had inky hair and fair skin that would have rivaled Isabel's, although she was much older, perhaps in her forties. Her eyes were a clear, pale gray or blue, striking with her dark lashes and brows. "You've come to see me, Miss Paredes," the woman said, "but who is your companion?"

Oriana shot a glance at Mr. Ferreira, who nodded. She turned back to the elegant woman. Was this Nela's mysterious Lady? How could she determine that? "Mr. Ferreira is my employer. I am his mother's companion. How did you get in here?"

The woman turned her attention on Mr. Ferreira. "*Duilio* Ferreira? I met Alessio back in Coimbra, years and years ago."

Apparently her question was going to go unanswered.

"I was not," the woman added, "one of his lovers."

Mr. Ferreira hid a smile behind one hand. Oriana couldn't see his mouth, but his eyes were laughing again. He managed a polite nod, but didn't respond to the woman's announcement otherwise.

The woman settled on one of the wine-colored couches, apparently unconcerned about rumpling her skirts. Her dress seemed to fade into the couch itself. "Mr. Ferreira, you spoke with one of my associates this afternoon, Inspector Gaspar. I am also curious to know why Mata is after you."

He ran one white-gloved hand casually along the top of the couch. "So, you're with the Special Police as well?"

Oriana held her breath. What sort of trap had she led him into?

"Let me be clear, Mr. Ferreira," the Lady said. "My team is here to investigate the Special Police, both abuses of authority by some officers and misuse of them by . . . well, that's one of the things we're trying to uncover. Someone other than the prince has been using members of the Special Police to his own ends. That must be stopped."

Oriana cast a quick glance at Mr. Ferreira. He didn't seem too surprised by those claims.

"Mata is, essentially, an assassin," she went on, "working within the ranks of the Special Police. We want to determine who's pulling his strings. For what it's worth, we have evidence that he was paid to kill your brother."

Mr. Ferreira's jaw clenched, but his face didn't relay any emotion. "Why would you think someone assassinated my brother? He died during a duel."

The woman shook her head with a sigh and turned back to Oriana. "Miss Paredes, will you come sit across from me? I don't think he's going to sit until you do, and I'm tired of looking up at him."

A valid point. Oriana settled in a chair across from the Lady, her handbag in her lap. With a quick scowl, Mr. Ferreira sat in the chair next to hers.

"It took him three tries to kill your brother," the Lady said, smoothing her wine-colored skirts. "We confiscated letters from Mata to a counterpart in Southern Portugal, detailing his difficulties with Alessio Ferreira. I suspect his seer's blood allowed Alessio to escape the first two attempts unharmed, just as yours allowed you to escape last night."

Oriana licked her lips and dared to look over at Mr. Ferreira. He shrugged apologetically, and without words she knew the Lady was right. Duilio Ferreira was a *seer.* Like his uncle Paolo Silva and his brother Alessio.

Oh, dear. She'd been rather insulting about seers, hadn't she? Now she wished she could take her words back. Had she offended him? Her eyes fell to the handbag in her lap.

"Why kill Alessio?" Mr. Ferreira asked.

"We don't know who wanted him out of the way, and unfortunately, Mata didn't reveal that in his letters. If we can catch him, we have a team who specializes in extracting information, who could get out of him whatever he *does* know."

Mr. Ferreira's face hardened. "Torture?"

The Lady laughed. "Not at all. They wouldn't lay a hand on him. But he will answer their questions."

Oriana leaned closer to him. "I could do that," she whispered. "I could coax answers out of a human if I had to."

His brows rose but he said nothing.

"So, what did you do, Mr. Ferreira," the Lady asked, "that would cause this group such dismay that they would send their assassin after you?"

He gestured toward Oriana's bag. "This might be a good time to show her the sketch."

He didn't look too upset, at least. Oriana opened her handbag, withdrew the sketch of the table, and unfolded it. She handed it to the Lady, who took it with careful fingers. "Are you a witch?"

"Not at all," the Lady said. "I study witchcraft but am not a practitioner." She turned the sketch about to read the Latin inscription. "Where did you find this? Nela wouldn't tell me, which makes me suspect this is a matter of import to your people."

How much was she willing to trust this woman? Oriana glanced over at Mr. Ferreira again, wondering how much she should reveal.

"Whatever you think is appropriate," he said, as if he'd read her thoughts.

He was letting her make the call, then, of whether or not to trust this unknown person. Oriana pressed her lips together, weighing the odds in the silence of the room. "It was in *The City Under the Sea*," she finally said. "It was inscribed on a table. My hands were tied to it."

"The place with the floating houses?" the Lady asked. "Where was this table?"

"Inside the replica of the Amaral house," Oriana said. She hadn't thought it would be difficult to talk about it, but it wasn't much easier this time than it was the last. "Isabel and I were both there, tied to chairs, our hands lying on the table. When the water came in, Isabel drowned." Oriana swallowed. "Then that side of the table lit up, those words inscribed in it."

"It's a scripture," Mr. Ferreira supplied. "*However, as for me and my house we will follow the Lord.*" When Oriana cast a quizzical glance at him, he said. "I apologize, Miss Paredes. My cousin recognized it, but I forgot to tell you."

Oriana didn't know if that made any difference, as the words still didn't make sense of what had happened. "I can't recall what the letters in the inner ring were. They were in a strange script that I didn't recognize. And I have no idea about the center. Do you know what this is?"

"The side of the table that the other young lady was touching, that side lit up when she died. Do I understand that correctly?"

Oriana nodded.

"I can shine some light on this, Miss Paredes," the Lady said, "but it doesn't make much sense." She laid the sketch on her knees and touched her fingers to the edge, a visual echo of Isabel's fingers lying on the edge of the table. "I have wondered, although admittedly not much, why someone would waste all that money building a silly collection of houses that would eventually rot away."

Oriana had to agree. "Is this a spell to keep them afloat?"

"I don't believe so. The fact that half the inscription lit when this girl died tells me we're dealing with necromancy. You were meant to die as well, I assume. You said this was a table. What was it made of?"

Well, Nela had been correct about hunting a necromancer. That didn't make Oriana feel any better. "It was wood," she answered. "I think the letters were inlaid in some kind of metal."

"Silver and gold are the most common for this sort of work," the Lady said. "The best for controlling magic. I suspect we'll find that the inner ring contained some manner of runic inscription, as necromancers seem to prefer that for their handiwork. This center design is nothing I've ever seen, though, and that's saying something." She pursed her lips and turned the sketch around again. "The main problem I'm having with this is that there's no apparent *recipient*. One of the basic tenets of necromancy requires that the recipient take the victim's life force at the moment of death. In essence, your tale makes this seem like the recipient is a table. There wouldn't be much point to that unless the table was actively using that power. Now, there are rare devices that can focus power or carry out a specific action, but this is . . . a table."

Oriana felt tears stinging at her eyes. "You're saying that Isabel died for nothing?"

"No," the Lady said. "I'm saying that I haven't figured this out yet. No one is going to go to this much trouble, to kill a girl, without a reason."

"It's not just one girl," Mr. Ferreira said, leaning closer to hand Oriana a fine linen handkerchief. She wiped her cheeks with it while he spoke. "We have reason to believe that each replica has a pair of victims in it, not all female. All servants who'd worked at the house replicated. Most were never reported missing. Some had allegedly gone home to the countryside or found other positions, but when the police traced them they found false trails."

The Lady sat back, her eyes narrowing. "Servants who worked at the corresponding house?" She turned to Oriana. "You and this Isabel worked at that house?"

Oriana nodded mutely. She didn't see a need to correct the Lady's misconception.

The Lady closed her eyes for a moment, as if mentally organizing what she knew. "I think what we have here is a mixture of necromancy and imitative magic, a rather unusual combination, but not unheard of."

"Imitative magic?" Mr. Ferreira leaned closer. "Is that like voodoo?"

The Lady looked up. "Have you run across voodoo before, Mr. Ferreira?"

"In Paris, I'm afraid."

"I see. We'll have to chat about that one day," she said. "In the instance that one item is used to represent another related item, yes. In this case, I suspect the houses and the people *in* them represent the will of that family. That's why the victims were chosen from among servants who worked in those houses—it gives them a spiritual tie to that house and that family. As they're using aristocratic households, I would suspect this installment, *The City Under the Sea*, is a symbolic representation of the entire aristocracy. Why they're claiming they serve the Lord, I can't fathom."

Oriana covered her face with her hands. She'd heard enough of this academic discussion of Isabel's death. She didn't care how they were doing this or why. She just wanted to know how to stop them.

Mr. Ferreira's hand touched Oriana's elbow, a scrap of reassurance. Oriana dropped her hands to her lap again, resolved to be calm.

"Are you insinuating that the Church is involved?" he asked the Lady.

She shook her head, earrings glittering with the movement. "Not at all, Mr. Ferreira. It's not their style, despite the use of a scripture. It's easy to appropriate words." She laid her arm across the back of the couch again. "And before you ask, it's not the Freemasons either. Neither group is forgiving about necromancy."

Oriana lifted her head and took a deep breath. "Then who? Who's doing this?"

The Lady continued to gaze at Mr. Ferreira, her intense regard belying her casual posture. "Is this what you're investigating? These houses? Miguel said you wouldn't tell him."

"I'm not sure whom to trust," Mr. Ferreira said stiffly.

"Miguel has been following Mata for days," the Lady said in patient tones. "This afternoon he let Mata get away because he was concerned you might not get out of that apartment alive. He was about to go up after you when you jumped from the window."

He jumped from a window? Oriana glanced at Mr. Ferreira's face. He was tense, frustrated. She could see that in the set of his shoulders. She didn't know which of the two of them had heard more unsettling news tonight.

"Yes, this is what we're looking into," Mr. Ferreira finally said, pointing to the sketch. "The regular police started investigating a few weeks ago. When they asked for permission to pull up one of the houses and open it, they were told to shut down the investigation."

"By whom?" the Lady asked.

"We don't know what level it came from. Captain Santiago directed the request to the Ministry of Culture, but there's no telling how many eyes saw that request before the order was handed down."

The Lady nodded slowly. "And if I went to Maraval and asked, he would probably say the paper had never gotten as far as his desk." Oriana had no idea how many people worked in the Ministry of

Culture, but any one of them could have alerted the killers to the request. "I'll ask anyway. I studied with him when I was younger," the Lady added. "He's familiar with this type of magic. If nothing else he can tell me who in the city might be able to put together a set of spells of this intricacy."

"Do you not know?" Oriana asked.

"I've been abroad for much of the past three years, Miss Paredes. Witches come and go, particularly where the . . ."

The latch on the library door clicked and began to turn.

"Go stand against the wall," the Lady ordered, pointing. "Stay behind me."

Mr. Ferreira grabbed Oriana's hand and hauled her out of her chair before she could protest. She barely managed to grab the sketch off the table with her free hand before he dragged her back toward the wall with him. The Lady went to stand behind the couch, one hand lying on its back, as the library door swung open, and a silver-haired man walked in, a young girl clutching his arm.

It was Paolo Silva.

CHAPTER 20

Duilio's whole body tensed when he saw young Constancia Carvalho being squired about on Silva's arm. He wanted to storm over there and plant the man a facer. The old lecher had a reputation for seducing young women that had never quite made sense to Duilio. Silva simply wasn't that handsome, and while he might be influential, it was usually older women who found power attractive, not girls of barely seventeen, like the one on his arm now.

Silva gave the library door a gentle push, not obvious enough to alert the girl she was closed in. It would be scandalous if the girl was caught here alone with Silva, even if the man *was* old enough to be her grandfather.

Miss Carvalho pointed at one of the shelves, fortunately not too near where Duilio stood, Miss Paredes still as stone beside him. It was clear that whatever the Lady was doing *worked*. Miss Carvalho showed no sign of seeing them there. *How fascinating.*

"I think the book is on that shelf," the girl said brightly, pointing. "Father keeps the keys with him, though."

"I only wanted to see the cover, my girl." Silva started in their direction.

Duilio heard a soft intake of breath from Miss Paredes. He grabbed her hand to reassure her. Silva didn't pose a true threat to them right now. Even if the man saw them in the library, his presence here was no less questionable than theirs. And Duilio wanted to know what the man was up to. The Lady moved silently to stand directly between them and Silva.

Silva peered into one of the bookshelves with locked glass doors. Duilio doubted Miss Carvalho could see Silva's right hand fiddling with the lock. Apparently skill with a skeleton key ran in the family. A muted click sounded, and Silva pronounced, "Oh, look. Your father's left it unlocked, my girl." He opened the door and extracted one leather-bound volume. "It is lovely."

"Father never leaves the doors unlocked," Miss Carvalho protested, sounding panicked.

Duilio felt sorry for the girl. She wasn't the brightest of the Carvalho daughters to begin with. Newly out in society and exuberant over her birthday ball, she must have made an easy target. The girl wrung her hands together, then raised one as if beseeching Silva to return to her side. "I said I would show it to you, but you can't look inside. Father would be livid."

"Your father's a friend of mine," Silva told her. "He won't mind."

Miss Carvalho chewed at her lower lip. She cast a glance back at the door, her eyes widening as she apparently realized for the first time it was closed. She knew she was in trouble. "Please . . ." she began, her voice fading to a whisper.

It was actually clever of Silva, Duilio thought. *Cruel, but clever.* For any young, unmarried girl to be caught alone with a man would be scandalous. Silva could have crept into the library on his own, but this way, if he got caught he could hold the girl's reputation hostage in order to get away unscathed. Surely Carvalho would protect his daughter before his books.

The Lady turned slowly to face them. She pointed at Duilio and indicated the chair farther from where Silva stood flipping through his confiscated book, then gestured for Miss Paredes to approach her. Duilio understood—his mere presence would protect young Miss Carvalho's reputation. He glanced at Miss Paredes and nodded. She let go of his hand and walked a few steps until she stood right at the Lady's side.

Duilio walked softly around the back of the couch to the chair the Lady had pointed out. The fabric made a soft whoosh when he sat, not loud enough to alert Silva, though. The man continued to flip through the book's pages.

Duilio waited. The Lady must be keeping him in reserve.

The library door opened a second time. Duilio turned his head and saw it was the eldest of the daughters, Genoveva—the one Carvalho wanted to palm off on him. Lovely in an elegant cream-colored gown, she seemed more mature than her twenty-one years. Her brown eyes flicked between her sister and Silva, and she regally extended one hand. "Come here, Constancia."

The younger sister darted over to her, but Silva didn't look up from the book. "Miss Carvalho, how will you explain where your young sister has been for the past quarter hour?"

The elder Miss Carvalho lifted her chin. "No one need know she was here, Mr. Silva."

"She disappeared from her birthday ball with a man," he said. "I, for one, would consider that a sign of overeagerness."

Genoveva strode over to where he stood, leaving the younger girl cowering by the library door. "You will not slander my sister," she hissed.

Silva's eyes rose to meet hers, and then he made a show of giving her a thorough appraisal. "I will do whatever I want, Miss Carvalho. Are you offering yourself in her place?"

"She's been in the ladies' retiring room," Miss Genoveva said coolly. "She and I were returning to the ballroom when we looked in the library and saw you pawing through my father's books." She held out one hand, clearly expecting him to place the book in it.

Silva didn't. "Two guests saw her come in here with me, Miss Carvalho. I made sure of that. So what will *you* give me to keep my mouth shut?"

Her nostrils flared. For the first time Duilio thought that if she hadn't fallen in love with Alessio long ago, an arranged marriage between them might have worked out after all. Genoveva Carvalho had nerve. Duilio glanced over at the Lady and nodded . . . and the Lady and Miss Paredes both disappeared from his view, as quick as the blink of an eye. He hadn't expected that.

Duilio heard a quickly stifled squeak from near the door. Evidently Miss Constancia had seen *him*, even if the other two inhabitants of the room hadn't yet. In as light a tone as he could manage in his current irritated state, Duilio said, "None of this is necessary, you know."

Miss Genoveva shrieked and spun about to stare at him wide-eyed. She pressed one gloved hand to her bosom. Silva chose not to acknowledge Duilio at all.

Duilio put on his blandest smile. "I've been here the entire time, Miss Genoveva. I sent my mother home from the dancing, you know, and I was going to meet with Pimental to chat later, only I came in here to find the newspaper and I must have fallen asleep. I guess I blend into the chair." He laughed as if he found himself amusing, then rose. "Whatever is that book you're reading, old man? It must be fascinating."

Silva snapped the book shut and set it back on the shelf. "I doubt that, in your drink-addled state, you would understand a word of it, pup. Likely not if you were sober either."

Ah, those rare chances to speak with Silva face-to-face. Duilio ignored the insult and turned to Miss Genoveva. "Isn't Miss Constancia missing her own ball? Nice of her to show him the library, but I expect she wants to get back to the dancing and"—he waved one hand in a vague circle—"whatever things, I suppose, that girls do."

Miss Genoveva gazed at him for a moment, her eyes uncertain. Then she seemed to snap back to attention. "Yes, of course."

Without a further word, she strode across the room, grabbed her younger sister's hand, and dragged the girl out of the library.

"You *are* inconvenient," Silva said acidly, dropping his pretense of civility. "Where were you hiding, pup? Under the couch?"

Duilio kept his eyes on Silva, praying he couldn't see either of the two female occupants of the room. Not that he thought Miss Paredes couldn't deal with Silva. He would simply rather avoid that confrontation. "I was there the whole time," he said. "Are your eyes going bad?"

Silva crossed his arms over his chest, lips pressed together in an angry line. "I don't know what you're trying to achieve here, pup, but forget it."

"You know what I want," Duilio reminded him. The pelt was all he'd ever wanted from this man.

"And I've told you I don't have it," Silva said. "I've never laid a finger on the thing."

That was what Silva *always* said. The one thing that made Duilio think there might be truth in those words was that the man had never asked him for a ransom. "Tell me about Mata," Duilio suggested. "What's he after this time?"

Silva laughed aloud. "Mata? You think *I'm* giving him orders? You don't understand what's going on at all, do you? Playing policeman again—I should have known. What a waste! If all that money had come to me instead, as it should have, I wouldn't be spending my time hunting for missing servants."

Duilio gazed at Silva wide-eyed, trying very hard to look stupid. The man clearly knew *something* about Mata. There was no telling what else he knew. "Missing servants?"

Silva tilted his head. "How *did* you find Miss Paredes first? I planned to have her in my quiver of arrows, so to speak. But, alas, now she's warming your bed, when I would have been using her as bait."

He hoped Miss Paredes wouldn't be offended, but he didn't intend to argue with Silva about that insult to her. "Bait?"

Silva patted him on the shoulder in a fatherly fashion. Duilio was hard-pressed not to sweep the man's hand aside. He did his best to ignore it.

"You see, pup," Silva said, "I don't know exactly what the Open Hand is doing out there, but when she escaped them, your fishling lover changed the balance of prophecy. The prophecy that Fabricio is destined to die at the hands of the sea folk? Every day that prophecy is growing stronger and stronger." Silva smiled with false affection, his hand heavy on Duilio's shoulder. "So, keep in mind that while she's powdering your sainted mother's cheeks and handing her fans, your little fishling is planning to kill your lawful ruler. That makes you treasonous just for harboring her in your house."

Silva dropped his intrusive grasp and strolled past him toward the door.

The Open Hand? Duilio hoped nothing showed on his face. He clenched his hands behind his back. Silva had just spilled far more information than he'd expected, which meant at best it was poisoned. It was more likely all false.

"By the by, I wasn't going to seduce the little one," Silva said as he went. "Too bland for my tastes. But the older girl might prove interesting. A bit of fire in that one." He paused at the door to see if Duilio was attending, then added, "Or perhaps I'll wait until *after* you marry her." With dramatic grace worthy of the theater, Silva swept out of the library.

Duilio closed his eyes. He could not begin to express how much he *hated* talking to that man. He took a couple of calming breaths, afraid that if he spoke to anyone too soon he would bark at them. Then he turned back to look for the two women who'd heard every word of that exchange. They still stood next to the couch, less than ten feet away.

Miss Paredes regarded him with wide, haunted eyes. "It's not true," she said softly.

"I know," he said, although he didn't know anything of the sort. She could be an assassin. It *was* possible, but the very fact that Silva asserted it made Duilio think it unlikely. If she'd posed a direct threat to his prince, Silva would never have let her go. "I take everything he says with a great deal of skepticism."

Miss Paredes looked relieved, her shoulders losing their tightness.

"Well, I found that informative," the Lady said, apparently unfazed by all the distractions of Silva's conversation. "Let's have a look at that book."

Duilio located the book Silva had set back on the shelf. It stuck out from the others just enough that he could readily spot it. He pulled it out, noting that no title appeared on the spine.

"Please hand it to me," the Lady said. "Carvalho may have given me permission to use his library, but he didn't extend that to you, Mr. Ferreira."

He had no way to verify that, so he didn't see any point in arguing. Duilio handed it over.

She opened it out and flipped through a few pages in the center. Then she shook her head. "I wonder how many times Silva's managed to get into this house. I suspect he's stealing most of his better prophecies. I don't know if you're aware, but Silva isn't a particularly strong seer. Stronger than you, Mr. Ferreira, but nothing like Abreu or Gardineiro." She turned the book so that Duilio could see the handwritten pages. "Whose prophecies are written in this volume. This belongs to the city's Freemasons and is not for public consumption—the reason Carvalho keeps it locked away. I will suggest a more secure arrangement for the future."

Miss Paredes had come closer, simply listening. Duilio hoped she was keeping track. It would give him the luxury of having someone with whom to discuss this bewildering evening. He turned back to the Lady. "Are you a member of the Freemasons?"

The Freemasons sought enlightenment in all things, and someone who studied the practice of witchcraft in the abstract might fit well into their ranks. But they didn't have female members here, even if they did in France and in the Americas.

"No," she said. "Carvalho is my contact, should I need information from them, but I am not a part of any of their organizations."

That was a nicely unequivocal statement. "What about the Open Hand? Who are they?"

"A secret society?" the Lady said musingly. "So far we've identified five officers within the Special Police who seem to be members of this Open Hand, Mata among them. There have to be others outside the Special Police, but we don't know yet who they are. At this point, we don't know exactly what their goal is, either."

Not very helpful. All Special Police officers bore the sigil of an open hand on their caps, a symbol modeled after a stone carving on the gate of the palace itself. It seemed only logical that this group might be found within their ranks.

"I find it interesting that your uncle handed that name to you on a platter," she added.

Ah, the Lady was aware of his relationship with the man. Duilio suspected she'd chosen those words to inform him of that. It increased the likelihood that she actually had known Alessio. "I did too," he said. "I've never heard that name before tonight."

"But he has," she pointed out. "Silva is like a spider, Mr. Ferreira, and his web touches on everything. He has friends everywhere, if you can call them friends. I suspect most of them tolerate him because he's pulling their strings; no more."

That was Silva's special talent: twisting people's words and intentions, provoking them to distrust one another. Getting them to dance to *his* tune. It was gratifying to hear someone else say it aloud. "So he wanted to assure the police heard that name, through me," Duilio surmised. "Why would he use Miss Paredes as bait?"

The Lady's pale eyes flicked toward her. "Most practitioners of witchcraft are very superstitious, Mr. Ferreira. A spell of this complexity—and I suspect there's much more of it than what appears on the surface of that table—it does not require a specific victim, save for the apparent fact that they lived in that house. However, if the witch involved wants to go back and fix this spell, fix the fact that one of the intended victims escaped, they will prefer strongly to recover the original victim."

Miss Paredes' eyes lowered to the carpet.

"So this Open Hand will be looking for her," Duilio said, "to try again."

"It's very likely." The Lady turned to Miss Paredes. "I would keep my distance from the Special Police, Miss Paredes, or you might be rejoining the other maid you mentioned in that house. I want you to appreciate the danger you stand in."

Miss Paredes' hands were shaking now. "Not a maid, Lady. It was Isabel Amaral, my mistress. *She* died there."

For the first time, the Lady appeared disconcerted. "I thought you said they were servants."

"Until last Thursday night," Duilio said, sparing Miss Paredes from repeating it. "Lady Isabel was planning on eloping, and decided that she and Miss Paredes should dress as housemaids to escape notice."

"Whose idea was that?" the Lady asked.

"She seemed to have come up with it on her own," Miss Paredes offered hesitantly.

"I don't trust anything that convenient," the Lady said. "If I understand correctly, they've chosen dozens of victims already, and managed to cover their tracks well enough that the police didn't catch on. Miss Paredes, you were the one person in the Amaral household not likely to die if put in the water, yet they chose you, a sereia? Does that not strike you as an unlikely twist of fate? It makes me suspect you were there intentionally."

Miss Paredes looked as haunted as she had when Silva implied she was an assassin. "I am *not* in league with them."

The Lady laid a gloved hand on Miss Paredes' arm. "I do not

imply that. But you and your mistress may have been chosen because someone within the organization wants to sabotage whatever the Open Hand is trying to achieve."

"My knife," Miss Paredes whispered, her eyes lifting to his. "They didn't take my knife. I had it with me, but whoever tied me to that chair didn't take it."

Duilio recalled her mentioning the knife, but before this moment he'd assumed it was a hurried oversight. He could tell she'd already worked her way to the conclusion: if she'd been put there to sabotage the spell, then Isabel had been selected intentionally merely to put *Oriana Paredes* in the desired situation. He set a hand under her elbow to support her. "We don't know what's true at this point, Miss Paredes."

She nodded jerkily. He hadn't driven that demon out of her mind, he could tell.

The Lady glanced across the library, and Duilio turned to see Inspector Gaspar standing in the doorway. Duilio nodded to the man but didn't bother with introductions.

"Are you ready to go?" the inspector asked the Lady.

"Actually," she said, "I need to stay a while longer and speak to Carvalho about his security. Could you see these two home safely and then return for me?"

The inspector nodded and stepped inside the library to wait.

Miss Paredes handed the sketch to the Lady. "Perhaps it will help."

"We'll talk again," the Lady said, tucking the folded paper into a handbag Duilio hadn't noted before. "I think we've all learned enough for one night."

Duilio mentally agreed to that. If they weren't running short on time, he would like to mull this over for a week or two. Possibly three.

Still looking shaken, Miss Paredes took his mother's shawl and settled it around her own shoulders. "I'm ready."

CHAPTER 21

Walking might not be the fashionable choice, but it was faster than sending for the carriage and waiting for it to come back. So she and Mr. Ferreira slipped out the servants' door in the back and walked down the street in silence, the unknown African man following them at a distance. Oriana hadn't caught who he was, although he was likely one of the Lady's *special* associates. Mr. Ferreira seemed inclined to trust him. For now that was enough for her.

Oriana drew the shawl up over her head to cover her hair. It was chilly out, although not nearly so much as this time last week. Her thoughts swirled. She didn't think she would sleep at all tonight, despite feeling worn to the bone.

Until tonight, she'd believed that ending up in that house with Isabel had been an accident. Not that those who put them there were unaware of their actions, but that the selection of Isabel Amaral and Oriana Paredes as victims had been an accident. Hearing that her placement there might have been intentional—*that hurt.* That Isabel had been killed merely for being with her. For befriending her.

If true, it also implied that the saboteur was aware of Oriana's identity. The killer hadn't been, although he might have guessed by now how she'd escaped. Would the killer even know that something was missing from the artwork yet? *How* would he know that?

And Silva, that . . . *bottom-feeder.* She hadn't believed for a moment that his rescue of her had been beneficent. But he clearly had ugly designs within designs. If that was what one used a seer's gift for, it was a crime.

The Lady had said it very clearly, though. Silva was a seer, not a particularly strong one, *but stronger than Mr. Ferreira.* The moon was almost full, allowing Oriana to see Mr. Ferreira's face. He was watching the pedestrians on the street. Not overtly, but she could tell from the way his eyes flicked from group to group, evaluating the danger each posed.

"I owe you an apology," she told him.

He didn't look her way, eyes still busy. "Why do you think that?"

"Because of what I said about seers being frauds."

He laughed softly. "No offense taken, Miss Paredes."

A carriage rattled by and she tensed, unable to quell the irrational fear that someone would jump out and grab her. It was foolish. She knew that.

Mr. Ferreira took her hand and laid it on his sleeve. "We will get home safely, Miss Paredes. That's about all my gift's good for, but it does tell me that."

Her tension slipped away like water rolling past. She wouldn't have believed those words if they'd come from Silva, seer or not. But she trusted Duilio Ferreira. They walked on for a moment in silence, and then she said, "So, you and Miss Carvalho are betrothed?"

"No, she and I are *not* betrothed," he said firmly. "Her father suggested that it would be a good match, but I refused his proposition. I wonder how Silva learned about it."

A good question. "She's a nice girl, although she and Isabel didn't associate much."

It was prying, she knew. She didn't have any business asking into his personal plans.

"Yes, Genoveva Carvalho is a perfectly nice young lady. When she was her young sister's age or so, she fell head over heels in love with Alessio. He never led her on. He was always very clear with women that he had no intention to marry, ever. But he was friendly to her, and that was enough. I would hate to marry a woman for whom I'm the second choice."

Like Pia, Oriana thought. Pia would have been Mr. Efisio's second choice. Oriana wholeheartedly agreed with the girl's decision to cut her ties with him. They stopped for a carriage to cross Clérigos Street, and then continued on. "Why did your brother not intend to marry?"

Mr. Ferreira let out a long breath, sounding almost vexed. "His scruples. He didn't believe he could be faithful to a wife and refused to take vows he couldn't uphold."

"Is that what he and your father argued over so much?" Pressuring a young man to marry and produce a legitimate heir was common in aristocratic families.

"They argued over everything possible, Miss Paredes. They would argue over whether the color of an invitation card was ivory or bone," he said with a sigh. "Alessio adored our mother, and it infuriated him that Father was unfaithful to her. Alessio took every opportunity to fling that in his face. Father actually threw him out of the house a few years ago. It took the theft of my mother's pelt to get them to work together on anything."

Oriana pressed her lips together. She had bickered endlessly with her own father. It didn't mean she hadn't adored him. But she'd always thought she knew better than he did, particularly where her younger sister was concerned. It had taken her years on her own to realize how often she'd been wrong as a girl.

She could see the front gate of the Ferreira house now, a reassuring sight, but in the moonlight the house looked Gothic, its dark stone haunted by the memories of angry quarrels and bitterness. "Your mother doesn't mention that about your father—that he was unfaithful."

"No," he said, "her people expect males to be promiscuous. She found it more troublesome that he lied about it and treated women like they were . . . I don't know . . . *whores.* Throw some money at them and his responsibility ends there. Just like his father before him."

Oriana felt the corners of her lips lifting. He definitely wouldn't have said *that* to Genoveva Carvalho. His irritated tone hinted that the lying must have irked him as well. And his grandfather's actions had to be part of what made Silva such a twisted man. "Do you have any other siblings?" she asked cautiously. "Like Silva, I mean?"

He paused at the gate before his house. "There's a reason I didn't refute Silva's claims about the nature of our relationship, Miss Paredes, despite the fact that I did so earlier when speaking to Rodrigo Pimental. Any scrap of information Silva picks up, he'll twist into a weapon. He has, in the past, hinted that I have two bastard brothers. He says he kept a closer eye on our father than Mother did. I have no way to know if it's true. But he used that to distract me, which was all he was after, I suspect."

Somehow she didn't think another member of the Ferreira family would be a bad thing. "Could it be true?"

"Of course it could," he said with a sigh.

He swung the gate open, and Oriana saw that Cardenas already stood in the doorway, as if he'd been waiting for them. Oriana went up the flagstone walkway to the house. He stopped at the front door of the house, nodded in the direction of their distant escort, and then led her inside while Cardenas locked up behind them. They silently made their way up the stairs, but when she stopped at her own door, he paused, laying one hand on her arm.

Oriana turned back to look at him in the glow of the gaslight at the head of the hallway. She couldn't read the expression on his features. He did look tired now, perhaps because he no longer needed to keep up the pretense. He opened his mouth to speak and then apparently thought better of it. She wanted to hear it, she realized, whatever it was he had to say. "Mr. Ferreira?"

He tugged off his gloves and brusquely said, "It isn't your fault."

She found herself staring at his patent shoes, surprised by his cross tone. "I . . ."

His fingers lifted her chin, forcing her to look up at him. "You survived," he said, speaking more gently now. "That doesn't make you complicit. You are not responsible for Isabel's death."

"If they wanted me," she said, "then Isabel—"

"No," he interrupted. "It doesn't matter *why* she ended up there. Neither of you deserved to die. You were both victims that night. You can't blame yourself."

She *could*. If she'd never come to Northern Portugal, Isabel wouldn't be dead. If she'd not taken a job in Isabel's home, if she'd refused to go with Isabel to Paris, if she had chosen . . . well, there were a thousand other paths her life could have taken, most of which wouldn't have tied Isabel Amaral's fate to hers. Life would be easier if she knew all the ramifications of each choice before she made it, but it seemed she had to make each one blind. And apparently Mr. Ferreira's gift hadn't made his life proof against that, either. On the other hand, they had gotten back to the house safely, as he'd promised.

His fingers still cupped her chin, forcing him to stand close. She breathed in and caught that scent he had, the smell she'd mistaken for cologne before. How long had she been standing there silent? His warm eyes weren't on hers any longer, fixed on her lips instead.

Footsteps on the stairwell made her jerk away, and Mr. Ferreira stepped back. Cardenas came up onto the landing only a second later, the keys to the house dangling in his hand. He nodded blandly and bid them both a good evening, no reproach in his expression. Oriana felt it anyway. "Good night, Cardenas," she answered quickly. "And to you too, Mr. Ferreira."

Mr. Ferreira tipped his head toward her. "Miss Paredes, try to get some sleep."

Oriana slipped inside her bedroom without answering. Once

she'd closed the door, she pressed her warm cheek against the wood. What had she been thinking?

She'd had to fend off enough attempts at seduction in the past two years. Duilio Ferreira had been considering kissing her. She was almost certain of that. Almost.

And she had been about to let him.

CHAPTER 22

FRIDAY, 3 OCTOBER 1902

Duilio liked to believe that he made his own destiny. He walked along Clérigos Street, heading toward Joaquim's office in Massarelos, frustrated at the tangle his mind was in. He suspected that Inspector Gaspar was somewhere nearby. He had that feeling of being watched again, but his sense of it was benign, so he doubted it was the man who'd murdered Alessio, Donato Mata. He had his favorite revolver clipped to his waistband, though, just in case.

At the moment, though, his main worry was *himself.* When he'd first laid eyes on Oriana Paredes, he'd felt she would be a pivotal factor in his life. Otherwise he might not have done any more than glance at her that spring day on the banks of the Douro. Instead he had watched her, bribed servants to learn her name, and sought her out when Isabel Amaral disappeared. He'd brought her into his household because she was a witness who might have valuable information, but also because he simply wanted her safe.

He liked her. He enjoyed talking to her. She was . . . challenging.

Last night he'd nearly kissed her. He had stood there in the hallway, his fingers cradling her chin, and the desire to kiss her—no, in all honesty, the desire to bed her—had almost overwhelmed his good sense. Part of that was simply the stress of the previous few days. Sex would have been a release, more than just literally. But somewhere in his mind had been a wish to simply lie in his bed with her afterward and discuss the confusing evening they'd had.

He *could* ask her to become his mistress, but he'd meant what he'd said to Rodrigo Pimental. He would never demean her that way. Beyond the impropriety of such a notion, he simply liked her too much. And given their talk the previous morning, he suspected her response to such a proposition would involve her sharp teeth.

Her people had always had a tense relationship with the Portuguese, one balanced on the edge of a sword. The violent introduction by rape—no matter how Camões had interpreted the event, it wasn't logical to believe that women who ran away were inviting courtship—had wrought terrible changes on their society. Several decades later, King Sebastião I *had* sent ships to help the sereia keep the Spanish from invading their islands. It had saved them from the slavery reportedly suffered by the sereia on the Canary Islands, but that hadn't been enough to wipe away the stain. The current banishment of her people from the Golden City had likely spoiled any progress in relations made since then. Duilio could well understand the antipathy Miss Paredes showed toward his people.

But yesterday Duilio had held her long-fingered hand in his. Staring down at that delicate, veined webbing, he had thought of more than tracking down one more killer. He had wanted all of this over with, because he wanted to take up his own life again. He wanted to see what destiny he could make for himself. Holding her hand, he'd asked himself if Oriana Paredes might play a part in it.

Surely that was impossible. She would be gone soon, returned to her own life on the islands . . . or maybe to some new assignment spying in the city. Unlike most of the noblemen's daughters and well-bred city girls he met at soirees and balls, Oriana Paredes—*Is that even her name?* Duilio wondered—had some purpose in her life other than waiting about for a man to claim her. He had no idea if her future plans included a man at all.

Yet standing in the dim hallway outside her bedroom, his fingers touching the softness of her throat, he'd believed she felt the same yearning he did. This morning he'd left the house before either she or his mother had risen, hoping to trade information with Joaquim before Joaquim's side investigation was shut down. If he'd gotten the chance to talk to Miss Paredes, he might have a better idea of her expectations. Now he could only wonder. There was someone out there who might want to kill her, which would render everything else moot.

He'd spent too much time stewing over this. He was at the Massarelos station already, so he worked his way back to Joaquim's office and installed himself in his regular chair, inordinately grumpy about everything.

"Silva showed up at the ball last night," he said before Joaquim could even manage a greeting. "He was unusually forthcoming."

Joaquim groaned. "Odd that you should start with that. You know better than to dwell on anything he says."

Duilio stretched out his legs and kicked at the desk. He didn't need Joaquim to remind him of that. "Fine. Did the Amaral servants have anything pertinent to tell you?"

"Did you enjoy nearly being burned to death?" Joaquim asked. "If I were picking, I would have started with that, Duilio. For God's sake . . ."

"What?" Duilio snapped. "Did you come by and have dinner with Cardenas?"

"No, I stopped by and chatted with Gustavo Mendes this morning." Joaquim peered at him narrowly. "Have you had breakfast? You're normally only this cranky if you haven't eaten."

Duilio sighed. *Cranky* wasn't the image he wished to portray. "No, I left before Mother and Miss Paredes woke, and I didn't want Mrs. Cardoza to prepare breakfast twice."

Joaquim shook his head, pushed a notebook over to Duilio, and rose. "Read. I'll ask one of the officers to go get you some food."

He suited actions to words, shutting the door behind him as he went off to procure food. Duilio picked up the notebook and found the marked page. Joaquim's notes were tidy, with a conclusion at the end of each interview of the Amaral servants. He'd spent the most time with the first footman, Carlos, and the lady's maid, Adela, shared by Lady Isabel and her mother. Then Joaquim's notes took a sidestep, moving to interviews with a few of the workers at a tavern frequented by servants up and down the Street of Flowers, The White Rose. Both Carlos and Adela, when asked if anyone had been inquiring about the activities of the Amaral staff, mentioned a woman who'd approached them at the tavern, offering positions in a more lucrative household. When Joaquim returned to his office a few minutes later, Duilio snatched one of the egg-custard pastries his cousin offered and asked, "What led you to ask these two—Carlos and Adela, I mean—about this woman at the tavern?"

Joaquim left the remaining pair of pastries on the desk near the notebook and went back to his side. "Both of them volunteered that information. They *wanted* to talk. The maid was genuinely distressed over her mistress' absence. She believed Miss Paredes' story about the bandits grabbing Miss Amaral, and said the bandits must have taken the missing jewelry—that Miss Paredes was above such things. She tried to think of anything that might have been related to the girl's disappearance, which took me to that point. Now, the footman is *not* grief-stricken over Miss Amaral's absence, but he seems to feel guilty over something regarding Miss Paredes and wanted to help clear her name. He might be responsible for the missing jewelry himself."

Duilio scowled down at the notes. According to the tavern keeper, the woman who had spoken with both Adela and Carlos—named Maria Melo, a name so commonplace that it meant nothing—had been visiting the tavern for almost a year, befriending servants from various households along the Street of Flowers. When pressed, the tavern keeper said he suspected she was hiring them away to Espinho or some other nearby town, as many of them stopped frequenting his tavern afterward. Duilio had a different interpretation of that coincidence. "She's been selecting the victims, hasn't she? So, Carlos and Adela might have been the two members of the Amaral household originally targeted," he told Joaquim. "But our killers changed their minds at the last moment and picked Lady Isabel instead."

Joaquim sat back and propped his feet up on his desk. "I don't think so. Both servants said Mrs. Melo first approached them about a month ago, and specifically asked about Miss Paredes. The maid had an impression that they were cousins, although this Mrs. Melo was much older than your Miss Paredes. Just checking up on a younger kinswoman, so to speak."

Duilio finished off the second pastry. This much sugar was going to sit heavily in his stomach later, even if that revelation didn't make his gut twist on its own. Miss Paredes felt guilty enough while only *suspecting* she'd been the target of the abduction. This confirmed that suspicion, and increased the likelihood that she was still being hunted.

"Gustavo told me you'd already asked him to keep an eye on Miss Paredes," Joaquim continued, "so you must believe she's not out of danger."

Duilio sighed and launched into as concise a retelling of the previous evening's revelations as he could manage, as well as outlining what he'd found at the apartment that had belonged to the artist Espinoza, and his first meeting with Inspector Gaspar afterward. "Miss Paredes might have some time this morning to start reading the journal," he added, "since Mother was very tired last night, from what Felis tells me."

"You gave it to *her* to read?"

"She has time to do so," Duilio pointed out.

"And I don't?" Joaquim shook his head and pointed to the pastry still on his desk. "Eat that last one before I give in to temptation. You must trust your Miss Paredes a great deal."

Duilio picked up the last tart. How could he respond to that? His instincts told him to trust her. And he *wanted* to trust her. Neither was actual proof that she was trustworthy.

"Are you bedding her?" Joaquim asked when he didn't respond immediately.

"Excuse me?" Duilio found it hard to believe that Joaquim had asked such a thing. He expected that sort of question from Erdano. Erdano didn't often think of females in terms other than bedding them. But Joaquim? "She's Mother's companion, for heaven's sake, Joaquim."

Joaquim shrugged. "Just asking. Gustavo thinks you're sweet on her, to use his phrase."

This would be a good moment to say something snide about Gustavo's deductive abilities, but Duilio didn't want to defame him unfairly. "She needs protection," Duilio said. "That doesn't extend to her bed."

Is she even sleeping in that bed? He hadn't heard any more scandalized whispers from his valet, so, if not, Miss Paredes must be dutifully rumpling her covers.

Joaquim nodded slowly. "I see."

Now he'd protested too much over the matter. Duilio sighed and took a bite of the last pastry.

"I prepared a list of the missing items," Joaquim added, "and I sent it over to your man of business so he can negotiate with Lady Amaral about compensation. . . ." A brisk knock at the office door prompted Joaquim to go open it.

"Are you going to let us in?" a now-familiar voice asked.

Duilio craned his neck about to see Inspector Gaspar standing in the doorway, Captain Santiago behind him. He stuffed the remainder of the pastry into his mouth and swallowed it with unseemly haste as he rose, brushing some pastry flakes off his frock coat as he did so. "Captain Santiago," Joaquim said, stepping back to allow the newcomers in. "What can I do for you?"

The two newcomers came inside, making it crowded once Gaspar shut the door.

"You're being reassigned, Inspector Tavares," the captain said. "I've received an official request for use of your services by the Special Police, signed by Commissioner Burgos himself. "That includes you too, Mr. Ferreira. I do understand this is temporary, though," he added with a glance at the silent Gaspar, who nodded once. "Good, then. Carry on."

And with that said, Captain Santiago let himself out of the office and shut the door.

Gaspar regarded Joaquim with that piercing gaze of his, then turned back to Duilio. "Well, gentlemen, where do we begin?"

Oriana woke far later than she'd expected. She quickly dressed and made her way down to the kitchens, only to discover that the staff had been given orders to allow her to sleep as late as she wished. Lady Ferreira was still abed, she was told, and Felis thought the lady wouldn't rise for hours yet.

After asking Cardenas to inform her when the lady needed her, Oriana made her way back up to her bedroom and stared at the rumpled covers of her bed. She'd actually slept in the bed the previous night, since her skin seemed recovered enough that she no longer needed to sleep in the tub. The temptation to crawl back under those sheets and stay there a while longer was strong, but she turned her back on the silk-draped bed and went into the dressing room instead.

The journal Mr. Ferreira had given her had dried overnight. Many of the pages were stuck together and a great deal of the ink had smeared, but most of it was legible. She located a letter opener in a desk drawer and settled on the leather settee near her bedroom door. She flipped through several pages, using the letter opener to pry apart pages that were stuck together. In the interest of thoroughness, she decided to start at the beginning.

After describing his original idea for the artwork—apparently provoked by a conversation he'd had, although he didn't specify with whom—Espinoza recorded his research. He listed his reasons for choosing that very spot in the river to locate his masterpiece: an easy depth and calmer tides, since it was on the Gaia side of the river, protected by the breakwater and out of the regular path of commercial shipping. He talked about taking measurements for the lengths of chain, calculating the approximate weight and buoyancy of the planned wooden houses, and then drawing the sketches of the houses he intended to replicate. Oriana hadn't given much thought to the technical aspects of building such a creation before, but she was beginning to understand the vastness of such an undertaking, even without its murderous aspects.

It wasn't long before she discovered that the charms on the tops of the houses *weren't* responsible for their buoyancy after filling. Espinoza hadn't trusted in the efficacy of the buoyancy charms, and had built the houses out of cork over a lightweight frame. The wooden exteriors were merely facades. Hadn't she tasted cork when she was inside the house? She was certain she remembered that correctly. That helped explain why she'd been able to so easily pry open the corner of the house.

At the beginning of the journal, there'd been no actual purchasing, building, or sinking. Then she hit upon the word that changed everything from planning to actualization: patron. The artist had found a patron whose funding had allowed him to rent an apartment and the vacant floor below to use as a shop. Only after that had he started building the first house.

The journal didn't tell her the patron's identity. The artist never used anyone's name in his writings, not even his own, guarding them as if they were state secrets. But as she continued to read, she began to spot hints that the patron was of the aristocracy.

And Espinoza didn't mention his victims at all. There was nothing about the chairs or the table, nor could she find anything about the kidnapping of the victims. It was as if Espinoza hadn't added that aspect until later. Or perhaps someone else added it. His mysterious patron might have made that change.

Oriana caught her lower lip between her teeth. The Lady had indicated that the Open Hand had members in the Special Police. Could the prince himself be directing them? After all, the mandate of the Special Police was to carry out the orders of the prince. They were known for hunting nonhumans and Sympathizers, but that didn't mean that was all they did.

Hadn't they been guarding the artwork? It was under the guise of patrolling the mouth of the river, but they still kept boats away, save for the scheduled visits by the submersible captains. The orders for the regular police to shut down the investigation of the artwork could have come from someone in the Special Police. And the newspapers hadn't questioned the artwork's presence at all, citing the guidelines that came down from the Ministry of Culture. But that body also answered directly to the prince.

What would happen if they could prove the prince himself was behind the deaths? Would that force him to abdicate, perhaps, if it became public? Would his younger brother, the infante, assume the throne and possibly overturn the ban? The journal in her hands took on new significance. She stroked the water-damaged cover with a fresh respect.

Then again, those with power and money had a tendency to stay in power, the worst of their sins swept under the rug. That was as true here in Portugal as it was back on the islands.

Sighing, Oriana rubbed her eyelids. She hadn't been such a cynic when she was younger.

CHAPTER 23

Joaquim and Inspector Gaspar got along well, although on occasion Duilio noted Gaspar aiming a narrow look at Joaquim when Joaquim wasn't attending. Given that Gaspar was a Meter, it made Duilio itch to know what the man saw when he looked at his cousin.

They went through the details of the case, starting with the very beginning. Duilio made his decision early on: he was going to trust Inspector Gaspar. So he told the truth about Erdano's complaints about the taste of death in the water near *The City Under the Sea.* He told Gaspar how his gift had warned him that Lady Isabel was dead, and delineated most of the steps they'd taken since. He even admitted he'd kept the journal and had Miss Paredes reading it. Joaquim followed his lead, volunteering his rather copious notes, including what he'd gleaned the previous day from the Amaral servants.

"So, your Miss Paredes was clearly the target, rather than her mistress," Gaspar said. "This Maria Melo must be our saboteur or working with him, but there have to be a thousand women with that name in this city. Likely a false name anyway. Is there anything more you can tell me about her?"

"Frequents The White Rose, although I suspect she'll hear about my inquiries and stop doing so. Dark hair, dark eyes," Joaquim read from his notes. "Always wears black—good-quality cloth, though. That would make her an upper servant at the least. Moderately tall, with a nice figure. Heavy eyebrows were the only distinguishing characteristic anyone could give me."

Gaspar puffed out his cheeks in disgust. "I suspect that's a dead end. I'll post an officer there and see if she shows up again."

"An officer of the Special Police?" Duilio asked. "Can you trust them?"

"My associates have vetted a dozen of them so far. They're not working with the Open Hand and admittedly have Liberal leanings, so we're safe using them."

"Your associates?" Duilio echoed.

"You haven't met Inspector Anjos or Miss Vladimirova yet," Gaspar said. "They've been working their way through the ranks while I was off hunting Mata."

Although Anjos was a Portuguese name, Vladimirova sounded Russian to Duilio. "Are they witches, like you and . . . the Lady?"

"Yes. You'll probably meet Anjos later, but you'd rather *not* meet Miss Vladimirova." Gaspar smiled grimly, not showing his teeth. "Unfortunately, they haven't turned up anyone associated with this floating-house business. With so many officers to question, it may take them weeks to root out the right men, and the ones whose names we did have all disappeared as soon as Commissioner Burgos gave us permission to start questioning them."

Duilio didn't doubt that. "What about Mata?"

"I haven't seen him since yesterday afternoon, Mr. Ferreira. I have no doubt he's still after you, but is keeping his distance because he's seen me." Unfortunately, Gaspar was difficult to miss in a country with relatively few representatives of its former African colonies.

Duilio licked his lips. Joaquim wasn't going to like this. "Silva spoke of using Miss Paredes as bait, Inspector. Why not use me that way?"

"No," Joaquim said immediately.

"I'm not suggesting standing in the middle of a plaza all day to be shot at," Duilio told him. "Just doing what I would be doing anyway."

Gaspar regarded him with narrowed eyes. "What did you have in mind?"

Duilio shot a glance at Joaquim. "Miss Paredes mentioned that Espinoza was raised in Matosinhos. I could go there and ask around about him."

Gaspar looked intrigued, but Joaquim wasn't placated. "Mata is not going to get on the tram out to Matosinhos with you," Joaquim pointed out. "You know what he looks like."

It was about four miles out to the town of Matosinhos on the Marginal line. "No, he'll know he has to take the *next* one, try to catch the steam tram out of Boavista, or find some other means of transportation."

Joaquim sat back, a scowl twisting his lips.

"I'll head up to Matosinhos," Duilio said. "I can ask a few discreet questions about Espinoza, and that should give Mata time to follow me. Matosinhos is small enough that he should be able to find me if he tries."

Joaquim sighed heavily. He didn't like it, but Duilio knew he understood. If this man *had* killed Alessio, Duilio wanted him brought in. "Start with Father Barros at the Church of Bom Jesus," Joaquim suggested. "He's been there forever and knows the parish better than anyone else. He can tell you whom to talk with about Espinoza."

One of Joaquim's teachers from his days in seminary, no doubt. "I'll do that."

"And watch your back," Joaquim added.

Duilio patted the pocket where his holster was clipped, his Webley Wilkinson revolver quiescent within. "I'll stay on my guard."

Mr. Ferreira showed up at the house near lunchtime, evidently wanting to change clothes. He came into the front sitting room, where Oriana sat on the couch, poring through the journal he'd left with her, gesturing for her to stay seated as he entered. "Miss Paredes, I hope you were able to get some sleep last night."

"Yes, sir," she said. "Your mother is still abed, and Felis is reading to her, so I thought I would give this a try."

He settled in a chair across from her, much as he'd done the day before. He seemed to have forgotten their . . . closeness . . . of the previous evening. Or he was pretending so to set her at ease. It was a pretense she was willing to join, as discussing the issue would surely be embarrassing for him. "Rough going?" he asked. "From what I glimpsed before I pocketed it, it looked fairly technical."

"I'm not mathematical, sir," she admitted. Languages, history, and literature: those all made more sense to her than this confusing tangle of numbers and symbols. "A great deal of this is calculations and plans that mean nothing to me."

"I'm more curious if there's anything useful in there. Names?"

"Not a one, I'm afraid. He's very cagey about the people he's working with."

Mr. Ferreira sighed heavily and sat back in the chair, crossing his legs and lacing his fingers over his knee. "Then we're wasting your time."

"Not at all," she said. "I've noted, for example, he doesn't mention the victims in his calculations. Or the table on which the spell was inscribed. Those had to have been added later in the process."

"That would throw off all his calculations," Mr. Ferreira said. "For buoyancy and weight, I mean."

She nodded. "Also, the houses aren't wood, as everyone thinks. The wood is a veneer, over cork. That's what actually makes them float. If the chain broke on any one of them, it would probably pop to the surface like a rubber ball."

He shrugged. "I *was* told those charms on the top were useless."

She told him then what she'd read about the patron who'd made it all possible, but didn't have a name for the man, which made the information useless. "I'll read more this afternoon, sir. Perhaps he'll say who's paying for his creation."

He nodded, his lips pursed, and then cautiously asked, "Does the name Maria Melo mean anything to you?"

It was a common name, but Oriana didn't actually know anyone who bore it. "No, sir."

"Have you ever been to a tavern called The White Rose?" he asked then.

That tavern was frequented by *servants* from up and down the Street of Flowers. Carlos had once suggested she meet him there, although at the time she'd thought it a joke. And it was one of Heriberto's favored haunts. When her master wasn't on his boat, he could often be found there. "I've never been inside," she said. "Can I assume that Mrs. Melo has?"

He looked grim. "My cousin talked to the Amaral servants yesterday. Both the first footman and the lady's maid said they met her there. They said she asked after you. How you were faring, how you liked the household. The maid thought Mrs. Melo was your cousin. Do you *have* any cousins here?"

Oriana laid one mitt-covered hand over her mouth. How should she answer that? He'd met Nela and so must suspect about the exiles, so it was a logical question, but her father was her only direct kin. No, the woman had to be lying. And given it was a tavern Heriberto frequented, he had to figure into this somehow. Oriana dropped her hand back to her lap. "She's your saboteur, isn't she?"

"We don't know that," he said swiftly, as if to reassure her again. "But if she is, then she had to know you're not human."

"*You* knew," she pointed out, and then felt guilty for withholding information he might need. "My master frequents that tavern, as well. It's possible he gave her that information, although I can't think why he would."

Mr. Ferreira pinched the bridge of his nose. "Would your master willingly put you in that position? In the floating house?"

Oriana thought of her father speaking of paying Heriberto more money. If Heriberto was willing to stoop to extortion, what else might he be willing to do? "He might," she admitted. "I'm not one of his favorites."

"And you *lived* in one of the houses in question," Mr. Ferreira said. "Are there other spies like you in comparable positions? Or some of your people who chose to live here? I don't need specifics—just a general idea whether you were one of a hundred or the only choice."

Oriana knew of six other spies currently in the city, none of whom worked on the street of the aristocrats. Of the exiles, the only one she knew who frequented the street was her own father. He visited the Pereira de Santos mansion often, but that house had already appeared in the water, so he'd been bypassed. He didn't actually live in that house anyway. "I may have been the only choice," she whispered, a sick feeling swelling in her stomach.

Mr. Ferreira pushed himself out of his chair and came to loom over her. He set a hand lightly on her shoulder. "I meant what I said last night, Miss Paredes."

She looked up at him. No, he hadn't forgotten last night's extraordinary discussion either. She could see it in his eyes, an awareness of her as more than a servant. He looked at her like she was a woman, perhaps even a lover. But opening that door would only lead her to pain. She wasn't the sort who could take a lover and then go on her way. She just . . . wasn't. Her scruples wouldn't allow it. Even for a male as fascinating as Duilio Ferreira. It would break her heart, and she refused to do that to herself. She nodded jerkily. "I know, sir."

His lips pressed together, possibly in vexation. She wasn't quite certain how to read that expression. Then he stepped back and left without another word.

As the tram drew closer to Matosinhos, Duilio could see the port of Leixões to the north. The port was an unfinished work that must either be considered art or an eyesore, progress brought to a standstill. The builders had begun constructing two stone "arms" intended to stretch out into the sea to act as breakwaters to protect the ships that would someday sail up the Leça River into the port. Silhouetted against the horizon, two Titans of iron and steel waited—giant steam-powered cranes that ran on rails to the ends of those breakwaters. One sat on each abandoned arm, capable of going back to work and moving giant blocks of stone . . . as soon as the prince should deign to give his permission. Duilio doubted that would happen while this prince was alive.

Not for the first time, Duilio wondered if it wouldn't be better for Northern Portugal if the seers were correct and the prince *was* doomed to die. Somehow Miss Paredes had changed the odds of that prophecy coming true. Not through her own choices, of course. She'd been forced into that position. He hated the price at which that had come. He sighed and returned to surveying the passengers of the tram.

The man in the dark suit was the one who concerned him. When he'd gotten on the tram at Massarelos, a prickle had gone down Duilio's spine. He'd settled a couple of seats behind Duilio and pulled a folded newspaper from under his arm. He didn't appear to be an immediate danger, but Duilio felt sure the man had no other business there other than to watch him.

Duilio dug into a pocket for his watch, flicked the lid open, and held the case to one side, trying to get a glance at the man's face in the mirror secreted inside the lid. He didn't look familiar. In his midthirties, dark-haired, and average in size, he wouldn't stand out in a crowd. Duilio studied him a moment longer while the man perused a copy of the *Gazette*. He closed the case then and slid the watch back into his pocket.

While at the house Duilio had changed into a more casual suit—one that Marcellin found plebian. But it would be better for running should he find that necessary. He'd changed into less-formal shoes and picked up a spare gun, just in case. If this man intended to chase him down, he'd make it difficult.

When the tram reached the end of the line, Duilio got off and began ambling toward the ships that bobbed on the river. He'd been to the area a few times in the past year, but wasn't nearly as familiar with it as he would have liked. The man in the dark suit followed in a desultory manner, confirming Duilio's suspicions.

The Church of Bom Jesus rose majestically in the midst of a public park. Duilio walked up the steps, stopped at the threshold of the church, and crossed himself. He'd been especially lax in his devotions since his brother's death, one of those things he occasionally resolved to change, usually following one of Joaquim's lectures. He waited a moment, allowing his eyes to adjust to the darkness and wondering if someone would come to renounce him. The lack of any divine rebuke reassured him.

He stepped forward into the gold-encrusted nave and spotted a fair-haired priest speaking to an elderly black-garbed woman. The priest nodded toward Duilio as if asking him to wait, so Duilio settled on one of the pews, determined to be patient. The young man eventually left the woman's side and came to lend his priestly ear to Duilio.

"Are you Father Barros?" Duilio asked without preamble.

"I'm Father Crespo. How can I help you today, my son?"

Duilio hoped his expression didn't show his amusement at being called *my son* by a man who must be younger than himself. The priest couldn't be much older than Cristiano. "I need to speak to Father Barros. Where might I find him?"

The young man's brows drew together. "I believe he's closeted with the books, but I'll inform him he's needed here." He scurried off toward the sacristy, much to Duilio's relief.

Not long after that, another priest emerged from the sacristy, an older man with graying hair and a stern visage. He presented himself to Duilio. "How can I help you today, son?"

This time *son* made more sense. "I've come to make some inquiries," he admitted. "Inspector Joaquim Tavares suggested you might be able to help me."

The priest's eyes narrowed. "And who are you?"

Well, he couldn't fault the man's caution. "I am his cousin, Duilio Ferreira."

"Hmmm . . . you certainly resemble him," Father Barros said. "Tell me, then, why did he not enter the priesthood after seminary?"

If that question was meant as a test, he was about to fail miserably. Joaquim turned stubborn at times, refusing to discuss certain issues, even with family. He had an overdeveloped desire for privacy. "I honestly don't know, Father," Duilio admitted. "He's never told me."

"He's never told anyone, so far as I know. I thought perhaps . . ." The priest shrugged. "Here, Mr. Ferreira, come with me. I've not had luncheon yet. Let's walk into town."

Duilio followed the man back through the nave and along a path that led to the back side of the church, away from its chapels and statues. They headed toward the town's center, walking along the narrow cobbled streets among the noontime press of carts and pedestrians. Much like the streets around the Ribeira back in the Golden City, these buildings were old and packed together, with painted walls and iron-railed balconies. The priest led him to the front of one building, its pink facade decorated with only a sign marking it the Restaurant Lindo. "My cousin owns the place, so we can sit in the back as long as you need. Is that man in the dark suit following you?"

"I believe so," Duilio said without turning to look. "Not being terribly discreet, if you noticed him as well, though."

Father Barros laughed and pointed out a table in a dark corner of the room. "I wasn't always a priest, son."

There had to be a story behind that short statement. If he weren't pressed for time, he would have liked to get to know the priest better. Duilio headed back toward the corner and picked a chair situated so that he could see out into the street. The man in the dark suit passed the front of the restaurant as Duilio settled at the table. He moved on without pausing. Duilio felt gooseflesh prickle along his arms, but his gift seemed unconcerned at the moment, so he shook off the odd feeling. He could deal with that problem later.

The priest settled across from him. "So, how does Inspector Tavares think I can help you, Mr. Ferreira?"

Duilio looked about for a waiter. He'd only had time to grab one of Mrs. Cardoza's meat pies at the house. He was still hungry. "We have a case that we're working on, and I'm gathering background information."

The priest set his chin atop laced fingers. "About what?"

"*The City Under the Sea*," Duilio said.

Barros sat back, shaking his head. "Ah. Gabriel Espinoza's creation."

A chubby man with a white apron tied over his garb finally bustled over and offered to tell them the specials. "Thank you, Eusebio," Barros said. "We'll need some privacy, if you please. Just bring us whatever the cook has prepared, and . . . tea."

The waiter cast a curious look at Duilio but took himself away promptly.

"So what about a bunch of floating houses could catch your interest?"

Duilio pressed his lips together, trying to decide where to start. "We know for certain a young woman was trapped inside the house that went into the river recently."

"Inside?" The priest leaned forward, sounding incredulous.

"Yes, tied to a chair. She was grabbed off the street, drugged, and placed inside the house while still unconscious. She had no chance of escaping alive once the house went into the water."

"You think Gabriel Espinoza did this?" Barros shook his head firmly. "No. He may be rather single-minded in the pursuit of his lofty artistic goals, but he wouldn't hurt a woman."

Duilio stared at the priest, weighing the conviction in his tone. The man *believed* Espinoza's innocence, so any mention of necromancy would get a similar appalled reaction. But given what Miss

Paredes had said about Espinoza's calculations not accounting for the victims, it seemed that aspect of the artwork wasn't his doing at all. Duilio tried another tack. "When was the last time you spoke to Espinoza?"

"January, right after Epiphany." Barros frowned. "He came back to his parents' home after some disagreement with his patron, and he came to see me. I'm not his confessor. It was just talk, but he was quite upset."

That had promise, and if it wasn't a confession, Barros was at liberty to discuss their conversation. "Upset?"

"Something about the artwork. He didn't want to tell me. And that his patron wanted to move him somewhere out of the city, away from prying eyes and . . . *nosy writers*, I believe he said. They had an argument that got out of hand. Espinoza even showed me a cut on his forehead where they'd fought over it."

Duilio recalled that dark spot on the floor in the apartment's dressing room. "He had a fight with his patron?"

"Well, not the patron himself. The man the patron sent to check up on him. I haven't seen him since he told me that, so he must have given in and moved out of the city."

That would put Espinoza's disappearance in early January, about the time the fifth house had gone into the water. About when he'd stopped giving interviews. So something had changed abruptly then. Perhaps Espinoza had learned about the victims and objected. "Father, did Espinoza tell you who his patron was?"

The priest mulled that over, his lips pursed. "He said the work was being funded by the government, the Ministry of Culture."

"I thought there was a single patron," Duilio said.

"I believe the Marquis of Maraval was personally overseeing the artwork. Espinoza considered him the primary patron."

The Marquis of Maraval? The Ministry of Culture performed functions like the installation of sculptures in the Treasury Building and the restoration of tile facades in older parts of the city. They kept a finger on what newspapers published. But they had no control over the Special Police. Duilio didn't see how the minister could be involved. "I see. Have you ever heard of a group called the Open Hand?"

Barros sat back. "Espinoza mentioned them once, although I wasn't clear who they were."

"In what context?" Duilio asked.

"It didn't make sense." Barros sighed. "Espinoza saw *something*. He wouldn't tell me what it was, but it made him think they were subverting his work."

That was an odd choice of word. "Subverting?"

"Yes. It sounded insane, but he truly believed it. Somehow they intended to use his work of art to make the prince into the king of all Portugal."

CHAPTER 24

The restaurant had filled with all manner of folk from the town, fishermen and laborers and tradesmen. The noise within the narrow room grew chaotic, but nestled where they were in the back, Duilio could still hear his companion's voice. Over a fine lunch, Father Barros painted a picture of Espinoza as a man obsessed with his art, but not evil at heart.

It seemed that Espinoza was as much a victim in this as Miss Paredes.

After paying for the meal, Duilio took his leave of the priest. "You've been very helpful, Father. Be cautious whom you tell about this. It would be better to say nothing."

The priest rose and shook his hand. "I understand. I hope you find the truth, Mr. Ferreira. And keep an eye out for the fellow I saw earlier."

Duilio hadn't forgotten the man in the dark suit. "I will, Father."

When he got out to the street, the sky had cleared considerably. People hurried by on the cobbles, and he fell in behind a group of fisherwomen, their embroidered aprons bright splashes of color over their floral-print skirts. By the time he'd turned onto Serpa Pinto Street, Duilio's gift warned him he was being followed again. It didn't feel like a warning of imminent danger, but a reminder he should be *aware.*

He ducked down Godinho Street. It was narrower and led only

to the harbor's construction yards and the southern breakwater, but would afford him a chance to see if anyone was behind him. There was little there beyond a few factory offices, which should minimize the number of bystanders who might be hurt should Mata appear and take a shot at him.

As Duilio expected, the man in the dark suit—the one who'd followed him from the tram—appeared at the end of the street behind him. It wasn't Mata, but there was no telling how many people were working with him.

Duilio reached inside his jacket, unsnapped his holster, and searched the area about him. There was no traffic in sight; too close to lunchtime. Ahead of him waited the abandoned construction yard with its neat rows of giant granite blocks. He could only hope he got there before anything happened . . . and that Inspector Gaspar and Joaquim were keeping an eye on him, as planned.

The granite blocks would supply excellent cover. The ocean beyond the yard presented an escape route as well; he could outswim most men. He would need to reach the water first, though. Duilio jumped the gate into the construction yard, edged between two rows of stone blocks, and headed toward the giant crane on its rails at the end of the unfinished breakwater.

His gift abruptly warned him, a spasm down his spine.

His mind raced, taking in everything about him. Shadows moved on the far left of his vision. From that direction his nose picked up the tang of perspiration. The man in the dark suit was behind him, still on the road, which meant someone else was in the construction yard already. Mata? Weighing the distance between himself and the iron base of the Titan, Duilio bolted that way.

He'd almost reached it when a shot rang out. Duilio crouched but kept moving. That shot went high, pinging off the body of the crane with a metallic whine.

Reprieved, he threw himself the final few feet toward the Titan's base.

He stumbled over the rail on which the crane ran but managed to get behind the iron wheels. His heart was racing, pulse thudding in his ears. He glanced up at the base of the crane that shielded him—terrifyingly huge now that he was under its bulk. A wave of dizziness assailed him and he quickly looked down, noting for the first time the revolver in his hand. He didn't recall drawing the thing.

There was movement in the yard. He could hear the scuffling of feet on gravel. One man called to another, confirming there was more than one person about. Duilio huffed out a breath, pressed the side of his face against the cool iron, and made himself breathe slower so he could listen. What was going on out there?

Another shot sounded. This one ricocheted off the ground near his left hand, sending a shower of rock chips spraying about. He jerked back, but not before a chip caught the side of his cheek. He hissed and pressed the back of his right hand against the cut. It came away bloody.

Damnation. He needed to get behind his attackers, however many there were. Out here on the end of the breakwater, they couldn't miss him if he made a run for it. They had him pinned down behind the Titan's wheels. He glanced toward the edge of the breakwater more than a dozen feet away. His mind spun, trying to weigh the odds.

He didn't want to kill anyone today, but he might not have any choice. He could swim back to the quay and get behind the man. The revolver would probably still fire, which gave him six shots, but he couldn't trust the old derringer once it got wet.

A third shot hit the iron wheel near him. Duilio jerked back and pressed himself against the wheel again. Two more shots followed. They sounded like they'd come from different spots, farther away, but he couldn't be sure. Duilio held his breath.

Above the wind and the clinking of the chains hanging from the Titan's boom, he heard moaning. He dared a glimpse in that direction and saw Mata slumped against the stones, clutching his belly.

"He's down, Mr. Ferreira," a man with a Brazilian accent shouted. "Come on out."

Duilio didn't think the Brazilian was in league with Mata. Surely he wouldn't announce himself that way if he were. That didn't necessarily mean he could trust the Brazilian, and his gift supplied nothing. But he needed the answer enough to risk going out there.

Mata lay next to the first row of giant granite blocks, with the man in the dark suit standing over him, his pistol trained loosely on Mata. Inspector Gaspar approached, jumping over the gate at the entrance of the construction yard. Once he reached them, Gaspar knelt down and began to check Mata's injuries.

Duilio walked cautiously along the rails toward them. His heart was still thumping erratically, but at least his breathing sounded normal. When he'd gotten within a dozen feet, he paused. "Who are you?"

The man in the dark suit came toward him, giving Duilio a better look than he'd gotten on the tram. He had slender features and a lean build, suggesting athleticism, but he seemed tired, worn. His dark gray suit was of a modest Portuguese cut, and his composure after a shoot-out suggested he'd seen the like before. "Anjos," he said in his Brazilian accent. "Inspector Gabriel Anjos."

Gaspar nodded curtly to Duilio, confirming that, and turned his attention back to the assassin. He'd opened Mata's waistcoat and shirt and was surveying a seeping injury that looked to be near the man's liver. A police-issue pistol lay a few feet away, ignored.

"Would have been nice to know who you were sooner," Duilio said to Anjos.

"There wasn't time," Anjos replied. "You've got a nick on your cheek."

Duilio tugged out a handkerchief and dabbed his cheek. It had nearly stopped bleeding. Still keeping his distance, he gazed at the assassin. A youngish man with a stocky build and regular features, there was little to distinguish him from thousands of other men in the Golden City—save that Duilio had been attacked by him in a tavern earlier in the week. "This is Mata, isn't it? The same man who killed my brother?"

Anjos regarded Duilio with narrowed eyes. "Yes. Don't get ideas. He's *our* prisoner."

Did the man think he was going to attack Mata? Duilio turned his eyes back to the assassin. Gaspar was attempting to staunch the wound with a handkerchief, but Duilio suspected it was already too late for a hospital. An internal injury like that was almost always a death sentence.

I should feel . . . more, Duilio thought.

"He's not going to make it until she can get here," Gaspar said, looking up at Anjos.

Anjos nodded grimly. "You ask him, then."

Gaspar grasped the wounded man's chin with a bloody hand. "Who ordered you to kill Alessio Ferreira?"

The assassin laughed wetly. "I don't know."

Gaspar shot a glance up at Anjos, who nodded. He turned back to Mata. "*How* did you get the order, then? Who gave it to you?"

Mata coughed, and blood speckled his lips. "No one."

"That's true," Anjos inserted quickly.

Duilio glanced at the Brazilian. How did he know that?

"*How* did you get the order?" Gaspar asked again.

The assassin laughed. "They're left on my desk in my home. Don't you get it? I can't tell you anything. You might as well shoot me now."

Duilio frowned, trying to recall where he'd heard such a story before—a note left on a desk.

"He means that," Anjos told his partner. "It's the truth, as much as he knows."

Aha! Duilio glanced back at the Brazilian. Anjos must be a Truthsayer, able to parse out the truth or lie in another's words. It wasn't a common gift, but not nearly as rare as Gaspar's ability. It explained why Anjos had been doing the questioning of members of the Special Police. They couldn't lie to him, not successfully.

Gaspar gripped the assassin's chin. "Same with Ferreira here?"

But Mata coughed, and blood splattered the back of Gaspar's hand. Duilio had a feeling they weren't going to get any more answers. "He's dying, man."

"I know." Gaspar wiped away the blood that now bubbled from Mata's mouth. Mata slumped to the ground, lacking even the strength to sit up. Gaspar propped him on his side, but Mata's coughing grew fainter.

Duilio watched Mata as the man's breathing calmed again. He'd expected to feel more anger, but Mata wasn't truly Alessio's killer. He'd simply been the tool that carried out the orders. No, someone else had pulled the man's strings.

Anjos glanced back toward the quay and waved to a group of uniformed police officers who approached from the town. Workers were beginning to return from their lunch breaks, and a few stood watching curiously at the construction yard gates. Two of the officers stopped at the gates and took up a position there, keeping the civilians out, while another pair entered the construction yard and approached them.

Anjos drew out a handkerchief and covered his mouth as he coughed. "I would rather have gotten him back to the city," he said as he folded the handkerchief, "but I don't think he would have spilled anything useful. The best way to keep an assassin from talking is not to tell them anything in the first place."

The two uniformed officers had reached them and knelt to inspect the body. Gaspar picked up the assassin's discarded pistol and came to Anjos' side. "He's unconscious."

Duilio watched as the officers prepared to carry Mata out

between them. "I had an investigator looking for something previously stolen from my house," Duilio said, figuring it was better not to say what was missing in front of the two unfamiliar officers. "*He* was warned off by a note left on his desk, in a locked house."

Gaspar snorted. "Someone picked his lock—nothing more."

He'd thought exactly the same at the time. "But the same method was used, which struck me as important. We have reason to suspect Paolo Silva was behind that theft, but no proof."

Anjos produced a cigarette case from a coat pocket. "I'm familiar with the case. We don't have any grounds to question Silva, but other recent developments suggest he doesn't have the missing item." He withdrew a cigarette, lit it, and put away the case with a fluid ease that spoke of long practice. "We do, however, intend to question Silva the first time he gives us an excuse. I suspect he knows a lot more than he's told anyone."

Duilio held his tongue. With a Truthsayer present, it would settle the matter of the theft permanently. It would be nice to know.

The two uniformed policemen carried a now-unconscious Mata out of the construction yard, leaving Duilio with the two foreigners. "They'll take him to the station," Anjos said once they'd gone. "They'll bring a doctor in, but I don't think he's going to regain consciousness."

Duilio had to agree. He touched his cheek again and found that the nick there seemed to have stopped bleeding. "Well, I got two things from Father Barros, who, as it turns out, is an old friend of Espinoza and talked with him back in January when he came here. First, Espinoza's work might have been subverted. And second, he thought the Open Hand wanted to use it to make the prince into a king."

Anjos ground out what remained of the cigarette with his foot. "How the devil is that supposed to work?"

"I don't know," Duilio said. "But Espinoza saw *something*. That's why Espinoza fled to Matosinhos in a short-lived attempt to hide from his patron."

Anjos nodded. "Did Barros know who that patron was?"

"Not exactly," Duilio admitted. "Barros thought the artwork was funded by the Ministry of Culture, overseen by Maraval himself."

Gaspar cursed under his breath and turned to Anjos. "She went to go talk to him. To ask about the table spell."

The Lady? Duilio recalled her mentioning she knew Maraval. "If he's involved . . ."

"Then she could be walking into trouble," Anjos said. "Miguel, go."

Gaspar tossed the assassin's discarded pistol to Anjos and took off at a run.

"Should we go with him?" Duilio asked.

"No." Anjos checked the safety on Mata's pistol and tucked it in a pocket. "If Maraval harms her, Miguel will kill him. The fewer witnesses, the better."

Duilio wasn't quite certain whether the Brazilian inspector was serious. Given the unforgiving look he'd seen in Gaspar's eyes, Duilio wouldn't be surprised if it were true. He wondered if the man intended to run the full four miles back to the city.

That question was answered before he asked it. Joaquim came jogging into the construction yard, a rifle slung over his shoulder by the strap. He held his hands wide. "Where did Gaspar just go? He took the carriage."

"Back into the city," Duilio answered him. "Where *were* you?"

Puffing out his cheeks, Joaquim pointed back toward the row of businesses that lined the road leading up to the construction yard. "Rooftop."

"Well done," Anjos told him. "You picked a good spot."

"Thank you," Duilio added. Joaquim did have a talent for being in the right place at the right time. "Good shot."

"No, it wasn't," Joaquim protested. "I was aiming for his leg. Damn. Please tell me he was the one who's been after you. The one who killed Alessio?"

"Yes," Anjos answered him.

Joaquim rubbed a hand over his face. "Good."

"He wasn't going to tell us anything," Anjos said. "I've seen that often enough, so I know what it looks like."

Duilio would bet money that a Truthsayer was indeed a good judge of whether a man was going to spill information. "So, where do we go from here?"

"Inspector Tavares, would you accompany me down to the station?" Anjos asked. "I doubt Mata has anything on his person, but you might be able to smooth things over with the locals for me if he does."

Joaquim nodded. "Come by later," he mouthed at Duilio.

Duilio watched as Joaquim and Inspector Anjos headed out of the construction yard, leaving him standing alone on the bloodstained gravel. A light drizzle began to fall, a reminder that they were headed into the rainy months of the year.

He was still holding his pistol. Sighing, Duilio holstered it. Now that the initial flush of adrenaline fostered by the attempt on his life had faded, he was tired . . . and hungry. He needed to consider everything he'd learned today, and try to work in the little bits with what they already knew. Hopefully the tram ride back to the city would provide him with time to do just that.

Oriana walked down the alleyway toward the Street of Flowers, her nerves on edge. Someone might be hunting her, but her conversation with Mr. Ferreira late that morning had given her more to worry about. How had that woman learned she wasn't human? The rain had stopped, but the street glistened with wet, a reminder to watch her footing—especially important given that the mantilla's lace obscured her vision. And she wished she had a warmer jacket or a shawl. She rubbed her silk-covered hands briskly along her arms.

She had almost reached the end of the Street of Flowers when she realized she was being followed. A man trailed behind her at some distance. She stopped and laid one hand on a wrought-iron fence, pretending that her heel was caught in the hem of her skirt. Turned to one side as she fiddled with the fabric, she could see the man wore a dark suit, but he was several houses away. She could lift the veil and squint to see him better, but that would surely alert him. She continued on toward the Customs House, noting with relief that he hadn't gotten any closer.

Once past the Customs House, she joined more pedestrians strolling along the tree-lined Alameda de Massarelos. She walked on slowly, being passed by workers on their way home for dinner, chattering loudly when she wanted silence to listen. She tried the same trick again, pretending she had caught her heel, and glanced behind her.

Thank the gods. Her pursuer had been joined by another man, and the two were walking companionably along the avenue. She dropped the fabric and walked on. It was probably just her imagination, along with an excessive dose of caution. While the mantilla hid her features from notice, it was *distinctive.* She wished she'd thought of that before leaving the house. But it covered her face, which might allow her to evade anyone looking for her.

I need to plan better. She strode more quickly along the avenue toward the spot where Heriberto moored his little fishing boat among a dozen others. Watching her footing, she made her way onto the ramp and down to the boat. The deck smelled of gutted fish, making it clear that Heriberto did occasionally pursue his stated occupation, if not tidily.

Careful of her skirts, Oriana climbed over the rail. She removed the mantilla, tucked it into her handbag, and banged with one fist on the low cabin wall, clenching her jaw to ignore the jarring vibrations that set off in her webbing. "Heriberto," she called down toward the cabin, "I need to talk to you."

Her words were greeted with a stream of invective that didn't surprise her overmuch.

"Wait a moment," Heriberto called back. A moment later he emerged from the small cabin, still tying the drawstring of his rough-spun trousers. He hadn't bothered with shoes. He wasn't even wearing a neckerchief to hide his gill slits. His hair was mussed, making Oriana suspect he hadn't been alone in that cramped cabin.

His eyes narrowed in the afternoon light. "What are you doing here?" He looked frazzled, which had to be better for her.

"I hear you're looking for me."

"Your father told you, did he?" he asked.

His casual mention of her father surprised her. After two years of never speaking of him, it was bizarre to have Heriberto say that so baldly. "I haven't had any contact with my father since I got here, as per our orders. Not a word."

Heriberto crossed arms over his bare chest. "And I went directly to *him*, so how else would you have found out?"

She could claim that Carlos, the footman she'd seen with him, had told her, but she was going to have to go with the truth if she wanted to get her father off Heriberto's hook. "I followed you Wednesday when you met him at the Golden Church. I was standing right under where you were talking. I believe what I heard was called extortion. If you're looking for me, there's no reason to bother him. He doesn't know my whereabouts." He didn't deny the charge of extortion, she noted. "Who is Maria Melo, and why did you tell her that I'm not human?"

Heriberto shook his head. "You're not entitled to that information."

"Extortion isn't in your orders," she reminded him. "My aunts are high up enough in the ministry that if I should happen to mention your extra source of income, it *would* come back to haunt you. There are other ways of getting correspondence out of the city than by going through you. I can go around you."

For her first attempt at blackmail, it seemed to work. "Do you think it's that simple?" he asked. "There are those in the ministry who outrank me. When she demanded a list of my people in the city, I didn't ask why."

Oh no. Oriana stifled the desire to walk away. The saboteur knew she was a sereia not because Heriberto revealed that fact . . . but because she was a sereia herself, a member of their intelligence ministry.

She'd been put in that house to watch Isabel die by one *of her own people.*

Oriana lifted her chin. "Where can I find her?"

"Thanks to your appearance in the gossip columns of this morning's *Gazette*, *she* knows exactly where to find *you*." Heriberto grabbed her arm and hauled her closer. "Don't think . . ."

Oriana bared her teeth and dragged her arm free from Heriberto's grasp.

He smirked. "It's all over the street whose house you're living in now, girl. If she wants to talk with you, she will. Take my advice: keep your distance. She's been undercover a long time, and we're *all* expendable if we endanger her mission."

Did her government have agents who'd been here longer than Heriberto? That was news to her. "What mission is that?"

"You think she would tell me? A male?" He laughed, a short bark. "I learned long ago there are times it's better to stay still under the water. Act like everything's normal, stay hidden, and perhaps the storm will pass without all of us getting killed."

Oriana had a sinking feeling in her stomach. The woman who'd handed her and Isabel over to the Open Hand had a greater mission, one so important that Isabel Amaral's death was acceptable. Putting Oriana Paredes in danger of exposure was also acceptable. Oriana couldn't think of too many missions important enough to warrant that much leeway, but assassination might be one of them. Perhaps Silva had been right about an assassination after all, although not about the assassin. It was hard to believe her people's government would condone such a thing. "Why were *you* looking for me, then?"

"She ordered me to," Heriberto said. "She claims someone's trying to kill you. If they succeed, it would spoil her plans, whatever those are. She said she wanted to warn you."

Oh, that much is true. "So you threaten my father, just to warn me?"

Heriberto crossed his arms over his chest and glared. "Girl, I don't like you. You think you're better than me. You think you don't have to do the things the rest of us stoop to because you're superior to us, because you've got old family ties in the ministry." He gestured at her mitt-covered fingers. "I notice you're not at the doctor's appointment I made for you to get your hands cut."

Was that today? Oriana had a vague recollection of him ordering her to do that the last time they'd spoken, but she'd had other concerns since. "I forgot."

"Of course." Heriberto set one fingertip under his eye, the sign for doubt. "The truth is that I don't like my people getting killed. Even you. If your getting killed by these other people would ruin *her* plan, then the easiest way to ensure that doesn't happen . . . is to kill you herself."

Oriana felt a chill run down her spine. Why had she not figured that out? She folded her silk-covered hands together to hide their shaking.

She'd come here to tear into Heriberto's fins, but instead he'd given her information he shouldn't have. If Maria Melo was his superior, he shouldn't have divulged the woman's intentions, not even obliquely. Yet he'd done it to warn her. It was possible he'd been guarding her all along, although she doubted that was the case. Instead, she suspected he didn't like this superior of his. "Thanks for the warning."

He waved away her words. "I haven't seen you. I haven't spoken to you. Just get out of my sight."

He didn't wait for her to say any more, but climbed back down into the hold of his boat. Oriana turned and carefully walked back up to the quay. Her mind was spinning. She pulled the mantilla out of her bag and settled it over her hair again, taking a moment to put the comb in firmly.

She'd been concerned about the mysterious Open Hand coming after her, but not truly afraid. The prospect of being hunted by Maria Melo worried her far more.

CHAPTER 25

Duilio walked along the quay, mulling over the death of Donato Mata. His gift lay quiet now, not a hint of concern for his safe journey back to the house, although it would be foolish to rely overmuch on that.

When he reached the road that wound behind the Customs House, he noticed a woman walking briskly some distance ahead of him. *Miss Paredes.* It wasn't her plain black dress that identified her, or even the mantilla that covered her head, an unusual choice for a Friday afternoon. He'd recognized her walk, the faint swing to her hips that he'd always considered enticing.

And then he spotted Gustavo lounging in one of the shop doorways, head down as Miss Paredes passed. Tomas must be somewhere nearby as well. He'd asked the two footmen to keep an eye on Miss Paredes. When he reached the spot where Gustavo waited, he nodded to the young footman and Gustavo headed back home. Duilio jogged to catch up with Miss Paredes' quick steps.

"Miss," he called when he got close enough.

She stopped and slowly turned, one hand clutching at the other wrist, preparing to draw her knife. She relaxed when she saw it was him. That damnable mantilla kept him from seeing her expression, but he was sure she was unnerved.

"What are you doing here?" she asked when he reached her.

"I could ask the same. Are you *courting* trouble?"

She frowned at him; this close, he could see that through the mantilla's lace. He must have had a snap in his tone. Without answering, she turned and walked on toward the Street of Flowers.

Duilio caught up to her in a few strides; ladies' shoes weren't made for walking fast on cobbles. "I apologize. I've had a trying day and was concerned."

"I thought a man was following me," she said. "I didn't realize it was you."

She'd slowed, so he walked alongside her. She even laid her hand on his arm when he offered it. "It probably was Gustavo, actually. Or Tomas. I asked them to keep an eye on you if you left the house. They weren't to interfere with you, only inform us if someone tried to grab you." She didn't protest that safeguard as he'd half expected she would, so he continued. "When I got off the tram near the Customs House, I saw you walking down the street. Sheer luck."

The mantilla rippled over her face in the faint breeze. He would rather she remove it—he preferred to see her face—but it was better to keep her hidden out here on the street. Just because Mata was no longer a threat didn't mean Miss Paredes was safe.

She walked on in silence for a moment. "I thought that if Maria Melo knew I'm a sereia, it had to have come from him. My master, I mean. So I went to talk to him."

Duilio couldn't fault her logic. "I see."

"I wanted to know why he'd revealed my identity," she said softly enough that he had to lean closer. "Why he'd compromised me."

"Did you accomplish your objective, then?"

"Yes." Her dark eyes fixed on his face. "I didn't like what I heard. I have never stepped out of line before, Mr. Ferreira, never truly defied my orders until Isabel's death. I have not been perfect, but I have tried. I am . . . on uncertain ground now, and don't know how far I dare go."

Duilio had defied orders enough times to grasp what she meant. "Doing what one is told," he said, "is far simpler than not doing so."

She gave him a sad smile, visible through the veil. "So I'm learning."

There were, at this time of day, far more pedestrians than last night. Even so, he thought they could speak safely without anyone overhearing anything important. He steered Miss Paredes out of the way of a group of tired-looking girls in maids' garb, walking down the street.

"There's a small café near the church," he said, pointing discreetly. "I'm famished."

She gazed at him through the veil, and he could almost make out her perplexed expression. "But it's only a couple of hours until dinner."

"Famished," he insisted. He'd endured a jarring day thus far. He and Joaquim had been loaned to the Special Police, a rather dubious honor. He'd been shot at, although, admittedly, he'd set the stage for that himself. He'd faced the man who'd killed Alessio but learned nothing. His day had left him with too many questions. What he wanted to do now was just sit and talk.

Being honest with himself, he wanted to talk to *her*. He could stop and eat by himself. He was supposed to go over to Joaquim's apartment later this evening and discuss the day's developments with him. But right now he wanted to talk to Oriana Paredes.

So he led her up São Francisco Street to the café near the Church of São Francisco. He picked a table with a view of the church's rose window, but far enough from any other patrons to allow them to talk freely. Miss Paredes finally lifted the damned veil when they were settled there, and he ordered a meal large enough to startle her, judging by her expression. She ordered creamed coffee.

"Did you not eat lunch while you were at the house?" she asked.

"Yes, but I seem to need more food," he offered.

Her dark eyes regarded him appraisingly. "Is that inherited from your mother?"

"Yes," he said, glad he didn't have to explain further. "Alessio inherited it as well."

"Ah. Your mother has a picture of you next to her bed," Miss Paredes said then. "With both your brothers and your cousins. She said you were twelve then. I had only one sister, so I can't imagine what it would be like to grow up in such a large family."

He knew exactly the photograph she meant. His mother had it taken when his father was away so that he couldn't argue with her inclusion of Erdano, Joaquim, and Cristiano. Over coffee Duilio told Miss Paredes the story of the taking of that photograph, including his mother's epic struggle to keep a fifteen-year-old Erdano still long enough for the exposure to take. That led to a few stories about Alessio's less-risqué adventures, and then about Joaquim and Cristiano, neither of whom was risqué at all. Miss Paredes imparted vexingly little about her own family. The topic seemed to pain her. She said only that she'd lost her sister and mother, and apparently her father had been exiled to parts unknown, so he let the topic drop.

Once the waiter brought the food, he managed to coax Miss Paredes into taking his croissant. She picked it apart with her fingertips while he finished his soup and fish. As she still wasn't ready to talk about her discussion with her master, he told her instead about his trip to Matosinhos and his conversation with Father Barros.

"Maraval?" Her brow knit at his mention of the Minister of Culture. "He gave me his card. He asked me to come by his office if I had any idea where Isabel was. He's a friend of her father's and has been looking for her. To quell rumors about her, I mean. He said he's been keeping her name out of the papers."

Duilio tried to recall if he'd seen any recent mention of Isabel's elopement in the newspapers. "He must be. I haven't read a word about her since the first notice."

Miss Paredes nodded pensively. When she didn't speak, he went on to tell her about his misadventure at the construction yard, meeting Inspector Anjos, and the death of Donato Mata.

She seemed to be worried for him then. Her slender brows drew together, her large eyes shadowed. "Your day was busier than mine."

Duilio laughed. He couldn't help it. He rubbed one hand over his face and laughed again. "My apologies, Miss Paredes. You either have a gift for understatement or sarcasm. I'm not certain which."

Her expression remained bland. "I have many talents, sir."

Which just set him off laughing again. Duilio wiped his eyes with a finger, hoping he hadn't attracted unwanted attention with his amusement. "Forgive me," he managed. "I'm not mocking you."

Her face was all seriousness, her lips pursed disapprovingly. "You wouldn't dare, sir."

This was why he'd wanted to talk to her, he realized. He'd known there was a hot temper buried under all that self-control. Now he'd discovered a sense of humor as well. How had she held her tongue all those months among Isabel's society friends? Duilio strove for an equally serious expression. "Yes, it was a busy day."

And *then* she smiled, her dark eyes turning toward the white tablecloth. Her hands curled around her cup of coffee, only the tips of her long fingers peeking out of the silk mitts with which she hid them.

Duilio suddenly decided she was lovelier by far than Isabel Amaral or Aga . . . or Genoveva Carvalho. Her full lips were surprisingly enticing, even when he knew there were sharp teeth behind them. Although she normally wore her hair down in the English style, she'd looked quite striking on the night of the ball with her hair pulled up to show off her delicate features and large, dark eyes. He would like to see her wearing something less stern.

It wasn't just that he would like to bed her. He would. He hadn't for a moment forgotten the vision of her in her bath. But he'd had lovers in the past and would never have dreamed of telling any of them of Mata's attempt to kill him. Most gentlewomen would be shocked and appalled. Oriana Paredes had *joked* about it.

Shocked and appalled would sum up Joaquim's reaction should

Duilio confess he was considering Miss Paredes as a potential . . . What *was* he considering her as? He'd already dismissed the idea of asking her to be his mistress. There was very little left beyond that: lover or wife. Friend? Did women on the islands from which she came have male friends? It wasn't usually done in Portuguese society, and he wouldn't be satisfied with that anyway.

Duilio pressed his lips together. Joaquim would protest that Miss Paredes wasn't a child of the Church. That didn't matter to Duilio; he lacked Joaquim's piety. And while Joaquim wouldn't care that Miss Paredes wasn't human, he would find it worrisome that she was a spy. That was probably why he hadn't introduced her to Joaquim yet. Joaquim would immediately pick up on his interest in Miss Paredes, and Duilio didn't need to be arguing with him. They had other things to worry about.

"Mr. Ferreira? Are you listening?" Miss Paredes lowered the lace veil over her face.

That made him want to snatch the thing off again. "I apologize, Miss Paredes. My mind was wandering."

She leaned over the table toward him, and something about her posture told him she was spooked. "I think we should go, Mr. Ferreira. We're being watched."

Stupid of him to forget that. "Where?"

"There's a woman over at the church, watching us."

He wasn't facing the proper direction to see that. "Do you recognize her?"

"I saw her the last time I was here," she said. "She was watching me then. I don't believe it was a coincidence."

He left more than enough money to cover their fare and, offering Miss Paredes his arm, led her away from the café in the direction opposite the church, back down toward the quay. She occasionally cast glances back over her shoulder. "Is she following?" he asked when they walked around the corner onto the Street of Flowers.

"Not that I can see," she said softly.

They crossed to the other side of the street, where the tram was beginning its trek up the steep hill. When it halted he drew her over and they both got on, which would spare her the climb. When they got near the house, she jumped down ahead of him. Once on the street, he offered her his arm again, but decided to go all the way up to the Gouveia house, then around to the alley and back down to his own. If someone was following them, it would provide a smokescreen, although not much of one.

Apparently Miss Paredes understood the ruse, as she didn't argue when he passed the house. She kept walking at his side, her heels clicking on the cobbles. Most of the pedestrians were headed downhill, since it was the end of the workday, so they walked against the traffic. He leaned closer to shield her from a large group of schoolboys approaching them. "What does she look like?"

"Average," she said, her voice barely audible above the boys' chatter. "Brown hair. Brown eyes. I don't know. Intense?"

They'd reached the Gouveia house. Duilio indicated that she should walk around to the side. "That's very vague, Miss Paredes."

Her head tilted in his direction. He could see her dry look even through the lace veil.

"I wondered if she might be this Maria Melo," he said.

"I did too," she said in return. Softly, as if it were a secret.

"Would this be related to your . . . master? Does she work for him?"

They had reached the back alleyway that housed the mews for the Street of Flowers, and she turned to go down that direction. He steered her around a pothole forming in the narrow cobbled road. "I don't know if it's her," she finally said. "But . . ."

They passed the back of the Queirós house in silence and neared his own. Gustavo stood on the back steps, sharing a cigarette with Ana. The footman glanced up when they walked closer, stubbed out his cigarette, and started toward them, but Duilio waved the young man away. Gustavo took the hint and went inside, urging the housemaid along with him.

"I wish I could help in some way," Duilio said.

Miss Paredes reached up and worked the mantilla's comb out of her hair. "I don't know whom I can trust any longer."

Duilio led her up the back steps and paused to turn up the gaslight there. The sun hadn't set yet, but it was already growing gloomy in the shadow of the house. He stood on the step, wrapped in the fading scent of cigarette smoke. "If there's anything you need of me, Miss Paredes, you need only ask."

Considering that she was a spy, the offer could be considered treasonous, but Duilio didn't care. He'd been walking that line for days now.

She sighed softly. For a moment he could have sworn she wanted to tell him *something*, but then she shook her head. "I need more time to figure this all out. I'll try to finish reading that journal this evening after your mother goes to sleep, sir. Given the way he writes, I don't expect we're going to learn more. But I'll try."

She wasn't going to open up to him—not tonight at least. He opened the door for her. "I promised I would go see Joaquim," Duilio said, "but perhaps we can discuss your findings tomorrow after breakfast?"

She nodded and headed upstairs to freshen up before dinner, leaving him alone in the kitchen. Duilio sighed. He needed to decide what he wanted of her. While the Open Hand threatened her life—and the lives of so many others—he didn't think it fair to press her. He just needed to remember to keep his hands off her.

CHAPTER 26

Fortunately, Anjos had given Inspector Gaspar the address of Joaquim's apartment in Massarelos. The Cabo Verdean man arrived there not long after Duilio and quickly eased their worries for the Lady's safety. Joaquim poured a glass of *Vinho Verde* for Gaspar, who settled in the leather chair near the window. It was the first time Duilio had seen the man sit down.

"She's not a fool," Gaspar said. "She didn't tell Maraval anything about our group or your association with us. And Maraval informed her himself about being linked with the floating houses. That bears out Espinoza's statement, as per your priest, that Maraval has been overseeing the installation."

Joaquim leaned against the apartment door. "But he's not the one behind the deaths?"

"I can't say that. I didn't get a look at him myself," Gaspar said. "And I would only have been able to tell if he's been practicing witchcraft himself. This entire thing stinks to me of an effort to keep someone's hands free of actual killing."

Duilio sat down across from Gaspar in his regular chair. "But she doesn't think he's behind it? Does she even have a name?"

Gaspar's lips twisted in a wry smile. "No."

Duilio had a feeling Gaspar could talk circles around him. He didn't think the inspector was more than five or six years older than him, but when he looked in Gaspar's eyes, the man seemed ancient. As if he'd seen everything in the world *twice*. "No, she doesn't think he's involved?" Duilio asked. "Or no, she doesn't have a name?"

Gaspar picked up his glass. "She does have a name but it's not recorded anywhere. No record of her birth, and as far as I know only one man alive knows that name. No, she doesn't believe Maraval could be involved. He's an old family friend, her godfather, although not officially, of course. The Church has no record of her birth or baptism." He took a sip of wine. "Speaking of which, what is your history with Silva?"

"He's my father's bastard brother," Duilio admitted with a shrug.

"There's nothing wrong with being a bastard," Gaspar pointed out.

"I agree," Duilio said. Joaquim had been born only six months after his parents' marriage; some might question his legitimacy as well, so Duilio chose his words carefully. "If Silva and my father had grown up as equals, Silva might have made a charming uncle. But my grandfather cast him out when his mother died, and Silva never forgave him. He made an enemy of my father, he baited Alessio endlessly, and he's spent the past year taunting me."

Gaspar regarded him with narrowed eyes. "Could he be involved in this floating-house business? Maraval dropped Silva's name at one point and then quickly took it back."

Duilio closed his eyes. Silva had the access. It was unclear how much money the man had, but with the Ministry of Culture doing the funding, that made the high cost of the installation less of a factor in who might be pulling the strings. And there had been that business with Mata getting notes similar to the one that had made Augustus Smithson back off the hunt for his mother's pelt. Duilio felt certain that linked the two cases, even if Anjos had reason to think Silva didn't have the pelt. Silva was on close terms with the prince, wasn't he? His pet seer? Silva would surely rise in influence if the prince became a king. "It's possible," Duilio finally said.

Joaquim shook his head. "I don't agree."

"I don't think it's *likely*," Duilio qualified. "If he was involved, he would have never let Miss Paredes go when he had her in his grasp. Nor would he have mentioned the Open Hand to me or told me about the prophecy. He knows I work with the police. Do you think Maraval was trying to deflect attention?"

Gaspar tilted his head to one side. "One reason that Anjos and I—and Miss Vladimirova—were brought in from outside the country was that we have no family ties here, no loyalties that might prompt us to false assumptions. So I'm inclined to reserve judgment on Silva and Maraval both."

Duilio had to admit the man was correct. He disliked Silva for their shared past history. Then again, until recently he'd believed Espinoza complicit in the deaths of dozens, which now seemed wrong. There was a benefit to keeping an open mind. "I'll try to do likewise."

The inspector drank the last of his *Vinho Verde* and rose. Evidently he'd said all he'd come to tell them. "Good."

"Anjos claimed that if Maraval hurt the Lady," Joaquim said, "you would kill him."

Gaspar chuckled. "Anjos underestimates me. I wouldn't do anything so obvious. Nor would it be that fast."

After bidding both of them a good night, he let himself out. Joaquim took over the chair the inspector had abandoned, looking intent. "They are an odd bunch. Do you think they work for the infante?"

"That's my best guess," Duilio said with a shrug, "although if it's true, then it's borderline treason, putting the infante ahead of the prince."

"But the infante is under house arrest up at the palace," Joaquim pointed out. "How could he possibly be pulling their strings? Anjos came all the way from Brazil, and Gaspar from Cabo Verde."

Duilio had been considering that. "I suspect there are ways of working around the infante's house arrest. There must be someone who can get in to see him, someone who knows his views and is willing to act on his orders. The Lady seems able to slip about unnoticed. She might be able to get in to speak with him undetected. And I'd bet there are plenty of wealthy men in this city who'd be willing to bankroll their future prince's whims."

"Meaning that they expect Prince Fabricio to die," Joaquim said. "Soon enough for their efforts to pay off."

It was a cynical thing for Joaquim to say, but Duilio wasn't surprised by his conclusion. "Yes."

"And do we believe Anjos and his crew?" Joaquim asked, pouring another glass of wine for him. "That they're who they say they are?"

Duilio picked up the glass, thinking he should make this one his last. "Do you see an alternative? The Lady clearly has more influence than we do. If nothing else, they might be able to get one of the houses pulled up, perhaps even get a newspaper to dare to write about it."

"Not a very ambitious plan," Joaquim said, pinching the bridge of his nose.

"It's more than we had a week ago," Duilio pointed out.

Joaquim sighed and set his glass on the table. "And now we're assigned to the Special Police. That's a distinction I never wanted to have."

"I know." Duilio rubbed a weary hand over his face. "I don't know that we've gotten anywhere for that price."

"Well," Joaquim said, "Mata died on the way to the police station, so Alessio's killer is dead. The officers watching the tavern say Maria Melo hasn't reappeared there, so the Open Hand either knows that we're watching the place or they've figured out about the sabotage and gotten rid of her."

"That's probably the reason for two weeks between the houses appearing in the water," Duilio said. "It takes her time to set up the next pair of victims and arrange for their 'departure' to their new employment."

Joaquim nodded. "That occurred to me."

Duilio shook his head. "I *want* to believe Silva's behind this, but it just doesn't fit."

"I know," Joaquim said. "It's getting late. Go home. I'll see you tomorrow."

Oriana turned over, pushing the heavy coverlet aside. The large bed, no matter how comfortable, couldn't entice her to sleep. Her mind kept replaying Heriberto's warning.

The Open Hand was, according to Mr. Ferreira's source, trying to make the prince into the king of Portugal. Oriana wasn't sure that made sense. Prince Dinis II of *Southern* Portugal certainly wouldn't agree to such a plan. After all, the two Portugals had been separate for well over a century, closer to two. Reuniting them would disrupt the politics of both countries.

And Maria Melo was trying to stop whatever the Open Hand was doing. That *almost* made sense. One of the things that had kept Portugal from asserting any claim over the islands her people called home was that the two Portugals didn't have the resources to manage warfare on a large scale individually. They'd relinquished most of their interests overseas, turned their colonies over to local governments, and kept only a small military presence in each one. A reunited Portugal might expand to exert influence on the international stage again. And while the Portuguese royalty didn't know the location of the islands her people called home, the Portuguese Church did. They might be persuaded to give up that information should a king rise and pressure them.

But would that possibility be enough for her people's government to opt for assassination? In Oriana's mind, it didn't quite fit. Her people had a long history of avoidance, not confrontation. Even their navy did so, using their magic to judiciously guide ships *around* the island chain without those ships realizing they'd been redirected. Why suddenly choose a violent option for Portugal?

Oriana shoved the coverlet down and got out of the bed. She wasn't going to sleep. Not now. The moon had risen, allowing her to see the minimal traffic on the Street of Flowers. Two inebriated young men walked toward the river, but otherwise the street was empty. She let the curtain fall.

She didn't know what time it was, but since she was awake, she might as well try to finish off that journal. It was exceptionally dry. She would rather be reading one of those overblown novels Isabel had favored. That tongue-in-cheek thought made her smile; some of those novels had been awful. But it was the first time she'd thought of Isabel without pain since that night.

Oriana went into the dressing room and took down the dressing gown she'd been using for the past few days. A rich burgundy velvet lined in a paisley-patterned satin, it had to have belonged to Alessio. The hem brushed the ground, but she didn't own anything comparable and didn't think Alessio Ferreira would mind. So she drew it on over her nightdress and settled on the leather settee near the bedroom door. She lit the lamp and picked up the journal. With about thirty pages to go, she might be able to finish it before it put her to sleep again.

She picked up the letter opener and began searching through the last pages, gently separating the ones stuck together when Mr. Ferreira was doused. The outsides of the journal were the most affected, and the last ten pages had to be carefully eased apart. She was surprised to note that a few were blank, as if Espinoza had been forced to abandon the journal before he finished it out. Given what Mr. Ferreira had said about the artist fighting with someone in his flat, that seemed possible.

She slid the letter opener between the last two pages and slowly jiggled it to pry the pages apart, and stopped. She grabbed up the journal in both hands and forced it open, the paper crackling ominously but not tearing. On one leaf there was a diagram of three circles, the outer comprised of Roman letters, the middle containing what must be a series of runes, and the inner circle holding a group of lines that meant nothing to her at all.

It was the table. Espinoza had *seen* the table, and it was the last thing he'd recorded in his journal. Was this what had spooked the artist, sending him fleeing to Matosinhos to escape his patron? Oriana licked her lips. The runes resembled the ones she'd seen that night, even if she didn't remember them properly. And the rest of the words in Latin were there: *Ego autem et domus mea serviemus regi.*

Her heart pounded against the wall of her chest. Here was the missing half that her own death had been meant to illuminate. She closed her eyes. *What can this do that makes it worth killing so many innocents?*

Oriana pushed herself off the settee and, journal in hand, walked out into the hallway. There was only one lamp glowing there, but it was enough. She strode past Lady Ferreira's room and stopped at the next door. Was this Mr. Ferreira's bedroom? It didn't matter; she would just try them all. She rapped on the door with the edge of the journal, sparing her webbing the worst of the vibration from knocking.

She heard movement within almost immediately. She stepped back, suddenly recalling that his selkie brother, Erdano, sometimes stayed at the house. For all she knew it might be him in that room. Oriana was relieved when, a moment later, the door opened slightly to reveal a disheveled-looking Duilio Ferreira. His hair was mussed, displaying a curl that he usually managed to keep tamed. Over a nightshirt he wore a dressing gown similar to the one she had on but without the paisley satin. He blinked at her, seemingly at a loss for words.

What was she thinking, coming to a man's bedroom in the dark of the night?

"I need to show you something," she blurted out before he mistook her intention. She held out the journal, opened to the diagram.

He took it, eyes fixed on the page. "They've altered the verse."

"What?" She leaned closer to peer down at it over his arm.

He seemed to shake himself. He stepped out into the hallway, closed the door to his bedroom, and went and turned up the one light in the hall. "Come here."

Oriana joined him under the hissing light fixture.

"That last word in the Latin verse," he said, pointing. "See? It should be *Domino*, but they've exchanged that for *regi*."

"King?" she guessed.

"Exactly," he said. "That's probably what gave Espinoza the idea that they wanted to make Prince Fabricio into a king. I guess the writing in the next ring is magic runes, but what in Hades' name is this business in the center?"

Oriana flicked her braid back over her shoulder. "I hoped you might know."

The center symbol was a grouping of perpendicular lines forming two Ts, one large, one small, with the tops parallel to each other. Between those were two parallel lines, one short, one long. And under one arm of one T there was a dash—or rather a minus sign, she suspected, since the other T had a *plus* sign under one arm. She pointed at that. "Could it be . . . mathematical?"

He ran a hand through his hair, smoothing it just a bit. "I don't know. But I know someone who would. Do you mind if I take this? I'll show it to him first thing in the morning."

As if the journal is mine. "Not at all, sir."

An uncomfortable silence fell. It was one thing for her to sneak out to report to Heriberto at night if needed. It was another thing to wake Duilio Ferreira in the middle of what must have been a sound sleep. He was a gentleman, and gentlemen lived by very specific codes of conduct. She'd had to study those rules before coming to Portugal. Meeting in the middle of the night with a woman not his wife—in his nightclothes—broke several of them. That was why he'd closed his bedroom door; he didn't want to invite impropriety.

She glanced down and noted that his feet were bare. They were nice feet. His dressing gown covered him to midcalf, and given that she'd seen him shirtless a few days before, she'd now seen almost as much of him as would be bared should he wear a pareu—little more than a length of fabric wrapped about the waist—as most of the males on her islands did. She could almost picture him wearing one.

She felt her cheeks growing warm. *What a strange thought!* She wasn't certain why that image had popped into her head.

"I couldn't find my slippers," he said in an apologetic voice, perhaps believing she was offended. "My valet has hidden them from me."

Oriana almost laughed then, at the image of Duilio Ferreira henpecked by his own valet. Of course, the elderly Frenchman *was* very snooty. She drew up the hem of her borrowed dressing gown to show her own silver feet. "I cannot reproach you, sir. By the way, are they black felt slippers, rather worn ones, with gold embroidery on the uppers?"

That got Mr. Ferreira's attention. "Yes."

"They're atop the high cabinet in the servants' workroom," she told him. "I wondered what those were doing there. I'll see if I can retrieve them for you tomorrow."

He took one of her hands in his own and lifted it to kiss her bare fingers. "I would be forever indebted to you."

It was done in a joking tone, so she knew better than to read anything into that gesture. He let go of her hand with acceptable readiness and stepped back, the journal tucked under one arm. "Thank you, Miss Paredes."

She headed toward her own room but turned back. Duilio Ferreira stood at his own door, apparently watching to be certain she made it there safely. Oriana took a deep breath. "The woman called Maria Melo? She's a sereia. A spy, but *much* higher in rank than I . . . or my master, evidently."

His lips pressed together as if he recognized the seriousness of what she'd just done. She'd exposed a member of her own government. She'd committed treason, although no one would ever learn of it. Duilio Ferreira would never betray her confidence. And she felt worlds better for having alerted someone else, someone other than Heriberto. It was as if a weight had lifted from her shoulders.

"Do you think she's the woman you saw at the church?" he asked after a moment.

Oriana shrugged. "I don't know, but I can't imagine why anyone else would be watching me. My master pointed out that she can't afford to let the Open Hand recapture me. That would endanger her mission."

Mr. Ferreira licked his lips. "Do you understand, then, why I had Gustavo follow you?"

Yes, he'd worked out that possibility—that she was in peril from both the Open Hand *and* the saboteur—when it hadn't even occurred to her. She was clearly in far deeper waters than she knew how to handle. She nodded. "I hadn't thought it through."

"So I'm forgiven for my interference?"

As if he needed her forgiveness. "Of course, sir." With a nod, she made her way to her bedroom and opened the door.

"Miss Paredes?" he called after her. "Is that even your name?"

Oriana paused on the threshold of her bedroom, bemused. Isabel had never thought to ask that question. After less than a week Duilio Ferreira seemed more of a friend than Isabel had ever been. "Yes, it is."

He smiled. "Good night, then, Miss Paredes."

"Good night, sir." She went inside her room and closed the door.

He'd said once he would like to visit her people's islands. Out of curiosity, that was all he'd meant. As a tourist. But it would be interesting to see how he adapted to her people's ways. Of any human man she'd met so far, he was the one most likely to be able to pull it off.

CHAPTER 27

SATURDAY, 4 OCTOBER 1902

Duilio left the house before breakfast with the journal tucked under his arm. He caught a tram heading toward the parish of Massarelos and got off in time to head down Campo Alegre Street toward the Tavares boatyard. When Joaquim's father had left the sea to pursue boatbuilding, Joaquim hadn't chosen to enter the nascent family business, but his younger brother, Cristiano, had. Now twenty and just returned that summer from the university in Coimbra, Cristiano possessed a genius for engineering and mathematics that Duilio could only admire.

Through the large open doors on the side, he entered the shop where the smaller boats were constructed and was immediately surrounded by the aroma of fresh-sawn wood and resins mixed with a hint of cigarette smoke. Several workmen were currently assembling the ribs of a smallish boat, no more than thirty feet long. It was, to Duilio's untrained eye, another of Cristiano's fascinating experimental designs. Duilio spotted Joaquim's younger brother standing above the pit where a boat was being assembled and called out his name. "Cristiano!"

The young man grinned widely and came around the pit to

embrace Duilio. He resembled Joaquim very little, having a more angular face, like their father's. "Cousin, it's been too long. How is your mother?"

"She's well," Duilio assured him, "although not changed from the last time you saw her."

"I'm sorry to hear that." Frowning, Cristiano waved at the workmen to continue their tasks and then drew Duilio to one side toward the office. "I haven't seen Joaquim in weeks. Tell him he needs to come for dinner."

"I'll nag him," Duilio promised. "Although I must admit now that I've come here for reasons other than social, to drag you into our investigation."

Cristiano opened the office door and gestured for Duilio to go in. A brown-haired English girl wearing dainty spectacles and an expensive tweed suit sat at one of the half-dozen wide drafting desks, a pencil behind one ear, scowling down at the page in front of her. Miss Atkinson was a scion of one of the British wine-trading families over on the Gaia shore, Duilio recalled, who'd come to work for the Tavares firm after leaving the university at Coimbra. She'd been the very first woman to study mathematics there. Although a couple of years older than Cristiano, her petite size made her seem younger.

Cristiano shut the office door. "Is this about the underwater houses?"

"Good guess," Duilio said, glad he didn't have to explain.

"Joaquim mentioned the investigation last time I saw him. Many of the same principles as submersible crafts or submarines," the young man said, "and I've been studying those. So, how can I help?"

One of the nice things about Cristiano: he didn't waste time. Duilio opened the journal, searching for the page that held the diagram in question. "My question is actually mathematical."

"Miss Atkinson's grasp is better than mine." Cristiano gestured for the English girl to join them.

As Duilio hunted for the right page, Miss Atkinson rose and

nearly tripped when her skirt was apparently caught under the leg of the stool. She jerked it free with one hand and came to join them, murmuring imprecations under her breath.

"According to this," Duilio told them, "the houses have walls of cork, thinly covered with wood, which is why they're still floating despite filling with water."

"I told you those buoyancy charms were meaningless," Cristiano said a bit smugly.

"I recall." Duilio finally located the page near the back and stuck on a finger to hold the place. "This is secret, so you can't say anything about it to anyone."

The girl nodded dutifully, and Cristiano did likewise.

Duilio opened it out to the diagram. "Is this symbol in the middle something mathematical? Some bizarre formula? It has a plus sign in it."

Cristiano and the girl exchanged a glance that appeared to condemn Duilio's ignorance. "No, sir," she said, "that's not mathematical."

"It's more my field," Cristiano offered. "Electrochemistry. That's a schematic for a pile."

"A pile?"

"A voltaic pile," Cristiano said, "although it might mean a different form. The symbols aren't standardized across Europe." At Duilio's blank look, he continued. "It's a form of battery, a way to convert chemical energy to electrical energy using two disparate metals, usually silver and zinc, with saltwater as an electrolyte—"

Duilio held up his hand. "Wait. Chemical energy converts to electrical energy?"

"Yes," Cristiano said patiently. "The two elements in each cell . . ."

"You're just going to say more words I don't understand. Let's go back. This is a symbol for a battery. Two parts linked by seawater, right?"

"That's one form," Cristiano said. "It depends on your needs. Dry-cell batteries—"

Duilio held up his hand again. "What if it converted something like *life force?*"

Miss Atkinson's brows rose. She cast a glance at Cristiano that plainly said Duilio was losing his grip on sanity. At his nod, she went back to her desk. Cristiano waited until she was out of earshot. "Are you serious?"

"Sadly enough, I am," Duilio said quietly. "We think there's one of these in each house. The middle ring is some form of necromancy. When the person touching the ring dies, their half of the diagram lights up. Two people die, it all lights up."

Cristiano gazed at him disbelievingly. "This is part of those houses? Sitting underwater? Most of them have been there for months, Duilio. Any electrical charge would have dissipated long ago."

"But this is magic, not electricity, so the rules wouldn't be the same, would they?"

"I have no idea," Cristiano said dryly. "We don't study magic at Coimbra."

Duilio closed his eyes, trying to figure out what was important here. "Each house had two people in it. Two elements in a cell, you said. So how many *cells* would they need to do something? If it were electricity, I mean."

"Just one," Cristiano said. "But more cells stacked together increase their power."

"How many cells would you need if you were planning something big? If you already have twenty-six."

Cristiano's lips pursed. "I guess for style's sake I would use thirty-two."

Hadn't Oriana's elderly friend said that the choice of two languages in the spell was a matter of *style* rather than content? "Why?"

Cristiano shrugged. "Twenty-eight is your next perfect number, thirty-four is your next magic number, but I would lean toward thirty-two. It's a power of two, which works well with current."

Duilio didn't know what he meant by *perfect number* or *magic number*, but he did understand powers of two. "One last question. Say one of the cells was broken. Only halfway lit. What would happen then?"

"That cell would be useless. I would just try to bypass it," Cristiano said. "It depends on how the cells are wired together, but if each is discrete, as those houses are, one cell should be easy to cut out."

"And replaced by another?"

"I don't see why not."

"But that wouldn't be tidy, would it?"

"No," Cristiano said. "I would just replace the broken cell . . . or recharge it."

Recharge. Which would mean finding Miss Paredes and sticking her back inside. Duilio closed the journal and stuffed it back into a pocket. He wasn't about to let that happen.

Oriana had enjoyed a leisurely breakfast with Lady Ferreira and had just settled in the front sitting room to read to her when Mr. Ferreira strode in, the leather-bound journal in his hand. He gestured for Oriana to join him at the doorway. She excused herself to the lady, who nodded vaguely, and went to go speak to him.

"It's a battery," he said. "The whole thing is a battery."

Oriana glanced back at Lady Ferreira to see if she'd overheard, but the lady's attention had wandered. "What?"

"This symbol in the middle is a schematic for a voltaic pile, which takes one sort of energy and converts it to another. But the energy isn't converted until the connection between the two halves is made by . . ." He closed his eyes. "Damn! I forgot what he called it."

"Duilinho, watch your tongue," his mother said softly from across the room.

He actually flushed at his mother's mild rebuke. "My apologies, Miss Paredes. Cristiano was speaking of seawater, although in this case I don't think that would be it, since we're dealing with magic and not silver and zinc."

Zinc? Hadn't the Lady said something about *silver and gold* being used for magic? "I don't understand."

He took a breath and visibly forced himself to slow down. "A battery doesn't do anything until you connect all the parts and then connect it to . . . a light, for example. What if *The City Under the Sea* is the same? It's not doing anything until everything is connected together and there's something to turn on. The Lady called it a recipient, right?"

"Yes," Oriana verified.

"So the table's storing the power," Mr. Ferreira said with a nod. "For now. I guess the plan is to use it all up at once."

That made sense in a twisted way. And it would neatly deal with the Lady's concern about a lack of a recipient. The recipient just hadn't shown up yet. "Would that be enough power to make the prince into a king?"

"I don't know . . ." A knock sounded on the front door, and they both turned to look. Cardenas came bustling down the hallway past them in response. The butler opened the door, and a voice outside said, "I need to speak to Mr. Ferreira immediately."

The butler drew himself up to his full height. "May I have your name?"

"Captain Pinheiro, Special Police."

Mr. Ferreira tossed the journal onto the ground and gave Oriana a not so gentle push. When she stumbled back a few steps, he swung the door closed, leaving him in the hallway, where the officer would surely see him.

What has he done? Heart pounding, Oriana pressed one ear against the door, hoping to hear what passed in the hallway. There wasn't any yelling going on, nor could she hear the sound of a scuffle. She could make out low voices talking, Mr. Ferreira and this newcomer, the officer of the Special Police. She wasn't going to be able to hear anything specific. She sighed and leaned back against the wall. She would have to hope he could manage the man on his own.

Duilio glared at the officer who stood in his hallway. Pinheiro was alone, a strange choice if he was planning to drag Miss Paredes away by force. The man was near his own height, although heavier. Near his age too, at best guess. "What can I do for you, Captain?"

"Anjos said it was up to me whether or not I told you, but I figure the best way to get you to trust me," he began, "is the truth. The seal pelt stolen from your house three years ago? My father doesn't have it. He never did, but he won't admit that to you. He knows you—rightfully, I have to point out—blame him for its theft in the first place."

Duilio felt as if a fog had abruptly filled his brain. "Your father?"

The captain shrugged again. "Yes. He told me about the theft only a couple of days ago. Inspector Anjos had questioned me about it because of my relationship to him. In a way this is my fault. When he found out about me he wanted to set things right, so to speak. He intended to have some paperwork stolen from your house, papers that might contain an acknowledgment by his father of his birth. But the man he hired took the pelt as well, intending to sell it to a collector. That collector apparently took the pelt *and* the paperwork and then killed the man for good measure, all before my father could get his hands on it."

Was this the evidence that made Anjos doubt Silva's culpability? Duilio could see a resemblance in the lines of Pinheiro's face—the square jaw and wide brow. His eyes were hazel, which he'd not inherited from the Ferreira family, but their shape was familiar.

"You're Paolo Silva's son?" Duilio asked, just to be clear.

"His bastard son, of course," the captain said. "My mother entered a convent when she fell pregnant, and I was raised by the brothers. Silva didn't even know of my existence. My mother decided to tell him on her deathbed."

The captain actually seemed sheepish about the whole thing. Duilio could hardly blame him. Pinheiro had grown to adulthood only to be saddled late in life with a father he undoubtedly didn't need: Paolo Silva. Had Gaspar been feeling him out about this police officer last night when he'd asked about Duilio's feeling about bastards? "So, you're my cousin?"

Pinheiro raised his hand. "I only told you so you would know I'm working with Anjos. That story wouldn't have come out without his interference. I neither want nor need anything from the Ferreira family. I do quite well on a captain's salary."

Duilio found this fascinating. Was Pinheiro a seer as well? "So, why did you say this is your fault?"

Pinheiro shook his head sadly. "Silva felt guilty about not providing for me or my mother, just as his father never provided for him. You would think that being a seer and on the prince's payroll, he would be wealthy, but he actually spends most of his funds paying off servants and police officers and whores to collect information for him. He has *tried* to be a father to me for the past few years, although he's frankly not well suited to the task."

The exasperation in the officer's tone was the thing that convinced Duilio. "Very well. Why are you here, then?"

Pinheiro shifted the cap under one arm to the other, his humor fading. "Unfortunately, I need you to come with me to the Carvalho house. I'm supposed to bring a Miss Paredes as well. One of the Carvalho girls is missing."

CHAPTER 28

Stepping into a carriage with the markings of the Special Police clearly gave Miss Paredes pause. "Trust me," Duilio offered. "This is not a ruse."

Her dark eyes met his, and she nodded and stepped up into the carriage. He joined her there, sharing her bench. He reached down and grasped her hand in his as Pinheiro climbed inside and pulled the door shut. Pinheiro settled facing them. "Miss Paredes? Is that right?"

"Yes, Captain," she said softly.

"I've not been informed on all aspects of this case yet," he said, "but I was told that you're to be protected at all costs, which is why the shades are down." The carriage began to move uphill after a jolting start. "We don't want to risk anyone seeing you."

She was trying hard not to betray any nervousness but watched Pinheiro carefully. Duilio shifted to place his revolver in his lap where she could see it. "I promise we will get there safely. I *know*."

Her eyes flicked down to the gun and back up. "What happened to the Carvalho girl?"

Pinheiro answered her. "I understand that on the way back from Mass, she fell back from her sisters to talk to the footman escorting them. A carriage stopped and two men jumped out, grabbed her, and hauled in the footman as well."

"In broad daylight?"

"Yes," Pinheiro said. "Someone has suddenly gotten very reckless."

"I see," Miss Paredes said cautiously.

Duilio gave her hand a squeeze. "Anjos told me he's cleared several officers in the Special Police of involvement. Pinheiro is one of them."

"Believe me, if I'd had a secret, I would have spilled it. The woman questioning me?" Pinheiro shuddered. "There's something unnatural about her. My flesh began to crawl the moment she walked into the room."

"Miss Vladimirova?" Duilio guessed.

"I did not ask her name," Pinheiro said, "but she had a foreign accent."

The carriage rattled over the tram rails, indicating that they were crossing to the Carvalhos' side of the Street of Flowers. That reassured Duilio. His gift had told him that they would get there safely, but it was nice to have it backed up by tangible experience. The carriage began to slow and came to a stop after a distance that seemed right to his mind.

"Lift the shade a bit," he asked Miss Paredes. She did so, and when he glanced up at the house revealed, he recognized the columns of the Carvalho home. "Yes, this is it."

He eased past her and opened the door. When he stepped down, everything looked perfectly normal, so he gestured for her to join him. She set her hand in his and jumped down without the step. Without waiting for Pinheiro, Duilio led her quickly up the steps. A footman waiting at the door allowed them inside once they gave their names.

"Straight to the library," Duilio said. Miss Paredes remembered the way, walking briskly ahead of him. The library door stood open, and they stepped inside the garish room, to be greeted by a crowd. The Lady sat on one of the couches, fully visible this time, wearing a smart-looking suit in green. Gaspar stood behind her, conferring quietly with Anjos. A pair of uniformed Special Police stood near the doors as if on sentry duty.

Carvalho, a barrel-chested man with graying hair, paced along his bookshelves. Sitting in one of the chairs was Genoveva Carvalho, her face grim and nearly as pale as her gown. Her fingers were splayed on the arms of the chair. She glanced up when Duilio entered, pistol still in his hand, and her brows drew together.

Duilio repressed a sigh. The young lady shouldn't be here.

She rose gracefully, wringing her delicate hands together. "Mr. Ferreira? What are you doing here?"

Her father turned at the sound of her voice. "Ferreira? What *are* you doing here?"

Anjos cleared his throat. "Mr. Ferreira and Inspector Tavares have been the lead investigators on a certain case for a few weeks now. Our investigations crossed paths recently."

Genoveva Carvalho sat down less gracefully, her expression nonplussed. She'd probably thought he was too idiotic to load a gun, much less use one.

"You work for the police?" Carvalho asked, stomping in his direction.

"Yes," Duilio said, "although I'm only a consultant."

Carvalho raised one beefy hand to indicate Miss Paredes. "And who is this?"

"My mother's companion," Duilio said. "Miss Paredes has knowledge of this case."

On hearing her name, Duilio could tell Carvalho stopped listening. The man pointed at Miss Paredes. "This is the woman they want to trade for my daughter?"

Duilio felt fury fill him. Had he led Miss Paredes into a trap? He stepped in front of her and hefted the revolver in his hand, deciding whether he should train it on Carvalho or the two Special Police officers at his back. A glint of silver on the edge of his vision warned Duilio that Miss Paredes had drawn her knife. Carvalho backed away.

"There will be no trade," the Lady said calmly. "Do you hear me, Carvalho?"

"She is my daughter!" Carvalho slammed his hands down on the back of the chair in which his older daughter sat. She went even paler than before.

The Lady didn't flinch, though. "And we will do everything in our power to get her back. But making a trade is out of the question. You have no right to sacrifice one life for another. Or do you not believe in the equality that your Freemasons espouse?"

Carvalho scowled, his anger deflated by the Lady's pointed question.

"It's unlikely they would return your daughter anyway," the Lady added. "They're desperate enough to court exposure now by snatching victims off the street. That tells me they mean to rush through the last of their preparations and enact the spell as soon as possible. They'll need two victims from your household, and Miss Paredes won't do for *that* purpose."

"Victims?" Miss Carvalho repeated softly.

Duilio flinched. She didn't know. He was willing to bet that Carvalho didn't yet know what had been happening in those houses either, what was planned for his daughter and the footman taken with her.

"Mr. Ferreira," Anjos said patiently. "Put the gun away. We're not going to permit Miss Paredes to be harmed. I give you my word."

"I'm here too," Joaquim's voice said from behind them in the hallway. Pinheiro had entered with him, and seemed prepared to follow Joaquim's lead.

Duilio mentally checked the numbers and slid the gun back into a pocket where he could get at it easily. Miss Paredes restored the knife to the sheath at her wrist, which, given Carvalho's reaction, showed remarkable faith on her part.

"Joaquim and I won't let anything happen to you," he promised her, catching Joaquim's eye as he did so. Joaquim gave him a nod, agreeing to his part in the pact.

"Everyone sit down," Anjos said. "We need to discuss this like civilized people."

"Miss Paredes found something last night," Duilio told him. "It might help."

She had apparently tucked the journal in the waistband of her skirt prior to drawing her knife. She tugged the journal loose and handed it to him wordlessly. He opened the journal to the diagram and handed it to the Lady, aware that Joaquim had taken his place at Miss Paredes' side. "This was found in an apartment formerly rented by Espinoza. It's the rest of that table. We think it might be what he saw that caused him to flee the city."

She took the journal. "The apartment Mata set afire with you inside it?"

"Yes," Duilio said. "I'm told the design in the center is a symbol for a battery."

"A battery? Oh, I see." The Lady took the journal and smoothed her fingers over the water-rippled page. One finger traced the inner circle, the one with the runes, her green eyes flicking back and forth. "I shouldn't be surprised someone has managed to convert this particular science to magical use, but I am anyway. I would never have thought of this."

"But what does it do?" Duilio asked.

"The runes in this middle circle aren't a spell," she said. "They're more like an outline for a spell, each symbol linking a portion of spell work into a whole. There's more than what we're seeing here, not only more runes, but probably also a component of the spell that must be spoken with the recipient in place to receive the power of the deaths. Given the symbols I do see and the words surrounding the outside edge, this *is* meant to do a work of Great Magic. It will indeed make Prince Fabricio king over Portugal, with all the northern aristocracy supporting him."

"The prince?" Gaspar asked. "Does this mean he *is* a participant?"

The Lady considered for a moment. "Actually, I think not. He would have to speak the words, getting everything correct. This isn't work for an amateur."

Duilio shook his head. While the prince was whispered to be mad, he would hope that something this macabre was beyond the man's imaginings. "So this is someone else making a grab for power?"

"Someone's doing it in his stead," the Lady said. "And it's a safe bet that the creator of this designed the spell to make himself second in command or an éminence grise. Not just that. From the limited bits I see here, I believe it would turn back the clock on the empire, bringing all the former colonies back under Portuguese control—Brazil, East and West Africa, Cabo Verde, Goa, Nagasaki—all of them."

Inspector Gaspar gazed down at the journal over her shoulder, displeasure on his features. Duilio could understand that; Cabo Verde had been independent for decades.

"Does that include the islands of the sereia?" Miss Paredes asked.

"I believe so," the Lady said with a nod in her direction. "Vasco da Gama claimed them, Miss Paredes, even if that claim's never been enforced." She touched one of the strange runes with one finger. "This symbol indicates *territories*, meaning anywhere Portugal has made a claim in the past. There's no date. We might even take back part of Castile."

"How is that possible?" Joaquim asked from across the room. "We can't just tell Brazil we're taking it back. Not after almost a century of independence."

No, Duilio couldn't imagine that any of the former colonies would enjoy a sudden return to Portuguese domination.

"This is a Great Magic," the Lady said patiently. "It's . . . an impossibility. A legend."

"You mean . . . this won't even work?" Duilio asked, aghast. "After all they've done?"

The Lady sighed and closed the journal. "I honestly don't know, Mr. Ferreira. It's difficult to explain. If they *can* make this work, then no one will know the difference. We will all wake up the next morning and never recall that there were ever two Portugals, not recall that the colonies were ever given autonomy. All evidence of it will be gone. Paperwork, buildings, artwork. Some of *us* will no longer exist. And no one will know any different, no one in all the world."

Once she'd worked her way through the concept, Oriana found it offensive.

No one could prove that a Great Magic had ever succeeded. It could be proven that some had failed, but if one worked, all evidence of it would have been consumed in the enacting of the spell itself. While Anjos claimed the Church condemned the idea of Great Magics because they flew in the face of God's Will, Oriana had a simpler objection: it was unfair. No one had the right to change things, not for the entire world.

While they were all arguing over the specifics of this particular magic, Carvalho had a cold luncheon brought in—a quick, informal meal. Mr. Ferreira had introduced Oriana to his cousin Inspector Tavares, who'd bowed nicely over her hand, and then had taken Tavares and Pinheiro to one side to have a quick private discussion. Oriana had caught Carvalho glaring at her a couple of times, which told her she shouldn't trust him. But he was glaring at Gaspar as well, apparently put off by the inspector's darker skin, so she wasn't alone in disfavor.

She sat now on the couch with the Lady, her black skirt and jacket no doubt looking threadbare next to the Lady's splendid wool walking suit in an apple green, its skirt hem wrapped with fine Valenciennes lace. Miss Carvalho occupied one of the side chairs, her hands clenched tightly in her lap, still wearing a morning dress of pale pink muslin embroidered with tiny rosebuds. Dirt marked the hem; it must be the same dress she'd worn to Mass that morning. Anjos sat in the final chair, his tired eyes on the table in the middle. Inspector Gaspar stood behind the Lady, remaining silent as Inspector Tavares summed up for Carvalho and the three Special Police officers what he'd uncovered in his investigation and the subsequent ending of that inquiry. Carvalho seemed horrified by the disappearances of the servants, but he hadn't heard the worst yet.

Mr. Ferreira set one hand on Oriana's shoulder. "Do you want me to tell them?"

My part, she realized. He was offering to tell them of their capture and Isabel's death, to spare her the anguish of telling the story yet again. It wasn't as if he didn't know everything, and this day had already made her weary. "Go ahead," she whispered.

He did so. On hearing of Isabel's death, Miss Carvalho crossed herself and began to cry silently, but Oriana felt numb.

There were three officers of the Special Police in this room, all listening to Mr. Ferreira's version of her story. She could see their eyes turn toward her when Mr. Ferreira explained why she'd been chosen to sabotage the artwork, because she was a sereia. For years they'd been hunting down nonhumans like her. None of them jumped to arrest her, though. It seemed unreal.

They moved on past her part in this, discussing what had been done since. Anjos had been put in charge of clearing undesirable elements out of the Special Police—a separate investigation altogether. He was meant to find officers who abused their power or acted for reasons beyond the group's mandate, most specifically members of a shadowy group called the Open Hand. "Our arrival on the scene, however," Anjos said, "was concurrent with the failed house going into the river. Word of our investigation traveled through the ranks, and several officers disappeared before they could be questioned, which only made us wonder what they were involved in. Captain Rios—who has now vanished as well—learned that Mr. Ferreira was following a new lead. Several attacks on Ferreira followed, meant, I think, to slow the investigation rather than end it. They needed time to complete the artwork and enact the spell. Once we learned what Mr. Ferreira and Inspector Tavares had been investigating, we realized there were ties between our investigations, so we attempted to capture one of the conspirators—Officer Donato Mata, who's acted as an assassin before—using Mr. Ferreira as bait."

Miss Carvalho gasped softly. Oriana glanced up at Mr. Ferreira, who merely shrugged.

"Unfortunately, that didn't work as planned." Anjos said. "They must have seen Mata's death as a sign that we're closing in on them. Today's abduction suggests they're now willing to risk exposure to complete this. After all, if they make it work, no one will recall the abductions or deaths."

"And we're sure now that the Open Hand is behind this?" Mr. Ferreira asked.

"Yes," Anjos said. "Of the officers we've questioned so far, almost all were aware of the group's existence and that it was a very small select body of officers, but none knew its purpose. All the information we've collected so far points to eight or so officers, along with a handful of outsiders who are providing the funding and strategic support."

"But we don't know who those outsiders are?" Inspector Tavares asked.

A hush fell over the room. Oriana joined the others in looking toward the library door, where Paolo Silva, resplendent in a frock coat of black superfine wool and an ecru waistcoat embroidered with gold thread, stood with one hand poised on the door frame.

"It might be beneficial at this point," he announced, "to put me under guard. I'm almost certain you'll find evidence pointing to me as the cause of this mess."

Genoveva Carvalho pushed herself out of her chair, cheeks flaming scarlet. "Get out of this house, you . . . you . . . devil," she demanded, her hands clenched in fists at her sides. "If you're responsible for this I'll shoot you myself."

Anjos rose as well. "Let's hear him out, Miss Carvalho," he said. "I believe Silva's had a finger on this longer than any of the rest of us. I want to hear his side."

Miss Carvalho sat again, her lips in a thin line.

"So gracious of you," Silva said acerbically. He strode into the room, as much at ease as an actor on the stage. He turned his gaze on the Lady. "You've got the Special Police turning themselves inside out, girl. Where did you find that undead creature you've been using to terrify them into talking?"

Undead? Oriana kept her mouth shut. *Could he mean this Miss Vladimirova?*

"In a library," the Lady answered coolly. "Where else?"

"I had little use for your father," Silva said. "Always tinkering around with his magical toys and collecting books. A dilettante, but at least he wasn't murderous. Your godfather, Maraval, is another matter. My prince would never approve of what Maraval has constructed, what he's doing. I want to assure all of you that no matter Maraval's intention, His Highness is not involved."

That statement set off murmurs about the room that died out when Silva raised a hand for silence. "This morning," he said dramatically, "I managed to find someone in the Open Hand who was willing to talk. *She* arranged for Miss Paredes to be abducted in hopes that her survival would trigger the failure of Maraval's witchcraft."

Ah, he'd talked to Maria Melo. Oriana didn't bother to look in his direction. Did he know that Mrs. Melo was a sereia spy? Would it make any difference?

"And what did she tell you?" Anjos asked.

"That they planned to grab one of Carvalho's daughters, since the young ladies walk to Mass every morning, and see if Carvalho would fall for the promise of a trade. But you already know that," he added, "else you'd not be gathered here. Still, they don't know that *you* know what they're doing. They know you have part of the spell—a very small part—but not enough to tell you the truth about what they're trying to accomplish."

"Enlighten us." Anjos drew out a handkerchief and coughed.

"They want to override reality," Silva said, sweeping one arm out grandly. "And change history—"

"We already know about the spell," Pinheiro interrupted. "Do you have something new to tell us?"

That was the first time the captain had spoken. Oriana wondered at the irritation in his tone. Mr. Ferreira laid a hand on her shoulder, warning her not to speak.

"That was hardly necessary, Captain Pinheiro," Silva rebuked him gently. "My source says they intend to start putting one house in the water per night. They're prepared to break into houses and steal victims from them if need be. They'll place the copy of the Carvalho house in the water tonight, and take the Amaral one back out of the water so it can be, shall we say, repaired."

Although he didn't say *how* they were planning to repair that house, Silva's eyes slid toward Oriana. She did her best not to react.

"So, how do I get my daughter back?" Carvalho demanded, arms crossed over his wide chest.

"We'll have to time it carefully," Anjos said, "but we might be able to rescue your daughter when they drop the house into the water."

"Why not just surround the boat and arrest them all?" Carvalho asked impatiently.

Anjos sighed wearily and rubbed one temple. "Because while they have your daughter on their ship—or, frankly, within rifle range—she's a hostage. If we try to arrest them, they will threaten to kill her outright. An impasse."

Silva nodded sagely. "You'll have to let the ship—it's a medium-sized yacht with a crane affixed to the deck, by the way, painted dark blue—slip away first, I'm afraid."

"You've seen it?" Inspector Tavares asked.

"I had a source on the inside," Silva said with a wicked smile. "The selkie they hired to attach the chains to weights on the riverbed. Astounding how easy it is to buy a selkie's loyalty. A few fish and a girl to bed and they're most cooperative. Unfortunately he seems to have changed loyalty again, so I've had to find other sources."

Oriana expected Mr. Ferreira was clenching his fists. Pinheiro rolled his eyes.

Anjos ignored the commentary, though, likely irritating Silva terribly. "Inspector Tavares, what grade of chain did you say they used?" Inspector Tavares supplied a number that meant nothing to Oriana. Anjos clearly understood it, though. "Good," he said. "That's not too large. We wait for them to drop the house in the water. As soon as the ship has pulled away far enough, we cut the chain. The main obstacle is getting a diver with bolt cutters into position without him being seen."

"I can row close in a dory," Mr. Ferreira volunteered.

"And I will cut the chain," Oriana added, and was gratified when Mr. Ferreira refrained from protesting her involvement. She wasn't going to let the threat of capture stop her from doing this.

"And how do you manage that without being seen?" Captain Pinheiro asked.

"Discreetly," Mr. Ferreira said. "If they come before the moon rises, they won't be able to see much. It's far enough from the city that we won't have any ambient light to contend with, and out of the way of river traffic. We just sit on the water, no lanterns, and wait for them to come to us. I might be able to find a selkie or two willing to give chase afterward."

"Why bother?" Carvalho asked.

"If we stop them tonight," Mr. Ferreira said patiently, "they'll know it's over. They'll start preparing to flee. We have to find the workshop where they're assembling the houses before they get a chance to destroy all the evidence."

"Maraval won't be there, even if the yacht is his," Silva inserted. "He lets Captain Rios do most of his dirty work."

Oriana wondered whether they were actually going to take Silva at his word—that Maraval was to blame and the prince knew nothing of what was being done in his name. Or were they going to put Silva under guard, as he'd suggested when he'd walked into the room? She wished she could see Mr. Ferreira's face to judge his reaction. Then Anjos tilted his head to peer up at Silva.

Of course! Anjos was a Truthsayer. He could weigh Silva's veracity.

Apparently Anjos believed him. "Leave Maraval to us," Anjos said. "It's well known that you have a long-running adversarial relationship with the man. Carvalho, do you have a room secure enough to keep Silva locked up?"

Carvalho made some growling noises that Oriana took for assent.

"Promise that you won't even try to escape," Pinheiro said, arms crossed over his chest.

"My dear boy," Silva said smoothly, "how can you think . . . ?"

"Promise," Pinheiro insisted.

"I give my solemn word," Silva said with a half bow in the captain's direction.

As the afternoon crept on, the police officers began to break down the new undertaking into tasks, finding boats, finding appropriate tools. Oriana listened, trying to remember where each person would be. Evidently the Lady couldn't join them, as being on water made her ill, but Gaspar would be in the patrol boat. They might be able to keep other patrol boats at bay. Carvalho insisted on being on the water as well, which Oriana didn't think would be helpful. Carvalho bellowed at them all until they agreed.

"I'll keep the rowboat behind the patrol boat until the yacht closes in," Mr. Ferreira said, "then row close enough to dive in."

Oriana lifted her eyes to meet his. Was he going to try to cut her out of the action? "For *me* to dive in."

"You don't need to do that, Miss Paredes," Inspector Tavares inserted quickly.

"I do," she insisted. It would be full circle for her, back into the death-laden waters near *The City Under the Sea.*

"I was counting on your company," Mr. Ferreira told her.

Thank the gods she didn't have to argue about this. She *was* the best choice for working under the water, but there was more to it than that. She hadn't been able to save Isabel. She was going to do whatever was needed now to save the Carvalho girl. It was her chance for redemption.

CHAPTER 29

Duilio needed a favor, and he suspected he was going to have to pay for it. As they were leaving the house, he asked Miss Paredes to wait for him in the hallway. Carvalho had already stormed out, dragging Silva along with him. Anjos had taken his crew of approved Special Police off in search of a patrol boat to commandeer, which left Duilio more or less alone, save for Miss Paredes and Captain Pinheiro, who was to escort them safely back to the house.

After a moment's consideration of the room, Duilio settled on the curtains . . . or, rather, the tiebacks. They were thick braids, burgundy shot with gold, each end capped with a tassel almost a foot long. He carefully picked one in a corner of the room and liberated the braid from its hook, allowing the drapery to fall loose. There was no way to stuff it in a pocket, so he coiled it up and tucked it inside his coat against his body. Perhaps the staff would be too busy to notice.

"What are you doing?" a soft voice asked from the doorway.

Duilio sighed inwardly. It was Genoveva Carvalho. He pulled the coil from under his coat and walked to where she stood. He could see Miss Paredes and Captain Pinheiro watching from farther down the hallway. "I need to make a trade, Miss Carvalho, and don't have time to stop by my own home to find something suitable. Your father can send me the draper's bill."

She nodded and stood to one side of the doorway to let him pass. He moved to join the others, but she laid one hand on his arm. "Thank you for going after them," she said. "This is my fault. I let Constancia fall back to talk to Tiago. I shouldn't have, but they're friends, and he's too kind to take advantage of her naïveté. Please . . . bring her back."

Duilio patted her hand. "We will do our best, Miss Carvalho. I promise."

Her hand slid off his arm, and he hurried to join the other two. Miss Paredes gave him a strange look, but said nothing about the encounter. A few minutes later they were all in the captain's carriage again, heading in the direction of the Bicalho quay.

Duilio figured Pinheiro had never met a sereia before, but the man seemed unfazed by the revelation of Miss Paredes' identity. "So, what will happen to Silva?" he asked Pinheiro cautiously.

Pinheiro sighed. "He'll probably get several fine meals out of this, have a nice nap, and gather a lot of gossip to spread about. I'm sure he'll come out of this smelling like springtime."

Duilio almost laughed at Pinheiro's vexed tone.

"Do you know Silva well?" Miss Paredes asked the policeman.

"I didn't tell her," Duilio inserted quickly.

"Ah," Pinheiro said. "I have the distinction of being his son, although he wasn't aware of that until about three years ago, when my mother died." He crossed himself at the mention of his mother's death.

"I'm so sorry," Miss Paredes said politely.

"That makes Captain Pinheiro my cousin," Duilio told her. "And it puts a different complexion on the theft at our house three years ago." He explained about Silva's attempt to create an inheritance for his son and its tragic, even if unintended, consequence. Miss Paredes shot a glance at the captain's face, possibly noting the resemblance to Silva. "So, some collector has my mother's pelt."

"Yet she still blames Silva," she said.

"It is, ultimately, his fault," Pinheiro said. "I won't make any excuses for him. I think larceny just comes more naturally to him than honest effort."

"So, how do we find this collector?" she asked.

Duilio was pleased that she'd automatically said *we*.

"My father," Pinheiro said, "has had an ongoing feud for decades, he claims, with the Marquis of Maraval, who has been slowly eroding his influence with the prince. Silva claims that Maraval has a huge collection of magical items secreted away in a basement, but that the item you want isn't there. He's checked; I'm afraid my father has a side career of breaking into others' homes. I expect Maraval knew he would come looking for it and hid it elsewhere, along with the stolen strongbox."

"And Silva knew my family would never deal with him while we suspected he had my mother's pelt," Duilio told her. "None of us would believe him if he claimed innocence, because he *did* arrange the theft in the first place."

"He didn't want to admit he'd lost that round to Maraval," Pinheiro said. "He hadn't told anyone until I became involved in this investigation. He told me only then to convince me that Maraval is behind these evil acts."

"I see," Miss Paredes said. "And Silva's not behind any of it?"

"To be honest, miss," Pinheiro said, "he's not clear of all of this. He suspected that murder was happening for a long time but wanted to tie it to Maraval first. He didn't report the crimes he suspected. Then again, to whom could he have reported them?"

Duilio had to agree. Silva couldn't report it to the Special Police because he wouldn't know which of those officers were part of the Open Hand, and the investigation by the Security Police was shut down. The carriage rattled to a stop. They'd reached the quay where his family's boats were moored.

"We'll just be a few minutes," he warned Pinheiro, and then opened the door and invited Miss Paredes to join him.

His family kept three boats here in a small marina that had been used by his father and his grandfather before. One of the three was a shallow-drafted paddleboat, one of Cristiano's experimental designs. It was good for river traffic and for travel near the coastline when the water was glassy, but in rough water the thing was prone to capsizing. There was also a twenty-six-foot sailboat, but the family's pride was the yacht, a long, graceful ship that Duilio had learned to sail as a young man. Commissioned by his grandfather, the *Deolinda* was nearly sixty years old, yet still tugged and bobbed at its moorings.

Miss Paredes seemed suitably impressed at the sight of the yacht. Duilio honestly preferred the smaller boats; they felt closer to the water. So the yacht had spent most of the last year moored here, only going out when Cristiano or Joaquim had the time to sail.

Fortunately, Aga was on the yacht with João, who rose when he saw them approaching. "I hope you don't mind my bringing her out here, sir," João said quickly, "but she was interested in the boats."

Not a surprise. His own mother found boatbuilding a subject of endless fascination. "I'm certain she would make an excellent boatman. Perhaps you could take out the sailboat tomorrow and show her how it handles under full sail."

João's eyes lit. "Yes, sir. She would love that."

"Good. I need you to gather any bolt cutters we have, and if you could have the dory ready by sunset, that would be helpful. Also, I need to ask Miss Aga a favor."

The young man nodded and held out his hand toward where she sat coiling a line on the deck. The girl was barefoot, wearing a pair of trousers, a man's shirt and vest, and a woolen cap. They weren't hugely oversized, so they must be João's spare garb rather than Erdano's. Aga took one look at Duilio and turned up her nose. Evidently she hadn't forgotten being passed over.

Duilio held up the tieback he'd liberated from the Carvalho library. "Aga, I need to ask a favor. Please?"

Her eyes flicked toward the heavy braid, and she returned to her coiling as if he hadn't spoken. Duilio handed the tieback to Miss Paredes. "I'm afraid you'll have to ask her."

She leaned closer to him. "Why won't she talk to you?"

"She's effectively queen of João's harem now, so she won't take gifts from me."

"I see," she said, a smile tugging at her full lips. "And what do you need asked?"

"I need her to go and fetch Erdano for us. We need his help tonight, and any of his harem that's willing. They can meet us here at sunset."

Miss Paredes crouched next to Aga. She asked the question, offering the braid in exchange. "It would make a nice belt," she added.

Duilio noted that she'd taken Aga's measure quickly enough.

Aga snatched the length of braid from her hand. "Now?"

"As soon as you can," Miss Paredes said. "Please."

Aga immediately began to unbutton her borrowed shirt, provoking João to rush over and launch into a lecture on where and when it was proper to disrobe, which made Aga turn her pretty pout on him. Feeling they'd created enough chaos for one day, Duilio led Miss Paredes off the yacht and up the ramp to where the carriage waited.

"She's very pretty," Miss Paredes noted as he helped her up the last step.

"Not very clever, though," Duilio added. "I'm afraid Erdano's father wasn't known for his deep thinking."

"My people tend to think of selkies as . . ." Her lips pressed into a thin line.

Duilio raised one brow as he opened the carriage door. "As?"

"Well, rather savage," she admitted. "They choose to live on the sea rather than in homes, as we do."

He helped her up. "Anything different is barbaric, Miss

Paredes. You should see the Scots." He stepped up after her, to be greeted by Pinheiro's quizzical look. "Of course, the Scots invented the steam engine, which shows that generalizations are made only to be defied."

"Did they?" she asked. "Amazing. Wearing skirts all the while?"

"Kilts, Miss Paredes," Duilio corrected. "Kilts."

Pinheiro rolled his eyes. Duilio had a distinct feeling that as much as he disliked Paolo Silva, he was going to find Pinheiro an excellent addition to the Ferreira family. "So, Pinheiro, do you sail?"

Oriana changed to the most worn of her clothing, the shabby black skirt and black shirtwaist that had made up her housemaid costume. It was the same garb she'd worn that night, bringing a sense of completion to the choice. She checked the knife's sheath to make certain it was securely strapped on, buttoned the sleeve, and tugged on her mitts. Everyone who would be on that patrol boat tonight already knew she was a sereia, but she didn't intend to rub it in their faces.

A knock at her door heralded Teresa's entrance. The maid waited until Oriana had emerged from the dressing room. "There's a woman in the sitting room who wishes to speak with you," she said. "A Mrs. Melo."

Oriana felt like the world shook. She gripped the edge of the door. "Is she alone?"

"Yes, miss," Teresa said.

She took a deep breath. "I'll go down directly," she said. "Could you advise Mr. Ferreira as well?"

Teresa headed off to find one of the footmen to talk to Mr. Ferreira, who must still be changing clothes. Oriana stripped off her mitts in case she had to get at her knife quickly and headed downstairs to the front parlor. When she pushed the sitting room door wide open, she found the woman from the church sitting comfortably on the couch.

Oriana stopped at the threshold. Should she go in? Would that put her in a more vulnerable position than standing in the doorway? But surely remaining outside would tell this woman she was afraid. She leveled her shoulders and stepped inside. "Mrs. Melo, I believe it is?"

The woman had been watching her, dark eyes hard as stone. She was an attractive woman, but not striking enough to draw attention. Her brows were thick, which lent her a look of intensity that Oriana had noted before. "You've done well so far, Oriana." The woman surveyed the contents of the sitting room with an appraising eye. "I have to say, I'm impressed that you managed to land in a wealthy household following the incident with the Amaral family."

The incident with the Amaral family? Is that how she saw Isabel's death? An incident? Oriana forced her fists to unclench. "What do you want?"

"I want to know if Silva spilled everything I told him," the woman said as she rose. "Did he tell you that we'll be putting out the new house tonight?"

Oriana suspected her reaction—or lack of one—gave away the answer to that. "Yes."

"And will Anjos and his collection of freaks move to rescue the girl?"

Collection of freaks? What an odd thing to say. "I'm sure they'll try."

"You'll have to leave here," the woman said, her eyes fixing on Oriana's. "You know that, don't you? Once the press gets wind of Isabel Amaral's death, they'll want you hauled in and questioned. You'll be exposed for certain, and the Special Police—well, most of them—haven't given up their persecution of our kind. I don't want to see someone who's done so much for the cause hanged."

Done so much for the cause. "You let them kill Isabel. You were there and didn't stop it."

"Oriana," the woman said softly, almost gently. "If you hadn't been there, the Open Hand might have succeeded with this insane idea. Yes, your employer died, but sacrifices have to be made."

Oriana couldn't look at her any longer. "She was my friend."

"Making you carry her handbag and read to her? I think not. One of the first rules of this occupation, Oriana, is never get too close to anyone. Never become attached to anyone. You haven't been in this game very long, so I understand your making that mistake. But there are some things you have to give up for your cause. People like us don't have friends or family. We can't afford them."

Oriana wanted to close her eyes, but didn't dare put that much trust in this woman. She felt ill, a minute away from casting up her lunch on the fine rug.

"I'll make arrangements," the woman continued, "for your extraction. I'll leave word for you here as soon as those arrangements are made. I expect them to be followed explicitly. Do you understand?"

She didn't have an answer. She wasn't ready for this. She didn't want to leave.

"And if you don't go," the woman continued in a reasonable tone, "I'll make certain that the press turns up enough evidence to prove that your father . . . well, let's say that it will make his life most uncomfortable."

Oriana looked up. "Leave my father out of this."

"Remember, Oriana, family is a liability in this occupation. You came to us with a built-in failsafe. I've always known that. Now . . . Heriberto, he's soft. All he wants is to gather enough gold to run away to Brazil, the impetus behind all his petty crime. I promise you, I am not soft. I will do whatever's needed."

No, Oriana had no doubt of that. Maria Melo must have witnessed, even participated in, the deaths of dozens of innocents in the last year. She'd handpicked the people who'd died. She'd chosen Isabel. If Oriana had been discovered by the Open Hand, this woman would have stood silently by and watched them kill her too . . . or done it herself. "I understand."

The woman inclined her head. "I'll send word." She walked around the sofa and paused while Oriana stepped aside to let her out of the sitting room. "You do have your mother's look about you," she said. "Unfortunately she didn't understand the rules of the game either."

And with that parting shot, she walked past a stunned Oriana and down the hallway. Cardenas opened the door, and Maria Melo strode down the steps as if she were queen of the world.

Duilio only caught the last few seconds of that conversation. He'd been half-dressed and still eating his dinner when Gustavo came in to tell him of Miss Paredes' unexpected visitor. He'd thrown on a jacket, bolted down the mouthful he was chewing, and run down the stairs to see that Miss Paredes was safe.

He'd been about to enter on the pretext that his mother wished to speak to Miss Paredes when he'd realized the visitor was emerging. He ducked into the library instead. Miss Paredes didn't need him to interfere, but he wished he knew what had happened. When he came out of the library, she seemed shaken by whatever her visitor had to say.

"Miss Paredes?"

She jerked to attention, her jaw clenched tightly. "Sir?"

Duilio wondered what it would take to get her to call him by his name. "Why don't you join me in the library? You look like you could use a brandy."

"I could, actually." She followed him meekly down the hall. He grabbed the decanter out of the liquor cabinet, and she settled in the chair while he poured. "Can you tell . . ." she began. "Do you know if someone will die tonight? If I can't save them?"

Duilio closed his eyes and concentrated, trying to call his gift into order. He posed a question to his mind, but his gift only had a tentative answer for him, as if there were too many variables that could change. He shook his head. "I don't know."

"Ah," she said, sobering.

"It's not just your responsibility, Oriana," he said. "There will be several of us out there, all working on it." She didn't object to his using her name. Perhaps she hadn't even noticed.

"She fed Silva all that information. She wanted to be sure he'd repeat it to us."

"That doesn't surprise me," he said. "If she's the saboteur, then she wants them to be brought down. She just doesn't want to be brought down with them, or have anyone know that she brought them down."

Miss Paredes nodded shakily. "She said that once the press gets hold of Isabel Amaral's death, I'll be exposed as a sereia."

He'd expected that, but had already planned to pay off anyone necessary to keep her name out of the press. "That can be worked around. I can assure you that your name, and possibly Isabel's, won't appear in the papers."

She shook her head wearily. "She's making arrangements for my extraction. If I don't go, there will be repercussions."

Duilio felt all the threads he'd pulled together slipping loose out of his hands. Why had his gift not warned him? He'd known she had a life beyond this household, but he hadn't seen her walking away so soon. "When?"

"I'm not certain," she said softly. "She'll send word."

Duilio reached across and touched her chin, trying to get her to meet his eyes, but she seemed determined to avoid his gaze. Leaning that close to her, he felt a sudden, wild desire to press his lips to her jaw. He need only lean forward a few more inches. He wanted to smell her skin, tangle his hands in that tightly braided hair. He firmly reminded himself that he was a gentleman in whom she'd placed a great deal of trust. She wasn't one of the demimonde to be pawed, or one of Erdano's girls looking for a night's entertainment.

Oriana Paredes was as much a lady as his own mother. So he sat back, putting some distance between himself and temptation. Heaven knew they had other things to do tonight than entertain his currently hotheaded desires.

"What sort of repercussions?" he asked. "Can I help?"

"No." She gazed down at her hands. "I've been used as a tool, nothing more."

That had to sting. "It happens to all of us at one point or another, Oriana. There are always people out there using other people to get their way."

"She let Isabel die," she said. "She made the choice. I don't think I could ever do that."

Ah, now he had an idea what was whirling around in her head. "Spies put their ideology ahead of everything else. One reason I'm not a spy. I don't think I could do it either."

She smiled then. "No, you would have tried to save Isabel."

He'd never been good at keeping up a subterfuge when it violated his principles. "Speaking of saving others, we should probably head down to the quay."

She picked up her brandy and tossed back the whole glass in one gulp. "I'm ready."

They left the library. On the table in the hallway lay the two overcoats that he'd asked Marcellin to bring down. Duilio pulled one on, picked up the second, and held it so she could step into it. "Too big, I think, but it will keep you warm. It'll be cold out on the water."

"I'm going to be *in* the water," she pointed out.

"The whole time? With whom will I talk?" he asked, allowing a plaintive edge to creep into his voice.

She rolled her eyes but let him help her into the coat. He hoped that look of exasperation meant he'd been forgiven any inappropriate ardor she might have perceived. "I can't promise to make conversation, sir," she said. "It's not one of my skills."

He couldn't resist the temptation to tease her, even though he knew he should. "That only makes me curious to know what your skills *are*."

At the quay where the lovely yacht waited, Mr. Ferreira inspected the bolt cutters that João had collected for him. They had a brief discussion and picked two out of the batch. The sun set while they prepared the rowboat to cast off. It actually served as the yacht's lifeboat, so they had to lower it down by winch to the water before Mr. Ferreira pulled it around for Oriana to join him in it. With João's help, she stepped from the floating marina's planks into the rowboat and swiftly sat. There was a shuttered lantern at her feet, so she made certain to keep her skirts away from it.

"Where is your brother, do you think?" she asked delicately. She'd half expected to find a dozen selkies waiting for them. She was disappointed when they weren't there.

"He'll be here," Mr. Ferreira said, using one oar to push away from the marina. "May be late, but he'll show up." He handled the oars easily, as if he'd done a lot of rowing in the past, and they were quickly away from the other boats clustered near the quay as darkness fell over the water.

The city proper was more than two miles inland, and *The City Under the Sea* had been constructed on the southern side of the river, between the large bend in the river's path and the breakwater that shielded that area from the sea. Mr. Ferreira rowed patiently, taking them along the river's northern bank and then heading across the lanes of river traffic at a southwesterly angle that would take them to where the houses floated. By the time they got close to the right spot, it was full dark.

Oriana disrobed quickly and slid into the water. She submerged long enough to identify the vibrations of another vessel—the commandeered patrol boat—moving slowly toward the breakwater. She fixed the direction in her mind and then returned to the rowboat.

Mr. Ferreira helped her over the side and wrapped the overcoat back around her. With her directions, they soon located the patrol boat. A few minutes later the rowboat was tied behind it, sparing his arms.

"I haven't rowed in a while," Mr. Ferreira whispered ruefully, rubbing at his left arm.

"So, what do we do now?" she asked.

"We wait," he said.

CHAPTER 30

In the darkness, the patrol boat floated along without lights, the rowboat drifting behind it on a towline. The moon hadn't risen yet. They were nearer the breakwaters now that sheltered the river from the open sea, well over a mile from the city itself. They could see the lights of the city still, but were closer to the dark Gaia shore with its high cliffs. Two lighthouses on the breakwaters marked the edge of the open sea.

The crew on the patrol boat had cut their engine, so the silence wrapped about them. They had been sitting there for a couple of hours now in the darkness but hadn't yet seen a single Special Police patrol—or anything else. There were no gulls out here, no seabirds at all, as if they knew what was under the surface of the water. The absence of their cries was eerie. In the darkness it was as if the two boats had fallen off the edge of the earth.

Oriana kept one hand in the water, feeling the currents in her webbing. Her clothes lay in a neat pile near the prow of the rowboat. She hadn't seen the need to don them again, since the borrowed overcoat kept her warm enough and hid the paleness of her skin.

The selkies Aga had gone to fetch never arrived, which meant that the freeing of the house was Oriana's task alone. She could do it. She wouldn't let herself think otherwise.

She could barely make out Mr. Ferreira's face a few feet away.

He'd kept the lantern shuttered to prevent anyone from seeing them, and true to his earlier words, he'd talked with her. Mostly trivial things, such as what books she liked, her favorite food, whether or not she cared for Mozart or Alfredo Keil. Had she read Eça de Queirós? Castelo Branco? Dickens?

He was trying to set her at ease, a kindness since she was so tense. "Is it my turn or yours?" she asked.

He laughed softly and whispered, "It *was* your turn, but you wasted it by asking that, so now it's my turn again. What happened to your father, Oriana? You told me he was exiled."

He'd taken to addressing her by name. It was a step further than simply using the familiar person, more intimate. She liked that. She took a deep breath and considered his question. Then she answered honestly, no matter how terrible it must sound. "He lives in Portugal now."

She opened her mouth to explain, but paused.

She sensed movement in her webbing. It was large—a ship, its screws churning the water. With the pitch-blackness about them, she couldn't *see* the approaching ship, but could feel its motion and hear the ripple of its wake. A shiver ran down her spine. She touched his hand to get his attention; he could see even less in the darkness than she. "It's in that direction. No lights."

He lifted one shade of the lantern, letting off a pair of brief flashes, the signal agreed upon with Gaspar. A single flash showed in response. They'd gotten the message.

The yacht continued on past them in the darkness as he cast off the towline. There were only a couple of faint lights on the yacht's deck, but Oriana could make out the arm of a crane affixed to the deck. A large, boxy shape hung from the crane, a house all ready to drop into the river. A chain draped from the underside of the hanging house to the deck of the yacht. It would have a weight attached—she knew that from the journal—even if she couldn't see it yet. When they got to the right spot, they would drop the chain, then lower the house into the water from the crane. The weight would drag it downward, and their diver—Silva's selkie—would guide the weighted chain to the right spot and attach it to an anchor set on the silt-clouded riverbed before the first house had been put in place.

It was eerie to see the instrument of Isabel's death.

They waited in silence a while as the ship found the right position, apparently being directed by the selkie, much as she'd led Mr. Ferreira to the patrol boat. Mr. Ferreira rowed quietly, moving them closer to the yacht.

Then Oriana heard the rattling of chains. The sound sent a cold wash of remembered fear into her stomach. She dropped the coat she wore and slid into the water, naked save for the knife strapped to her wrist. She reached over the edge of the rowboat to grab the bolt cutters from the bench.

"Be careful," Duilio told her.

She submerged in time to feel the house hit the water, its chain dragging it down. As she got closer, the water was full of death. Oriana breathed it in, felt it in her gills and tasted it in her mouth, the flesh of dozens of innocents rotting away in this slow eddy of the river. The taste of corruption in the water sent the terror and pain of that night surging back into her mind. Isabel was among those whose bodies were slowly decaying in this watery graveyard.

Isabel had died in this place, but *she* hadn't. Oriana was going to make use of that.

She forced herself on, swimming awkwardly with the heavy tool in her hands. Her large eyes took in more light than a human's, but in the moonless dark, distorted by the water's movement, the house was little more than a blur.

Oriana reached the floating house and immediately swam downward to locate the chain. She brushed against columns, a triangular pediment—definitely the Carvalho house. She couldn't hear voices within, so the captives might not even have woken yet. Perhaps they would be spared the worst of the terror.

She located the chain. It was taut, which told her the selkie must already be pulling it downward to affix the chain to the weight on the riverbed. Oriana wrapped one leg about the chain for leverage and worked the bolt cutters into position. She pulled on the long handles as hard as she could, but couldn't get them to bite through the chain.

And then a body slammed into her from behind, breaking her grasp on the chain. She managed to keep her grip on the cutters and swung them slowly through the water at her attacker. It was the man from the boat that night, the one who'd chased her through the water and tossed her into a rowboat with Silva—the selkie.

Set free, the house began easing back upward, fighting the weight pulling it down. It wouldn't last. Water was filling the house, and that weight would force it back down.

The selkie grabbed the bolt cutters and ripped them from her grasp. Then he swung them toward her head.

Duilio listened to the sounds over *The City Under the Sea*. He'd heard the slap of the house hitting the surface of the river. He dropped his own anchor over the side and held his breath. How long would it take before the house sank far enough to be safe from stray bullets? Should he dive in and help Oriana? Or would he be in her way?

The rowboat rocked suddenly when Erdano levered his bulk up onto the side of the boat. "Am I too late?"

Duilio let out a frustrated sigh. Erdano had probably been playing in the water all this time. "Miss Paredes needs to cut the chain on the floating house they just put in. She's got a tool to do that. Can you go help her?"

Erdano nodded and slid back into the water, leaving Duilio in the dark again. He could only pray that between them, Oriana and Erdano could cut that chain.

The patrol boat was waiting for the yacht to move away from

the vulnerable house. Duilio could make out one lantern on the deck of the yacht, alerting him to its position. Its first task done, it began to move, likely hunting the waters over the Amaral replica so it could retrieve it. Where would that be?

The crew on the patrol boat opened their lanterns suddenly, and Duilio saw the yacht *had* changed course, heading directly for them. With their engine cold they had no hope of getting out of the way, so the patrol boat blew its horn. Barely visible, the yacht changed course again, now trying to pass *behind* the patrol boat.

Oh, God! Duilio made a panicked grab for the anchor line, but before he could cast it off and move away, the yacht caught the rowboat broadside.

Oriana pushed out of the way of the selkie's wild swing. In the water everything moved more slowly. The cutters passed within inches of her face and she kicked farther back, her heart pounding hard.

And then another body hurtled past her in the water, slamming into the selkie's form. The cutters spun out of his hand, immediately sinking. Gasping in water, Oriana dove after them, pursuing them down toward the riverbed. She would lose them in the silt if they hit the bottom. She made a desperate grab and managed to catch one handle.

She headed back up toward the surface. She had no idea where the selkie or his attacker had gone. She took in a large breath, relieved to be above the clouds of silt near the bottom. She located the chain and followed it upward. Would she be in time?

She could see the house itself then, so she grabbed the chain and wrapped her leg about it again. She hauled the cutters around, positioned them, and clamped them down on the chain, but the blades didn't cut through. *Damnation!* She wasn't going to give up. She ground her teeth together and tried again.

Then a warm body enveloped hers, two large arms coming around hers and grasping the handles of the cutters. The taste in the water told her it was a selkie. His muscular arms strained, and the cutters sliced through the chain. The house was free! It began to float upward, turning now that it was loose, like a fish righting itself in the water, which must be terrifying for the victims inside.

Oriana shoved at the warm body holding her. The selkie released her, although one of his hands squeezed her left buttock before he swam away. She was too relieved to bite him. She let go of the cutters and swam after the rising house, trying to guide it upward. Gods grant that those inside were still alive. She broke the surface only a second after the house did and bobbed in the ripples there. Her throat opened and she tried to catch her breath.

Lights told her where the patrol boat was, and the yacht. Voices carried across the water, a spate of urgent cries. She didn't see the rowboat. A gunshot sounded, but she couldn't tell from which vessel. The house, now on one side, began moving in a stately fashion toward the patrol boat, and she realized the annoying selkie—it had to be Erdano—was propelling it in that direction.

She treaded water. Where had the rowboat gone? She felt cold from more than just the night air. She twisted about to look the other direction, thinking perhaps she'd mistaken where he'd been. He wouldn't just leave her out here.

The floating house banged against the side of the patrol boat, and with shouting that carried over the water, the crew reached down with hooks and a long metal pry bar to break into it. The selkie moved away, his dark head coming in Oriana's direction.

"Go after the yacht!" she yelled at him. "Follow it!"

He jerked about in the darkness and slipped under the water again.

She swam closer to the patrol boat. A bright flash of light momentarily blinded her. They must have found a photographer willing to bring his precious gear out on the water with them. She blinked to clear her eyes and yelled at the top of her lungs. "Where is the rowboat?"

In the chaos on the deck of the patrol boat, someone must have heard her. "Down," a voice called back—Inspector Gaspar. He yelled something else. ". . . yacht hit it. Go after . . ."

Oriana's heart slammed against her ribs. The yacht had hit the rowboat? *Oh, gods, no!*

None of the humans would be able to see in this water. They would never find him.

Another explosion of light came from the deck of the patrol boat. Oriana clamped her eyes closed, took a large breath, and submerged again. She swam down a dozen feet and then held her depth, her fingers spread wide to sense movement. Frantic tremors came from above where the patrol boat and the floating house banged against each other.

There was nothing on her own level save for the motion of the tide. No, there was something . . .

Below her she sensed a struggling movement, like that of a dolphin caught in a net. He was still alive! Oriana whirled in that direction and tracked the source of the movement.

She saw a flash of whiteness far below—his shirt. The current was pulling Duilio out to sea, while an anchor was dragging him lower each second. Could he hold his breath longer than a human?

She pushed herself downward until she reached him. His leg was caught in the anchor's rope. Oriana wrapped her arms about him and pressed her lips to his, giving him the mouthful of air she held. It surely wouldn't be enough. She *had* to get him loose.

She found the rope tangled about him, caught in the wool of his trousers. It must be crushing his leg, the weight of the anchor and undertow pitted against his will to survive. She patted his knee to reassure him and began to saw at the taut rope with her knife. After a moment only a thread was left, and then that thread snapped.

Unanchored, Duilio began to drift upward through the dark water. With a thankful prayer to whichever god was helping her, Oriana swam up after him, wrapped her arms about his body, and kicked hard.

When they broke the surface, he gave a ragged gasp. He choked and coughed while she supported him. "Be still," she said, tears stinging her eyes now that he was safe. "Let the water hold you."

There was panic in his eyes, visible this close. "Where are we?"

He couldn't see the nearby shore, she realized, and had no innate sense of the direction. Following the lights of the city would mean swimming *across* the river, more than a mile against the current, a foolish choice when the unlit Gaia shore was closer. They'd drifted far from the patrol boat, certainly far beyond the crew's ability to see two people stranded in the water. She could hear its engine chugging away. They must be heading back toward the city to get the victims to a doctor. At least she hoped that was the case. They had trusted her to save Duilio.

"I know where the land is," she reassured him. "Here, let me get this coat off you."

She could tell he was fighting to keep calm, his breathing still ragged. She worked the buttons of his coat, the wool swollen with water and stubborn. Once she finally had it undone she pushed it off his shoulders. Freed from its weight, he seemed better able to stay afloat. She tugged off his sodden tie, just to be certain he could breathe.

"I'm going to tow you to shore," she said in his ear. "Don't fight me."

He coughed again but nodded, so she wrapped one arm about his chest and began hauling him toward land. He let her carry him most of the way, but after a time insisted on swimming on his own. It wasn't far. Even so, it seemed to take forever.

They ended up on the Gaia shore, almost all the way out at the breakwater. Her feet found purchase in fine sand, and she pushed herself upright, walking the last little distance to the beach. She slid down on one side of a large rock, where she would be hidden from view from passing traffic on the river. "Just let me rest a while," she mumbled.

Only a few steps behind her, Duilio didn't argue. He sat next to her on the damp ground and coughed up more water. She caught him in her arms when he slumped to the sands.

CHAPTER 31

The green hills rolled gently down to the Douro at the Marialva estate, allowing all the guests a fine view of the sparkling waters peeking between carefully manicured stands of trees. Tidy rows of grape vines climbed the far bank of the river. It was a mild spring afternoon, and Oriana had gone with Isabel to an informal picnic on Lord Marialva's grounds.

Pia walked with them, her white-gloved hands fluttering as she spoke. She wore pink, and with her blond hair down she looked sadly insipid next to her vividly alive cousin. Isabel's dark green walking suit made her seem more forceful and real. Oriana held a parasol to shade her mistress' alabaster skin.

They walked past a blanket where a young woman reclined next to the prince's seer. As they walked closer, Silva took the girl's hand in his, slowly drew off her short glove, and ran a bare finger across her palm. The girl's mouth opened in a surprised O at whatever he said.

"I don't know why anyone listens to that man," Isabel said loudly enough for the girl to overhear. "He's wrong more often than the astrologers." She lifted her chin in the air, the feather from her cap curving around to touch her cheek, and walked on past.

They'd nearly reached the river's bank by then, the comforting smell of the water filling the air. Marianus Efisio, Pia's betrothed, stood speaking with another man, one Oriana didn't recognize. Dark brown hair, medium build, slightly taller than average—not much to distinguish him.

"Who is that with Mr. Efisio?" Oriana asked.

"Mr. Ferreira, the younger one," Pia whispered, and crossed herself reverently, white gloves fluttering like gull's wings. "The elder passed recently."

Isabel laughed under her breath. "You wouldn't want your handsome betrothed talking to the older Ferreira," she told Pia, a waspish note in her voice. "They say he took a different lover every night, sometimes more than one . . . and not only women. Scandalous. He was sinfully handsome, Pia, and might have stolen your swain from you. At least with boring Duilio there, your betrothed's chastity is safe."

Pia flushed bright red, her cheeks clashing with her pink dress, while Oriana wondered what had made Isabel's tongue so sharp that day. She extended her arm to keep Isabel's face shaded by the parasol, and turned her eyes toward the two men in question. The newcomer looked in their direction, his gaze settling directly on Oriana.

But Mr. Ferreira looked away quickly, leaving her with only the impression of warm brown eyes in a serious face. Yet when she saw his face more clearly, his expression seemed fatuous . . . vacant. He went on his way a moment later.

She turned to watch his escape . . . and realized she stood on a seashore instead. It was the beach she'd lived near as a child. She closed her eyes. A cool breeze off the water set her at ease, the smells of flowers and the cries of the birds familiar. It was home.

A musky scent touched her nostrils. She opened her eyes to see Duilio Ferreira standing only an arm's length away, his bare feet on the sand. He was bare-chested and wearing a black pareu tied in the manner that proclaimed him chosen. Scratches ran across his back and one shoulder, and a number of rose-gold cuffs adorned his ankles and his arms, enough to show his mate held him to be of great value. He turned toward her, revealing that his chest had been painted with the Paredes line mark. His kohl-rimmed eyes laughed. "It *is* beautiful."

Oriana stared at him, captivated. *What is he doing here?*

"As are you," he added. He stroked her cheek with gentle fingers. She held her breath, waiting for him to kiss her. His warm lips touched hers, soft and patient. His left hand spread on her bare skin below her breast, and then slid around to her back, pulling her closer.

But his grasp suddenly turned cold and wet. His other hand tangled in her loosened hair, just as sodden.

SUNDAY, 5 OCTOBER 1902

Oriana felt cold water in the shell of her ear, and that jarred her out of whatever strange world of dreams she'd inhabited. She lay on the sands at the edge of the river, warm on one side, chilled on the other. The tide had begun to overwhelm the river's usual good sense, coming in with icy morning fingers; that was what she'd felt threading its way through her hair.

Duilio Ferreira lay half-across her, with his head pillowed on her breast. His hand rested on her stomach, his legs tangled with hers. Oriana lay still, trying to decide what she should do. She had never lain with a man in her arms before, and hadn't realized the warmth a male body would carry with it.

She didn't understand why she'd dreamed such things, why that day by the side of the river had surfaced in her memory. It had been the first time she'd realized Isabel intended to steal away Pia's betrothed. But she'd forgotten seeing a man named Duilio Ferreira that day.

Or, rather, he had seen her. A man who had seemed otherwise unremarkable had noticed her as a person, rather than a nameless servant. He had *looked* at her. She recalled wondering about him later, but he'd already gone. And then she'd forgotten all about him.

She swallowed, tasting river water on her tongue. She didn't want to dwell on whatever had made her cast him in the dream as her mate, dressed and painted as a man of her people would have been. It was laughable. He was wealthy and a gentleman; he would never display himself in such a way. Nor would he take someone like her—a sereia, and a penniless woman who'd spied on his people—as a mate.

She'd been told for years that she would never have a mate, that she was destined for service to her people instead. Was she so unhappy with her current life as to conjure a mate from among the humans?

Oriana closed her eyes, hearing the denial spinning through her thoughts. Presented with the truth, she didn't want to face it; the numinous thread that her people believed bound her soul to another's—that thread of Destiny she'd always believed didn't exist—was tied to *him*. She knew the way he smelled, the twist of his lips when he held in some clever comment that made her wish she could blush.

She did believe in Destiny after all.

Duilio woke when water soaked through his shirt anew. The morning tide was coming in. The sun had begun to rise. Birds screeched in the rocks above them, barely visible in the fog that blanketed the shore.

He was tangled in Oriana's arms, one of his wool-covered legs between her bare ones. Desire flushed through his body, leaving him almost painfully aroused. His left hand lay just below her breast, and for a traitorous second he wondered if she knew he'd awakened. But she had one hand loosely atop his head; she must have felt him move. He lifted his head slowly from her shoulder.

He'd awakened in a woman's arms often enough before that it didn't shock him. Normally this would be the moment to kiss her, to shift his body closer and move his hands to caress her. Normally it would be a good time to make love and perhaps to sleep again afterward. His body surely found that an excellent idea. Unfortunately, nothing was normal with Oriana Paredes.

So he eased himself off her and into a sitting position with a sharp mental reminder not to stare at her breasts. He coughed and moved to one side, his eyes averted. His leg ached fiercely. That helped distract him. Mystified, he peeled back his trouser leg. Blue and purple bruises wrapped his leg where the anchor line had been, crushing the little derringer in its holster against his ankle. He hadn't realized how tightly the anchor had held on to him. And where were his shoes?

Oriana moved, drawing his eyes back to her body. She settled on her scale-patterned knees and touched his ankle. "Is it broken?"

Her hands on his skin brought his body back to full attention. Duilio felt his face go warm with embarrassment. Her wet hair hung in sand-encrusted tangles, and her eyes seemed deeper set with exhaustion, but she still stole his breath away, just as she had the first day he'd seen her so. He was close enough to lean in and kiss her. Instead he fixed his eyes on his leg. "I don't think so."

She insisted on running her fingers along the bones to be certain, coolly and clinically, as if she hadn't noticed his discomfort. He leaned back while she unstrapped the holster, which actually set off another flare of pain. "What happened?" she asked.

She didn't seem offended, a small recompense. "The yacht hit my boat," Duilio said. "I was casting off the anchor when it hit. My foot must have tangled in the anchor line, and it dragged me under."

He took another deep breath and decided that he finally had his body under control. And if he wasn't going to ravish Oriana Paredes on this fog-veiled beach, then what was the point of staying? Fog clung to the cliffs, but he could see enough. They had fetched up on the beach near the breakwaters. Without a coat or tie he must look disreputable, but boats did go down in the river from time to time, stranding people. He would simply plead that as an excuse.

Oriana could hardly walk through the streets naked, though. "Wait here," he told her. "I'll come back with something."

He started to take off his shirt to offer it to her, but she shook her head. "I'll stay in the water," she said. "I'll be fine."

He would have felt silly wearing only sodden trousers anyway. Duilio peered at the rocks, trying to decide how to get up onto the heights. A narrow wooden stair ascended the cliff's face, likely property of some homeowner. Duilio headed toward the stair.

"Ferreira," a voice called across the water. "Ferreira!"

Duilio stared out into the fog. He couldn't make out a boat, but he heard oars cutting the water, the noisy splash of an inefficient rower. "Gaspar? On the sand."

"Coming," Gaspar called back.

Oriana half rose out of the water. "I'll go find him."

She didn't wait for his response. She dove into the water and disappeared into the fog. Duilio leaned against the rocks, his ankle throbbing. The splashing grew closer, and then he saw a small boat sliding toward the sand. Gaspar sat inside, Pinheiro with him. Duilio waded out to them. "Do you have a blanket?"

Chuckling, Gaspar dug one out of the bow and handed it over. Duilio helped Oriana settle it about her and lifted her up into the boat. He pushed the boat away from the shore and then clambered over the side and settled on a middle plank facing her. She managed to work the blanket around so that not even an inch of her silvery feet showed. After fending off a spate of questions from both of the other men, Duilio finally got to ask a question of his own. "What happened to the two in the house? Was it Miss Carvalho and the footman?"

"Yes, both are alive," Gaspar said.

Duilio saw Oriana's shoulders slump in relief. She'd saved them.

"The boy was in rough shape," Gaspar added as he rowed toward the city. "It looks like he fought them, trying to keep them from the girl. A couple of broken ribs, and his face was so swollen he could hardly breathe, which is why we had to leave you out there. We needed to get him to a doctor."

Duilio didn't blame them. They would never have been able to see him in the river in the dark anyway. "And the photographer? Did he get any pictures?"

Gaspar grunted. "Yes. It's a matter now of developing them and convincing his editor to run them. Anjos is already meeting with the City Council, bypassing the Ministry of Culture altogether. We expect that, given the evidence, they'll agree that the remainder of the houses must be cut loose."

"Good," Duilio said. "What did Maraval say?"

"Nothing so far," Gaspar said. "Anjos and his team didn't find the man. They did, however, find an extensive collection of magical artifacts in a secret basement, which bears out Silva's claim. The Jesuits have volunteered to catalog the collection, but they haven't found your missing pelt yet. Maraval wasn't at the ministry either, which leaves . . ."

"The mysterious workshop?" Duilio asked.

"Yes. If he's on the run, it's likely he'll go there. Miss Vladimirova is questioning the servants at his home. If any of them know the location, she'll get it out of them—I promise."

"I told the selkie to follow the yacht," Oriana told Gaspar. "If he did, he'll know where it is."

Duilio was glad to hear that Erdano had gone after them. He hadn't dared to ask.

"We'll have to hope that one plan or another gives us an answer," Gaspar said, "or Maraval will get away before we have a chance to get our hands on him."

They planned to take no more than an hour to return to the house, change clothes—or, in her case, put some on—and head back out to find Erdano and his harem. Oriana only hoped that

Erdano had been able to follow that yacht. Inspector Gaspar claimed that the regular police were watching all train routes out of the Golden City to prevent Maraval from escaping that way. But why bother with a train when he had a yacht at his disposal?

The police had a carriage waiting when the rowboat reached the Bicalho quay, so a couple of minutes later they were rattling across the cobbles, heading toward the Ferreira house in the morning fog. The road was rough, causing her shoulder to bump against his. Oriana clutched the blanket closer; it was chilly.

"I did offer you my shirt, Miss Paredes," Duilio reminded her.

"And how would you explain *your* returning to the house half-naked?" she asked. "Would that be any easier?"

"I will, of course, replace the garments you lost, Miss Paredes," he said magnanimously.

"So you don't have an answer either," she surmised. If he'd been caught in this situation with a young Portuguese woman of any social stature whatsoever, he would be expected to marry her to protect her from scandal. No one would expect the same for a hired companion.

"We should simply say nothing," he said mischievously, "and let the servants wonder."

Well, they would probably come up with their own interpretation anyway. "I am far more comfortable in this situation," she said, "than you would be. More accustomed to such garb."

"You mean wearing a blanket?" He regarded her with raised brows. "What exactly *do* people wear on your islands?"

She smiled, gazing down at the one hand in her lap. She still had the dagger's sheath strapped to her arm, but the blade had been forgotten in the river. "That book you read as a boy was right in that those who work near the water often do so unclothed. Otherwise one usually wears a pareu." When he opened his mouth to ask, she explained. "A length of fabric wrapped about the waist. It would cover from the waist to the knees, or just below."

"Ah," he said. "Do you mean the men? Or the women?"

"Both," she said with a shrug. "When it becomes cooler, one wears a loose vest over that, or even a jacket."

He shifted in his seat to look at her. "The islands *must* be warmer than Portugal. No shirts?"

"They come into fashion now and then but aren't essential." She shot a swift glance at him, trying to gauge his reaction. "A human would be quite uncomfortable dressing so."

His lips pursed. "Probably at first. I suspect I would enjoy it after a while. No need for a valet, certainly."

She plucked at the blanket with her free hand. "Yes, the many layers your people wear are rather . . . redundant."

"You must hate our clothing."

"At first I did, a bit," she admitted. "But I've grown accustomed to it."

It was an ordinary conversation, a break from all the other things they didn't want to discuss. *As if we'd simply met at a café*, she thought, wishing with a sudden pang that her life could be that simple. Would she have the nerve to court this man if she had the chance?

The carriage drew into the alleyway behind the houses on the Street of Flowers, getting them quite close to the back door. Cardenas was outside on the steps, sneaking a cigarette, as he did when upset. The butler stubbed it out on the wall and came to meet the cab. When Duilio opened the door and stepped down, Cardenas embraced him and burst into tears. He drew back quickly, though, apparently recalling his station. "We feared the worst, sir, when João told us the rowboat hadn't returned."

Oriana stayed in the carriage, giving the butler a private moment with his master. Duilio kept his hands on the man's shoulders, reassuring him. "I'm well enough, old friend. I need to get Miss Paredes inside," he said. "We're only here to change clothes and get right back out on the water."

Cardenas nodded and stepped back. Duilio returned to the carriage and insisted on helping her out, lifting her down with an ease that surprised her. She might expect that of the big selkie, but perhaps Duilio was stronger than he looked. He set her on the ground, and she clutched the blanket close. Cardenas went up ahead of them, clearing the servants out of the kitchen so Oriana could dash through in her inappropriate garb.

Duilio led her up the back stair to the second floor, and fortunately no one intercepted them. "I'll wait for you in the library," he said when they stood outside her bedroom door.

She showed him her wrist. "Do you have another spare dagger?"

"I'll find something," he promised, opened the door for her, and then headed down to his own room.

Oriana went inside. She was short on clothing. If she were staying she would have to ask for an advance on her first quarter's pay, but she knew better. She closed the bedroom door, dropped the blanket across the settee, and paused.

There, on the small table next to the settee, lay a notecard addressed to Oriana Arenias Paredes.

Her breath went short. It had come from someone who knew both of her mother's surnames, Paredes *and* Arenias. Most people paid little attention to the surname a female received from her father. Oriana picked up the note, impressed by the fine quality of the paper and the author's neat hand. Surely this was from Maria Melo, who'd implied an acquaintance with her mother. *Her orders.* The ones that would tell her how to get out of the city, where she would be sent, and to whom she would report. Perhaps they would say she had to leave *now.* How long had this been sitting here?

She ran her fingers over the lettering and then turned the envelope over to break the blue wax seal marked with the letter M. She slid one finger under the flap.

What if I'm supposed to leave immediately? This could order her to leave this morning, an hour ago or an hour hence.

I am not letting Isabel's killer get away.

Oriana set the note back down on the silver salver on the table and went to the dressing room to find something to wear.

She'd hated these garments at first, so tight and uncomfortable. Now she saw them as a symbol of all the things she would miss from this place. She'd even miss the silk mitts that pinched her webbing. She would miss . . . many things. Once dressed, Oriana gazed at the tired face in the mirror, determined not to let her emotions get the better of her. She inhaled deeply, taking in the masculine smell of her borrowed room. Then she plastered a serene look on her face and went down to the library to meet Mr. Ferreira.

CHAPTER 32

Duilio brought his last knife for Miss Paredes to use. His favorite revolver had been in the pocket of his frock coat last night, now lost forever in the water of the Douro. He would miss that gun, but he had an Enfield revolver that would do well enough until he could get a replacement sent over from England.

The carriage was waiting for them behind the house and bore them out to the quay, where Gaspar and Pinheiro were still waiting. Gaspar had a wooden box about the size of a football in his hands. He opened it up to reveal a golden device sitting atop what looked like a pincushion. A collection of gears with a coil of metal inside, the device ticked and trembled like the works of a watch. "I'd like you to take this along with you," he said.

Duilio surveyed the clockwork device doubtfully. If it was valuable, he didn't want to take it out on the water, not on the paddleboat. "What is it?"

"It's called a blood compass. A clever little device that Anjos and I have found useful," Gaspar said. "They come in a pair. The other follows this one. In essence, it mistakes this one for the northern pole. Sadly, it only works one way."

Oriana came to look into the box with him, her brows drawn together. "You can track us up the coast?"

"Precisely," Gaspar said. "Wherever you end up, we can follow."

How incredibly clever. Duilio wondered if the box might be one of the magical "toys" that the Lady's father had tinkered with. Unfortunately, magical items usually came with a price tag. "Do we have to wind it?" Duilio asked cautiously.

Gaspar grinned. "It won't bite you, Ferreira. I've already wound it, so to speak. Or, rather, Pinheiro did."

Pinheiro held up a bandaged hand. "I had to bleed on it. On both of them."

Duilio cast a quizzical look at the African inspector.

"Magic doesn't work on me," Gaspar said, "so it had to be him. Just try not to lose the thing."

Duilio grimaced. "If it gets wet?"

"It will still work," Gaspar said, "unless all the blood is washed off."

Duilio glanced at Oriana, who just shrugged. He closed the box and tucked it under one arm, nodded once to Pinheiro and Gaspar, and then led Oriana down the ramp to the paddleboat. At least this increased the chance that if they did find Maraval, they wouldn't have to face the man alone.

Half an hour later, they'd pulled out past the breakwater and traveled north up the coast. The wind was lacking and the water glassy, the reason he'd chosen the paddleboat rather than the sailboat. Oriana had taken off her shoes to keep them from the water, exposing her silvery feet again. From what he could see, the black dorsal stripe came to a point on the inside of her heel. Duilio could make out a rippled edging between the black and silver skin, a narrow border of brilliant blue. She looked up from where she sat by the wheel compartment and caught him staring at her bare feet. She immediately tucked them back under her skirt.

He didn't know if he should be blushing or not. She had been with him the entire morning—unclothed—and had somehow managed never to turn her back to him, as if she were hiding her dorsal stripe. Was there some risqué aspect to curiosity about a sereia's dorsal stripe? Her behavior was beginning to make him think so.

And that made him burn with curiosity

"So, where will we find your brother?" she asked.

"I expect he's gone back to Braga Bay," Duilio answered. "Where his harem lives."

"A harem? Truly?"

"It's the way they live," he said, feeling a flush creep up from his neck. "The way they've lived for centuries. Males are rare, so there are sometimes as many as fifty females in a harem."

"Fifty?" she asked, sounding appalled. "With one male?"

"Well, to be honest, I don't think Erdano has nearly that many in his harem. But he does have a number of human lovers as well. It's natural for selkies to compete."

"I see," she said, then shook her head. "No, actually, I don't. Why would a female share her male with another? Or fifty others?"

"I've never understood it," he admitted. "Selkie charm?"

"What exactly *is* selkie charm?" she asked.

"Selkies don't talk about it," Duilio said. "It's not a talent or a skill; it's just the way they are. Their powers of seduction are quite real, but I don't know to what they can be attributed."

She looked at him from under a lowered brow. "Do you . . . Have you . . . ?"

He clamped his lips together, holding in the urge to laugh at her hesitance. She was apparently shy when it came to matters of sex, which suggested a modesty sailors believed sereia didn't possess. If he recalled correctly, the English even used the symbol of the sereia to indicate houses of prostitution. It pleased him that Oriana Paredes didn't fit that stereotype. "No," he answered. "I don't have it, whatever *it* is. Alessio did, though. No one could resist him."

She smoothed her skirt. "Is it something to do with the way you smell, perhaps?"

He felt warmth creeping up his cheeks. "Well, we do smell."

She looked up then, her lips falling open. "I didn't mean that badly. It's just that I thought at first you were wearing cologne—ambergris cologne. It took me time to realize you weren't. Your mother, as well."

Duilio supposed he should be relieved she hadn't meant that as an insult. "I do bathe regularly, which limits the smell, but you should hear my valet grumble about it."

"*I* am not complaining," she said.

Duilio chuckled. "So, may I ask, is your ability to *call* something that your people simply do or a skill?"

Oriana didn't answer immediately. They'd passed the port of Leixões and were nearing Braga Bay, so Duilio watched the cliffs more carefully. He didn't want to miss the narrow opening. But he stole a glance at her face and decided she was still unsure whether to answer his query. "You don't need to answer," he said. "I'm simply one of those inquisitive people who wants to know everything."

"I've noticed," she said in a dry tone. "We're all born with a voice, but we must learn to use it. It's a combination of natural talent and skill. Some females can *call* ships from afar. Others can't get the attention of a man two feet away."

He was tempted to ask into which category she fell, but decided it would be rude. She'd said she could coax a human into answering questions, so she must have *some* talent. But she probably wasn't supposed to have said as much as she already had. "Why do you suppose it affects humans?" he asked instead. "I've always wondered why selkie charm seems to be aimed at humans rather than other selkies. Does the *call* affect males of your own kind?"

"Not as much," she said. "It is specifically pitched for humans. Our lore says it's because you're the main danger to us. We're relatively harmless. Before your Vasco da Gama, we simply distracted sailors into sailing *past* our islands."

Even when he couldn't see the webbing, he liked watching her hands. They were long and slender. Capable hands. "Being half-selkie," he said, "I must have some immunity."

"I know we're not supposed to affect them," she said. "Or the otterfolk, for that matter."

"Good to know," he murmured.

Oriana wished there had been more time, but they'd reached their destination. Braga Bay was surrounded by cliffs, the narrow strip of sands melding into rock. It was more of a cove than a bay, but the name had stuck, Duilio told her. Despite the storm clouds rising out at sea, the water was calm and crystal clear. Inaccessible to larger boats, it made an ideal spot for seals to bask in the sun.

Duilio drew the boat up onto the shore before helping her to the beach. She waited, enjoying the feel of the sand under her bare feet while he grabbed a chart from the boat. Then he directed her toward the center of the narrow beach, where at least two dozen seals waited. They grunted in surprise at the humans' approach. Then the largest rose on its flippers and began to strip off its pelt.

Oriana stared, mouth agape. She didn't see how it happened, but one moment she was looking at a large seal; the next at a man unwrapping a pelt from about his body.

"I still can't figure it out," Duilio said in her ear. "It's magic."

She turned back to the seal man. He was definitely the selkie who'd fondled her rump after helping to cut loose the floating house the night before. He cast his pelt onto the sand, and two female seals moved to stand guard over it.

Erdano approached them then, eyeing her. No, he was *leering* at her. Several inches taller than Duilio, he was broader as well and heavily muscled. There wasn't much resemblance to Duilio, save about the eyes. They both had their mother's eyes, clear and warm, with thick, dark lashes. He *was* a strikingly handsome man, but even so, he wasn't to her taste.

He grinned down at her. "You're much prettier than I remember."

Oriana could smell the seal musk on him too. If that *was* a component of selkie charm, it didn't work on her. However, having seen Erdano nude, she'd begun to formulate a new theory about selkie charm, one she wouldn't embarrass Duilio by discussing. Hoping to discourage the selkie at the outset, Oriana firmly told him, "I am not interested in being part of your harem."

Erdano cast a sly smile at her, one surprisingly like his brother's, and then turned to Duilio. "Are you still not . . . ?"

"No," Duilio interrupted him sharply, flushing. "Thank you for helping Oriana with the house."

Oriana tried to catch Duilio's eyes, wanting to know what Erdano had been about to ask. Duilio seemed determined to avoid her gaze.

Erdano crossed his muscular arms over his bulky chest. "You didn't tell me Kerridan was there."

Kerridan? "Who?" she asked.

"The other male that was trying to kill you," Erdano said, giving a name to the selkie who'd been working with the Open Hand. "Thought I'd scared him out of my territory before. Got him this time."

Erdano leered down at her as if expecting her to be impressed by that. Duilio cleared his throat and asked, "Were you able to follow the ship?"

"It went far down the coast to the green stone cove," Erdano answered.

"Which one is that?" Duilio asked, unfolding the chart.

His brother scowled dramatically at the chart. "On that? I can't tell you."

"The one with the hooked cliff, right?" Oriana asked Erdano. When he nodded, she pointed it out on the chart. It had to be the site of the workshop.

Duilio's expression went pensive. "This map doesn't show any buildings there."

"Well, there is one now," Erdano said. "I can show you where."

Half an hour later, Erdano lounged in the boat's prow, dressed in a loose tunic and trousers. After another conference with his brother, Duilio came back to the rear and settled on the wide bench next to Oriana. He took the tiller from her and thanked her for holding on to it while he spoke with Erdano. The motor rumbled as the paddles splashed quietly in the water.

The green stone cove was farther up the coast, and she'd only seen it from a ship before, but a layer of copper deposit made it distinctive. It would take some time for this paddleboat to reach it. The clouds that had been gathering all afternoon had come closer, blocking out much of the sun. They consumed the meat pies that Mrs. Cardoza had packed for them, and after a time Erdano fell asleep, snoring loudly, in the prow of the boat. The boat's paddle splashed on as the afternoon waned toward evening, and they could only hope that Gaspar was following. Oriana pushed her skirts aside to double-check the box tucked under the bench on which she sat. It was still there and, fortunately, not wet.

"I know you're expected to leave soon," Duilio said, startling her. "But our house is open to you for as long as you need it. We should be able to keep your name out of the papers. You'd be safe."

Such a tempting offer. She could hide in the Ferreira home, pretending to be a companion just as she had with Isabel. Perhaps no one would come asking questions about Isabel. But Maria Melo would know she hadn't obeyed orders and would make her father pay—a threat that Oriana didn't doubt. She stared down at her webbing.

She wanted out of the intelligence ministry, she admitted to herself, but she didn't know if they would let her go. And until she could extricate herself, her presence in the Golden City would only be a danger to her father. She couldn't afford to take Duilio up on his offer. "Thank you," she said. "I will remember that you offered."

"Do you *want* to leave?" Duilio asked softly then. "Are you being blackmailed?"

She clenched her hands together, wishing she dared to give him the true answer. "I must go home," she said instead.

Erdano shifted suddenly, making the boat list, forcing Oriana to grab the side rail to steady herself. He yawned widely and pointed at the cliffs. "There. That's where the ship went in."

Duilio turned his eyes to the rocks. They were approaching the mouth of the cove, so he cut the motor. He and Erdano each took an oar and rowed, and the paddleboat slipped quietly into the cove in the twilight. And once inside, Duilio saw what he'd expected. At the end of a wide pier built in the center of the cove, the blue yacht was moored.

Erdano pointed. "There it is, the boat from last night. See the strange arm?"

They guided the small boat behind the larger one, so that someone on the shore wouldn't be able to see it. Duilio slipped off his frock coat. He laid it across the quiescent motor's housing, then climbed atop that and jumped to catch the ship's railing. He pulled himself up enough to scan the yacht's deck and glanced back. "I'm going to see if anyone's aboard."

Oriana had her mouth open to protest, but he'd already swung one leg over the rail and pulled himself up. He signaled for her to stay in the paddleboat and slipped over to the side of the cabin. When he didn't hear any movement within, he climbed the ladder into the steering compartment of the ship.

Dusk had fallen, but in the dim wheelhouse, he spotted a chart on a low table—a map of *The City Under the Sea.*

It was evidence. Duilio rolled up the chart and tucked it under his arm. He quickly surveyed the wheelhouse but decided that anything of value would be in the cabins below, so he headed for the stair leading down to the captain's cabin. It was dark, but on a shelf fixed to the wall near the door, he spotted a box of matches. He struck one and in the sudden flare of light could make out the entire room for an instant.

That was all it took, showing him exactly what he'd hoped he might find, the item that Maraval hadn't left behind in his collection. He must have hidden it *here* to frustrate and annoy Silva, with no care whatsoever for the damage his actions had. Tears stung Duilio's eyes.

On the wall above the captain's bed, a seal's pelt hung.

CHAPTER 33

Oriana stepped into the center of the paddleboat. A wave of seal musk warned her a second before Erdano came to stand next to her. His hand touched her shoulder in an overly friendly fashion and then slid down to the small of her back.

"I've never had one of your women before," he said, "but I hear you're not as cold as you appear."

Of all the times! Oriana gave him a hard look. "I have very sharp teeth."

He smiled down at her, apparently undeterred. "Perhaps later, then."

She stepped out of his grasp. "I wouldn't make any plans."

Duilio slipped over the yacht's rail and dropped to the paddleboat's decking then, a bundle tucked under one arm. "Plans for what?"

"It doesn't matter."

Duilio turned a vexed expression on his brother. "Erdano, keep your hands off her."

"She's too pretty not to have a man," Erdano said, hands wide. "I had to try."

"No, you didn't," Duilio snapped.

"Don't argue over me." Not wanting to further discuss Erdano's heavy-handed attempt at seduction, Oriana pointed to the bundle. "What is that?"

Duilio inclined his head as if to acknowledge her ability to take care of herself. He set a rolled chart atop the boat's engine housing and shook out the dusty bundle he held—a pelt. Oriana reached out to touch the soft fur, glancing up at Duilio's face.

His expression was hesitant—hopeful. "Erdano, is this what I think it is?"

Oriana stepped back, not wanting to intrude.

Erdano leaned down and sniffed the pelt almost reverently. "It's Mother's." Then he slapped Duilio hard on the shoulder. "You found it!"

Duilio rocked forward from the force of the blow but didn't protest. He embraced his brother, laughing. Erdano let out a whoop. Oriana feared he would alert anyone listening to their presence, but Duilio pulled away and grabbed Erdano's shoulder to get his attention. He lifted one section of the pelt for Erdano to see it more clearly. "There are nail holes in it."

"They'll heal," Erdano said, sobering. He stroked the recovered item and then tugged it from Duilio's grip to embrace it like it was his mother herself. "They'll be painful," he said, "but in time they'll heal."

Any damage to the pelt must translate into damage to the wearer, Oriana realized with a pang. She hated the idea of gentle Lady Ferreira suffering such pain. It was bittersweet, but still a victory for Duilio. *One good thing to come out of all this horror.*

"My father's stolen strongbox was also there," Duilio told her. "Filled with ashes. Silva's destined to disappointment, it seems." He frowned and added, "I was expecting more than just the yacht."

Erdano pointed toward the beach that would be on the other side of the yacht. "There's a big building in a space inland. I saw it when I came here last night, all lit up. People moving around."

That had to be the workshop where the houses were being built. After a quick conference, they rowed the boat to the shore where a large boulder gave it cover, although not much. They had to hope that would hide it from casual observers. Duilio pointed toward the pelt his brother grasped. "Can you take that out into the water and wait for our return? I don't want Maraval recapturing it."

Erdano didn't argue. Still clothed, he slipped into the water and a second later was gone from Oriana's view. She climbed from the boat and stood barefoot on the sand next to Duilio. "Getting rid of him?"

He cast a glance after his brother. "I don't want to lose that pelt. But, yes, he's not a quick thinker, even when he's being shot at. It would be better if he's not around to run into any of Maraval's Open Hand."

She should be pleased he considered *her* a quick thinker. "This could be a trap."

"Oh, I'm sure it is," Duilio said with a short laugh. After donning his coat, he drew his revolver and checked to be sure it was loaded. "Maraval would expect us to come here. It's just a matter of how well we anticipate him."

Oriana grimly drew her knife. "Let's find him, then."

A wide pathway led inland from the center of the beach and the pier where the yacht waited. After a brief consultation, they decided that it would be safer to approach the workshop obliquely, so they would skirt the cliffs instead and climb up to where the scrub gave way to cultivation. The crescent moon had risen, granting them just enough light to guide their steps without making them visible to watchers. No one appeared on the sands in response to their presence. It looked like the gods were granting them luck.

After a moment they reached a fall of rocks that looked scalable. Low scrub grew there, not lending much cover, but only a stone's throw inland stood high trellises for grapevines. The landowner must produce *Vinho Verde* by squeezing trellises into every spare inch of his land.

Duilio reached a hand back to help Oriana up a steeper stretch. "Will this hurt your feet?" he whispered.

"No, they're very hard." That was one advantage of growing up rarely wearing shoes: her feet could handle rough terrain. They hurried to the cover offered by the tall trellises. Oriana let loose a breath of relief when they got there. A few brown leaves lay scattered across the ground, but she could see that the grapes hadn't been harvested yet. Did the grower know of the workshop built on his land? Was he staying away because of it?

Duilio pointed toward a light visible through rows of vines. "That's got to be it there."

She crept under the trellis and they skirted the rows of vines. As they got closer they could see the light came from a new-looking building. Wholly utilitarian, it had no embellishment, simply plain wooden walls with wide-opening doors, more like a warehouse than anything else. Holding his revolver ready, Duilio gave her a quick nod. He edged around the side of the building toward the large open door on the nearer side. Oriana stayed back out of the way until he peered around the corner and then straightened and waved her closer.

"I don't see any movement," he told her. "Come on."

The workshop was indeed empty. Lamps blazed inside, casting a flickering glow over the wooden rooftops. Duilio stepped over the threshold into the big main room, where six completed replicas waited. With the house dropped into the river the previous night, that would make thirty-three houses constructed. Duilio had said something about thirty-two being a likely total, but she supposed one could have been built as a failsafe. He walked around them, glancing between them to see if anyone hid within. Nothing moved.

"It looks abandoned," Oriana said, which didn't explain why all the lamps were burning.

Duilio nodded, his eyes still roving the room. Oriana slid her knife back into its sheath. He walked on toward the far wall of the workshop's main room, so Oriana followed. He leaned closer to examine the roof of one of the houses—the Cordes manor house,

Oriana guessed—inspecting the metal framework extending from the roof that would be attached to the chain.

She walked on toward the far wall of the building. There it smelled of sawdust. A dozen tables and benches arranged into working areas held neat collections: saws, hammers, and nails, as well as dozens of tools for which she had no names. She stopped cold a few feet from the outside wall.

Several small casks were stacked at the base of the beam that stretched up to and across the ceiling, rags stuffed between the casks. Each of the major support beams had a similar adornment. Oriana's stomach fluttered with anxiety. "Duilio," she called over her shoulder. "You need to look at this."

He jogged over to her side. "Oh. That can't be good."

A concise assessment.

Duilio picked at one of the yellowed labels. It was a cask of turpentine. A slender cord emerged from the top cask and led up the wall. Fuses wrapped the entire ceiling, he realized, connecting all the weight-bearing beams. "I'd definitely call this getting rid of evidence."

Oriana pointed. "There are a couple of rooms at the back. We should check to make sure there aren't any hostages back there."

He could make out the two doors to which she gestured. One was an office, with windows that would allow the occupants to look out over the workroom floor, much like those at the Tavares boatyard. The other was windowless, perhaps a storeroom. Oriana went ahead of him, her bare feet making no sound on the clean-swept floors. When they reached the windowless door, she gestured for him to wait.

"Be still," she whispered. She laid one hand against the door, her fingers spread wide, showing the webbing. "I don't sense any movement inside."

She'd told him before that her senses didn't work as well through the air as in water. "Are you sure?" he whispered back.

She stepped to one side of the door. "I didn't feel *movement.* That doesn't mean they're not very still."

Duilio raised his revolver as she turned the latch. He shoved the door inward and quickly stepped over the threshold. No bullets greeted his entry into what appeared to be a tidy bedroom. Lining one wall were piles of foolscap, a practice he recognized. "This looks like the apartment that burned."

Oriana hadn't entered the room with him, he realized then. Worry streaked through him and he stepped back into the main room, but she stood only a few feet away, peering into one of the office windows.

"I believe I've found Espinoza," she said sadly.

Duilio joined her, holding up one hand to cut the glare from a flickering kerosene lamp overhead. A lean, white-haired man lay facedown on the floor amid a dark pool of blood. His feet were cuffed, joined by a couple of feet of chain. *Poor fellow.* Duilio sighed, wondering if Maraval had kept Espinoza prisoner here since January. Clearly the man hadn't been a willing participant in his plans. "I'll go see if he's alive."

"I don't think he is," Oriana said. "I don't see him breathing."

He still needed to check. It was the proper thing to do. Duilio made his way to the office door. He turned the latch, pushed open the door . . . and the room exploded about him.

CHAPTER 34

Oriana instinctively dove for the floor. She'd been far enough from the door that she wasn't thrown by the blast itself. The window nearest her was unbroken but shattered a moment later with the building heat in that office, raining glass onto the floor. With a yelp, she scrambled away backward on her bare hands and feet like a crab.

She managed to get off the floor then, and scanned the room wildly. The office was completely afire, but the rest of the workshop was still intact. *Where is he?* "Duilio?"

A groan reached her ears, and she ran that way. He was alive, at least. She dropped to her knees next to him. The explosion had knocked him backward over one of the houses, sending him sprawling onto the far side, a drop of several feet. His white shirt was darkened with soot. He seemed dazed, but his wide eyes focused on her when she yanked on his good arm. "We have to go," she yelled at him, her pulse racing. "Now!"

He blinked up at her, dazed. "What happened?"

Oriana grabbed his braces and hauled him to a sitting position. "Come on!"

He got to his feet, stumbling against her. She set one arm about his waist and steered him toward that distant open door, wishing he would go faster. They had to get out.

"The fuses," Duilio mumbled.

And then his urgency matched hers. He grabbed her wrist and bolted along the center aisle of the workshop in the direction of the water. Fleeter of foot, he dragged her along then. They had almost reached the end of the rows of houses when the first incendiary pile went with a boom louder than the first.

Letting him guide her, Oriana looked over her shoulder. The beam nearest the office fell, dragging the ceiling of the workshop with it. It crashed down right where Duilio had lain dazed after the initial explosion.

"Come on!" He pulled her toward the open door, drawing her out into the night air just as another explosion sounded.

They ran down a rutted pathway that led all the way to the pier. When they stopped, Oriana leaned against one of the posts, her breath embarrassingly ragged. They were alive. She closed her burning eyes for a moment. Now that they'd escaped, she was shaking all over. She clung to the post.

Another explosion shook the air, less terrifying now that they were some distance from the building. They could see another portion of the roof cave in. The contents of the building were starting to burn now, a roar building.

Duilio came to her side and laid one hand on her back. "Are you hurt?"

Oriana turned to face him, shaking her head. Her lungs felt ready to burst and her gills had begun to sting from the smoke drifting their way. "No. I'm fine. You?"

He was breathing hard. The scab on his cheek had begun to bleed again, and his clothes were ruined. She suspected he would be horribly bruised by morning. "I'm well enough," he said, though, wrapping his hand about her own. "Thanks to you."

His eyes on hers, he opened his mouth to say something else, but the words seemed to be caught in his throat. Oriana waited, desperate to know what he meant to say. It was as if they were alone in that darkness. The roar of the fire retreated, all sounds fading as if the world waited for those stalled words.

Then a voice forestalled whatever he meant to say. "Well, Ferreira, a thorn in my side until the last. I had hoped that you would be caught in the explosion, but alas it seems the fuses were too long."

Duilio turned back toward the flames. Maraval strode down the rutted pathway toward them, a gun in one hand and a portmanteau dangling from the other. Oriana's hands clenched into fists. Maria Melo might have chosen Isabel to die in *The City Under the Sea*, but he was the one whose mania had started this nightmare in the first place.

Four Special Police officers flanked him, cutting off any chance of retreat into the vineyard. Duilio gave her a gentle push toward the water. She didn't know if Maraval had seen her standing behind him. Was there enough light coming from the fire? The man must see her skirts, if nothing else.

Maraval came closer, apparently undaunted by the revolver in Duilio's hand. When he stood a few feet away, he said, "Do you have any idea what you've done, Ferreira? If you'd let the case alone, as ordered, Portugal would once again be the empire it was meant to be. Now I'll have to start over. Brazil awaits, with as many loyal servants of the empire as this tired old city, perhaps more."

Start over? Oriana shuddered. Did the man think he was simply going to walk away?

"There's no point, Maraval. You can't turn back the clock," Duilio said.

"Are you going to say next that it's God's will?" Maraval asked with a snort. "We have grown beyond letting God decide history for us."

"And so you decide who lives and who dies?"

"Sacrifices have to be made," Maraval said with a blasé shrug.

Oriana swallowed, fury rising in her gut. It was *exactly* what Maria Melo had said about choosing Isabel. Was a spy no different from this man, playing at being one of the gods? Perhaps Maria Melo was different in her espoused cause, but both valued their goals above innocent lives.

She laid one hand on Duilio's back so he would know she was behind him. Keeping her eyes on the four police officers, she backed away. She was in the water then, up to her knees. She turned and dove into the shallows, pushing away toward the edge of the cove.

Duilio heard a splash behind him; Oriana had fled to the safety of the ocean.

Good. She would be safe, and he could count on her and Erdano to get the pelt back to his mother. He wasn't going to get out of this alive, not facing five armed men. He could take two, possibly three. He took a deep breath, feeling remarkably calm. "I'm not a religious man, Maraval," he said, "but don't you worry you're inviting divine retribution?"

"God doesn't concern me," Maraval said blithely. "Now out of my way, Ferreira. We have a tide to catch. Rios, you lost control of him. You finish him off."

Duilio tore his eyes away from Maraval long enough to see that one of the four officers was indeed Captain Rios. The captain gestured with his pistol for Duilio to clear the way to the pier for his master. Duilio gazed at the muzzle of the gun, knowing Rios wasn't going to hesitate. Rios had never liked him.

He was going to die now.

And then a sound made him spin about, eyes drawn toward the sea.

Duilio felt his heart slow as an ethereal song tore his attention away from the fire, from Rios, from Maraval. He tried to quiet his own breathing so he could hear it better. He needed to find the source.

He scanned the dark water with desperate eyes. At the edge of the cove he could see a swimmer, only a dark silhouette of a head above the water. He had to find her. . . .

Then he realized what he was hearing. Wordless, keening, it wasn't a song after all. Duilio ground his teeth together and jammed fingers into his ears, trying to block it out, trying to concentrate.

His pulse pounded in his shut-off ears and his head buzzed as if a fly were trapped inside. He wanted nothing more than to remove the fingers from his ears and let it out, but if he did he would surely find himself swimming toward that open ocean, unable to help answering Oriana's *call*.

CHAPTER 35

It was her only weapon against the man who held a gun on Duilio.

Oriana wove the *call* from memories of childhood longing, from every bit of homesickness she'd felt in the last two years, of the yearning to have her family whole again. She didn't weave a spell of sexual desire, but of comfort and home and love. It was her only magic, her only way to protect him—to *call* them to her.

He stayed on the shore, hands on either side of his head. He recognized what she was doing and didn't come to her. *Thank the gods!*

But the others did—all of them, the four police officers and Maraval. The marquis resisted her only for a second before his desire for the comfort of fond memories led him to the edge of the pier. He dropped his bag and leapt into the water. He swam toward her, drawn as straight as an arrow.

Two of the police officers didn't swim. They were going to drown.

Oriana didn't let that stop her. She couldn't let them go and still *call* Maraval. So she sang on, kicking farther away from the beach as she did so. She swam out to sea, the three of them—no, only two now—following her *call*. How far out did she need to draw them?

She submerged, skirts buoying about her, and dropped her *call* to a hum. She spread her hands wide so that her webbing could sense the movement of the two remaining pursuers. There was a disturbance in the water behind her, but with a flash of dismay, she realized one of her pursuers was almost on her. She kicked desperately backward, only to collide with Erdano. Suddenly her arms were full of pelt and he was gone in a flurry of bubbles, the policeman in his grasp. He might not be all that clever on land, but Erdano *was* fast in the water.

Oriana turned her attention back to her lone pursuer: a slower swimmer moving doggedly in pursuit. Clutching the pelt to her chest with one arm, she sank lower. Then she started back to the beach, cutting around her adversary with a dozen feet to spare. It was Maraval.

Was this her chance? She could use her *call* to draw him down in the water, to cause him to follow her deeper to his own death. It would be a proper repayment for what he'd done to Isabel, a death by drowning. She could pull him down and then release her control of him when it was too late for him to make it to the surface but not too late to understand that he was drowning. It would be *justice.*

She could almost feel the pleasure that watching the terror on his face would hold. Her free hand curled into a fist, nails digging into her palm.

They needed him. If they were going to find everyone involved in this plot, they needed the head of the serpent. So Oriana swam back toward the beach, coming out of the water at the side of the pier.

But Duilio was no longer alone. A petite woman dressed and veiled in black stood near the water's edge, easily visible on the pale sands.

Duilio grabbed Oriana's arm and drew her back away from that dark form. "What happened?" he asked, pointing with his chin toward the sodden pelt clutched under her arm.

Oriana could sense the tension in him. "Erdano gave me this. Maraval's still out there."

The woman turned her black-veiled head in Oriana's direction and in accented Portuguese said, "Bring him back."

Her voice was flat, without emotion. Oriana felt a chill not due to the cold air, until Duilio set a hand on her shoulder to steady her. "She's on our side. She's with Gaspar."

Had Gaspar managed to find them with his compass? She spotted him then, walking along the path toward the beach.

Reassured, Oriana took a deep breath, turned to face the sea, and *called* again. Duilio turned his head, plugging one ear with his free hand; he held his revolver in the other. Apparently her *call* had *some* effect on him, but Duilio managed to resist her, keeping his gun trained on the waves lapping at the edge of the beach. Gaspar seemed completely unmoved. After only a few minutes Maraval stumbled onto the sands, his fine clothes ruined. Oriana closed her mouth, letting him go.

Duilio kept his gun trained on the man. But upon seeing the woman waiting for him on the shore, Maraval struggled to his feet. Grimacing, he swung one arm toward her. She merely touched him with one slim hand. Maraval whimpered. She said a word in a foreign language, and he collapsed to the sands. His ragged breathing showed he was still alive, but the black-veiled woman knelt down, apparently unconcerned by any threat Maraval might pose. "I can take your life away," she told him, "bit by bit, drag you down into the waters and hold you there till you drown in my arms. But first you and I have much to talk about."

Oriana felt ill. Hadn't she just thought of doing the same thing?

Gaspar strode directly over to the woman's side and proceeded to put cuffs on the prone Maraval. As if they'd been waiting, Joaquim and Pinheiro appeared at the end of the path, both tugging wads of cotton or wool from their ears.

"Don't try anything on me, old man," Gaspar said as he dragged Maraval to his feet. "It won't work."

Oriana suspected Maraval was too worn or too terrified to try anything on anyone. He was clearly frightened of the slender woman in black, who walked away toward the burning building without a backward glance.

Gaspar dragged Maraval to his feet. "Pinheiro, take your team and search the area for any others. We'll send the regulars out to investigate further when there's light. I'll take this fellow and Miss Vladimirova back to the city. Mr. Ferreira?"

"Yes?" Duilio said.

"There's a storm coming in. That flat-bottomed thing you came out here in won't like that. You should probably tie it off and come back for it in a day or two."

Duilio looked seaward at the dark sky. No stars were visible through that thick cloud cover. "I think you're right."

Two more police officers appeared at the end of the pathway as a carriage drew up to the edge of the beach, its dark sides gilded by the fire's light. A second carriage drew up behind it. "Tavares, why don't you head to the city with them? Get some rest," Gaspar suggested as two of the officers wrestled the marquis into the carriage. "Anjos will want you back on the beach tomorrow."

Inspector Tavares looked relieved to be joining them instead of heading back in that coach with Maraval and the strange Miss Vladimirova. He volunteered to help Duilio secure the paddleboat while Pinheiro and his crew boarded the moored yacht to look for evidence. Duilio took off his soot-stained coat and settled it around her shoulders, saying, "You must be freezing."

"Thank you," Oriana managed without her teeth chattering. She *was* cold now that she was out of the water. The pelt she clutched against her chest was still wet. Her clothes were sodden, and if they hadn't been headed back into the city she'd remove them, but she didn't want to cause further consternation.

So Oriana stood on the sand, her skirts dripping onto her bare feet. She just wanted to leave this place. She didn't want to be around to watch the bodies of the three police officers she'd lured to their deaths wash in on the tide. It was a cowardly thought, not wanting to face up to what she'd done. But she would do it again if it meant keeping Duilio safe. What sort of person did that make her?

Returning from tying off the paddleboat, Duilio took one of her hands in his. "Let's get back to the city."

She had the strongest feeling he knew exactly what was bothering her. She nodded wordlessly.

After walking up to the burning workshop, they transferred the wooden box with its blood compass to the carriage. A handful more of Gaspar and Anjos' officers had arrived to help with the search. Apparently Tavares knew them already and verified their identities. Then they were finally in the carriage, heading back to the city.

How late was it? Ten? Midnight?

Oriana wearily settled next to Duilio while his cousin took the seat facing backward. He took the pelt from her and arranged it on the empty spot on the bench, allowing some of the water to drain off. She listened while they talked of Anjos' effort to convince the City Council to allow the floating houses to be pulled up from the river's grasp. Apparently the inspector had been persuasive, and the effort was scheduled to begin as soon as the storm passed. The police suspected few of the bodies would be identifiable, so they were counting on Joaquim, with his knowledge of the case, to give names to the victims and help contact the families involved. She didn't envy him that job.

They went on to talk about newspapers and which were sending writers and photographers out to cover it, whether the prince himself would comment on the whole affair, and whether Maraval would be charged or if he would quietly disappear. *Just as long as he doesn't go free*, Oriana thought.

And that was the last thought she remembered until Duilio shook her shoulder to wake her.

CHAPTER 36

MONDAY, 6 OCTOBER 1902

Oriana had been sleeping, her head on his shoulder, for most of the trip. When they reached the house Duilio hated to wake her, but she probably didn't want to sit there in damp clothing any longer than necessary.

Joaquim had been a font of information, mostly about what they'd learned in going through Maraval's private papers. The papers cleared up any doubt of his having Alessio killed, as he'd kept thorough records of all Alessio's movements for a few months prior to that date. Maraval had feared that Alessio might—at the infante's request—seduce the prince out from under Maraval's thumb. Ironically, it was Alessio's death that had led the infante to bring in Anjos and his people, ultimately causing Maraval's downfall.

Over the past few days, Joaquim had also learned a great deal about Anjos and his people. Having spent more time with them, he had several interesting observations. Duilio was most interested in Miss Vladimirova, though, whom Joaquim told him was a Russian water nymph called a rusalka. Camões might have referred to Oriana's people as sea nymphs, but Duilio suspected the similarity ended there. According to Joaquim, Silva had apparently been correct in calling Miss Vladimirova *undead*. And while Duilio had read several lurid stories about vampires, he wasn't sure he believed that something could be both dead and alive.

"All I know," Joaquim said, "is that I'm glad I'm in this carriage, not the other. Just being around her makes me nervous."

That Duilio *did* understand. Of course, if Joaquim had been in the other carriage, then he might have had a chance for a private talk with Oriana. He could tell she was shaken after what had happened at the cove. He didn't know whether she'd ever caused another's death before, but he suspected not. He understood that. He'd never liked killing, no matter the situation.

But the carriage had been standing for a couple of minutes now, and they should let the driver get his horses back to the police stables. Duilio sighed and gently shook Oriana's shoulder. She blinked at him but obeyed his instructions when he helped her down onto the cobbles behind the house. He dragged the nearly dry pelt out as well, and then sent the driver on with orders to take Joaquim to his apartment. They could talk more later.

It was the one thing Duilio didn't think should wait until morning, so in the early hours of the morning they stood next to his mother's bed. The lady slept silently, looking almost like a painting in a museum, her braid trailing off the edge of the bed. Oriana touched her shoulder lightly. "Lady Ferreira?"

The lady moved as if in a dream, sitting up and stretching out her arms. Her eyes never saw Oriana there. She looked right past her.

Duilio held out the pelt. "See what we've found, Mother?"

He surrendered the damp pelt into her hands . . . or perhaps it moved into Lady Ferreira's arms; Oriana wasn't certain which she'd just seen. The lady gathered it close to her chest and curled around it like it was a lost child finally found. Under her fingertips, it seemed almost as though the pelt came alive, the fur shining again. "Mother, there are nail holes in it," he warned, "so don't try to wear it immediately."

"No wonder my fingers always hurt," Lady Ferreira said under her breath.

Tears stung Oriana's eyes, and she wiped them away with the side of her hand. Now Lady Ferreira's life could resume. It must be an incredible relief to be able to move on. Oriana didn't know when, if ever, her own life would be hers to direct again. She sorely wanted that.

"It'll be better soon, Mother," Duilio said, touching her hair lightly. "Rest now."

The lady breathed in the scent of her pelt as if it were the sweetest perfume. She seemed too enraptured to speak at all.

"I'll stay with her for a while," Duilio told Oriana as he dragged over a chair and set it next to the head of the bed. "Why don't you try to get some sleep?"

She nodded, feeling dull and drained. She left him there and headed to her own bed, only bothering to remove her waterlogged garments before crawling under the warm coverlet. And then it was morning, a dim light piercing the curtains and bidding her to wake. Oriana crawled from her borrowed bed and dressed in her black serge skirt and blue vest. She braided her hair and was relieved when Teresa showed up with her morning coffee tray.

A short time later she left her room, unsure whether anyone would be awake this morning. Before she reached the stairs, Cardenas came up. "Good morning, Miss Paredes," he said cheerily.

"Is anyone else up?" she asked.

"Mr. Duilio has an early caller," he said, "but the lady apparently plans to sleep late."

It *was* early for a caller, but Oriana supposed it might be his cousin, Inspector Tavares. Or Gaspar or Pinheiro. "Very well."

Cardenas reached into a jacket pocket and produced an envelope. "I have a letter for you, Miss Paredes. It was left last night, but . . ."

Oriana cringed inwardly. She knew what that letter must be. She took the envelope Cardenas handed her and thanked him, and he walked on toward the end of the hallway. This card had a different seal from the other, Oriana noted as she made her way more slowly down the stairs. In fact, it looked like Heriberto's seal and wax. Oriana stopped halfway down the stairs and popped open the envelope.

There will be a ship waiting for you, south-southwest of the mouth of the river. Be there by noon on Monday, or I will do as I promised. MM

Oriana sighed and closed her eyes, fighting back the sting of tears. *Today.* She had known this was coming. She had known it would be soon.

She turned to head back up the stairs when she saw Duilio emerging from the front sitting room with his guest. It was Genoveva Carvalho, her companion trailing behind her, clutching a parasol in her hands. Miss Carvalho lifted tear-filled eyes toward Duilio, then leaned up and kissed his cheek, one of her gloved hands lingering on his coat lapel. Oriana couldn't make out what the young woman said, but the admiration in her eyes was plain to see. Duilio was likely blushing. Then Miss Carvalho turned and led her companion out the front door.

Miss Carvalho was from a wealthy family, an aristocratic one with ties here. And there was an understanding already, was there not? Even if Oriana had the time left, even if she wanted to court Duilio Ferreira, he had other choices for a mate—much better choices than a sereia with no money and no prospects.

Swallowing, Oriana darted back up the stairs, not wanting him to turn and catch her watching. But Felis stopped her at the landing and asked if everything was well. Oriana managed to blurt out something about packing because she had to leave. She edged past the elderly woman to reach the privacy of her bedroom. Once inside, she closed the door and rested her back against it.

She was nearly out of time. If she was going to swim the distance from the city out to the mouth of the river and from there to wherever the ship waited for her, she needed to go soon. And she hadn't swum a long distance since coming to the city. What would have been easy when she was two years younger seemed daunting now. She was already so tired. She covered her face with shaking hands and began to cry in earnest. The note slipped to the table, atop the other, unopened note, forgotten.

Duilio ached all over. His back hurt now too from when he'd slammed into one of the miniature houses, slid over its top, and then dropped to the floor. His hair was singed on the ends. Fortunately, he hadn't lost his eyebrows, which would have made him look ridiculous.

He sat back, moaning when his sore back touched the chair. He'd had to endure an uncomfortable interview with Genoveva Carvalho, who seemed to believe he'd saved her sister singlehandedly. He told the girl that Miss Paredes had done the difficult part, but she must have mistaken that for modesty on his part.

She'd called at his house far earlier in the morning than was proper, apparently on her way to Mass. Duilio sighed. Apparently she *had* transferred her affections from Alessio to him, which might have been desirable a year ago. Now it only seemed an annoyance. He was going to have to start avoiding her.

He picked up the newspaper Cardenas had left on the table. The *Porto Gazette* had run an article on the front page, complete with a photograph of young Tiago Coelho, the footman, taken while he was still bound to the table in the house, blood staining his swollen features. In the photographer's flash Duilio could make out a few of the now-familiar symbols on that table. Markings ran along the pedestal of the table and across the visible walls of the house as well. The Lady had been correct about that—there was far more to the spell than just the table itself. And despite the scripture binding the edge of the table, it was clear that this was the sort of magical invocation that the Church found unacceptable.

The people of the city wouldn't permit this to go on, no matter how their prince felt about the work of art. The City Council had recognized that fact. *The City Under the Sea* wouldn't be growing. According to the paper, the police were making plans to dismantle it. They would bring up the houses and their contents onto the Gaia beach near the breakwater, far from the city, where fewer eyes would witness the grisly sight of bodies that had been in the water too long. Setting aside their usual antagonism, the Jesuits and the Freemasons were set to take possession of the houses to study the spell written on the tables and the walls, determine its intentions, and decide whether it would work at all.

He should be elated. They'd won. No more bodies would be buried in the river, and his mother had her pelt back. He'd even found his missing slippers hidden under his pillow last night, no doubt thanks to Miss Paredes.

Instead he felt a vague worry, as if his gift couldn't yet define the threat that waited for him. Their actions tonight had unleashed something to wreak havoc on the city. He asked his gift for some guidance but got nothing. He didn't know what questions to ask. He'd just lifted his glass of brandy to his lips when Felis strode into the library, a militant expression on her face

Duilio wondered what he'd done to offend his mother's maid. He rose, fully expecting to get his ears boxed.

Felis set her hands on her hips. "Duilinho, Miss Paredes tells me she has to leave. For God's sake, boy, stop her."

He had hoped it wouldn't be so soon, but somehow, given the way things were going, he wasn't particularly surprised. He *was* shocked that Felis had used such strong language. "She needs to return home, Miss Felis. I've known for some time she would have to leave. I can't force her to stay."

The elderly maid thrust one hand into her apron pocket and drew out a tattered playing card. She held it up in front of Duilio's face—the king of hearts. "Don't you know what this means, boy?"

She had never told him the meaning of that card, the one she'd drawn for him the day he'd asked her to help him find Oriana, but he didn't need her explanation. The import of the card was all too clear in his mind now. He nodded, his throat tightening. "I know what it means."

Felis threw the card on the table. "Then why would you let her go?"

She turned and walked out of the library, leaving the card behind.

Duilio slumped into his chair again.

A book might tell him a dozen different interpretations of that card's meaning. Whatever Felis had seen in it didn't matter. Like all fortunes, the only thing that mattered was what he saw in it now, what it meant to him: that Oriana Paredes was the great love of his life.

And he was about to watch her walk away.

Should Oriana simply ignore her orders to return home, she would be in violation of her people's law. Much like a military man who fled his post. For some that would be acceptable. For her, he didn't think it would be, and he was not going to attack her resolve. That would only belittle her.

He had to hope that she would return to the Golden City. He didn't care if she was assigned to spy on his people. He didn't care if there was a scandal tied to her name, if she was exposed as a sereia. He just had to hope she would come back.

He picked up the card and slid it into his jacket pocket. Then he did take a drink of his brandy, letting it burn down his throat. It didn't chase away the malaise of victory and despair that clouded his thoughts.

"Mr. Ferreira?" Oriana stood at the door, her expression somber. "How do you feel?"

He'd gone back to being Mr. Ferreira, as if a polite distance would make this easier. Duilio swirled the glass before glancing at her. "I'll be fine. Just bruised."

"I suspect that Miss Carvalho has changed her mind about you," she said then. When he gave her a curious look, she added, "I think you're no longer her second choice."

Ah, she must have seen that exchange in the hallway. "It doesn't signify," he said. "She would be *my* second choice."

He waited for her to say something, anything, but she just stood there with her eyes on the floor. "Did you receive orders to go?"

"Yes." She still didn't meet his eyes. "I need to leave immediately if I'm to make my rendezvous."

Immediately? He'd hoped she would be able to rest for a day or two. He'd hoped they would have time to talk, that he would have time to work out all the confused yearnings in his head. He set the glass on the table. She had her hands folded together tightly, knuckles white.

"Must you go?" he asked, even though he knew what she would say. She had never told him whether she was being blackmailed, but he suspected so.

"Yes."

"Any time you need a safe haven, our house will be open to you. I meant that."

She closed her eyes, as though she couldn't bear to look at him.

Duilio stepped closer and set his hands on her arms. "Oriana . . ."

"I'm expected to be at my rendezvous by noon," she said in a tight voice. "I need to leave now."

She no more wants to go than I want her to leave.

He should be pleased by that knowledge, but instead it hurt, an ache in his chest that must be his heart breaking. There was so much more he wanted to say, but he wasn't going to batter against her resolve. He finally settled on, "I'll walk you down to the quay."

EPILOG

Spray lashed up over the prow of the rowboat, the waves at the mouth of the river rougher than Oriana had expected. The sun's first light streamed across the water, a red dawn. She cast a glance back to where Duilio sat at the oars, his face grim. His linen shirtsleeves fluttered in the wind; as chilly as the autumn morning was, he'd given her his frock coat anyway to keep her warm until she dove.

The boat breached a low wave and landed hard as they passed the stone breakwater that protected the river's mouth from the open sea. "The storm is coming," he called to her.

"I'll be under," she called back. "I'll be safe." She looked eastward, past Duilio at the city rising on its hills in the sunrise. The whitewashed walls of myriad houses gleamed in the morning light. But the time had come to leave it behind.

It wasn't the city she would miss.

Duilio shipped the oars, and the boat began to drift outward on the tide. "This thing doesn't fare well on the open sea, not if it's rough."

Meaning that this was as far as he could take her. Oriana rose cautiously. She looked out at the red-stained waters to the west, smelling the salt and the coming storm, still hesitating. She turned back to Duilio, trying to decide what to tell him.

She didn't know what would happen to her once she got home. She couldn't even be sure that her leaving would keep her father safe. The only thing that seemed clear to her was that she wanted to return to the Golden City, to come back for *him*.

Duilio had risen to stand next to her. The boat heaved as another wave came, and he steadied her with a hand under her elbow. He regarded her as if he suffered the same lack of words she did. He ran fingers through his dark hair and then said, "Please come back."

Oriana reached up and set one bared hand against his cheek, feeling the feathery warmth of his breath on the webbing between her fingers. Duilio turned his head and pressed his lips to her palm, his eyes drifting closed. She pulled away, afraid she would lose her resolve.

"I will try," she said, her voice breaking. It was the most she could promise. And then, because no more words came to her, she drew off his frock coat and passed it into his hands, shivering as the cold air clutched at her bare skin.

"Go," he said softly.

Oriana dove, going deep beneath the waves. She didn't look back.

ABOUT THE AUTHOR

J. Kathleen Cheney is a former mathematics teacher who has taught classes ranging from seventh grade to calculus, with a brief stint as a gifted and talented specialist. Her short fiction has been published in such venues as Fantasy Magazine and Beneath Ceaseless Skies, and her novella *Iron Shoes* was a Nebula Finalist in 2010.